THE CACTUS

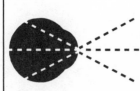

This Large Print Book carries the
Seal of Approval of N.A.V.H.

THE CACTUS

SARAH HAYWOOD

THORNDIKE PRESS
A part of Gale, a Cengage Company

GALE
A Cengage Company

Farmington Hills, Mich • San Francisco • New York • Waterville, Maine
Meriden, Conn • Mason, Ohio • Chicago

Copyright © 2018 by Sarah Haywood.
Thorndike Press, a part of Gale, a Cengage Company.
Cover art Copyright © 2019 by Harlequin Enterprises Ltd. Cover art used by arrangement with Harlequin Books S.A. ® and ™ are trademarks owned by Harlequin Books S.A. or its affiliated companies, used under license.

Thorndike Press® Large Print Core.
The text of this Large Print edition is unabridged.
Other aspects of the book may vary from the original edition.
Set in 16 pt. Plantin.

LIBRARY OF CONGRESS CIP DATA ON FILE.
CATALOGUING IN PUBLICATION FOR THIS BOOK
IS AVAILABLE FROM THE LIBRARY OF CONGRESS

ISBN-13: 978-1-4328-7010-2 (hardcover alk. paper)

Published in 2019 by arrangement with Harlequin Books S.A.

Printed in the United States of America
1 2 3 4 5 6 7 23 22 21 20 19

For Simon, Gabriel and Felix

■ ■ ■ ■

AUGUST

■ ■ ■ ■

1

I'm not a woman who bears grudges, broods over disagreements or questions other people's motives. Neither do I feel compelled to win an argument at any cost. As with all rules, of course, there are exceptions. I won't stand idly by while one person's being exploited by another, and the same goes when *I'm* the one being exploited; I'll do everything within my means to ensure that justice prevails. Not surprisingly, then, the events that have unfolded this month have left me with no choice but to take immediate and decisive action.

It was my brother, Edward, who informed me that our mother had died. Although it was only five thirty, I was already awake; I'd just been hovering over the toilet bowl wondering whether I should make myself vomit or endure the nausea. Vomiting relieves the feeling for a few minutes, but it

9

soon comes back, so, having carried out a cost-benefit analysis, I decided endurance was the best option. While I was examining my bilious reflection, the phone trilled from the kitchen. So few people ring my landline that I sensed immediately that it must be an emergency relating to my mother. It was not, however, an emergency. In fact, there was no reason why my brother should have called so early other than to catch me off guard.

"Suze, it's me, Ed. I've got some news, and it's not good. You might want to sit down."

"What's happened?"

"I don't know how to say this, Suze. I'm afraid . . ."

"Edward, get a grip. Is she in the hospital?"

"Suze, she's gone. She passed away last night. I didn't get in until about two — I was at a mate's house having a few beers. Her bedroom light was still on, so I knocked and stuck my head round the door. I could tell straight off from the way she was slumped. The GP's been — massive stroke, she said. I can't believe it."

I gulped back the surge in my throat and sat down at the kitchen table. I took a moment to sweep a few stray toast crumbs into a pile with the side of my hand.

"Suze . . . Suze?"

"She *was* seventy-eight," I said, eventually, "and she *had* already had two strokes. It's not exactly unexpected." I hesitated. I was aware that I should say something sympathetic, but it didn't come naturally to me where my brother was concerned. "I understand it must've been unpleasant to find her, though," I added. "Sorry, I haven't got time to talk now, I need to get ready for work. I'll phone later. And, Edward."

"Yes, Suze?"

"Please don't call me Suze."

I didn't expect to find myself orphaned at forty-five, an age at which most people still have both parents, but my mother and father were into their thirties when I was born, and my father had a certain weakness of character that cut short his life. I didn't see my mother as often as I should have in her final years. I'm a civil servant, working on Project Delivery (analyzing reams of complex data and producing in-depth reports on performance), and I find that, when I'm not spending long hours wrestling with large numbers and small print, I'm running just to stand still.

Another reason for the infrequency of my

visits was that Edward was living with my mother yet again, and he and I don't — to put it nicely — share the same outlook on life. In fact, we go well out of our way to avoid each other. My brother is only two years my junior in age, but at least thirty years my junior in emotional and psychological development, which in his case ceased in his teens. Not, I should add, because he has any sort of diagnosable mental condition, but because he's weak-willed and self-indulgent. While I've worked hard to establish a secure career and stable lifestyle, Edward's staggered from useless job to meaningless relationship to seedy flat. No surprise, then, that he ended up crawling back to my mother in his forties.

It's a shock to be told that a close relative has died, even when they were old and had been unwell, and I found that I needed to spend several minutes sitting quietly and gathering my thoughts. With me being in London, though, and my mother's body being in Birmingham, there was little of any practical use for me to do. I therefore decided to go to work and carry on as normal, or as normal as I could fake with this relentless nausea. I wouldn't tell anyone at the office of my mother's death. I could imagine the orgy of fussing and sighing, the clammy embraces and the expressions of sorrow for the loss of someone they'd never met and didn't even know existed. Not really my sort of thing.

Emerging from the Tube station near my office building, I was struck by the heat, which had already risen to a level sufficient to soften the fresh tarmac outside the exit. The noise and fumes from the crawling traffic seemed amplified, and the piercing intensity of the sunlight stung the backs of my retinas. Once at the relative sanctuary of my desk, which is in the quietest corner of a large open-plan office, I switched on the fan and trained it on my face. Somewhat revived, I spent a few minutes, as I like to every morning, checking the cacti that I have ranged across the front of my desk. I ascertained that there were no areas of rot or any parts that looked shriveled or dry, dusted them with a soft paintbrush, ensured that the moisture levels in the compost were correct and turned them to maintain an even exposure to daylight. When that was done, I opened a case file. I hoped that grappling with the particularly challenging report that I needed to submit to my head of department at the end of the following week would help me elbow the events of earlier that morning to the back of my mind.

Mine might not be the most exciting of jobs for someone with a law degree, but it suits me. Most of the students in my course went on to train as solicitors or barristers, but I found myself drawn to the security of a government career: the predictable, if ungenerous, pay scales, the tolerable pension scheme and the fact that I wouldn't be subject to the whims of senior partners or heads of chambers. Although my work doesn't make use of my degree, and although I don't have the kind of expertise I'd have if I'd gained a professional qualification, my broad knowledge of the law and the workings of officialdom come in remarkably useful whenever I need to pursue a complaint.

If it wasn't for the fact that I have colleagues, office life would be bearable. That day, however, even more than usual, I had a catalog of annoyances and irritations with which to contend. For example, it was barely ten thirty when the smell of leftover Chinese takeaway, which one of my stockier workmates likes to microwave in our tiny kitchenette and eat mid-morning, wafted across to my desk. The bile was rising in my throat, and I needed a long, cold drink if I was to avoid an emergency dash to the lavatory. I made it over to the watercooler, where I was less than delighted to encounter Tom, a bouncy, recently joined administrative assistant, who still had evidence of a breakfast baguette in his luxuriant beard. He was to be the next source of irritation.

"Hey, Susan — just the woman. I've been meaning to say, I've set up an office Facebook group for organizing pub sessions and sharing stuff that's going down. Fling me a friend request and I'll add you to the group."

"You haven't been here long, have you?" I managed, as the water glugged into my glass. "Everyone knows I'm not on Facebook."

"Wow, for real? So how do you connect with people? Are you on Instagram or WhatsApp? I can set up groups on there, too."

"I'm not *on* anything. I find picking up the phone or sending a text usually works."

"Yeah, that's okay for, like, your *mum* or whatever, but how do you keep track of all your old mates from school and uni? How do you organize your social life?"

I wasn't in the mood for this. For some reason my eyes were pricking — perhaps it was the harsh overhead lighting. I explained, briskly, that I had no desire to maintain contact with people I'd had a fleeting connection with many years ago, and that I kept my life very simple. If he felt compelled to inform me of office get-togethers or an important piece of workplace intelligence, he should email me. I could have suggested that he walk the fifteen paces from his own desk to mine, but I don't like to encourage that sort of thing.

Just after one o'clock, as I was binning the white-bread-and-butter sandwich that I'd hoped I'd be able to tolerate, and struggling once more to corral my thoughts, I was irritated by the sight of Lydia — a recently single thirtysomething colleague — striding around the perimeter of the room. Every minute or so she peered at a wristband. I needed to begin work on analyzing a table of figures I'd printed out before my short break, but my colleague's perambulations were making it impossible.

"Lydia, are you being *deliberately* infuriating?" I snapped, the fourth time she passed my desk.

She told me she'd been given an activity tracker for her birthday and was doing her ten thousand steps a day. She needed to get in shape, now that she was back "on the market" — not words I would choose to describe our shared status as single women. On her fifth approach, I asked why she wasn't walking outside, like any normal person. Apparently, she couldn't; she had a blind date that evening, and didn't want to end up covered in sweat and grime from pounding the streets. At the sixth time of passing, she said I seemed so interested in what she was doing that I might like to join her. I declined. Circuit number seven, and I felt like throttling the woman. I was in desperate need of silence and calm, so I could focus on getting though this gruesome day. I suggested she try walking up and down the stairs; that way she'd shift the excess pounds from her rear twice as fast.

"Getting the message, Susan," she snorted, altering her course and pushing through the swing doors. I'm sure I couldn't have been the only one to breathe a sigh of relief.

Midafternoon, and Tom — vying with Lydia for the title of most annoying colleague of the day — sidled up to my desk. I tried ignoring him, but it seemed he was determined to stand and wait until I acknowledged his presence.

"I'm doing a charity pub crawl next month, and wondered if you'd sponsor me," he said. "I can email you the fund-raising link direct, seeing as you're not joining the twenty-first century anytime soon."

"What charity is it for?" I asked, throwing down my pen.

"I haven't decided yet. I just know I need to do something meaningful with my life. I might do it for pandas — I love pandas — or I might do it to stop global warming, 'cos that's something I really care about at the moment. There are so many good causes, though. Where should a guy start?" He pulled an exaggeratedly sad face.

"I hear the Stroke Association does very good work," I said. I don't know why, but my eyes started to prick again.

"Maybe, but it's not very sexy. And anyway, I think my mate shaved his beard off for stroke victims last year. I want to do something different."

"Well, come back and see me when you've made up your mind," I said, swiveling my chair away from him.

Everyone's raising money in my office these days. It used to be a once or twice a year thing, but now it's a constant stream of charity-this, sponsored-that: walking, running, cycling, swimming, climbing, bungee-jumping, trekking, wading through mud. This isn't a complaint, you understand. I wholeheartedly approve of people using their energies for the good of others, rather than for themselves — well, if you don't count the associated health benefits and impression of virtue. Having said that, though, the personal interactions that seem to be part and parcel of these things *do* have an impact on office productivity. I decided I should have a word with my line manager, Trudy, even though I wasn't really up to it. I wished I hadn't bothered; she turned out to be yet another source of frustration.

Trudy joined the department on the same day, and at the same level, as I did, more years ago than I care to think about. At first, she would nag me to join her for a cup of coffee in our lunch break or for a glass of wine after work, but she soon realized she was wasting her time. Since then, Trudy's clawed her way up to the dizzying heights of team management, while also having four interludes of maternity leave. Photographs of the end products of those interludes were prominently displayed on her desk, in all their buck-toothed, freckle-faced glory.

While she leaned back in her chair and smiled indulgently, I explained how it would make sense, in terms of efficiency, to have a single allotted time every month at which colleagues could promote their charity, sign up sponsors and collect in any real physical money. Trudy, who I assume was trying to be amusing, said it would make more sense in terms of efficiency to have a single allotted time every month at which I was allowed to make my productivity-enhancing suggestions. She chuckled; I didn't. Perhaps she sensed my dissatisfaction with her reaction, because her expression changed from one of mirth to one of concern. She asked if I was alright, if I'd caught the summer cold that was doing the rounds. As she proffered her box of tissues, I made my excuses and left her room.

Six thirty: the only sound was the distant buzzing of the vacuum cleaner, getting louder as it approached the now-empty office, and unruly thoughts were jostling their way back into my head. I was switching off my computer and putting my phone in my bag, when our Romanian cleaner, Constanta, pushed open the door and came huffing in. I braced myself for our usual exchange.

"Evening, Susan. How are you today?"

"Excellent," I lied. "You?"

"Good, good. I always good. You last person in office?"

"As usual."

"Ah, you hard worker, Susan, like me. Not like other lazy layabouts."

She came over to my desk, and bent down to whisper conspiratorially, her breath hot on my ear.

"That one over there. He drop dirty tissues on floor. Tissues full of snot and bogies. Yuck. And that one over there. She leave mugs all over her desk, covered in thick, greasy lipstick. Why she not put them back in kitchen? She got half a cupboardful. I used to clear desk for her, now I not bother. I'm not her mama. Big babies." She straightened up. "So, Susan, you still not got husband?" If it was anyone else, I'd tell them to mind their own business, but she and I have the same conversation every day, and I've learned my lines. I told her she must be joking.

"Very sensible lady. Men! We slave away to earn money, then get home and start slaving there, too. And what do they do when they finish work? Put their feet up and expect to be waited on, or disappear God knows where with their wages and come back with empty pockets. My own husband, Gheorghe, he vanished, just like smoke — poof. Left me with four daughters to bring up. They all married now, all their husbands waste-of-spaces, too. I got three cleaning jobs so I can send money back to them. I tell them to hide it under the floorboards."

"They're lucky to have a mother like you," I said, checking I had my Oyster Tube travel card in my pocket and switching off my fan. I stopped; the words felt different today.

Constanta was beaming. "We the same, you and me. We know what we want from life and we know how to get it. We not care what other people think. You a good person, Susan."

She went to pinch my cheek, remembered that I always dodge such physical contact, then headed across the room to plug in her vacuum cleaner. As I left the office building and was assaulted once more by the heat radiating up from the paving slabs, I was pleased with the front I'd managed to put up all day, despite the constant onslaught from my colleagues. No one would ever have guessed. But, then again, I have no difficulty concealing my feelings from others. You'll see — it's a talent I have.

Once home, I called Edward. It was odd to be conversing with him twice in one day, and to be doing so civilly for once. Circumstances dictated that we had to heave our sizable differences to one side and work together, at least until the funeral had taken place and the estate had been dealt with. He informed me that the undertakers had been, and that he'd provisionally arranged the funeral for Friday of the following week. A cremation, he said. I had no objection to that; it's beyond me why someone would want their family member's body to putrefy in the sodden earth, or why they would want a shrine to frequent, as though the soul of the deceased will perch on the headstone waiting for a visit and a chat. So, good; we were in agreement.

"I don't expect she left a will," I continued. "She never mentioned anything. There'll just be the proceeds of sale of the house and some savings to be divided between the two of us. I'll deal with all that."

A pause. "She did write a will, actually, Suze. A few weeks ago. She'd heard some program on the radio about how everyone should have one. I told her I didn't think she needed it, but you know what she was like." I remember a defensive tone entering his voice, or is that just hindsight?

"Really? She didn't mention anything to me."

He'd already contacted the solicitors to inform them of our mother's death, which I thought showed remarkable practicality on the part of my brother, whose executive skills generally went no further than placing an accumulator bet or ordering a pizza.

"They told me they'd dig out the will and be in touch with us. I'm leaving it all in their hands. I don't know anything about this kind of thing."

I was going to be tied up at work that week so was forced, very much against my better judgment, to rely on Edward. I gave him meticulous instructions concerning the registration of the death, provided a list of suitable venues for the wake and directed him to my mother's address book for details of friends who should be notified. He snorted when I asked if he was capable of doing all that.

It was nine o'clock by the time I finished speaking to Edward. I'd had nothing to eat all day, apart from two Rich Tea biscuits for breakfast, and I felt dizzy. I cooked a small portion of plain rice and sat down at the kitchen table to conquer the rising queasiness. The French windows to my courtyard garden were ajar, and the howls of upstairs' new baby and the reek of next door's bins drifted in. I should explain, I live in a flat — the ground floor of a converted Victorian terrace — in South London. I rented it for over ten years until the landlord decided to sell, by which time I'd saved up enough from my measly civil service salary for the deposit. So I'm now a property owner, or, more significantly, the holder of a colossal mortgage.

While I summoned the willpower to raise fork to mouth, I watched my neighbor's cat Winston, a sturdy ginger tom, meticulously grooming himself on my terra-cotta paving tiles. I'm not usually fond of cats; I dislike the way they scuttle under parked cars or squeeze through railings when you make friendly overtures. Winston, though, is an exception. He stands his ground when you approach him, and tolerates stroking and petting until he's had enough, at which point he yawns, stretches and pads away at his leisure. He's intimidated by no one and feels no need to ingratiate himself. He calls to mind Kipling's "The Cat that Walked by Himself," one of my favorite stories as a child. I remember my father, in his more lucid moments, sitting me on his lap and reading it to me from a battered volume of the *Just So Stories.* As I watched Winston, I wondered where that book was now. Probably in a forgotten box in the loft of the family home, which reminded me of the work that lay ahead in clearing it for sale. That thought, in my present condition, was overwhelming.

■ ■ ■ ■

When I called Edward a few days later to check on his progress with my list of tasks, the phone rang out for an inordinately long time. I was about to hang up when a voice that wasn't Edward's mumbled, "H'lo?" I hesitated, apologized for dialing the wrong number and ended the call, before remembering I'd rung my mother's number on speed dial. I immediately phoned back. Again, the same off hand greeting.

"I rang a moment ago. Is this the Green household? Patricia Green — the late Patricia Green — and her son, Edward?"

"Yeah, it is."

"This is Edward's sister, Susan. I'd like to speak to him immediately."

"Oh, Susan. Yeah, er, right. I'll just see if he's around."

The sound of murmuring, followed by an unnaturally cheery, "Hi, Suze, how're you doing?"

"Edward, who's that man, and why's he answering our mother's phone?"

"Oh, it's just Rob. I said he could doss down for a few weeks while he sorts himself out. He's just got back from traveling. He's a great guy."

"I don't care how great he is. I don't want strangers staying in our mother's house. Tell him he'll have to leave. She's only been dead three days, and the house is full of her valuables."

"Look, Suze . . ."

"Susan."

"Look, I've known Rob since college. You met him yourself a few times, years back. He needs a bit of help at the moment. He was there for me when I was going through a tough time and now I'm there for him. I'm not turfing him out — he's got nowhere to go." My brother's loyalty to his drinking pals is really quite touching.

I decided to pursue the matter in person on my visit to Birmingham. It wouldn't take me long to have this Rob character back on the streets. I turned the conversation to the more pressing matter of the funeral arrangements. Edward told me I'd be pleased to hear the wake was sorted; he'd hired the back room at a pub called The Bull's Head.

"We can bring our own food if we want, and have a tab behind the bar," he said with pride in his voice.

I explained that that was completely inappropriate; he'd have to cancel the booking immediately. "Mum was teetotal. She would've been horrified to think her wake would be in a pub."

"Bollocks. She wasn't teetotal. She liked a sherry or a half of shandy from time to time. And she'd want to know people were enjoying themselves, which they will at The Bull's Head. She wouldn't've wanted china teacups and polite conversation."

"That's *exactly* what she would've wanted. That's the sort of person she was. She wasn't a pints-of-beer-and-a-knees-up kind of woman."

"Well, that's what it's going to be, Suze, and everyone's going to have a good time, and swap funny stories about her, and get a bit pissed if they want to. And if you don't like it you can bugger off."

2

Deciding on the correct attire for an occasion is simple. First, know yourself. I'm petite and angular, so I look best in neat, fitted clothes. Second, make sure that any item you buy coordinates with everything else you own. I do this by only buying clothes that are charcoal gray or black, colors that contrast with my blond hair. Finally, glance occasionally at the style sections in the newspaper. I'm not against modifying my purchases if a trend makes sense. You might dismiss this as time-wasting frivolity, unworthy of a serious-minded woman. However, it's precisely so that I *don't* have to spend time worrying about my appearance, but am always dressed appropriately and well, that I've devised this simple modus operandi. And, of course, applying such organizational techniques to other aspects of your daily life, as I try to, considerably reduces the likelihood of being ambushed by unforeseen circumstances.

I smoothed a plain black shift dress front-down on my bed, laid a piece of A4-sized tissue paper on top of it and carefully folded it around the paper. I then wrapped the dress in another piece of tissue and placed it in the bottom of my suitcase. I did the same with a black cashmere cardigan. I packed tissue paper into the front of a pair of black patent leather heeled court shoes, put each one in a separate shoe bag and positioned them at the sides of the suitcase. The forecast for Birmingham was for dry, warm weather for the next two days but, never liking to leave anything to chance, I repeated the folding exercise with a light-weight gray trench coat and placed it between the shoes. After adding a black linen skirt, a charcoal T-shirt and a thin gray cotton sweater, I rolled up my underwear and fitted it into the remaining gaps.

As I locked my front door and turned to wheel my suitcase to Clapham North Tube station, the postman handed me a wad of mail, mainly catalogs from shops I have no recollection of ever having visited and pleas to change internet provider. I squeezed most of it through my letter box to be recycled on my return, retaining the two proper letters. When, half an hour later, the stifling Tube train slowed to a crawl, then to a halt, just after Leicester Square station, I had no reason to think it wouldn't start moving again soon. Using a folded tissue, I dabbed at my forehead, then unfastened one of the buttons at the top of my black cotton sundress. I lifted my hair away from the back of my neck, but the air was too stagnant to provide any cooling relief. My breath, when I exhaled through my mouth, felt like a hairdryer. It wouldn't be legal to transport livestock, let alone humans, in such conditions.

"Apologies for the delay to this service," crackled the driver's voice over the loudspeaker. *"I'll let you know as soon as I have any information."*

On looking around, my immediate impression was that a swarm of butterflies had been trapped with us; many of my fellow passengers were using their tickets to fan themselves, an act that must have been more symbolic than effective. I was thankful I'd managed to grab a seat when I boarded the train, unlike more than half of the carriage's occupants, who were packed into the spaces by the doors. I caught my reflection in the darkened window opposite. My recent inability to eat had taken its toll: I looked deathly pale; there were hollows under my cheekbones; the sockets of my eyes were cavernous. If my appetite didn't return soon, I'd be skeletal within days. Was this entirely normal in my condition? I wondered.

Time flowed like lava, and the temperature continued to rise. People were shifting in their seats, pulling their clothing away from their damp skin and slipping their feet out of their sandals. It occurred to me how humiliating it would be if I were to vomit in this situation, and the thought made me feel more nauseous than I already was.

"No effing phone signal, as per usual," grunted the bodybuilder type next to me, who had rivulets of sweat running down his exposed lower legs to his saggy leather deck shoes. He jabbed, futilely, at the screen of his mobile, huffing that it would have been quicker to walk.

"Apologies once more for the delay," came the announcement. *"Rest assured I'll update you the minute I'm able."*

Two gray-haired old women sitting opposite me were gripping the handles of the holdalls on their laps, their knuckles white.

"There's no way we can make it in time now."

"We might not make it at all."

"What are you talking about?"

"Everyone's thinking the same. There's all sorts of dreadful things happening in big cities these days. This could be a terrorist incident. That's why they haven't given us any information — they don't want to panic us. They could've found a suspect package, or they could've had a warning that there's a suicide bomber on the train."

"Oh, lordy, Jan, don't talk like that." The woman's hand went up to her mouth.

I don't make a habit of interacting with strangers, particularly on public transport, but I feel duty-bound to be of assistance wherever I can, even if it's at a cost to myself. I leaned forward.

"Excuse me, but I couldn't help overhearing your conversation. I live in London, and this happens all the time. Not usually for this long, but I promise there's nothing to worry about."

"How can you possibly know that for sure?" snapped the doom-monger. "You can't. You don't know any more than we do. I just want to get off this train *right now.*"

I often wonder why I bother.

"Once again, sorry for the severe delay, which I've just been informed is due to the preceding train breaking down outside Tottenham Court Road station. The engineers are in

33

attendance, and we hope to have you moving again shortly."

The announcement seemed to shatter the general mood of forbearance, and everyone started talking at once.

"I've got a train to catch from Euston in fifteen minutes."

"I'm supposed to be meeting a group of overseas students at the British Museum at half past."

"I'll miss the start of the film if they don't get a move on."

"This is getting a bit claustrophobic."

"I'm dying for the loo."

I could have said, "My mother's dead, it's her funeral tomorrow, I haven't slept for days and I want to vomit." I never would, of course; I'm not a person who courts sympathy.

"You know they had to do an emergency evacuation of a train last month, don't you?" said the smart black woman sitting the other side of me, putting down her magazine. "It was stuck between stations for hours, just like this one. Everyone had to climb out through the driver's door and trudge for miles along the track in almost total darkness. I bet we'll have to do that."

There was a general murmur of unease, during which a skinny man in cargo shorts, who had taken off his shirt and tied it around his waist, sauntered into our section of the carriage. He was holding up a mobile phone, which he panned across us.

"What do you think about the delay, friend?" he asked the bodybuilder next to me, zooming in close. In response, the man raised his newspaper in front of his face.

I was the next target. "What do *you* think about the delay, lady?"

"Are you videoing this?"

"Yeah, of course. If this turns out to be a major incident I can sell the footage to the TV or the newspapers. Even if it's minor, someone might be interested. If not, I'll just stick it on YouTube, anyway. You'll be able to see yourself on-screen, lady."

"Turn that thing off, please. I have no wish to be on the news *or* on YouTube."

"That's right," said the woman sitting next me. "I don't want to be on the telly either. I haven't done my hair or anything." There was a general nodding of heads.

"Look, son," said the bodybuilder, "I'm asking you very politely, but very firmly, to stop filming. Pronto."

"Or what? Are you going to make me?"

"If you want to push it that far, yes, I am."

"Wait a minute," I said, making a valiant effort to rally myself. "I'm sure that won't be necessary. If this young man's got any sense he'll stop before he gets himself into trouble. I'd just like to point out to you," (I turned to the skinny man), "that this is a violation of our statutory right to a private life. We haven't consented to being filmed. We could take you to court for a breach of the Human Rights Act. Are you sure you can afford to pay us all compensation?" Complete rubbish, of course.

"That can't be right," he said, looking less sure of himself. "What about all those people you see on the news, in wars and stuff?"

"Yes, but the footage you see on the news is recorded in the public arena. We're all here in a private and personal capacity. It's entirely different in the eyes of the law."

He wavered, muttered something under his breath, then switched off his phone and put it in the pocket of his cargo shorts. He stomped off back down the carriage. It's incredible how easily people can be intimidated by the mere mention of the law. My fellow passengers looked relieved, but the incident had done nothing to help the way I was feeling. I rummaged in my handbag and found a supermarket carrier, which would be my only option should I be unable to contain the sickness any longer. I bowed my head and tried to block out the inane prattling around me.

Abruptly, there came the noise of an engine starting; a wheeze and a lurch, and the train crawled off. There was a muted cheer and a smattering of applause. Within a minute or two we were at Tottenham Court Road station, where the carriage cleared a little, and not long afterward I arrived at Euston. I'd missed my train to Birmingham, of course, and after an argument at the booking office, for which I didn't have the energy, I had no alternative but to buy a ticket for the next one, in just under an hour's time. The train company would be hearing from me.

On the concourse, in front of the electronic information boards, my fellow passengers and I waited like greyhounds in the slips for the "train now boarding" message and the announcement of the platform number. I resent the indignity of sprinting to the train to grab a seat, but, in the absence of a reservation, I had no alternative but to hurtle down the ramp and along past the almost-empty first-class carriages. Once on board, I settled myself, breathless and sweating, into a forward-facing window seat, placing my jacket and handbag next to me to ward off any unwelcome physical proximity. That ploy was effective as far as Milton Keynes, after which a pudgy young woman, dressed in gray jogging bottoms and a tight pink T-shirt became my traveling companion. Her jersey-clad thighs overflowed onto my seat, and every time the train swayed, which was often, her flesh pressed against mine. I shuffled as far over to the window as I could.

Contemplating the steady progress of the Grand Union Canal, sometimes veering away from it, sometimes hurtling toward it, I remembered the two letters. I wrestled my bag from the floor and took them out. I could see that the type-face through each address window was the same; one had been franked on Tuesday and one on Wednesday. I opened the older one first. It was from the firm of solicitors Edward had mentioned on the phone. The writer, a Mr. Howard Brinkworth, offered his condolences for the recent loss of my mother. He said she'd named him as executor of her estate; that he intended to carry out a valuation of her assets and apply for probate; and that he'd write shortly with details of the will. I was very surprised my mother had chosen to appoint a solicitor to act as executor, a role I could easily have fulfilled myself. I put the first letter back in its envelope and turned my attention to the second. After the usual preamble, Mr. Brinkworth got to the point:

> Under the terms of the will, your late mother has given your brother, Mr. Edward Green, a life interest in the family home (22 Blackthorn Road). This means that Mr. Green is entitled to live in the house for as long as he wishes; the sale will take place, and the proceeds divided equally between the two of you, only upon his vacating it or upon his death.
>
> The rest of your mother's estate, which consists of bank accounts, furniture and personal effects, is to be divided in equal shares between Mr. Green and yourself.

I found myself saying out loud, "For God's sake, Mum." The pudgy woman remained inert, headphones plugging up her ears, but several other passengers swiveled in their seats to see whether some entertainment was brewing. Finding no prospect of an argument or a fight, they turned back in disappointment. I carefully placed the letter back in its envelope, folded the two envelopes in half, in half again, then twisted them together as tightly as I could. I shoved them to the bottom of my bag and stuffed it back down by my feet. What on earth could have possessed my mother, letting Edward keep the house for as long as he liked? It was *inconceivable* that this had been her idea.

My traveling companion had by now opened a bag of cheese and onion crisps, and I found their pungent smell, mixed with that of the chemicals from the nearby toilet, unbearable. I took a sip from my bottle of water and tried to order my thoughts. Perhaps my mother's mental state, after her first two strokes, had been worse than I'd realized. Or perhaps she'd deteriorated since I'd last seen her, somehow managing to put on a show of lucidity when I'd spoken to her on the phone. That would have left her vulnerable to pressure from Edward. I'd need to act quickly if I wasn't to be deprived indefinitely of my rightful, and now much needed, inheritance.

3

I've single-handedly created the ideal life for myself in London. I have a home that is adequate to my current needs, a job that is appropriate to my skills and easy access to cultural stimulation. Except for my working hours, I have control over every aspect of my existence. I did, until recently, have what you might loosely term a "partner," but it was a relationship of convenience for us both; a simple arrangement that delivered the benefits of an intimate association with a member of the opposite sex but at no emotional cost. As soon as I discovered that chance, fate, bad luck — call it what you will — had seriously compromised my position, I severed our association cleanly and swiftly. My world remains impregnable, although that description seems a little ironic in the current circumstances.

In contrast, as my taxi pulled away from New Street station and headed toward

Blackthorn Road, I felt the disquiet I've always experienced on returning there. Perhaps that feeling derives from my almost pathological phobia of suburban life, of its seductive insularity and mesmerizing obsession with the mundane. Perhaps, more than that, it derives from the stirring up of memories of a past that I'd much rather forget. I have the terrifying sensation that my carefully constructed life in London is simply the dream of an unhappy girl, a dream from which I'm about to be woken. Irrational, I know.

Watching the familiar streets passing by through the taxi window, I cast my mind back to last Easter. I'd traveled up to Birmingham in time for my mother's usual Saturday tea of ham sandwiches, fruit salad and Victoria sponge. Reluctantly, I agreed to accompany her to church the following day. She had never, to my knowledge, had any religious faith, but in the last couple of years she'd started attending St. Stephen's, a church that I walked past countless times as a child. I wondered whether my mother's strokes had made her think about her mortality, prompting her to hedge her bets with God. Or maybe she was starting to lose her faculties and was becoming more susceptible to the influence of other people;

Margaret and Stan had been trying to lure her through the doors of St. Stephen's for as long as they'd been her neighbors.

"You'll enjoy it, Susan," she assured me as she put on a flimsy lilac cardigan and took a clean handkerchief out of the kitchen drawer. "I was nervous before I went, but straightaway it felt so familiar. It takes me back to when I went to church as a youngster. You'll feel the same, I'm sure."

"We didn't go to church when I was a child, remember?" I replied, heading to the hallway for my jacket, which was hanging on the peg rack by the door. "You never took us. You and Dad were atheists. You reap what you sow, isn't that what they say in the Bible?"

My mother joined me in the hallway, fumbling for the keys in her handbag. I spotted them on the hall table and handed them to her.

"I'm sure I did take you when you were little. And I've never been an atheist, Susan. Your father maybe, but not me. I've always had faith, but life's so busy, things get pushed to one side. And it might've helped your father if he'd believed in something. Anyway, I'm glad you're coming along — I can't get Eddie to give it a try."

"That doesn't surprise me. He doesn't get

out of bed until midday. And he's never exactly been the spiritual type. Mum, are you forgetting something?" I held up her coat like a waiter in a restaurant. She turned back from the front door and slipped her arms into it.

"He thinks about things much more deeply than you imagine, Susan. He's very sensitive. Religion can be a great comfort if you're troubled or afflicted. It can give you a lot of strength."

"The only things Edward's afflicted by are acute laziness and fecklessness," I said, following my mother out of the house.

"Susan, listen to me." She stopped halfway down the crazy-paved path and turned to me. "Eddie needs supporting. If anything were to happen to me, I want to know you'll keep an eye on him, make sure he doesn't go off the rails."

"He's forty-three years old — he's an adult. He doesn't need his big sister looking after him. Not that he's ever taken my advice on anything, anyway. He does his own thing. I might think he's a complete waste of space, but that's how he's chosen to be. He's absolutely fine in his own useless way."

I closed the curlicued wrought-iron gate behind us, and we walked down Blackthorn

Road, past the other neat 1960s semis and occasional self-effacing detached house. My mother kept falling a step behind me.

"He's not like you, Susan," she said after a while. "You've always been so sensible, so capable. I've never had a moment's concern about you. But Eddie, he's got an artistic temperament, like your father. The slightest thing can destabilize him."

We'd reached the squat church at the junction between our road and the high street. Margaret and Stan, who were lurking under the portico, spied us and waved.

"Happy Easter, Patricia." They beamed in unison, taking it in turns to kiss my mother's powdery cheek. "And happy Easter, Susan," Margaret continued, lunging toward me. I took a step backward and put out my hand.

Walking into church, I found myself being cross-questioned on the minutiae of my life in London. Fortunately, the service was about to start, and I managed to edge into the pew ahead of my mother, using her as a bulwark between myself and the tenacious Margaret. The service passed painlessly enough: the hymns were upbeat; the vicar was businesslike; and, more important, it was over quickly. Afterward, Margaret and Stan tottered back up the road with us, making the half mile feel like ten. Margaret engaged my mother in a detailed discussion about which variety of potato was best for roasting, while Stan regaled me with the teething troubles they were having with their new boiler. As we said goodbye and my mother headed for the front door, Margaret clutched my arm.

"So what do you think about your mum? We're a bit concerned about her," she hissed. "She seems to be getting a bit forgetful. She doesn't always remember things we've told her, or arrangements we've made."

It came as no surprise to me that my mother forgot what Margaret and Stan said to her; their subjects of conversation weren't exactly captivating. And her failure to remember arrangements to meet them could simply have been expediency. I had, however, been noticing an increasing absentmindedness on her part, although I had no intention of admitting that to the neighbors.

"She seems fine to me. Perhaps it's *you* who's getting confused."

I prepared the Sunday roast while my mother set the dining table. Edward, not surprisingly, had arranged to be away for the weekend — or, as my mother believed, had an invitation he was unable to turn down — so it was just the two of us. Over lunch she told me about the new block-paved driveway at number 25, of which she approved, and the goings-on at number 18, of which she didn't. Afterward, I washed the dishes and my mother dried, then I phoned for a cab. It came sooner than expected. I gave her a quick peck on the cheek before hurrying down the path. My last sight of my mother, ever, as it turned out, was of her bending down to pick up a chocolate bar wrapper that had blown onto the doorstep.

I was unsure whether to ring the bell or simply let myself in. When my mother was alive, I'd ring first out of politeness, only using my key if it appeared she was in the garden or otherwise occupied. To ring the doorbell in these altered circumstances, however, would have felt like conceding something I wasn't prepared to concede. I let myself in. I could hear music blaring from the kitchen, at a volume never heard during my mother's reign. It was something I recognized from my far-distant student days: *London Calling* by The Clash. Opening the kitchen door, and preparing to confront Edward about our mother's will, I was disoriented by the sight of a man stooped over an iPad, naked except for a small white towel wrapped around his waist. He was swaying from side to side, elbows flapping in time to the music. His jaw-length hair, like wet fleece, was flopped forward, hiding his face from me. I did what it's traditional to do in such a situation and coughed. He straightened and looked over with the startled look of a man caught in flagrante.

Now he was upright, I couldn't help noticing how ridiculously tall he was. Some people might find such height attractive, but, as far as I'm concerned, anything over six feet is excessive and smacks of attention-seeking. I also couldn't help noticing that he looked surprisingly toned for someone so slim. I'm aware, too, that this might be considered a positive attribute, but, if you were to ask me what *I* thought about it, I would tell you it's simply evidence that a person spends too much time on the physical and not enough time on the intellectual. The color of his skin suggested that he'd wasted a lot of time lazing on a beach in the recent past; his long, straight nose dominated his other features; and he had what are commonly known as laughter lines radiating from the corners of his eyes, probably caused by squinting in the sun. It occurred to me that he wasn't entirely unfamiliar.

When he saw me, his face relaxed.

"Hi, Suze, really sorry about your mum. She was a lovely person, a true saint. Ed's just gone down the shops. I'd offer you a cuppa, but we're out of milk." He brushed his hair back from his face and stood there without a hint of shame for the fact that he was squatting in the home of a recently deceased old lady. "Apologies for the state of undress, by the way. I've just got in from work."

"You must be Rob. I don't believe we've met."

"Oh, yeah we have, a few times, when you were going out with Phil. It was before, you know, the accident. So it must've been years ago." He picked up the kettle and filled it at the sink. "I noticed there's some herbal tea if that floats your boat."

"I know what my mum keeps in the cupboard. I'll make my own drink once the water's boiled. There's no need to trouble yourself."

"Cool, just do your thing, Suze."

"Please don't call me Suze. My name's Susan. The only person who calls me Suze is Edward, who has his own warped agenda."

"Oh, okay. Whatever."

I'm sure you can imagine how I felt, returning to my mother's house — my childhood home — for the first time since her death, only to find it had been invaded by an uninvited guest. Not just uninvited, but occupying twice as much space as could be considered polite. I excused myself and went into the sitting room. It was only a week since my mother had died, but the room already looked like it belonged to a gang of slovenly students rather than a fastidious elderly lady. The regency stripe curtains, instead of being held neatly by their tasseled tiebacks, were pulled only halfway across, as though the effort required to open them completely was too much. The scatter cushions on the olive Dralon sofa, rather than being plumped and propped at regular intervals across the back, were squashed to one side, obviously having been used as pillows. There were newspapers strewed on the carpet and beer cans imprinting rings on the mahogany coffee table. The final touch was an ashtray — an amber-colored glass one that I remember my father using — that contained, not only cigarette ends, but telltale butts constructed from a torn Rizla packet. As I stood there surveying the debris, Rob, now in a bathrobe, strode in.

"I'll give the room a quick clear up," he said, throwing the papers and cans into a carrier bag and picking up the ashtray.

"I'd appreciate it if you'd refrain from smoking in my mother's house," I said, struggling to keep my voice calm and even. "She loathed cigarettes — she couldn't bear to be in the vicinity of anyone who was smoking. She was very proud of this house, and look at the state of it."

"I don't smoke myself, just the occasional . . . you know. We stayed up a bit late last night watching an old Hammer horror, and then I've been on-site this morning, so . . ."

Sickened by the sight of the room, and unsettled by the presence of Edward's friend, I edged past, picked up my suitcase and went upstairs. The door to my mother's bedroom was ajar. I put down my case and pushed it open. Immediately the familiar smell hit me; a mixture of camphor, lavender bags and lily of the valley eau de toilette. Mercifully, the bed had been stripped, but other than that the room looked exactly as I assume it had done on the night she died; there was still a half-full glass of water on the bedside table, along with my mother's pill case, a National Trust magazine and her reading glasses.

I began to feel light-headed, so I perched on the edge of the Lloyd Loom chair, across the back of which my mother's balding pink chenille dressing gown laid abandoned like a shed skin. The bedroom was dominated by the six-piece bird's-eye maple suite of which she was excessively proud. I remember her telling me that it cost over three months of my father's wages in the 1960s. On the dressing table was a silver-framed photograph of the four of us standing in front of a traction engine. I walked over and picked it up. In it, I looked about nine years old and Edward looked about seven. My parents were in the center of the picture; I was holding my father's hand and Edward was holding my mother's. We were all smiling, just like a fully functioning normal family.

I replaced the photograph on my mother's dressing table, next to a dish of potpourri, and drifted to the bay window behind it. Pushing back the net curtain, I saw my mother's navy blue Volkswagen Polo approaching the house and turning into the driveway. For a moment, I felt a spasm of guilt at the prospect of being caught by my mother snooping in her room, and then I remembered.

As I watched through the window, Edward got out of the car, stretched, hitched up his black jeans and reached across to the passenger seat for his trademark leather biker jacket. He plainly hadn't shaved for at least a week, or combed his hair for that matter. Skinnier than Rob and far shorter, he has, to my mind, a weasel-like sharpness to his appearance, which amazingly seems to render him attractive to some women. Until they get to know him, of course. Edward opened the boot of the car, took out a couple of supermarket bags, then, no doubt with a sense that he was being observed, looked up to the bay window and saluted. I let the net curtain fall back.

When I entered the kitchen, Edward was crouched by the fridge unpacking the shopping, and Rob — who had changed into jeans and a T-shirt — was leaning with his back to the sink. The CD had been changed; there was now some discordant modern jazz assaulting my ears. Edward stood, screwed up the carrier bags and threw them into the corner by the bin.

"Hi, Suze, looking a bit peaky. Been making yourself at home?" he said.

"I've got just as much right to as you."

"Touchy. I didn't say you hadn't, did I?"

I walked over to the kettle, reboiled the water and made myself a cup of peppermint tea.

"We've got things we need to talk about, Edward. In private."

"Shall I make myself scarce?" Rob asked.

"No, you're fine where you are. I'm not getting into anything heavy now. We've got the funeral tomorrow, Suze. That's what we should be focusing on. Not going over old ground."

"I have no intention of going over old ground. I'm talking about Mum's will and sorting out her affairs."

"Well, that can definitely wait until after the funeral. I'm not getting into any of that until she's resting in her grave."

"She's being cremated, Edward."

"I think Ed was speaking metaphorically," said Rob, helpfully. My brother snorted with laughter.

Rob started lumbering around the kitchen, noisily removing things from drawers and cupboards. I found his patent familiarity with my mother's belongings offensive.

"I'll get started or we won't be eating 'til midnight," he said.

"Rob's cooking us a spinach balti. He's a vegetarian, picked up some great recipes on his travels."

"Wonderful. However, I'm off curry at the moment, so I regret to say I won't be joining you. I'll make myself some toast later. I assume you have bread."

"We're pretty domesticated here, you know."

"Talking of which, what do you think you're doing smoking in Mum's house? And leaving beer cans on the coffee table? The place looked like a doss-house when I arrived."

"Mum isn't here anymore, is she? So it's *my* rules now. And according to my rules, smoking is allowed in the house. I agree with you about the mess, though. I prefer a tidy place. I'll have a word with Rob about that." He winked at his friend, who smirked, then turned away.

"You've got no respect, Edward," I told him. "You never have. This conversation will be continued."

I picked up my drink and left the kitchen.

"See you later," Edward called after me.

There wasn't the slightest chance of my joining Tweedledum and Tweedledee that evening. I was outnumbered, and it was clear my brother and that friend of his were gaining considerable enjoyment from seeing me at a disadvantage. I contemplated repacking my bag and moving to a hotel, but was aware that that would be playing into Edward's hands. Instead, I'd remain in my room, go over my reading for the funeral and make a list of the issues I intended to raise with him. It would be a taxing day tomorrow, particularly in my current state, and I had no desire to be unsettled any further by the infantile behavior of two supposedly grown men.

4

To say the funeral didn't proceed as I'd planned would be an understatement. I'd ask you to bear in mind, however, that I haven't been myself recently for several reasons, some of which you know, and some of which you may have guessed. At least, though, I can say I have a legitimate explanation for my part in what transpired. Unlike Edward.

I woke uncharacteristically late that morning; it was after nine thirty and the funeral cars would be there in less than half an hour. I struggled to ride the waves of nausea as I threw on my clothes and ran a comb through my hair. Edward and Rob were already in the kitchen when I entered, my brother sitting at the table, legs stretched out and arms crossed. I was pleased to see they'd both shaved. That was the only pleasing thing about Edward's appearance, though. While Rob had managed to conjure up a dark suit, albeit a crumpled one, Edward was sporting black jeans, a black shirt, a metal-tipped bootlace tie and black cowboy boots. His sleeves were rolled up, displaying his gallery of tattoos. I shook my head. Rob seemed determined to engage me in a conversation about the readings for the service, but I made it clear that I didn't wish to play along with his charade of cordiality.

I poured a glass of water, made a piece of dry toast and sat down opposite Edward. He put his elbows on the table and began drumming his fingers together. I noticed, for the first time, a tense look on his face, as though his usually pliant features had become ossified overnight. While I was tackling a corner of my toast, Edward suddenly pushed back his chair, went to the dishwasher and pulled out a heavy-bottomed cut glass tumbler that my mother used to keep in the rosewood display cabinet. He took a half-full bottle of whiskey from a cupboard, sat back at the table, poured himself a very large measure and drank it straight down.

"Anyone else?" he said, lifting the whiskey bottle by the neck, a defiant look in his eyes.

"Oh, that's really going to help the day pass smoothly, isn't it?" I said. "Are you intending to get drunk and make an idiot of yourself?"

"I might get drunk, and then again I might not. I haven't decided yet. And it's nothing to do with you anyway, Suze. I'll deal with it my way — you deal with it yours."

"Of course it's something to do with me, Edward. You and I are representing the family. You have a duty to behave in a befitting manner."

"What fucking family?" he grunted, pouring himself another large measure.

"You might want to pace yourself, mate," Rob joined in. "I mean, long day and all that."

"Yeah, Rob, I'm fine. I know what I'm doing." He took out a packet of cigarettes and a lighter from the pocket of the frayed suit jacket hanging on the back of his chair and picked up the tumbler. "I'm going outside for a fag. See how considerate I am, Suze?"

After the back door had slammed, Rob set about knotting the tie that had been hanging loose around his neck.

"Maybe cut him a bit of slack," he said, "he's finding it tough."

"Do you think he's the only one?"

"I just meant it'd probably help if you could both stay calm and support each other on a day like this."

"Edward and I support each other? Do you actually *know* anything about our family?"

Rob held his hands up in front of him.

"Okay, okay. Just trying to help. I remember going to a funeral with my ex-girlfriend, Alison. It was her uncle who'd died, and two of his brothers ended up having a fistfight in the cemetery just after they'd lowered the coffin. Family deaths bring all sorts of resentments to the fore."

"I assure you, nothing like that will be happening today. I don't generally engage in public brawling." I was about to continue when the doorbell rang. I went to open it. The undertaker, a Mr. Rowe, was standing on the doorstep, displaying a well-practiced expression of professional gravitas.

"Good morning, Miss Green," he said solemnly. Behind him I could see two black limousines: the hearse containing my mother's light wood coffin, and a second car for Edward and me. The sharp morning sun was cast back by the oil-slick surface of the vehicles, causing me to squint as I took in the scene. On top of the coffin I could see the simple, tasteful wreath that I'd informed Edward I'd order in our joint names. Propped up on the side, however, was a hideous bubblegum-pink arrangement of carnations spelling out the word *M-U-M.* That could be nothing other than deliberate provocation on Edward's part. Even *he* would know it was ostentatiously vulgar. He was unable to put his childish animosity on hold even for one day.

I'm not, as you're aware, prone to irrationality. However, as I stood on the doorstep looking at the coffin through the shimmering late-summer heat, the thought of my mother's pale, rigid body encased in that wooden box hit me like a sudden squall. I felt myself sway, and reached out to the door frame for support.

"There's no hurry, Miss Green," Mr. Rowe intoned. "Take your time. We're ready whenever you are."

"Just a couple of minutes," I managed, closing the door. "It's a body," I told myself. "Just a body, not your mother. An empty shell." While I was leaning with my back to the door and endeavoring to regain my composure, Edward strode out of the kitchen, shrugging on his jacket as he went. He stopped in the middle of the hallway.

"Well," he said, "let's get this show on the road."

The slow, inching journey to the crematorium passed in complete silence. I could have challenged Edward there and then about the ghastly wreath, but I was determined to maintain the decorum of the occasion. An argument in the back of the funeral car would be unseemly. Edward, who took the view that the seat belt laws didn't apply to him, was leaning forward, picking at the skin around his fingernails. I sat back on the cold leather seat and observed the parade of high-summer city life. When I was a child, I remember people stopping what they were doing and bowing their heads as a funeral procession went past. It was clear, however, that no one was paying us the slightest attention: young women showing off their tans in sundresses chatted to each other as they ambled down the street; businessmen with short-sleeved shirts and loosened ties barked into their mobiles; children tugged the sleeves of their harassed mothers or fathers, pestering them for ice creams. It was all offensively inconsequential.

Entering the cemetery through the iron gates, I watched the progress of row upon row of headstones, some weathered granite, some gleaming marble with brash gold lettering. Many looked abandoned, unvisited for decades; others were laden with gaudy artificial flowers. In death, as in life, you can't always choose your neighbors. I was glad my mother's body wouldn't be interred in this showground of death. I began to feel a chill creeping through me, despite the increasing heat of the day. As we advanced along the baking tarmac driveway lined with municipal flowerbeds, I rubbed my hands up and down my arms, trying to get some warmth back into them.

We rounded the last bend and the crematorium heaved into sight; a square, redbrick building, its functionality bringing to mind a power plant or electricity substation. Milling in front were about fifty or sixty people; more than I'd anticipated. Among the crowd, I spotted trusty old Margaret and Stan, standing arm in arm; my mother's brash younger sister, Aunt Sylvia, in animated conversation with her two like-minded daughters; and my father's brother, Uncle Harold, standing apart from the general throng. Rob must have taken a rat-run to the cemetery, as he was already there nattering to a couple of men who looked like his and Edward's type. Spotting the cortege, people ceased their conversations and put on their best mourning faces.

The moment I stepped out of the limousine, Aunt Sylvia scurried over and clasped me in a crushing embrace. Her intense, musky perfume caught the back of my throat and I wanted to retch.

"Such a sad day for you both. But she's gone to a better place."

I stood stock-still, waiting for the moment to pass. Eventually she released me and grabbed Edward. I wasn't out of the woods yet, though; Aunt Sylvia was followed close behind by her twin daughters, Wendy and Christine, who administered more hugs and stale words of sympathy. I was disconcerted to see, standing in my cousins' wake, a number of their offspring, and it occurred to me that I should have specified that there were to be no children present at the funeral.

"This is my Leila and Cameron," said Wendy, pointing to two bored-looking children of somewhere between eight and ten. "And these are Chrissie's twins Freddie and Harry," she continued, pointing to a couple of small blond boys dressed in identical suits and bow ties. "We thought we'd make a day of it, seeing as we don't come to Birmingham so often. We're off to Cadbury World this afternoon."

Fortunately, before I had a chance to reply, Mr. Rowe indicated that it was time to enter the crematorium, my mother's coffin having been hoisted onto the shoulders of the pallbearers. Edward and I followed behind to the echoing arpeggios of Vivaldi's *Four Seasons.* As we processed slowly down the central aisle of the gloomy crematorium I found I was becoming increasingly light-headed. My legs felt unsteady and I wondered whether I'd be able to make it to my seat at the front. This sudden overwhelming dizziness was a shock to me; I'm not a person who's prone to feebleness, either physical or mental. When I thought back over the last few days, however, I realized I'd eaten and drunk only the barest amount necessary to settle my stomach or quench my thirst.

I had a vision of my blood having turned to clear liquid as the nutrients were leached from it. This thought made me feel even weaker, and I half staggered to the row of seats at the front, collapsing in the first one I reached. Edward looked at me quizzically, but I turned my face away, not wanting him to sense my momentary vulnerability. Aunt Sylvia, my cousins and their offspring, and Uncle Harold joined Edward and me in the front row, while the other mourners filed into the seats behind.

The bearded vicar from St. Stephen's coughed, smiled and began the service. To be perfectly honest, I couldn't take in much of what he was saying, as I was concentrating on my breathing. In addition, a squabble had broken out between the twin terrors, who Christine was trying to separate and reprimand with loud hisses. I managed to lean forward, catch Christine's eye and put my finger to my lips.

"Sorry," she mouthed, giving one of the twins a sharp shove.

"And now for our first hymn," said the vicar.

We all stood as the opening chords of "How Great Thou Art" filled the crematorium. As soon as I was upright I realized that that wasn't a position in which my body wanted to be. I felt the blood draining from my head, like water from a sponge. I contemplated sitting down, but had no wish to draw attention to myself. Instead, I linked my right arm with Edward's, and held tightly on to his sleeve with my left hand. He was startled by this, understandably so as our last physical contact must have been decades ago. To give him his due, he didn't shake me off as I'm sure he would have liked to have done, but remained standing as stiff as a guardsman, self-consciousness written on his face. As the hymn came to an end I dropped Edward's arm and fell back into my seat.

"It's time now for our first reading, which will be given by Patricia's son, Edward," said the vicar.

Edward slouched up to the lectern, coughed hackingly and began reading from the Bible in a monotonous drone. With my brother no longer sitting next to me, and the aisle on my other side, I felt even more vulnerable. I could sense myself swaying. When Edward returned to his seat, I leaned against his shoulder, my natural self-possession having by now dissipated. The vicar intoned a few more words, while I silently timed my breaths: "In, two, three, four. Out, two, three, four." I suddenly became aware that the vicar was saying my name.

"Susan . . . Susan . . . ?"

He was holding out his arm, gesturing to the lectern. I fumbled in my bag for my copy of Thomas Hardy's poem, "If It's Ever Spring Again." Finding it, I got to my feet and climbed the two steps to the platform where I was to give the reading. As I tee-tered, I cursed myself for wearing heels; a solid flat sole would have given me much more stability. I placed my sheet of paper on the lectern and looked at my expectant audience. All attention was on me, apart from that of the twins who were rolling on the floor at Christine's feet, and the two older children who were playing computer games on handheld consoles. I was having difficulty making out individual faces, as the scene appeared to be smudging before my eyes. I turned to my piece of paper.

"If it's ever spring again, spring again," I began.

"Yes!" one of the computer-players yelped in a pause between my lines.

I looked up, fleetingly, found that the audience had become one great blur of color and turned my attention back to the poem. The words were now swimming around the page.

"I shall go when I went there. Sorry, I shall go where I went. Excuse me . . . I shall go where I went when . . ."

My vision had become pixelated. All I could see were tiny dots of light and dark pulsing in front of me, and all I could hear was a high-pitched buzzing noise deep inside my head. I was engulfed by a wave of tiredness that I no longer had the strength of will to fight. Sleep seemed like the most delightful, the most enticing thing in the world. My eyelids closed and I succumbed to it.

I gradually became aware of Aunt Sylvia's

voice clucking away from a great distance. I wondered vaguely what she was doing in my flat in the middle of the night.

"She's as white as a ghost. She needs to get the blood back to her brain. We've got to get her head between her knees. Carry her to the edge of the platform and sit her up. I've seen it happen before. It's the grief. She's overcome, poor thing. It takes some people like that. You grab her top half and you grab her legs. That's right, hoist her up to the edge."

I felt hands under my armpits and around my ankles, and was conscious of being lifted and bumped about. Despite having some awareness of what was happening, I found myself unable to move or speak. I was maneuvered into a sitting position, my knees were parted and my head was pushed down. The thought, *Oh, God, I hope nobody can see my underwear,* passed through my head. I could feel someone's arm around my shoulders and again hear Aunt Sylvia quacking.

"It's all going to be fine, Susan. You've had a funny turn. It happens to all of us. Take your time. Breathe deeply. Wendy's gone to get you a glass of water. Don't worry, you'll be back to normal in a minute. Just take your time."

Consciousness was returning to me now, but I didn't want to open my eyes. I had no desire to confront what had just happened, or its aftermath. I lifted my head slightly and closed my legs.

"Look, she's coming round. Susan, love, can you hear me?" Aunt Sylvia shouted in my ear. "It's Auntie. You're in the crematorium. It's your mum's funeral and you've just fainted on the stage in front of everyone. Can you hear what I'm saying?"

Mustering all the dignity that was left to me, I opened my eyes and said, "I'm fine. Absolutely fine. I'll just go back to my seat. Carry on with the service, please."

I looked up and saw Edward, still sitting in the front row, arms folded and a wry look on his face. He raised his eyebrows, unfolded his arms and clapped silently. An easy chair was produced from somewhere and I was helped to it by Rob and Aunt Sylvia. I was given a glass of water, asked several times if there was anything else I needed and then the service continued. Edward offered to read the Hardy poem; I'm sure he loved stepping into the breach left by my feebleness. There were prayers, another hymn — for which I remained seated — and then the curtains closed on my mother's coffin to the strains of her

70

favorite song: Doris Day singing "Que Sera Sera." As the song finished Edward leaned across to me.

"So," he said, "what was it you were saying about making an idiot of oneself?"

With the receding of the tide of nausea and dizziness to which I'd been subject to all morning I was left beached with my humiliation. It was a relief to me finally to close the door of the funeral car on the interminable solicitous inquiries concerning my wellbeing. My place of sanctuary, however, didn't remain such for long. Within moments, salmon-pink fingernails were tap-tapping on the window, the door was yanked open and Aunt Sylvia launched herself onto the seat next to me. Deaf to my protestations, she insisted on accompanying me to the wake; anyone with a modicum of sensitivity would have realized that a person who's just fainted at their mother's funeral would need time alone to compose themselves.

"Oh, I know you want to be brave, love, but it's no trouble. Chrissie'll cope without me for once. She'll just follow behind in the Merc with the twins. You're the one that needs me at the moment."

Strangely, Edward decided to travel in

Rob's mud-spattered van rather than in comfort with Aunt Sylvia and me. My aunt kept reaching across the leather seat to stroke my hair or pat my knee, her flashy rings and bracelets glinting in the sunlight as she did so.

"I understand you must be absolutely mortified by your behavior. I know I would be. But these things can happen to anyone. Nobody'll think any the less of you. Nobody'll think you're having a nervous breakdown, or that you've got some kind of genetic weakness or anything."

"I know that. Why on earth would they think that, anyway?"

"Well, you know, with your family history. On your dad's side, I mean. But nobody at all'll be thinking that, so don't you worry."

My parents' backgrounds were very different. While my father was from a solidly professional, metropolitan family of lawyers and accountants, my mother was from a hard-grafting Midlands family of manual laborers and factory workers. My father, himself, was a lecturer at a redbrick university, and was well-respected before his decline. It was at the university, in fact, that my mother and father met. My mother, a typist in the faculty office, had had her eye on my father for months before they ever spoke. He always dressed in a smart but jaunty manner: well-tailored tweed blazer, bow tie, suede shoes. They were both in their late twenties, and my mother's family had begun to think she would remain an old maid. When my father sidled up to her desk one day and asked whether she would like to go for afternoon tea with him, she felt like a character in one of the silly romantic novels she continued to devour until the end of her life.

After six months of afternoon teas — which later became trips to museums and stately homes and talks by the university's classical music society — my father's proposal of marriage was eagerly accepted. The tearooms, museums and stately homes turned out to be a smoke screen, though. Following my parents' picture-book church wedding, and despite my mother's pleas, their outings became limited to pubs, inns and taverns, indeed anywhere that had a bar.

In contrast, Aunt Sylvia, who's fifteen years younger than my mother, was always ambitious for a life of luxury. She began her hoped-for ascent at the tie counter in Rackhams department store; apparently, she'd applied to work at the makeup counter but had been turned down, which surprises me greatly considering how much of the stuff she's always troweled on. Although Aunt Sylvia managed to mesmerize a number of wealthy young men with her charms while wrapping their neckwear, she was always peremptorily discarded once they'd got what they wanted from her, or so I deduced from her conversations with my mother.

Eventually, giving up on her dreams, my aunt decided to take her chances with the builder who was sorting out my grand-parents' rising damp, had a low-key wed-ding at the local registry office and nine months afterward gave birth to my cousins Wendy and Christine. The builder, Uncle Frank, despite his unpromising beginnings, turned out to be exactly what Aunt Sylvia had wanted all along: a person whose main aim in life was to accumulate as much money as he possibly could. His line of busi-ness went from domestic repairs and main-tenance, to buying, renovating and reselling properties, to building housing develop-ments. The family went from a modest three-bedroom semidetached house on a suburban estate, to a 1960s detached house on a cul-de-sac, to an architect-designed ranch-style bungalow on a country lane. The upward trajectory of Uncle Frank's career was in exact opposition to the down-ward trajectory of my father's. I wonder if that gave Aunt Sylvia a flicker of satisfaction, despite her conspicuous displays of support and sympathy.

The funeral car pulled up outside a turreted Victorian pub, a peeling sign declaring it to be The Bull's Head. Aunt Sylvia expressed surprise that this was the venue for the wake, and for once I had to agree with her. In the potholed car park there was another flaking sign, indicating that the function room was down an alley to the side of the pub. Somebody, presumably one of the publican's minions, had stuck a sheet of A4 paper below the sign with drawing pins. On it was written *Patrisha's do this way,* with a smiley face drawn underneath. The narrow alley between the blackened sandstone of the pub and the breezeblock wall of the builders' yard next door was littered with cigarette ends, broken glass and something rubbery from which I averted my eyes. There was a smell of urine and blocked drains, and an insistent buzz of flies. I dreaded to think what our more genteel guests would make of this.

At the end of the alley was the function room, a pebble-dashed single-story extension. Walking from the fetid heat of the alley to the coolness of the room, I was hit by a new smell: a cocktail of stale beer and disinfectant. In the glare of the flickering fluorescent strip lighting I surveyed the room. The linoleum-tiled floor was the color of congealed blood, the sparse, high-up windows were laced with cobwebs and the wood-effect Formica tables lining each side of the long room were pocked with cigarette burns. There was a buffet table set up in the middle, on which was laid a selection of stodgy, carbohydrate-dense dishes and tooth-rotting, sugary drinks. Edward and Rob were already propping up the pine-clad bar at one end of the room. An almost empty bottle of red wine stood between them, and my brother was talking much too loudly. A few other people had arrived already and were standing in small groups, looking uncomfortable. Leaving Aunt Sylvia inspecting the buffet table, I marched over to Edward and his friend.

"What the hell were you thinking?" I hissed. "I trusted you with this. I was against the idea of holding the wake in a pub from the start, but I thought at least you'd choose a decent one, as you're such an expert. This is an insult to Mum's name. I'm ashamed, Edward. How am I going to face our guests?"

"Careful, Suze, or you'll have another funny turn," he replied, gulping down the dregs from his glass. "I know the landlord. He's done us a good deal — mates' rates. It means more money in your pocket at the end of the day."

"It's not about the money. It's about doing the right thing."

"Have a glass of wine and lighten up. We've got four cases to get through." He reached behind the counter and pulled out another bottle, which he unscrewed and sloshed into his glass.

"Don't mind him," Rob said in a low voice. "He's got his drinking head on. It's not surprising, today of all days."

"He's always got his drinking head on, and you're just encouraging him. You're as bad as each other."

"I'm keeping an eye on him, as a matter of fact."

"Ha."

Turning away, I spotted Uncle Harold entering the room. Until today, I hadn't seen him since my father's funeral more than twenty-five years ago, although he and my mother had stayed in touch by letter and had paid each other the occasional visit. His military demeanor was unchanged, despite the fact that he was now in his eighties. It was evidently down to me to welcome our more important guests, it being apparent that Edward had no intention of moving from the bar. I crossed the sticky floor to greet my uncle, who was accepting a glass of wine from a heavily pierced girl holding a tray of drinks.

"Feeling better now, are we, Susan?" Uncle Harold asked, grimacing as he took a sip from his glass.

"Oh, yes, back to normal. A bit of a stomach bug."

"Good, good, that's the spirit. Chin up, old girl. Your mother wouldn't have wanted you moping about and feeling sorry for yourself. Never helped anyone, that sort of behavior."

"Absolutely, Uncle Harold, I agree. I'm focusing on the practicalities, sorting out the estate and so on. No time for self-indulgence. By the way, I must explain — this choice of venue is due to an embarrassing error. We were supposed to be booking The Bull, which is a lovely old Tudor coaching inn, but Edward got in a muddle when he looked for the number in the Yellow Pages and ended up booking The Bull's Head instead, which, as you can see, is totally unsuitable. I hope you don't think this is the sort of place we'd choose deliberately."

"No, no, Susan, I quite understand. I realized straightaway that there must've been a terrible mistake. You have my sympathy. And for the death of your mother, too, of course."

"Thank you. And how are Aunt Julia, and Hugo and Sebastian?"

"Oh, everyone's doing splendidly, but very busy as usual. Julia was devastated that she couldn't make it today, but she has charity fund-raising commitments that she couldn't possibly cancel. You know how it is. Hugo's in Antibes at the moment on the yacht and Seb's on some tedious business trip to Brazil, otherwise I'm sure they'd be here, too."

I wasn't quite so sure. I've always had the distinct impression that Uncle Harold's family regarded ours with a mixture of haughty disdain and condescending pity. No doubt Uncle Harold kept in touch with my mother, and had attended her funeral, out of some old-fashioned sense of familial duty.

As the conversation was foundering, Edward appeared, swaying at Uncle Harold's side, bottle in one hand and glass in the other.

"Great to see you, Harry," he roared, putting his right arm plus wine bottle around Uncle Harold's shoulders. He clinked glasses with him with such ferocity I was surprised they didn't shatter.

"Good afternoon, Edward. Deepest sympathy, and so forth. You seem to be bearing up. Been raising a few glasses, have we?"

"It's what Mum would've wanted. I keep telling Suze that, but she's got no sense of fun at all, have you, darling sis?" He attempted to put his left arm plus glass around my shoulders to link the three of us together, but I managed to duck out of the way.

"I'm sure Susan is dealing with things her own way, Edward. And between you and me, although I understand that you want to give your mother a good send-off, I'd suggest that you have a little break from the pop."

Edward was put out by Uncle Harold's lack of bonhomie and removed his arm. I looked around the room. There were small knots of people chatting quietly, eating white bread sandwiches and drinking cheap orange juice from plastic cups. There was one group consisting of my mother's neighbors, most of whom I knew by sight; another group of slightly more arty types, who I assumed were from my mother's reading circle; and a third group, centered around the vicar, who were clearly from St. Stephen's. Aunt Sylvia, Wendy, Christine and the children, who had just finished loading up their plates from the buffet, came over to join Uncle Harold, Edward and me. While I made the necessary reintroductions — my father's and mother's sides of the family not having met for many years — Edward, who appeared to have forgotten he had a glass in one hand, took a slug from his bottle.

"Wendy, Chrissie, looking as luscious as ever," he slurred, leering at them. "You'd never know you two were such scrawny kids." They both tittered, uncertainly.

"You remember the twins, don't you, Harry? Last time we were all together, at Dad's funeral? What would we have been then? Early teens, late teens? Not you, Harry, you've always been old." He sniggered, then continued on his theme. "Wendy and Chrissie were plain Janes back then. And now look at them with their long blond hair and curves and everything." He waved his wine bottle in an undulating motion. "It's legal, isn't it, to marry your cousins? Not that it's necessarily marriage I'm thinking about." Nobody knew quite what to say to this.

"Yes, very charming young ladies," Uncle Harold volunteered. "So nice to meet you again, and your delightful mother." Aunt Sylvia blushed through her pancake foundation.

"Well, Sylvia was a bit of a looker in her day, too, weren't you?" Edward continued. "I remember when I was a boy, and you'd come visiting with your tight skirts and your slinky tops and your high heels." He sighed and closed his eyes for a moment. "Very confusing to a growing lad, all of that." Aunt Sylvia blushed a deeper shade of pink and instinctively fastened an extra button at the top of her blouse.

"Shut up, Edward, you're embarrassing yourself and everyone else," I told him.

"What was I saying earlier, Harry? No sense of fun, my big sister. She's like a black hole into which all joy and pleasure is sucked."

"Now, look here, Edward," said Uncle Harold. "We can all see that you've had a few drinks, but I'm not sure any of these ladies are enjoying the way this conversation is going. Perhaps you'd like to go outside for a breath of fresh air and come back when you're feeling better."

"Feeling better?" shouted Edward. "There's nothing wrong with me. It's just all these boring old farts getting me down." The conversations in the small groups ceased, and everyone turned to see what was going on. Edward found he had an audience. "All you lot," he continued, gesticulating around the room. "You should be having a knees-up, you should be getting pissed and having a party. Celebrating a life. And all you can do is stand around making polite conversation and nibbling sandwiches. Bloody well enjoy yourselves, can't you? It's free booze, for fuck's sake."

"Edward, listen to your uncle," urged Aunt Sylvia. "You've gone too far. You're upsetting everyone."

"Oh, put a sock in it, you dozy cow."

"Edward, that's enough," I said, grabbing his arm. He shoved me away with more force than was necessary, and I stumbled backward on my stupid heels. Rob, who had joined our group at the start of Edward's outburst, caught me before I fell to the ground.

"Take it easy, Ed," he said, helping me to steady myself. I shrugged him off.

Uncle Harold, who was used to dealing with obstreperous underlings, endeavored to take charge of the situation, but was regaled by Edward with a barrage of obscenities. Eventually Rob persuaded Edward, still cursing, to retreat with him to the bar, where he attempted to wrestle a fresh bottle of wine from my brother's hands. I apologized profusely, of course, to Uncle Harold, Aunt Sylvia and the room in general. It was clear, however, that nobody wished to prolong the debacle further, and people soon began to make their excuses and leave.

"Going the way of his father," I heard Aunt Sylvia whisper to Wendy and Christine as they and the children scuttled off to their appointment at Cadbury World.

"All be right as rain in the morning, you'll see," muttered Uncle Harold, undoubtedly relieved to be heading back to his impeccable family life.

Within minutes, it was just Edward, Rob and me in the room. I stormed over to them as Rob was trying to insert the arms of my swaying brother into his jacket.

"You've ruined things for me for the very last time, Edward. If you think I intend to let you stay in that house, your brain's even more addled than I thought. I'm going to make you regret you've got a sister, just like I've always regretted having a brother."

Back at our mother's house, while my cab was waiting outside, I threw my clothes into my suitcase and grabbed an old holdall from the cupboard under the stairs. Into it I shoved my mother's jewelry box, a set of silver dessert forks and a few other small items of value that I thought Edward might be tempted to sell. Slamming the door and heaving my luggage down the garden path, I felt a surge of strength from the pure hatred I felt toward Edward.

■ ■ ■ ■

SEPTEMBER

■ ■ ■ ■

5

On the first Saturday of this new month I set about drafting an email to Mr. Brinkworth, the executor of my mother's estate. Although it was only a few days after my mother's disastrous funeral I was feeling livelier than of late, perhaps because the morning sickness was abating, because I was becoming accustomed to it, or because the air was cooler and fresher. As I was about to click Send, there was a ring on my doorbell. I assumed it was the postman, as visitors to my flat are rare, particularly uninvited ones. Opening the front door, and expecting to have to sign for a parcel, I was astonished to find my erstwhile "escort" Richard standing there, as formal as a Jehovah's Witness. Before I could close it again, he inserted a highly polished brown brogue between the door and its frame.

Regrettably, it isn't just my mother's highly

suspect will and Edward's offensive behavior that I have to contend with at the moment. I haven't, until now, been inclined to address the other matter directly, not because I'm ashamed or "in denial," but because it takes time to come to terms with a new situation: to assimilate the facts, to mull them over and to decide how best to proceed. You will have realized I'm in the early stages of pregnancy. *But you're forty-five years old, single and of limited financial means,* you might well be thinking. I am, of course, acutely aware of those facts, and have been considering very carefully the options available to me.

I want to make it crystal clear that I've never had the slightest desire to become pregnant. I decided a long time ago that neither a husband nor children would feature in my life, valuing as I do my complete autonomy. That's why the understanding I had with Richard suited me so well. We first met over twelve years ago. I happened to be glancing one day through the "lonely hearts" column in a copy of the *Evening Standard* that someone had left on the Tube — not because I was lonely or was looking for a partner, but simply from boredom and idle curiosity — when a particular item caught my attention. I can still remember the wording:

Highly presentable man, midthirties, no desire to settle down, seeks independent, strong-minded woman for commitment-free mutual appreciation of the dramatic, artistic and gastronomic highlights of London and of each other.

I checked that no one was looking, tore the listing out of the newspaper and put it between the pages of my diary, where it stayed for the next few days. I must admit, I was feeling a little jaded by life at the time. I was thirty-two or thirty-three years old; living in London no longer seemed to be offering me the possibilities for excitement it once had; and my acquaintances from school, university and work were all rushing like lemmings into marriage and parenthood. "Why not?" I thought. "What have I got to lose?" It would be pleasant to attend the theater, galleries and restaurants with a companion. There would also be the ancillary benefit of having more intimate contact with someone on a regular and reliable basis.

I should explain, and I'm not being arrogant here but simply stating a fact, that I've never been short of male attention. Being petite, blonde and presentably turned-out seems to guarantee a certain degree of interest (a colleague once described me as looking like Kylie Minogue, if she'd spent her career working as an actuary. I'm not sure whether he intended it as a compliment). I find, though, that men invariably expect more than I'm prepared to give. Some want romantic love, a meeting of minds, a sharing of thoughts and feelings; others want veneration, deference, subservience. I'm not cut out for any of that kind of nonsense, which is why I was drawn to the listing in the newspaper. Here appeared to be a cultured man who wanted the companionship of the opposite sex with no hidden agenda. It would be like having an extramarital affair, but without the inconvenience of a husband back at home.

After weighing the matter up for a week or so, I replied to the PO box number. A couple of days later, after a businesslike phone conversation in which we agreed to the rules of our encounter — no long-term commitment, no emotional investment, no invasion of personal privacy — I met Richard at a fashionable restaurant in Chelsea, where I happened to know it was a struggle to get a table. He turned out to be surprisingly good-looking, in an uncomplicated sort of way. Everything about him was orderly and well-proportioned: his nose was neither too big nor too small; his medium brown hair was neither too long nor too short; his build was neither muscular nor slight; his eyes (which held my gaze as an equal) were a modest hazel; his skin had a wholesome glow; he was taller than me, but not excessive in height. His way of dressing was equally orderly: crisply ironed cotton shirt, pale chinos, a navy blue blazer and the aforementioned polished brown brogues. His manners were impeccable without being ostentatious and his conversation was interesting. After offering to pay for my meal, he made no fuss, and showed no signs of irritation, when I insisted on paying my share.

Richard informed me that he was a freelance arts critic and columnist, that he lived in Sussex and that he came up to London for one or two days each week. He said he was a busy man, dedicated to his interests and with no desire to be tied down by a family. He proposed that we meet every Wednesday evening, with the arrangements being made the Sunday before by phone. I told him I'd consider the matter carefully and let him know my decision. Two days later I called him to say I accepted his terms, on the understanding that either of us could terminate the relationship at any time with no questions being asked. The following Wednesday we went to see *La Traviata* at the English National Opera, and then went back to his room at a smart hotel, where things were more than satisfactory.

As I say, that was over twelve years ago. I'm sure neither Richard nor I envisaged the arrangement lasting quite so long, but it suited our needs perfectly. I enjoyed the gallery openings, the first nights and exclusive restaurants to which Richard had access by virtue of his professional contacts. Richard enjoyed having a reliable companion at those venues and events. We both appreciated having an intimate "relationship" that in no way compromised our independence. The only downside for me was the financial cost; I insisted throughout on paying my way, other than when tickets were complimentary or for the hotel rooms that Richard would have had to book in any event. In addition, I had to have a wardrobe of evening clothes, shoes and handbags, which I might otherwise not have bothered with. Such expenses made saving difficult for me, but I decided that the benefits justified the financial outlay.

Richard and I agreed early on that we wouldn't ask questions about each other's upbringing and family; the enjoyment of the time we spent together was the only thing that mattered. Because of his well-groomed appearance, his disciplined behavior and his precise, slightly old-fashioned manner of speaking, I formed the impression that he came from a military family — perhaps had been in the military himself. I hinted as much on a couple of occasions, and he didn't deny it.

I have no idea whether Richard saw other women during that time; I never asked as I didn't consider it to be any of my business. Because I knew nothing of Richard's intimate life outside our encounters, however, I insisted that it was he who employed the appropriate safeguards when we were together in his hotel room. I'd always assumed that such barrier methods were foolproof, but I've learned to my cost that they aren't. Perhaps I should have made doubly certain that nothing of this nature could occur by also taking precautions myself, but I thought that, if I did so, I might become less vigilant about policing Richard's obligation in the matter of personal protection. Anyway, something evidently went wrong, although I had no inkling at the time.

The manifestation of my current predicament began in what I understand to be the usual way: missed period, metallic tang in my mouth and then, a couple of weeks later, the onset of debilitating nausea and sickness. As soon as I found myself retching into the toilet bowl one lunchtime at work I knew without a doubt that I was pregnant. I took a test later that day, which confirmed the fact. With the tester stick lying on the table in front of me, and with hands that I couldn't stop from shaking, I picked up my mobile and sent a text message to Richard to inform him that it was over. I immediately received a reply, and an exchange of messages ensued:

Richard: This is completely out of the blue, Susan. I suggest we discuss it when we see each other next Wednesday. Shall we meet for drinks before the concert?

Me: There's nothing to discuss. We agreed at the start that either of us could end the arrangement when it no longer suited us, and that's what I'm doing.

Richard: That was years ago. Don't you think I deserve an explanation?

Me: That wasn't part of our agreement.

Richard: Just meet me next Wednesday

and we'll thrash this out. I had no idea you were unhappy.

Me: I'm not unhappy. Thank you for twelve pleasant years and good luck for the future. All the best. Susan.

My mobile phone rang half a dozen times during the following hour, but I let it go straight to voice mail. Eventually, there was one further exchange of text messages:

Me: Please stop ringing this number. There's nothing to be gained by further dialogue.

Richard: Fine. But don't expect me to be here when you change your mind.

You might wonder why, since I had no wish to have a baby and no moral or ethical objections to abortion, I was so quick to sever my connection with Richard. I could easily have carried on seeing him as normal, perhaps passing the morning sickness off as a stomach bug, while I organized the termination of the pregnancy. The truth is I felt angry with him. He had done this to me; it was because of my association with him that I was in this invidious position. It's a simple biological fact that the woman pays the price while the man gets away scot-free. In addition, I was keen to avoid any possibility of our falling into the clichéd roles adopted by people in cases of unplanned, unwanted pregnancies; the needy, vulnerable woman and the cold, disdainful lover. I could imagine the scene being played out: I tell Richard I'm pregnant; he assumes I've done it deliberately because I want a baby or some kind of permanence to our relationship; I try to convince him that it's the last thing on earth I'd want to happen; he offers gallantly to pay for the termination and accompany me to the clinic; I seethe with anger at his condescension and pity. No, much better to end it cleanly and swiftly.

I thought I'd successfully dispatched Richard, perhaps with a scintilla of regret on my part for the loss of our Wednesday evenings, but it wasn't quite over yet.

"Richard, this is harassment," I told him firmly, as he stood on my doorstep. "Please remove your foot and go away."

"Not until you've heard what I've got to say. Let me in and we'll sort this out."

I wavered. We might as well get this over and done with, I thought. I stood aside and let him enter.

"Well?" I asked, once he was ensconced in

my sitting room.

"Susan, the time we've spent together has been very valuable to me," he began. "It was only when I received your text message that I realized what an established part of my life our Wednesday evenings have become. I understand why you sent it. You want something beyond what we currently have, some guarantee that you won't be alone as you enter middle age. I didn't think I'd be able to make a commitment, but if not doing so means I'm going to forfeit our time together, then I'm prepared to give you what you want. Susan, I'd like to propose that you sell your flat and buy an apartment in a more central location, somewhere at the heart of things, within walking distance of the places we enjoy. I'll undertake to stay with you on Wednesday and Thursday nights, and spend the rest of the week in Sussex. I can't see any reason why this shouldn't be our new long-term arrangement."

Richard's uneasiness had dissipated, and he had a beneficent smile on his face. We'd really only ever seen each other in the rosy glow of a candle or a bedside lamp, under the dimmed lights of an auditorium or bar. Sitting on my sofa at eleven o'clock on a Saturday morning, he looked incongruous, like a fine old master hung in a modern gallery. He was someone accustomed to organizing his life exactly the way it suited him — using his decorous manners and his modest good looks to charm people when needed — and it clearly hadn't occurred to him that I wouldn't be won over by his petition. I couldn't help but laugh at his misplaced self-assurance. My anger with Richard ebbed away. I knew that the forthcoming scene wouldn't play out in the way I'd dreaded. It was I who held the cards. I might be pregnant, but I wasn't vulnerable.

"Well, Richard," I said. "That's a lovely idea. But obviously it'll have to be an apartment with a garden, for the baby that's on its way. And a decent size, too, to accommodate the prams, cots and whatnot that we're going to need. How much does a central apartment with a garden cost? I'll have to give up my job, of course, but I'm sure you'll be more than happy to pay the mortgage, and support me and the child. And we won't be able to go out in the evening anymore, because the cost of babysitters in London is astronomical. But don't worry, when we're together we can just cozy up on the sofa in front of the television and order takeaways. We'll have each other — at least, we will for two nights a week — and that's all that matters, isn't it?"

Richard's face was a picture. As I was speaking, his eyebrows rose higher and higher, and one corner of his mouth began to twitch. Sweat broke out on his forehead, despite the coolness of the day, and his normally glowing complexion turned a sickly yellow.

"What, you're pregnant?" he managed to stutter.

"Got it," I said. "Now, if you don't mind, I have an urgent email to send. Let me see you to the door."

Wordlessly, and with a stunned expression, Richard allowed himself to be led along the hallway. I opened the front door and stood aside to let him pass. He turned as if to say something to me, but then changed his mind. Reaching the front path, he turned again.

"You're not going to . . . I mean you wouldn't actually want to . . ."

"Goodbye, Richard," I said and closed the door.

And, although it's as much of a surprise to me as it would be to anyone who knows me, I think I *am* going to; I think I actually *do* want to.

6

Another visit to Birmingham, but this one
very different from the last. It was odd to
think that only a short time ago I was
debilitated by morning sickness and the
inevitable reverberations following the death
of a close family member. As far as my
physical condition was concerned, I was
almost back to normal. Emotionally — well,
I was on the up. Having dealt with Richard
and made a decision about the pregnancy, I
could address my mind to securing what
was rightfully due to me. Sitting there in
the reception area of Brinkworth & Bates, I
was fired up and ready for battle.

I know some people think of me as a difficult woman, but they would have to agree
that I never set out to be rude to anyone,
with the possible exception of Edward, who
deserves it. In fact, I pride myself on my
good manners: I relinquish my seat for the
elderly on public transport, often prompt-

ing feelings of shame in those who are younger and fitter; I'm meticulous about sending thank-you messages when I receive gifts, however ill-chosen they might be; I never push into a queue, even if people are obviously queuing in the wrong direction; and so on. I admit, though, that I don't believe in pussyfooting around. Ambiguity, at best, leads to misunderstanding and embarrassment; at worst, gives others the opportunity to take advantage of any vulnerability they sense on your part. I could tell that I would have to be dogged when it came to Mr. Brinkworth.

I'd sent the solicitor an email demanding details of the circumstances surrounding my mother's will so that I could establish the exact extent of Edward's involvement, but he hadn't had the courtesy even to acknowledge receipt, let alone address its contents. I'd discovered, however, that, as an interim measure, I could ask the court to block the grant of probate that Mr. Brinkworth would need in order to deal with the estate. Although the resultant delay would inconvenience me as well as Edward, I had no doubt that I'd be able to hold out longer than my brother, whose income is somewhere between unpredictable and non-existent.

It's a matter of constant frustration to me that I don't have a private office at work, which is clearly unjust given my level of experience and expertise; in my public-sector department, only those with managerial responsibilities have the honor of an office to themselves. Strangely, whenever I've applied for a supervisory role, I've been passed over. I've been told that that isn't where my talents lie, and I must acknowledge that there's no one else in the organization who's as conscientious as I am in analyzing complex data. The consequence of my not having my own office is that my colleagues can hear every word I say when I make a personal phone call at work. Whenever I chased Mr. Brinkworth for a response to my email, therefore, I had to take my mobile phone into the corridor by the lavatories; a very sorry way to conduct an important conversation.

Eventually, the solicitor allowed my call to be put through to him.

"Miss Green," he began, "you must *try* to understand that I'm not acting for you in this matter. Neither am I acting for your brother. Let me explain to you — my sole duty is to deal with your mother's estate in accordance with her wishes. To engage in lengthy telephone conversations or correspondence with you would simply incur unnecessary legal costs, which, as executor, I have an obligation not to do."

Mr. Brinkworth spoke slowly and deliberately, as though I might have difficulty following what he was saying, and I could sense that he had to restrain himself from adding "dear" to the end of his speech. I know the type very well. Mr. Brinkworth had almost certainly been educated at some minor public school, which overpriced, second-rate education had succeeded only in endowing him with the belief that he was entitled to deference from those less expensively educated. Unable to secure that deference in his everyday life, he'd qualified as a solicitor so that he could set up his own firm and rule it like the potentate of a tin-pot realm. I had no doubt that he treated his secretaries like his personal harem, and his female clients like imbecilic children.

"Well, *you* should understand, Mr. Brinkworth," I said, "that I won't take this lying down. I have a very strong suspicion that my brother plotted this whole thing to get his hands on my mother's property, and you share at least some of the guilt for allowing her to put her name to something which didn't reflect her true wishes."

"This nonsense will get us nowhere. I'm

aware that you've taken the misguided step of blocking me from dealing with the estate, so, in an effort to move things forward, I'm prepared to agree to a meeting with you. For the sake of transparency, your brother should also be present. I shall clarify any issues which you're struggling to grasp, after which I would expect you to remove the block and allow me to carry on with my job."

I was more than happy with the prospect of thrashing the matter out in person, and the necessary arrangements were made.

It was now a quarter past two; the meeting with Mr. Brinkworth had been scheduled for two o'clock. I arrived at the solicitors' offices on the dot, despite the fact that I'd traveled almost a hundred miles by underground and train that morning. There was no sign, however, of Edward, who only had to saunter along a few streets or take a five-minute cab ride if that proved to be too much exertion for him. On inquiring with the receptionist, I was told that the meeting couldn't begin until my brother had arrived. I expect he'd got so drunk or stoned the night before that he had no idea what day it was. I hadn't seen Edward since the fiasco of our mother's funeral, and I had no wish to do so that day. It appeared, however, that his presence would need to be secured. I tried calling the family house, but after a few rings the answering machine cut in. It sickened me to hear on the recording not my mother's courteous greeting, but Edward's would-be-hilarious gibberish backed by raucous laughter. I left a message requesting that he make his way to the solicitors' offices without delay. I may not have put it in quite such polite terms.

In the intervening days between my phone conversation with Mr. Brinkworth and our meeting I'd turned my attention to the antenatal rigmarole. I don't believe in seeking medical advice other than when absolutely necessary, preferring instead to research and treat any minor ailments I might have. Hence, other than when I registered with a general practitioner sometime in my late twenties, I hadn't had cause to visit my local surgery, and couldn't even recall its location. I was aware, though, of the necessity to notify the medical profession of my condition, and so left work early on the pretext of a dental appointment. The surgery turned out to be a tatty, converted, pre-war house, with frayed bottle green carpet, pale yellow walls and maroon gloss-work. Obviously, it was hazardous to have carpet on the floor, rather than a covering that could be disinfected, a matter that someone really should raise with the senior partner of the practice.

The doctor looked hardly older than a student, and was so fidgety that I wondered whether he'd ever encountered a flesh-and-blood patient. He spent almost the entire appointment picking at raw, flaking skin on the back of his hands and staring at a point somewhere above my left shoulder. When I told him I was pregnant, he raised his eyebrows and peered at my details on his computer screen, which can have revealed little other than my name and date of birth. Presumably he thought it would be more appropriate for me to be consulting him about the onset of menopause rather than the birth of a baby. After a stilted discussion during which the doctor tried to elicit information about my personal circumstances and I demurred, he finally completed the necessary formalities. Once all of that was out of the way I decided to take advantage of having a doctor before me to make some inquiries concerning the rights of a deceased person's relatives to access their medical records. He turned out to be a mine of useful information, despite his youth; perhaps they concentrate more on matters of paperwork than bedside manner at medical school these days.

I left the surgery with a handful of glossy leaflets about pregnancy and childbirth, which I skimmed through when I got back to my flat later that afternoon. They were invariably illustrated with photographs of content-looking, heavily pregnant women with their hands placed protectively on their bellies, or radiant new mums smiling proudly down at the precious bundles in their arms. More often than not there was a proprietorial male lurking in the background with a hand on their partner's shoulder. The women all looked youthful and radiant, glowing with the delight of appropriately timed procreation. I was at a loss to see what these instinctive breeders had in common with me; I felt like someone attempting to infiltrate a fundamentalist group with a less-than-believable cover story.

The leaflets brought home to me the reality of what would be happening over the course of the forthcoming months, not only to my own body, but to that of the growing creature inside me. The upside was that the nausea was due to abate completely within the next few days. There was, however, a multiplicity of downsides. I couldn't imagine my abdomen, which I consider to be well-toned for a woman of my age, distending to such gargantuan proportions. Neither could I imagine my modest breasts transforming into giant milk-producing udders. The bodily convolutions involved in the birth process itself didn't bear thinking about. I went to the sitting room and stood on the sofa in front of the overmantel mirror with a cushion stuffed between my blouse and my slip. I turned sideways, laced my fingers together under my cushion-belly and put on a placid, bovine, expectant-mother expression. No, it didn't look right. It most definitely did not.

I threw the cushion back onto the sofa and returned to the kitchen to study the leaflets. It surprised me to discover that what was referred to as my "baby" was already about three inches long and an ounce in weight. I'd been so preoccupied with the fallout from my mother's death, and with the clamorous physical symptoms of my morning sickness, that I'd failed to address the fact that what was growing inside me had gone beyond simply a clustered mass of cells. I didn't think of it as an actual person, but the information I read awakened in me a visceral sensation unlike any I'd experienced before. What I was now dealing with wasn't simply an abstract dilemma; at the end of this process — which the doctor had informed me would be in late-March next year — I'd be walking out of the hospital with a flesh-and-blood baby. That was so laughably surreal that my mind balked at the fact. I scooped up the leaflets and put them in the tray I keep for matters pending.

Later that day, as I was typing an email to the senior partner of the surgery giving him the benefit of my advice on the service provided by his practice, there was a knock on my front door. Fearing that I'd failed to put the wind up Richard sufficiently, I peered round the bay window curtain. It was only my neighbor, Kate, from the upstairs flat, who'd no doubt locked herself out yet again. I've reluctantly agreed to look after a set of keys for her in case of just such eventualities. When Kate and her partner, Alex, moved in five years ago, she was a well-groomed young professional woman working in an investment bank — something to do with personnel or communications, or that sort of thing. Both she and Alex had worked extremely long hours, and I'd barely seen or heard either of them. Kate was now the flustered, disheveled mother of a two-year-old and a baby, both of whom she had in tow. Alex continues to work the same hours, and must be as much a stranger to his family as he is to me.

"Oh, great, Susan's in," she said addressing the toddler, a small ginger-haired girl clinging to her mother's leg. "We didn't think she'd be back this early, did we? She'll never guess what we've done, will she?"

"I'll just get the keys for you," I said.

The baby, who was only a few weeks old, was fast asleep, cocooned in a portable car seat that its mother had hooked over her arm. Kate had a smile on her face that was patently the product of sheer willpower, rather than happiness, and her once voluminous pre-Raphaelite tresses were hanging around her face like limp seaweed. It occurred to me that this might be a good opportunity to carry out some scientific research, so I asked whether she and her offspring would like to join me for a cup of tea. Kate hesitated and her expression faltered, no doubt because in all the years we've been neighbors we've never stepped over the threshold of each other's flat. A moment later she reconstructed her smile and turned to the toddler.

"Ava, shall we have a little drink in Auntie Susan's house? Would you like that?"

Surprisingly, the toddler, rather than backing away in horror, beamed and nodded. I led the family through to my kitchen, made the tea and poured a glass of orange juice. It was a pleasant early-autumn afternoon and the French windows were open onto my tiny courtyard garden. Winston was stretched out on the back wall, soaking up the last of the day's warmth. The toddler wandered out.

"Auntie Susan's so lucky having a garden flat, isn't she, Ava?" Kate called after her, slumping into one of the kitchen chairs and placing the car seat on the floor between her sensibly shod feet. She smiled at the baby in an exaggerated fashion, and started making "mama baba dada" noises at it. "We should've thought more about a garden when we were buying a flat," she continued, addressing the baby, "but we didn't know we were going to have you two little ones at the time, did we? Not that Mummy and Daddy could've afforded a garden round here anyway, could we?" The baby began to grizzle, so she unstrapped it from the car seat, picked it up and bounced it rhythmically in her arms. I assumed it was a boy, as it was wearing the obligatory pale blue romper suit.

"What's it called?" I asked, reminding myself that that was the sort of inquiry that parents expect.

"You're called Noah, and you're an absolute angel, aren't you?" she said, gazing into the baby's eyes, which were starting to close again. "Except when you wake up at three o'clock in the morning and we've only just got you off to sleep."

I sensed that this was my entrée into a few more probing questions.

"What does it feel like being a mother? Are you glad you did it, or do you feel it was a terrible mistake?"

Kate laughed.

"We love it, don't we? We're tired all the time and it's tough money-wise, but we wouldn't be without you and Ava for the whole world, would we?"

It was now or never. I held my breath, tensed my muscles and dived in before I lost the nerve.

"Would you mind if I held it?" I asked.

A look of panic crossed Kate's face, as if I'd asked whether I could take it white-water rafting, and she instinctively held it closer to her chest. It was apparent, however, that she couldn't think of how to refuse my request.

"Are you going to have a cuddle with Auntie Susan, sweetheart?" she said to the baby, reluctantly passing it over to me. I

held it in the same way that Kate had —
horizontally in my forearms with its head
resting in the crook of my elbow. It was
much heavier than I'd anticipated; I'd
naively expected it to be the weight of a
handbag, whereas it was more like a full
briefcase. It was soft and clammy, and its
smell was a mixture of clean washing and
warm milk, with faint undertones of urine.
No doubt the baby could sense my awkwardness, as it started to contort its face,
which was darkening from rosy pink to a
sort of puce. I tried to bounce it in my arms
as Kate had done, but perhaps my move-
ments were too jerky and uncoordinated. It
began to howl.

"Oh, come back to Mummy, precious. I
think you're a bit tired and hungry, aren't
you? Would you like some milky?"

And then a disconcerting thing happened.
Kate's top obviously had some sort of
concealed opening, like a doorway in an old
mansion hidden by a revolving bookcase.
One moment she was sitting at the table
looking perfectly normal, the next moment
a flap was lifted, a catch undone and her
left breast was on full display. Now, I must
say that I don't consider myself to be a
person who's prudish or easily shocked; one
body is pretty much like another body as

far as I'm concerned. I was entirely unprepared, however, for having my neighbor's breast displayed in my own kitchen, and I'm sorry to say I found myself declaring that there was an important call I absolutely had to make before five o'clock. Kate did the revolving bookcase trick, and normality was restored. The baby, however, was not impressed by the withdrawal of its food source.

"Ava, time to go now. Auntie Susan's got things to do," she called through the French windows. Strapping the baby into the car seat she cooed, "We had a lovely time, didn't we? It's so nice to talk to some grown-ups for a change, isn't it? We'll have to do this again, won't we?"

My encounter with Kate had been far from successful in convincing me either that I had a hitherto undiscovered maternal streak, or that the life of a mother was something to be desired. Having said that, I've found from experience that I'm able to turn most situations, however unpromising they might be, to my advantage. Although Kate might be sinking under the stresses and strains of the maternal life, there's no reason why I should do the same. For one thing, I don't have a male partner to look after, which, I've observed, is often like having another child (witness my father and brother). Furthermore, the baby will have inherited my genes, and I'd therefore expect it to be reasonable and moderate in its behavior. Finally, I have absolutely no intention of giving up my job; I believe there are very good day nurseries that take babies from a young age. All you have to do is deposit the child first thing in the morning, collect it in the evening and the nursery does the rest. The downside, naturally, is the cost; another reason why it's imperative that I secure my inheritance within the next few months.

I looked at my watch again; it was now a quarter to three. After answering the intercom, the receptionist turned to me to say that if Edward didn't turn up within the next five minutes the meeting with Mr. Brinkworth would have to be canceled and rescheduled for another day. I was about to object when the door was thrust open and in strolled Edward. I was surprised to see Rob just behind him.

"Suze, my darling sis, how're you doing? Brought your boxing gloves, have you?"

"You're late. Where have you been?"

"Just didn't see the point of the meeting — we all know what the will says — but I was dragged here. Likes to keep the peace, old Rob . . . always trying to increase the positive karma in the world."

Edward threw himself down onto one of the low vinyl chairs and began rolling a cigarette.

"Ed Green, here to see the boss," he called over to the receptionist. "Don't worry, it's for later," he added, finishing his construction job and tucking it behind his ear.

"Hi, Susan," said Rob, still loitering by the door. "Hope you two get this sorted today."

He smiled, as if we were on friendly terms with each other. *Not a chance,* I thought. His appearance was that of a man who'd been tunneling through a bog: mud-caked boots, filthy combat trousers and some kind of donkey jacket affair. I was sure it wasn't necessary for a manual laborer to get into quite such a state; maybe he thought it made him look solid and dependable. If so, it wasn't working.

"I hope you don't think you're coming into the meeting — with us," I told him. "This is a family matter."

"Are you joking? Look at the state of me. Plus, I'm knackered. I've been knee-deep in mud since seven this morning. Project-managing work on the grounds of a care home up the road. If you need a lift back to the station after the meeting, though, give me a bell. I can be here in five." He came over to where I was sitting and pulled a business card out of one of his many pockets:

Robert Rhys, BA (Hons), Dip. PSGD
Garden Design and Landscaping Services
From Planning to Completion

I read it, then handed it back to him. "That won't be necessary, thank you. I have the number of a local cab company."

"Don't bother trying to be nice to her, Rob, mate. She'll only kick you in the teeth."

The receptionist's intercom buzzed.

"Miss Green, Mr. Green?" she said. "Mr. Brinkworth will see you now."

7

The receptionist ushered us down a low-ceilinged, windowless corridor. It was lined from floor to knee-height with piles of overflowing buff-colored folders held together with elastic bands; black lever-arch files marked with words such as *Exhibits, Statements* and *Evidence;* and bundles of yellowing papers tied together with pink string. For an establishment that claimed to have expert knowledge of the law, their indifference to tripping hazards was telling.

Framed by a doorway at the end of the corridor, I could see a portly, red-faced man sitting behind a mahogany desk, the surface of which was barely visible under mounds of the same folders, files and papers. This pompous-looking man was unmistakably Mr. Brinkworth. The solicitor, hearing our approach, raised his eyes from a document he was ostentatiously perusing and peered over the top of his half-moon glasses. If he thought this action would impress me with its air of judicial authority, he was mistaken. I'm not unused to dealing with such puffed-up types, and know how easily they can be popped. As we entered his office he stood up and extended his hand, first to Edward and then to me.

"Ah, the Greens, at last. I was wondering whether this meeting was going to happen today. Sit down, sit down." Mr. Brinkworth gestured to two sagging tub chairs, both of which were lower than his own regal throne by a good three or four inches. His back was to a large picture window, and I had to squint to focus on him. Such obvious strategies, and ones that would in no way unsettle me. Edward, putting on his usual act, slumped in the chair next to me with his arms folded across his chest and a defiant expression on his face.

Flanking the room were bookcases crammed with dusty brown-spined volumes of *Halsbury's Laws of England,* gray-spined *Halsbury's Statutes* and blue-spined *All England Law Reports,* probably bought for effect by the meter and never opened. At a small desk crammed into the farthest corner sat a scrawny young man whose liberal peppering of acne scars and dandruff was apparent from a distance of several feet. He was introduced by Mr. Brinkworth, with a dismissive wave of his hand, as Daniel, his trainee solicitor, who would be making notes of our meeting. The unfortunate youth blushed at hearing his name and focused his attention on smoothing back the cover of his blue counsels' notebook.

"Right, Mr. Brinkworth," I began, "let's start with the question of how my mother came to make this will, which couldn't possibly have reflected her wishes."

"All in good time, madam. Let me just locate the paperwork and we'll see where we're up to."

Mr. Brinkworth rummaged through the massed ranks of files on his desk, wheezing from the exertion involved. With the help of Daniel, who had scampered over, he finally pulled out a thin cardboard folder from the bottom of the furthermost pile, almost causing an avalanche.

"Ah, that's right. The late Mrs. Patricia Green. House, bank account, building society account, two beneficiaries. All very straightforward. Here's a copy of the will for each of you, so you can settle your minds as to the exact terms." He launched the two documents across the battlefield of his desk, my own copy overshooting and landing at my feet. "Nice little sum in the accounts, by the way. As an illustration, certainly enough to buy each of you a new car — midrange — with a bit left over. I should be able to send checks out to you very quickly once this little difference of opinion is resolved."

Mr. Brinkworth's dangling in front of me a hypothetical Ford Focus or Vauxhall Astra was ludicrous. I have never felt the need to learn to drive, living, as I do, in London. Only a masochist would want to contend with ill-mannered metropolitan drivers who believe themselves empowered, by their metal armor, to act like crusading warriors. On the underground, you can usually avoid engaging with your fellow travelers if you're careful not to make eye contact. I ignored Mr. Brinkworth's silliness and repeated my request for an explanation of how such a dubious will came to be written. I told him it was obvious to me, and should have been obvious to him, that there was someone else at work behind this.

"Yes, yes, I'm aware of your misgivings, but before we waste time discussing all that, I have a proposal to put forward." He turned to Edward. "As you know, Mr. Green, my hands are tied whilst your sister's block is in place. The fact is," he continued, "that the will was properly drawn up and executed, and you're entitled to remain in the former family home. I'm sure, however, that we'd all like to settle this matter without legal proceedings. What I propose is this — you, Mr. Green," (here he pointed at Edward with a blue plastic Biro), "agree to vacate the property by a certain date — say twelve months hence — and on that basis you, Miss Green," (here he waved the Biro in my direction), "withdraw the block and allow me to deal with the estate. You might both wish to seek your own independent legal advice, but I think you'll find that any lawyer you consult will tell you it's the perfect solution."

Mr. Brinkworth threw down his pen and leaned back in his chair with the ostentatious self-satisfaction of a man who's just finished *The Times* crossword and wants everyone to know about it. Daniel raised his pockmarked face from his scribblings and all but applauded his brilliant mentor.

"No need to see a brief, mate," said Edward. "I'm not agreeing to it. I've got to think about Mum's wishes. If she'd wanted me to be turfed out after a year she'd have said that."

"I'm not agreeing to it either. I intend to prove that my mother's will is the product of a criminal plot. If you won't admit that, we'll have to see what the court makes of it."

Waiting for the solicitor to assimilate my words, I felt a peculiar sensation in my lower abdomen; a delicate fluttering, as though a small bird was trapped inside me and was trying to escape. Its wings beat, then stopped, beat, then stopped. It was quite different from the feeling you get with an unsettled stomach or from hunger — more teasing and ticklish. Perhaps, I thought, it was a side effect of the adrenaline that primes a person for battle. I shifted my position in the chair and crossed my legs, hoping that that would make it stop.

"Miss Green," said the solicitor, picking up a brass paper knife and tapping it irritably on the file before him, "Daniel's notes of my meeting with your mother record that she gave me very specific instructions regarding the contents of her will. Perhaps I could quote a section to you, 'Client wants to leave estate equally to son and daughter, open brackets Edward and Susan close brackets. E lives with her. Client thinks E will need time to make alt living arrangements. HB explained to client poss of giving son life interest in family home. Client said sounded like excellent idea and thanked HB for his advice.' So you see, your mother was quite clear in her mind that she wanted your brother to be able to stay put in the short-term."

"Quite right, mate." Edward raised his thumb approvingly.

The fluttering was there again. Images of hummingbirds, dragonflies and giant hawk moths flew through my mind. A supreme act of will was required to chase them away and focus on the flaws in Mr. Brinkworth's argument. I tensed my abdominal muscles and straightened my spine.

"But it's not just in the short-term, is it?" I countered. "Edward can stay there for as long as he likes. My mother may have appeared to be clear in her mind, but she'd recently had two strokes. She was vulnerable to pressure. Did you know about that? Did you take the time to find out about the state of health of the frail, elderly woman who was consulting you?"

"Whether or not I knew about the strokes is irrelevant. Your mother, I recall, was a very astute, very lucid lady. The fact that her wishes don't accord with your own does nothing to cast doubt on her mental capacity."

"Couldn't have put it better myself," agreed Edward.

By now the miniature vivarium in my

abdomen was becoming a distraction and annoyance to me. I shifted position again, perching on the edge of the seat and leaning forward. I was anxious that, in my agitated physical state, Mr. Brinkworth and Edward might wrest control of the meeting from me. I must confess I began to lose my composure.

"Look, Edward," I said, turning to my brother. "Just keep your mouth shut unless you've got something useful to contribute to this discussion. In fact, if you want to contribute, why not just come clean about your part in this? It's obvious you got Mum to make the will. Did you think up the plan alone, or did you get Mr. Brinkworth to help you?"

"Yeah, me and the brief, we're down at The Bull's Head together every night. Sleeps over at mine if he's had a skinful. What do you think, Suze?" he said with a sneer on his face. "For your information, my involvement is this — Mum told me a few weeks ago that she was writing a will. That's the whole story. That's the beginning and the end of it. I've never met this guy before, never been to this place before, never told Mum to write a will, never said I wanted to stay in the house after she died. Do you want to make a note of all that,

Suze? And you, too, Danny Boy?" Here he turned briefly to the unfortunate minion, who blushed once again. "Mum must've just wanted to help me out. And maybe she wanted to thank me for being there for her over the years, and not just swanning off down to London."

"Being there for her, that's a joke," I said, standing up in a final attempt to subdue the fluttering. Edward must have taken my rising as an act of aggression and stood up to face me — an instinctive reaction, I'd imagine, after the number of pub brawls in which he's engaged. I'm a petite five foot one; Edward, although undersized for a man, is a good six inches taller than me. I took a step back. "She couldn't get rid of you," I continued. "Every time she hoped you might finally be making a life for yourself you'd go crawling back home. You didn't do it for *her*, you did it so you could lounge around and live rent-free. You're a parasite."

"Miss Green, Mr. Green . . ."

"Crap," Edward shouted, jabbing me in the chest with his finger. "I took her to the supermarket. I mowed the lawn. I did jobs around the house. And I kept her company. Who looked after her when she was ill? What did you do? Visit every few months, just so you could tell yourself you'd done your duty. No wonder she decided I deserved a bit more than you."

"I was closer to her than you ever were. I spoke to her on the phone once a week, without fail. I knew everything that was going on in her life. It's just that, unlike you, I've got a job."

"Enough." Mr. Brinkworth slammed his palms down on the desk. "If you don't put a stop to this behavior immediately I'll have to ask Daniel to escort you from the premises." The minion shrank into his seat.

The fluttering was now insistent, and it finally dawned on me that it wasn't just a *sensation* that something was moving inside me; something was, indeed, stirring. The thought wasn't a pleasant one. A scene from *Alien* leaped into my mind — the one where it is revealed, rather dramatically, that John Hurt's character has become a human incubator. I instinctively slipped my hand below the waistband of my skirt, which I noticed was snugger than usual. Nothing appeared to be breaking its way out.

"What do you need the dosh for anyway, Suze?" Edward continued, oblivious both to my agitation and to Mr. Brinkworth's entreaties. "You're always saying what a great career you've got in London and what a fantastic flat you own. *I'm* the one who needs it, not you."

I hesitated for a moment. I'd had no intention of informing Edward about the pregnancy. It was none of his business, particularly as I intended to cease contact with him once the issue of our mother's estate was concluded. Besides, there was nothing I could possibly gain. It was clear that Edward's position was entrenched, and it was highly unlikely that the prospect of a niece or nephew would do anything to change that. On the other hand, telling Richard had been surprisingly fun, like playing a trump card or pulling a rabbit from a hat.

"For your information, Edward, I'm pregnant," I said.

Edward looked me up and down wordlessly, then ran his fingers through his greasy hair, shook his head and laughed.

"Nice try, Suze, but I'm surprised you can't come up with anything better than that. D'you think I'm a complete idiot?"

The meeting with Mr. Brinkworth and Edward hadn't gone entirely to plan. Perhaps it had been a little optimistic of me to expect the solicitor to admit his negligence or my brother to admit his scheming.

Nonetheless, at least we all knew exactly where we stood, and I'd left Mr. Brinkworth in no doubt that I was a woman who wouldn't stop until she achieved justice.

On the train back to London later that afternoon, I took out the photocopy of my mother's will and examined it. The provisions were exactly as Mr. Brinkworth had stated, and I could see nothing obviously amiss with the wording. I turned to the final page, where the will had been signed and witnessed. My mother's signature looked different from how I remembered it, not necessarily in its overall shape but more in its character; it was fainter, shakier, written with less flourish and more hesitation than usual. I wondered whether that was because she was confused about what she was signing, or because she was doing so under pressure.

I directed my attention to the identity of the two witnesses, which Mr. Brinkworth, so far, had neglected to make known to me. One was Aunt Sylvia. That surprised me, as she and Edward aren't natural allies. I could only assume that the contents of the will were kept from her, or I'm sure she wouldn't have put her name on the document. The other witness was Rob, my brother's best friend and soul mate. *Ha, got you!* I thought.

If my brother had wanted to cover his tracks and be certain that the will would stand up to close legal scrutiny, he really should have ensured that neither witness was intimately connected to him.

I'd need to interview and take statements from both Aunt Sylvia and Rob in preparation for my legal challenge of the will. In the case of my aunt that wouldn't be a problem, but Rob might be trickier; I would have to think very carefully how I was going to coax information out of him. I was more than well equipped to put an end to Edward's little game, but, nonetheless, it might not be a complete waste of an hour or so to meet up with my old university flatmate Brigid (the possessor of a fine legal brain, reputedly, although you would never guess from the state of the body encasing it) and get a little pro bono advice.

I put the document away in my bag and turned to the parcel occupying the seat next to me. I'd had a phone call from the funeral directors the previous week to inform me that they'd made several unsuccessful attempts to contact Edward. They wanted to know when he wished to collect my mother's ashes, and wondered whether I could either pass a message on to him or pick them up myself. Not being a sentimental person, and also having been preoccupied recently with other more pressing concerns, I hadn't given any thought to my mother's ashes. Having been prompted to do so, however, I concluded that it would be far better for me, rather than Edward, to take charge of the matter. If I allowed my brother to do so he'd end up leaving the ashes on a bus or in a betting shop, or would decide to scatter them somewhere completely inappropriate like a beer garden. After the meeting at the solicitors' offices, therefore, I'd collected from the funeral directors a weighty and rather unwieldy cardboard box sealed with parcel tape.

It had been strange to be ringing the brass doorbell of the funeral directors' premises once again, twenty-seven years after I last did so. There was no reason for me to attend there in the aftermath of my mother's death, as Edward dealt with the funeral arrangements and I felt no desire to see her body. Why would I? Edward had carried out the identification and the doctor had certified her death. While my brother is capable of all manner of nefarious practices, I considered it unlikely that he'd murdered or imprisoned my mother and produced for the doctor the body of a different old lady who had died of natural causes. Standing in the reception area, waiting for my mother's ashes to be brought out to me, I recalled that I'd felt quite differently about my father.

I was seventeen years old when he died. In those days, I was less pragmatic than I am now — I'd liken my adolescent self to a young plant that has yet to toughen fully — and it felt important to me to see my father's body. Perhaps it was because my relationship with him had been complex; perhaps because of the nature of his final years and demise. Whatever the reason, a couple of days after my father's death, I decided to call in to the funeral directors on my way home from school.

The last time I'd seen my father alive his unruly mane reached his shoulders and his beard was unkempt. Now, lying in his coffin, he was clean shaven with neatly trimmed hair brushed back from his face. Instead of wearing the shabby clothes in which I'd become used to seeing him, he was shrouded with a silky white fabric, gathered around his neck like a choirboy's ruff. It's a cliché to say that the dead look peaceful, but he did, finally. The harmony of the scene was disrupted only by a short piece of cotton thread, perhaps half an inch long, protruding from between the lashes of his left eye. I couldn't allow that to remain. I gripped the end between my thumb and index finger and pulled. I found, when I did so, that it wouldn't come. It was clamped between his upper and lower lids. As I pulled harder I had visions of his eye springing open and a ball of wadding coming away in my hand. I let go of the thread, pushed past the undertaker's assistant who was skulking outside the room and ran. My mother had to call in to the funeral directors the following morning to retrieve my schoolbag.

Sitting on the train I was curious as to exactly what was in my charge. I slit the parcel tape with the metal nail file I keep in my makeup bag and folded back the lid of the box. Inside I found not the plastic, screw-topped jar I'd expected, but a tasteful rectangular wooden casket. I lifted it out of the box and placed it on the table in front of me. The grim-faced woman sitting diagonally opposite, who I noticed had been engaged for the last half an hour in Googling the various grounds for divorce, stared at the casket, then gave me an odd look. Some people are unable to mind their own business.

I turned the casket around, examining it from every angle. The wood was smooth, polished oak. Attached to the lid was a silver plate engraved in simple lettering with my mother's name and the dates of her birth and death. It was not unlike the sort of thing I might have chosen if I'd addressed my mind to it. I was surprised Edward had gone to the trouble of ordering such a casket. It goes without saying, however, that if he was really so concerned about the ultimate fate of the ashes he should have returned the funeral directors' phone calls more promptly. I had no idea what I, myself, would do with the container and its contents. At least, however, they were safely in my possession, which was the most important thing.

The following afternoon I had an appointment at the maternity hospital. I resigned myself to notifying my line manager, Trudy, about my pregnancy so that my absence would be classified as maternity-related. Early that morning, before my colleagues arrived, I went to see her in her office. I hoped to keep things as brief and business-like as possible, not relishing the prospect of divulging intimate details of my life. I rapped on her office door, entered and came straight out with the fact that I was pregnant and required the afternoon off.

"Oh, Susan, I couldn't be happier for you, I really couldn't," Trudy said, coming around to my side of the desk and embracing me. Her arms were as strong as navvies', which I assumed was from the manual labor involved in ministering to small children. The seconds passed, and a sense of panic rose within me as I wondered how I could extricate myself. Eventually her grip relaxed, and she stood back to look at me. "I always hoped something like this would happen to you one day. Just let me know what I can do to help, whatever you need. Oh, this is fantastic news."

Trudy's reaction was so out of proportion to the information I'd just imparted that it startled me. As soon as I could escape her pawing and burbling, I returned to the still-deserted office. I straightened my stationery, made sure my piles of paperwork were parallel to the edges of my desk and carried out the usual checks on my collection of cacti. I noted that there was just enough room for one more, if I shuffled them along a little.

That evening, as I sat on my sofa listening to the soothing, mathematical cadences of a Mozart violin concerto, I examined the three ultrasound photographs that had been taken at the maternity hospital. When I'd looked at the monitor, I'd been unable to discern what the sonographer, with her practiced eye, could see distinctly. Now, with the benefit of my reading glasses, I could make out a curled shrimplike organism with a large head, a dark patch suggesting the presence of an eye, and wispy arms and legs. It bore very little resemblance to a human being, but everything was in the right place — or so the sonographer told me as she pummeled my jelly-slathered abdomen with the scanner.

After the ultrasound scan, I'd been prodded, poked and verbally probed by a breezily efficient midwife. Contrary to my expectations, she was completely unconcerned when I told her I was forty-five years old.

"Oh, there're lots of girls in their forties having babies these days," she said, jabbing a needle into my arm to extract blood. "It's really not as uncommon as some people think. In fact, there're as many fortysomethings having babies as under eighteens. I even had a girl in yesterday who was fifty-two. You obviously keep yourself nice and healthy. Just carry on doing what you're doing."

There was, however, one little matter that

the midwife needed to mention; it seemed that I was likely to be in the high-risk category for having a baby with Down syndrome, although I wouldn't receive the final calculation of that probability for a couple of days. I really shouldn't worry myself, as it was still more likely than not that everything would be fine. If, however, having a baby with special needs would be a problem for me, I might want to consider having an amniocentesis test just to be sure one way or the other. There was a small risk of miscarriage attached to the procedure, and I should go away and take some time to think carefully about what I'd like to do. I told her, without hesitation, that it was only logical to have the test; it's important to have all the facts to hand when weighing up a matter. Plus, having a baby would be a fresh challenge for me (although one to which I knew I'd rise), and I wouldn't want to be caught unawares by unplanned-for complications. I could tell the midwife was unused to such quick and confident decision-making.

Looking at the blurry ultrasound photographs, I was quite sure I'd made the right decision. I remain so. If the test causes the termination of the pregnancy, then so be it.

I'll simply return to the position I was in a few weeks ago, and I was perfectly content with my life then. More than content.

It was getting late, and I was shattered. I carefully placed the photographs on the mantelpiece, propped up with the help of an ammonite fossil that I'd found on a childhood beach holiday. I straightened the sofa, switched off the lights and pushed aside my new polished oak doorstop to close the sitting room door. The casket is exactly the right size, shape and weight and matches my coffee table perfectly. My mother wouldn't have minded. She was a very practical woman and would be delighted to be of use.

■ ■ ■ ■

OCTOBER

■ ■ ■ ■

8

October is my favorite month, and its arrival signals a boost to my energy levels. I'm not someone who enjoys the summer; hot weather and its associated shedding of clothes and inhibitions hold no attraction for me. Colleagues often try to badger me into taking a "proper" summer holiday, but I find the length of time people waste lazing on a beach or by a pool incomprehensible. When I explain this, my colleagues simply laugh and say, "Oh, Susan!" Fortunately, by October, even the threat of an Indian summer has passed, and a woman can happily wear heavyweight fabrics and thick cardigans — and behave in a sensible fashion — without drawing attention to herself. This month, however, began in a less than invigorating manner.

It was after three o'clock — the early hours of a Saturday morning — and I was finally drifting off into an uneasy sleep. The teenage children of the fitness-crazy couple across the road were having a raucous party, and the deep thud of their dance music had been hammering away at my head since eleven o'clock the previous evening. I can only assume their parents were away at an Ironman race, or something similarly masochistic.

Over the years, I've become accustomed to the constant noise besieging my flat: the squeal of car alarms and police sirens; the grumble of buses and trains; shouts of rage or mirth from the street. All of these I accept without complaint as an unavoidable consequence of living in London. The teenagers, however, had turned the volume of their music up to such an extraordinary level that my patience was pushed to the limit. I'd contemplated calling the police to report the nuisance but, having done that in the past, I've found that the authorities generally act as though it's *I,* rather than the person I'm reporting, who's the problem. Even if they did take action on this occasion, which was highly unlikely, the youths would no doubt turn down the racket until the police were out of earshot then turn it up even louder than before.

At first, the insistent banging and ringing seemed to be part of the music but, as I was hauled out of my almost-sleep, I realized that someone was at the door of my flat. I assumed it was a prank by a delinquent partygoer who had somehow managed to get into the communal hallway. On opening my door to tell them exactly what I thought of their behavior I found not the expected drunken youth, but Kate, ashen-faced. She was clutching the car seat in which lay her baby, wearing nothing but a nappy. Kate, herself, was sporting an odd combination of red polka-dot pajamas, flip-flops and a Barbour jacket.

"Susan, thank God you're home," she said above the insistent drumbeat. Although I knew there must be something seriously amiss, as she was addressing me directly for once, I regret to say I was unable to muster up my usual courteousness.

"Surely you haven't locked yourself out in the middle of the night."

"It's Noah," she said, breathlessly. "He's got a raging temperature. I can't get it down. I've tried everything — paracetamol, ibuprofen, stripping him, cold flannels. I've just phoned the emergency helpline. They told me to take him to A and E. I'm not waiting for an ambulance. I'm going straight there in the car. It's just — Ava's asleep. I can't take her with me. Can you look after her while I'm gone? You can climb into my bed and go back to sleep. At least there'll be someone there if she wakes up. Tell her I'll be back soon. I'm sorry about this. I've got no one else to ask."

I looked at the baby. His cheeks were crimson, his sparse hair was plastered to his tiny head and his limbs looked floppy. He appeared neither awake nor asleep. I felt an odd lump in my throat.

"What about Alex?" I said, hoping there was an alternative to my involvement in this domestic crisis. "Can't he look after the child?"

"He's not around. It's a long story. Please, Susan, please. I've got to go. Straightaway. You've got my keys. Just let yourself in. Help yourself to whatever you want. I'll ring and let you know what's happening." She was backing away down the hallway and then down the path to her car, which she always parks directly outside my bay window. I followed as far as the front door.

"I don't mind helping out for an hour or two," I called after her. "But find someone to take over from me as soon as possible. I've got a very full schedule tomorrow. I hope everything's alright," I added, as she strapped the car seat in place and jumped in next to it. With a screech of tires, she was gone.

This really was an unfortunate situation. It was vital that I wasn't below par the following day as I'd meticulously planned a shopping expedition. The morning sickness was now a distant memory, and I'd very quickly gone from looking like a marathon runner to looking like an Eastern European shot-putter. The stage had now been reached where I was no longer able to wear my usual outfits, even if I left the top button of my skirt or trousers undone. I therefore urgently needed to invest in some suitable attire.

I'd taken the time carefully to research the subject of maternity wear and had planned a capsule wardrobe that would see me through from October to the birth in March, viz: two pairs of black trousers (one wide-legged and one slim-legged) with stretch panels; two black skirts (one above the knee and one below) with same panels; seven long-sleeved jersey tops, variously in black, gray and white; two charcoal knit cardigans (one fine gauge and one heavy gauge); and certain items of expandable lingerie, the details of which I'll omit. All that needed to be done was to try said items on for size and purchase them. I'd planned to leave my flat at eight thirty in the morning and be back by one thirty so I could spend the afternoon carrying out legal research. This disrupted night was going to have an impact on my carefully structured timetable.

I went back into my flat and picked up Kate's front door keys. I also bundled up my duvet, sheet and pillow; under no circumstances would I sleep in someone else's used bed linens. Once inside Kate's flat, I dumped my bedding on the sofa and surveyed my surroundings. The sitting room, which was directly above my own and of identical dimensions, seemed considerably smaller, probably because of the baby and child paraphernalia scattered over the floor: a muddle of jigsaw pieces, an avalanche of building blocks, heaps of lurid plastic in various configurations, enough ravaged synthetic creatures to fill a veterinary hospital, together with a play mat, changing mat, bouncy chair, potty and the like. I don't see why having children should be an excuse for letting your domestic standards slip. I'd be very surprised if my own did.

I tiptoed down the corridor and peered into the bedroom. A night-light in the shape of a giant mushroom was giving out a soft glow. I could make out the shape of an unmade double bed against one wall, with a Moses basket at its foot, and a toddler-sized bed against the opposite wall. It was all horribly cramped. I was pleased that I'd soon secure my inheritance and be in a position to buy a two-bedroom flat. My charge was spread out like a starfish on the smaller bed, breathing deeply and rhythmically despite the thumping music from across the road. I picked up a grubby toy from the floor (some character from a popular children's television series), placed it next to the sleeping child and covered her with the duvet she'd kicked off.

Next I crept to the kitchen, which I found to be as chaotic as the sitting room; unwashed dishes in the sink, spilled food on the kitchen table and surfaces, overflowing bin. I knew I'd be unable to go straight to sleep in such a strange environment after being so thoroughly disturbed, so decided to engage in some physical labor to tire myself out. I donned a pair of yellow rubber gloves that I found in an unopened packet in a drawer and set to work with soapy water, scouring cream and floor cleaner. Once the kitchen was spotless I tackled the sitting room, finding receptacles for the various scattered items, organizing the clutter on the shelves and mantelpiece, straightening the rug and plumping the cushions on the armchairs. By the time I'd finished it was five thirty, the music had stopped and I was exhausted. I switched off the standard lamp in the corner of the room and settled down on the sofa.

I've always had difficulty falling asleep at night, even when not bombarded by noise pollution. The moment I closed my eyes, the irrational feeling creeps over me that something dreadful might happen if I'm not vigilant. As I tried to summon sleep, I thought about the years I'd lain awake as a girl, waiting for my father to return from the pub. My bedroom was above the front entrance and hallway of my childhood home, and I could tell from even the smallest sounds that drifted up through the floorboards what state he was in. If he found the lock with his front door key straightaway it was good; if he dropped his keys or fumbled to find the lock it was bad. If he closed the front door quietly it was good; if he slammed the door it was bad. If his footsteps across the hallway were light and even it was good; if they were heavy or irregular it was bad. If there was a gush of water being poured into a glass it was good; if there was a clink of a bottleneck against a tumbler it was bad. If he came straight up to bed it was good; if he started playing Italian opera at full volume it was bad. I sometimes wonder if Edward lay awake thinking the same thoughts. I don't know. I never asked him.

As I pushed the memory to the back of my mind, I felt a tap on my shoulder. There, standing in the half-light filtering in from the street, was the child. She was clutching her stuffed toy and looking down at me with an expression of curiosity on her face.

"Hello, there," I said, "I'm Susan, your neighbor from downstairs. Do you remember me?" The child nodded, as though there was nothing at all unusual in the situation. "Your mother had to go somewhere urgently so I'm looking after you for an hour or two. Do you understand?" She nodded once more, climbed over me and squashed herself into the limited space between my recumbent body and the back of the sofa.

"I'm sorry, there's not enough room for the two of us. Go back to your own bed, there's a good girl," I told her. She shook her head and squeezed her eyes closed. "Go back now, please. I need to sleep and so do you," I added, with more authority. She shook her head again and closed her eyes even more tightly. I must admit, I'm not particularly experienced in dealing with small children; I'd far rather engage with people who are amenable to reason and logic. After a further concerted effort to get the child to comply with my instructions, I abandoned the sofa, went to the bedroom and climbed into the toddler bed. It was so tiny that I had to curl up like a fetus to fit into it. Within a couple of minutes, the child reappeared, clambered over me and squeezed herself into the narrow gap by the wall.

"Young lady," I said, "this is unacceptable behavior." But she'd already closed her eyes and was feigning sleep. After remonstrating with her to no avail, I returned to the sofa, and once more she followed. Her doggedness might be considered an admirable quality if she was using it to more constructive ends. Cursing under my breath I headed for the bedroom yet again. I had no doubt that the stubborn creature would follow me. I contemplated barricading the door, but decided that that might result in tears. Exhausted, I climbed into the double bed — used bed linen was no longer quite as repugnant to me as it had been a few hours earlier. As predicted, there was soon a patter of feet and a bounce on the bed, but at least there was ample room for the two of us. Just as I was beginning to drift off — and the child appeared to be, too — the phone on the bedside table rang.

"Susan, it's Kate. I haven't woken you up, have I? I just wanted to check everything's okay."

"Nothing to worry about here," I managed. "The child isn't missing you."

"Noah's got tonsillitis," she said. "They've given him antibiotics. They're going to keep him in for observation for a few hours until his temperature starts coming down, so I'm going to stay with him. I can't get hold of Alex but I've left a message explaining the situation and telling him to call me as soon as he can."

"Is he far away? How long will it take him to get here? I've got important things to do."

"I haven't a clue where he is. He's left me. He'll probably be with his girlfriend."

I expressed appropriate regret at the situation in which she found herself, but asked her to ensure that she found somebody — anybody at all — to relieve me at the earliest possible opportunity. Kate informed me that her parents lived in the Midlands, so they couldn't help out, and her friends were all tied up with family commitments or were away from London. I gave her my mobile number and instructed her to let me know the moment a rescue party had been dispatched.

By the time I finished speaking to Kate the child was sitting bolt upright, bright eyed and ready for the day.

"It's not morning yet," I explained to her, trying to push her gently down onto the bed. "Let's go back to sleep for an hour or two." She wriggled away from me, ran out of the bedroom and returned a minute later with an armful of books. I endeavored to ignore her. Her persistence was such, however, that in the end I capitulated and read story after story about creatures, places and situations that couldn't possibly have any basis in reality. After what felt like an hour, I decided that, while I was awaiting a phone call to signal the end of the ordeal, I might as well stick to my original schedule for the day, albeit that the timing would need to be adjusted. I therefore dressed the child in a manner appropriate to the weather, gathered up a selection of the less garish toys and returned to my flat. As she insisted on trailing after me, I parked her in front of the television — something I wouldn't, of course, do with a child of my own — so I could prepare our breakfast. She didn't eat much of her muesli or drink much of her grapefruit juice, which I knew she'd regret later. After breakfast, I explained to her that we would be taking a trip on a train, and that I expected her to be on her best behavior. She nodded her assent.

At the Tube station, I asked the birdlike woman perched behind the ticket counter — who I've always found to be sullen and grumpy — for a one-day travel card for the child.

"You don't need to pay for the little one, love. How old is she?" she inquired, her face breaking into a luminous grin. She waved her bony fingers at the child in the buggy, who shyly waved back.

"I've no idea. How old do *you* think she is?"

"Don't you know?" Her eyes narrowed with suspicion.

I cast my mind back to when I'd first encountered the child.

"Well, I suppose she can't be more than three."

"I'm two."

"Oh, she talks," I said, taken by surprise.

Managing a buggy and a toddler on the underground is more of a challenge than I'd anticipated. Each time we approached an escalator I had to stop, unstrap the child, fold up the buggy (easier said than done) and hoist it onto the moving staircase while simultaneously keeping hold of, and maneuvering, the child. Each time we alighted from an escalator I had to do the same in reverse. All this as other passengers were bearing down on us like a stampede of buffalo.

I couldn't believe how many escalators needed to be negotiated just to travel a short distance. There were also two changes of trains and numerous flights of stairs (which required a tricky backward operation with the buggy on its rear wheels) before we reached our first destination. I resolved to email those in charge of the underground to pass on my thoughts regarding their transportation system. Once sitting on the train, I found it was much harder than usual to avoid engaging with my fellow passengers; people were continually beaming at the child, then looking up and smiling at me. Some even asked me her name or age, information that I could now provide confidently. I expect we appeared to be a mother and daughter having a fun day out together. I, myself, have little interest in children, but I suppose she's quite winsome to look at, with her golden curls, rosy cheeks and big blue eyes. If you like that kind of thing.

We arrived at the first shop on my list

seventy-two minutes later than timetabled. I picked up the items of maternity wear that I wished to try on and went to the changing rooms. The buggy wouldn't fit in the cubicle, so I had to park it in the corridor and deposit the child on the floor in the corner. No sooner had I started undressing than she began whining that she was hungry. I explained to her that it was her own fault for not eating her muesli; *I* had finished all *my* breakfast and was still feeling satisfied. She was unable to accept responsibility for the situation in which she found herself, and continued to grouse. I paid no attention and proceeded with the important job of assessing the quality, functionality and appearance of the items of clothing. As I did so, the shop assistant put her head around the curtain and asked, in a concerned voice, whether everything was alright. I explained that the child was the author of her own misfortune, but the woman looked sorry for her nonetheless.

Armed with two large carrier bags, we headed back to the underground station. In an effort to put an end to the whining, I stopped at a fruit stall to buy some bananas, peeled one and gave it to the child. She squished it between her fingers, which she then wiped on her coat, dress and the sides of the buggy. I explained to her calmly why her behavior was unacceptable, but she proceeded to bawl unintelligibly. The only words I could make out were *mummy, home* and what sounded like *sweeties.* I regret to say that the rest of the shopping trip could only be accomplished with the judicious employment of chocolate buttons, which I drip-fed to the child at five-minute intervals.

This behavior called to mind Edward, who was also a very difficult toddler. I have an enduring image of him sitting in his push-chair, kicking his legs, writhing and scream-ing at the top of his voice until he got what he wanted. My mother overindulged Ed-ward in a way she never did me. Perhaps that was because he was unwell when he was small. I'm not sure exactly what was wrong with him; nobody explained it to me at the time and I haven't subsequently thought to ask. I believe it was a genetic disorder, something to do with his stomach, which involved several operations to cor-rect.

My mother was a distant figure to me dur-ing the summer Edward spent in the hospi-tal; most of the time it was just my father and me. Surprisingly, he managed to rise to the occasion and assume responsibility for domestic affairs in my mother's absence.

He even found time to play with me. In my memory, it was sunny for the whole of that summer. My father and I spent our lunchtimes in pub beer gardens, and I had chicken flavor crisps and lemonade every day. Dinner was always something slightly wrong like marmalade sandwiches or spaghetti hoops with sweet corn. When my mother brought Edward home, my father went back to his usual ways and the fun stopped. I had to creep around the house so as not to disturb my brother when he was sleeping, and wasn't allowed to play with him in case I hurt him. Instead of having the full attention of an adult — my father — I had to vie for the odd moments my mother was able to give me when she wasn't running around after Edward. Even though he was only two years old, my brother was aware of the power his status as a convalescent gave him and took full advantage of it.

It was midafternoon by the time we made it back to my flat, and there was still no word from Kate. The return journey had been even more challenging than the outward one due to the number of carrier bags that had to be heaved onto and off the escalators in addition to the buggy and child. Having been kept awake for the whole of the previous night, I was by now utterly worn-out. I therefore dumped the bags in the kitchen and curled up in bed with the child. We both fell asleep immediately.

That evening we were eating our meal of roast chicken with mashed potato and peas, which turned out to be acceptable fare, when relief finally arrived. As I showed Kate into the kitchen, the child flung herself at her mother. Anyone would have thought they'd been parted for months. Kate placed the car seat containing the now-peaceful-looking baby on the floor, and sat down next to the child while she finished her dinner. Kate explained that the baby's temperature was down and he'd been discharged with a course of antibiotics.

"Thanks so much for helping out," she said. "Alex is in Sardinia, according to his boss. I owe you one."

"That's quite alright," I said, getting up to clear the table. "I'd suggest, however, that you draw up a rota of emergency contacts in case of future family crises."

Standing to help, Kate spotted the heap of maternity-shop carrier bags in the corner of the kitchen. She glanced down at my belly.

"Oh, you're pregnant. Congratulations," she said. "Is there a father lurking somewhere?" she added, as though I might have one hidden in a cupboard.

"No. No father."

"Well, we can look out for each other. Two single mums together. We'll have some fun."

"That would be lovely," I said. She seemed to think I meant it.

I worked late on Friday evening, preparing a lengthy submission for the monthly departmental meeting. I'd come up with some novel ways of improving personal efficiency and thus increasing individual targets. I was sure my colleagues would be pleased. There's far too much inadvertent time-wasting going on in my office. I've noted that the quantity of beverages consumed during the working day greatly exceeds the number necessary to keep a person properly hydrated. No doubt people are making drinks simply because they think it's their turn to do so, rather than because they're thirsty. In addition, I've often observed two or more people standing next to the kettle at the same time, when it clearly only takes one person to make a round of tea or coffee. I'd therefore devised a strict timetable for the making and imbibing of drinks, the scientific validity of which was beyond dispute.

I've also noted that a considerable amount of time is wasted by my colleagues carrying documents across the open-plan office from their own desk to someone else's. They then feel obliged to loiter at that desk talking to its occupant, and I suspect that such talk veers away from matters that are strictly work-related. If people were required to email paperwork to their colleagues, rather than physically taking it, their perceived obligation to chat would be eliminated. I'd documented several other such ideas, which I'd calculated would save an average of twenty minutes per day for each employee. This would enable Trudy to increase personal targets — including her own — by 4.5 percent.

By the time I left the office, it was already dark, and the rain, which had been threatening all day, was thundering down. While I was fiddling with the stubborn mechanism of my umbrella, a familiar face loomed out of the shadows at the side of the doorway, where the smokers usually huddle. Richard. It was some time since I'd seen or spoken to him; he'd phoned on several occasions, but I hadn't picked up. What was there to discuss? He must have been lurking in the smokers' corner for some time, but although his hair was slick with rain, his midnight-

blue overcoat was sodden and he had drop-
lets of water clinging to his eyelashes, he
still somehow managed to look impeccable.
He called to mind a scene from an old
black-and-white film: a dapper Orson Welles
emerging from the darkness in *The Third
Man.* Something stirred in me, despite
myself. I suppressed it.

I was in no mood for a tricky conversation, particularly one for which I hadn't
prepared, so I turned to head toward the
underground station. I suppose it was a little
optimistic to hope that Richard would
simply dissolve away. Before I could make
good my escape, he grabbed my sleeve.

"Susan," he said, above the drone of the
post-rush-hour traffic, the drumming of the
rain and the fizzle of car wheels through
puddles. "Don't you think it's high time we
talked?" He lowered his gaze to the level of
my belly. "About our baby."

I pulled my coat around me.

"Please don't feel obliged to think of it as
our baby," I told him. "You've played your
part."

"Why don't we go somewhere dry, where
we can discuss things properly? It seems
silly to do this in the street."

"We don't have to do this anywhere. You
can rest assured — I don't need your as-

sistance."

"Susan, I just want you to know, I realize you were trying to frighten me off when we last met, because you wanted to demonstrate your independence. I admire you for that. But if I were to have some regular involvement, think how much easier you'd find it, both financially and practically. I've thought it all through and done a few calculations. I'm ready and willing to assume joint responsibility for the baby, with all that that entails."

I reminded myself that I'd made my decision, and that I was not a person to waver. It had been a long day, though, and I was weary. I needed to get rid of Richard before any chinks started to appear in my armor.

"You're wrong. I'm not trying to demonstrate anything. I'm just making it crystal clear that you're free to walk away. Our interactions were based solely on a businesslike agreement, which has now ended. You have no further obligations."

"But there's no reason why the terms of the agreement shouldn't be renegotiated if that's the desire of both parties," he said, with the air of a seasoned diplomat. "The initial purpose of our understanding was mutual entertainment and pleasure. The purpose now should be to raise a well-balanced and healthy child. I'm sure, if we work together to that end, it will be a most successful, mutually beneficial enterprise."

"Look, Richard," I said, brushing the dripping hair from my eyes. "I know you have no wish to be a father, and I also know that the child will be absolutely fine without you. If you think about it properly, you'll realize it would be absurd for us to continue to interact with each other for the next eighteen years simply because of an accident of biology. I doubt very much that that's what you really want, if you're honest with yourself."

"But what do *you* want?"

"I want to get out of this rain. I want to go home and have my dinner."

"That baby has my genes," he said, waving his finger in the direction of my abdomen. "It doesn't just belong to you. Half of it belongs to me. It might very well look like me, think like me, walk and talk like me. I'm not about to relinquish my share of control over its future. I owe a duty to my mother to ensure the welfare of her grandchild."

"It's not up to you," I said, batting his hand away, irritated now. "I understand you want to do what you believe is the right thing, but please trust me to know what's best for all of us. Now, if you don't mind . . ."

I thrust the useless umbrella into an overflowing rubbish bin and hailed the vacant black cab that had fortuitously loomed out of the darkness.

"If you don't come to your senses soon, I regret to say you'll be hearing from my lawyer," he called after me.

It's remarkable how people fall into clichés when they haven't got a leg to stand on.

9

I'd been endeavoring, for several days, to speak to Aunt Sylvia, but whenever I phoned I was greeted either by Uncle Frank's nicotine rasp, or Wendy's or Christine's giggling trills. On a couple of occasions, I heard, in the background, Aunt Sylvia asking her gofer to tell me that she was really, really sorry but she was completely up to her neck in it, and that she'd definitely give me a buzz later. Her avowals, however, were as false as her nails, her eyelashes and the dazzling blue of her eyes. During one call, when Aunt Sylvia supposedly couldn't speak because she'd had her teeth laser-whitened that morning, I managed to gather from Wendy that she, Christine and my aunt were coming down to London the following weekend to treat themselves and see a West End show. What about my giving their mum a tour of the sights while they had a "pamper day" at a spa?

"But I want a pamper day, too. I don't want to waste my time looking around a load of gloomy old museums," Aunt Sylvia managed to whimper through her dental distress.

In the end, it became clear that the only way I was going to pin down my elusive aunt was by agreeing, very much against my better judgment, to join her and the cousins at the spa. I've never before frequented such a place; I've always considered them to be a self-indulgent waste of time and money for the type who believe their worth as a person is directly proportionate to the amount they spend on themselves. Like my aunt and cousins. I was reassured by Wendy, however, that I need purchase only a half-day pass and wouldn't be obliged to be handled by anyone.

I arrived at the spa — which was located in a slick London hotel where I'd once stayed with Richard — at nine thirty in the morning. My relatives weren't yet there; it was evidently too early in the day for them to face the arduous task of being pampered. Everything in the reception area was gleaming, from the marble floor to the mirrored walls to the receptionist's flawless skin. The ecclesiastical silence was broken only by the gurgle of water spouting from a font-like stone basin opposite the entrance. The air hung heavy with oils and unguents sliced through with the smell of chlorine.

"Would you like to book some treatments today, madam? You can choose from our à la carte menu or you might be interested in our 'Serenity' or 'Vitality' packages," the glossy woman intoned. I informed her that I didn't believe that either state could be achieved from a morning at her establishment, and that I simply required access to the inner sanctum. The cost of such access was astounding.

I was given a monogrammed towel and robe and directed to the communal changing room, where a number of women were wriggling into the most impractical swimwear I'd ever seen. I hadn't worn my black Speedo costume since I'd become pregnant, and was aware that the way it stretched over my belly and squashed my newly fulsome breasts wasn't particularly flattering. That didn't overly concern me; I had much more important matters on my mind.

I wrapped myself tightly in the robe, and tied the belt in a secure double knot. Picking up my briefcase containing the hefty *Tristram and Coote's Probate Practice* that I'd collected from the library the previous day, I made my way to the poolside "tranquility zone." Its decor was similar to that of the reception area, with the addition of palm trees, lush trailing plants and sun loungers, and its atmosphere was sultry and airless. The place was already half full; it amazes me how many people have nothing constructive to occupy them on a Saturday morning. Crossing the room, I noted that the men reclining on the loungers were as portly and hirsute as the women were skinny and hairless. All looked equally vacuous. I found a secluded spot in a corner, put on my reading glasses and opened my law book.

An hour or so later Aunt Sylvia emerged from the changing room with Wendy and Christine a couple of steps behind. The usual kisses had to be tolerated, along with declarations of how brilliant it was to see me again so soon after the funeral. Sun loungers were pulled up to my own — Aunt Sylvia's on my left and the cousins' on my right — and robes removed. The cousins were both dressed in jade green swimsuits, wore matching gold bracelets around their ankles and had their brash blond hair arranged on top of their heads in a similarly elaborate manner. For twins to be dressing identically at the age of thirty-nine, and to be spending so much time together when they have their own families, is clearly an indication of deep-rooted identity problems, no doubt caused by their self-obsessed mother. My aunt, who was wearing a tropical-print costume to match the theme of the pool area, must have recently returned from her holiday home in Spain; her plump body was as brown and leathery as an old boxing glove. So very different from my pale, petite late mother.

The cousins and I spent more childhood afternoons together than I can bear to remember. Before my aunt and her family moved away from Birmingham to their showy spread near Worcester, she and my mother visited each other at least once a week. As children, we had no choice but to trail along. Strangely, even though my mother and aunt had very little in common, they managed to spend unfathomable amounts of time chatting and gossiping. In order to do so without the inhibiting presence of their offspring, Aunt Sylvia and my mother would usher us out to play in the back garden or in the street. When it was time to say our goodbyes, my mother would often be red-eyed and blotchy. I knew, then, that they had been addressing the perennial subject of my father's behavior.

I'm six years older than the cousins, so I was nominally in loco parentis when my mother and aunt were otherwise engaged. I say "nominally," because controlling those spoiled, sneaky little brats was impossible. My seniority in age held little sway with them, and neither did my superior size, strength or intelligence. The cousins were indulged by their mother to an extent even greater than Edward was by ours. So long as they treated her with fawning reverence, they were given whatever they requested — sweets, toys, pets. They made no secret of the fact that they disliked me, which was probably because I wasn't susceptible to their wheedling and whinging. Conversely, they hero-worshiped Edward; his subversive behavior gave him an air of excitement and rebellion. If there was an argument or disagreement when the four of us were together, which there invariably was, it would always be Edward and the cousins against me.

I offer up the following as an example: I must have been about thirteen years old, which would put Edward at ten or eleven and the cousins at seven. It was late summer, and I was simultaneously dreading and longing for the return to school. "Dreading," because even at that age I already preferred my own company; and "longing for," because my success with schoolwork was the one aspect of my life over which I had complete control. The cousins, Edward and I had been told, as usual, to play outside so the grown-ups could chat. I was much too old to "play," wanting instead to sit and read my book, but I knew that my mother needed me to mind the younger children. A new patio was being laid in our back garden, and there was a swarm of flying ants on the pavement in front of our house, so we decamped to the local park. When we arrived, Edward started larking about: hounding the Canada geese and their goslings; lobbing stones into the pond where the old men had set up their fishing rods; scaling trees far beyond a safe height. The cousins were squealing with delight at his antics. I did my best to bring him into line, but to no avail. I might just as well have been trying to reason with a baboon.

At the playground, Edward entertained himself by scrambling the wrong way up the slide when there was a queue of children waiting to come down and spinning the roundabout so fast that toddlers were almost hurled off with the formidable centrifugal force. Shooed away by angry parents, he then decided to play a version of chicken. This involved standing in front of a swing that was hurtling toward him and jumping out of the way at the last possible moment. I shouted to him to stop, that he was going to hurt himself, but he simply made a hand gesture that I won't merit with a description. As he was doing this, his timing went awry, and the corner of the swing caught the side of his forehead.

The amount of blood was alarming. The cousins were in tears, pale and trembling, and Edward fainted with the shock. Fortunately, a neighbor was in the playground with her young daughters. She stanched the flow of blood with one of their cardigans, bundled us all into her estate car — the cousins sitting in the open luggage space behind the rear seats — and drove us home. After Edward had been stitched up at the hospital, the inquest began. I gave my version of events, including an inventory of my brother's mean, stupid and dangerous behavior, and he gave his. According to Edward, an older boy had pushed one of the cousins in front of the swing. As my brother had bravely rescued her, his head had been caught. The cousins backed up his story. Apparently, I'd been sitting on a bench with my nose in a book the whole time. My mother told me, with moist eyes and a crack in her voice, that she was very, very disappointed in me. I'd been the one in charge. I should have taken more care of my brother and cousins. I was usually such a sensible, dependable girl. Who in the world could she rely on, if not me? Edward and the cousins could hardly suppress their grins.

"Well, ent this nice," said my aunt, squeezing my arm through the thick toweling of my robe.

"It is, it's lovely," chimed the cousins from my other side.

"Your uncle Frank's treating us to a girlie weekend to celebrate my birthday. I'm sixty-three, you know." She opened her eyes wide, as if it was a revelation even to herself. "No one believes it when I tell them. Everyone thinks I'm in my early fifties. It's because I've always looked after myself. 'Keep young and beautiful,' as they say."

"You're doing brilliant, Mum," said one of the cousins.

"Hope *we* look as good at your age," said the other, turning to examine herself in the mirrored wall behind her. Aunt Sylvia smiled, satisfied that her remarkable youthfulness had been registered.

"Are you totally recovered from your funny turn at the funeral?" she asked me. "It must all've bin too much for you, poor thing. It was for me, too. I almost keeled over myself, but then again, I've always bin a very emotional person. 'You wear your heart on your sleeve, Sylvia,' Uncle Frank always tells me."

I explained to her that I've never had any difficulty keeping my feelings in check, and that I'd simply been suffering from physical incapacitation.

"There's no shame in being taken queer at your mum's funeral, you know. Everyone makes allowances. Like for Ed's shocking behavior at the wake. We don't hold it against him, do we, girls?"

The cousins shook their heads in unison. "No, Mum, not at all."

"He didn't know what he was saying," said Wendy.

"Bin drowning his sorrows," said Christine.

I had to endure several long minutes of my relatives' inane prattling about the funeral and wake, including an analysis of the character, behavior and dress sense of each of the mourners, before they eventually paused long enough for me to explain that the sole reason for my joining them at the spa was to discuss the circumstances surrounding the signing of my mother's will.

"Did she write a will, love?" said my aunt.

"You must know she did. You witnessed it."

"Did I? I don't remember. When was that?"

I told her it was a few weeks before my mother died. Aunt Sylvia did the best impression of a thoughtful frown that is possible to achieve when your forehead's been paralyzed with botulinum.

"Edward's friend Rob was the other witness," I prompted. "Presumably he signed the will at the same time as you."

"Oh, Rob, yes, it's coming back to me now. Lovely man, real gentle giant. I could tell he took quite a shine to me. Gave me his business card with his personal number on the back. I think I'll get him to come over and take a look at our place. Our gardener's good at mowing and weeding, but he just ent got any artistic flair. I keep telling Uncle Frank I want a gazebo and a sunken garden, and he keeps saying, 'Anything you want, bab,' but then I'm so busy I never get round to organizing it. You've reminded me now. I'm going to give that Rob a bell when I get back home."

I could see it would require a supreme effort to keep my aunt's mind on the matter in question.

"So who asked you to be a witness?" Again, the barest whisper of a frown.

"Let me think. Yes, I remember now. Ed rang me the day before. That sticks in my mind 'cos it was the first time he'd ever called me. Not one for the family stuff, is he? I thought it was going to be bad news, 'cos your mum had had those two strokes recently, but then he said no, he just thought I might want to come over for a chin-wag. Said your mum seemed down in the dumps and needed a bit of cheering up. Knew I could always lift her spirits. That's what everyone says to me. 'Sylvia,' they say, 'you always bring the sunshine with you wherever you go.' Well, that's how you should be, isn't it? No point spreading doom and gloom. Do you remember Great-aunt Gladys? Face like a sour lemon? Nothing was ever quite good enough for her. I remember once . . ."

"Did he say anything else on the phone? Did he mention the will?"

As she was about to reply, what appeared to be a very glamorous psychiatric nurse — her starched white coat and air of clinical efficiency contrasting with her clownishly exaggerated makeup — emerged from the foliage and bent over Aunt Sylvia.

"Mrs. Mason? Sorry to disturb you. It's time for your manicure now, if you'd like to follow me."

"Ooh, nonstop here, isn't it?" my aunt said with a giggle.

Time was ticking away. I didn't want to waste the money I'd spent on the half-day pass, so I put the *Tristram and Coote's* book back into my briefcase and followed my aunt to the treatment area. She was already perched on a stool in front of a small table, on which her pudgy fingers were splayed.

"Getting your nails done, too, are you, Susan? I have mine done every two weeks, without fail. Uncle Frank always likes me to look my best."

"No, I'm not. I'm quite capable of clipping my own fingernails. About Edward's phone call and the signing of the will . . ." I pulled up a stool next to my aunt.

"Well, I'm pretty sure Ed didn't say anything about a will on the phone. But I remember he was quite insistent that I come over soon. Said he didn't want your mum to sink any lower. So I said I'd come the next day, 'cos I wanted to do a bit of shopping in Birmingham, anyway. I was looking for a fascinator to go with an outfit for my friend Jacquie's wedding. The shops in Worcester aren't up to much. That's the only thing I miss about Birmingham, the shops. And I was due to visit your mum, anyway. We liked to meet up regular."

"And when you visited Mum, what happened?"

"Nothing special really. Your mum didn't seem particularly down, as far as I can remember. A bit vague, maybe, but then she *was* after the strokes, wasn't she? Only to be expected. We had some lunch and a cup of tea, and then I headed off to town. Do you know, I trailed round every shop in Birmingham, but do you think I could find a fascinator in chartreuse? Not for love nor money could I."

"Yes, but what about *the will*?" I said.

"Well, after we finish our lunch Rob turns up. He's very tall, isn't he? I've always liked a tall man. So Ed tells your mum Rob's here now, and she looks a bit confused. And then he says, 'Remember, you need two people,' and she says, 'Oh, yes, that's right. Where is it?' And Ed goes out of the room and comes back a minute later with a big brown envelope. Then he says he's got to go out and he'll leave us all to it. That was the last time I saw him until the funeral. Your mum says she wants me and Rob to witness her signature, so she gets out a document and signs her name and I sign mine and Rob signs his, then we all have that cup of tea and I tell Rob about the gazebo and sunken garden idea and that's when he gives me his card. Such a charmer."

"Did my mum say anything about the terms of the will?"

"What color would you like today, Mrs. Mason?" the psychiatric nurse interjected. "We've got some fabulous new polishes that came in yesterday. I think you'll be very excited when you see them." She presented my aunt with a rack holding a multicolored array of tiny bottles.

"Ooh, it's just like a sweet shop, isn't it? I don't know what to choose. It's like asking me whether I want Turkish delight or sugared almonds or violet creams. I love them all. I'm feeling drawn to flamingo, or maybe watermelon. What do you think, Susan? I'm hopeless at making my mind up. My girls are always saying, 'Mum, it's 'cos you're just so positive about everything.' Positive to a fault, that's me."

"I don't know. I have no opinion on the matter. Just close your eyes and point to one."

"What a good idea. Like a game. Let's just leave it to fate."

She closed her eyes and jabbed a finger at the display. Her face fell at the sight of the natural-looking shade that fate had chosen for her.

"No, I think I'll go for flamingo instead. Trust your first instincts, I always say." She pulled a lurid bottle from the rack.

"That's an amazing shade. What a marvelous eye for color you've got, Mrs. Mason," said the psychiatric nurse, as though my aunt had formulated the nail polish herself.

"The will," I said. "Did my mother say anything to you about *the terms*?"

"Now, what did she tell me? Just that she'd been mulling over what was going to happen after she was gone. That she wanted everything to be fair, you know, between you and Ed. So there wouldn't be any arguments. She knew you two were like chalk and cheese. I think she said she'd been talking it over with someone to get it straight in her head. Can't remember who. It might've been the vicar. He was always calling round. Met him a few times when I was visiting. Lovely, but a bit of a sissy boy, if you know what I mean. You can tell, can't you? Hardly paid me any attention at all."

"Did she say she was going to give Edward a life interest in the family house?"

"A what, love?"

"A life interest. It means he can live there for as long as he likes."

"I don't know anything about that. She didn't mention 'live interests.' Or maybe she did and I wasn't concentrating. Are you feeling a bit cheesed off about it? Is that why you're asking me all these questions?"

"I'm not 'cheesed off,' I'm furious. There's no reason at all why Mum would do that. It's obvious Edward's tricked her or bullied her. I'm getting hold of her medical records and interviewing everyone who knew her. I'm going to prove that Mum was confused and vulnerable. And that she wasn't the sort of person who'd do something so manifestly unjust."

Aunt Sylvia turned her attention away from her garish fingernails and looked me in the eye. For once she had a solemn expression on her face.

"Susan, maybe you just need to accept what's in the will. Your mum must've had her reasons. Who knows what goes on in other people's heads? Why waste your time digging around in her personal affairs? Sometimes it's best just to accept the hand you're dealt in life and make the best of it. I know that from experience. Otherwise you just upset yourself. And other people."

"All done, Mrs. Mason," said the psychiatric nurse, putting away her equipment. "Do you like them?"

"Ooh, I do. I've got hands like a movie star now, haven't I?" She beamed, wiggling her fingers.

When we got back to the sun loungers, the cousins announced they were bored. It was half an hour until their first appointments (inch-loss body wraps — evidently it hadn't occurred to them simply to exercise or eat less) and neither of them had thought to bring a book to read. Assuming they're able to read, that is. They proposed that we all retire to the hot tub for a change of scene.

"Think I'll give it a miss, girls," said my aunt, stretching out and closing her eyes. "I've just had my nails done and I need a rest."

"Come on, Susan, it'll loosen you up," Wendy said. "We're not taking 'no' for an answer."

I've never felt the desire to share a bath with anyone, let alone two such awful women. As I was declining the invitation, Wendy deftly untied the belt of my robe and Christine pulled it off my shoulders. Their efficient teamwork was probably the result of years of debagging less popular children at school. As my robe fell to the floor they looked at my belly, then at my face, then at my belly again. I hadn't realized it was quite so obvious.

"Mum, Susan's having a baby," said Wendy. There was an expression of horror on her face.

"But she can't. She's forty-five," said Christine.

"Ooh, that's brilliant. I couldn't be more chuffed. That means I'm going to be a great-aunt," said their mother, always finding the personal angle. "Sounds very old, though, 'great-aunt.' "

The cousins were determined to get to the bottom of it. They thrust their little faces in front of mine.

"How did it happen?"

"Was it an accident?"

"How far gone are you?"

"Isn't it dangerous at your age?"

"Sit down, girls, and let Susan give us the whole story," said my aunt.

Before I could tell them to mind their own business the glossy woman from reception sidled over.

"Miss Green," she intoned. "Just a gentle reminder that half-day passes expire at midday, but you're very welcome to upgrade to a full-day pass if you'd like."

There was much more that I wanted to discuss with Aunt Sylvia, principally her views on my mother's mental capacity prior to the signing of the will — although bearing in mind her own questionable capacity such an assessment might not hold much sway in court. Further probing of my aunt, however, would have to wait. I was prepared neither to subject myself to the cousins' intrusive questioning nor to squander any more money.

"What a shame, I have to go now. It'll have to wait until next time," I told my eager relatives. I grabbed my robe and briefcase and bolted for the door before any of them could restrain me.

"Don't be a stranger, Susan," Aunt Sylvia called after me. "You'll have to spend Christmas with us now that your mum's gone. We're going to take you under our wings, ent we, girls?"

"Don't go. It's not fair. I want to hear all about the pregnancy," called Wendy.

"Stuck up madam," I heard Christine mutter.

10

That evening I made detailed notes on my discussion with Aunt Sylvia. I'd need to draw up a witness statement in her name, and I wanted to ensure that my recollection of what she'd told me was unswervingly accurate. Wherever possible I'd use her own words in any such court document, but would correct her ungrammatical speech and peculiar colloquialisms to make her evidence more persuasive. I wouldn't want the judge to think they were reading the testimony of an imbecile.

From the modicum of pertinent information I'd managed to sift from Aunt Sylvia's ramblings, I'd now established beyond doubt that Edward's involvement in the will went beyond his simply being informed by our mother of its existence. He knew where the will was kept before it was signed and had unfettered access to it. Not only that, but he had personally organized its signing by our mother, and its witnessing by his best friend, Rob, and our easily befuddled aunt. His desire to get Aunt Sylvia over to the house as a matter of urgency spoke volumes. In the circumstances, it's inconceivable that he wasn't aware of the contents of the will. I can imagine his breathless excitement and sweating palms as he handed over the brown envelope to my mother, knowing he was minutes away from securing what would, in effect, be a guarantee of virtual sole owner-ship of the family home. I'm not surprised he left them all to it. He would have wor-ried that his febrile eagerness would show on his face, which might cause our mother to hesitate and question what she was about to do.

I wondered why Edward had been so determined to secure a life interest. I'm not a vindictive person. If my mother's estate had simply been divided between the two of us, as it should have been, I wouldn't have thrown him out onto the streets the day after her death (however much pleasure I might have taken in doing so). No, I'd have given him a couple of months to find alter-native accommodation while I cleared and readied the house for sale. He could easily have found somewhere to rent temporarily pending that sale, after which he'd have had a sufficient sum from his share of the proceeds to buy a flat in a reasonable Birmingham suburb, or even a modest house in one of the less desirable districts. It seems that that wasn't good enough for dear mollycoddled Edward. He was installed in a very comfortable, carefully maintained, four-bedroom semi-detached house on a quiet road in a sought-after area, with all essential amenities — including a pub, off-license and betting shop — only a short walk away. He was happier to plot and scheme rather than drop a rung or two on the property ladder. This despite the fact that, having regard to the amount of remunerative work in which he's engaged since leaving college, he should, by rights, be living in a cardboard box under the railway arches.

Fortunately, my case against Edward was now taking shape. It was as if I'd scratched away the top layer of grime from the surface of an old painting. A hazy image was beginning to form before my eyes. I'd work on it until the complete picture was revealed, however monstrous it might turn out to be.

Finishing my notes and closing my portfolio, I heard a knock at the door and a sheepish "Hi, Susan, it's only me," through the letter box. It was Kate, once more in her pajamas (as was I), but this time with the addition of slippers and dressing gown, and with a bottle in hand.

"Look, it works down here. I can get a signal," she said, waving the receiver of a baby-monitoring device in the air like a winning raffle ticket. There was a low hiss, a faint rustle and a momentary flicker of red-and-green lights across the screen. "I can listen out for them upstairs while we share a bottle down here."

"I'm sorry, my condition precludes me from joining you in a drink."

"Oh, no," Kate laughed, reddening. "It's not wine. I know the score by now. It's sparkling elderflower pressé. I used to drink it all the time when I was pregnant. I'd try to convince myself I was getting drunk on champagne. Come on, share it with me. I don't often get a night out."

From the evidence so far, Kate didn't appear to be the type of woman for whom social intercourse with anyone over the age of two came easily. She was clearly making a huge effort. I took pity on her, invited her in and directed her to the sitting room.

As you know, I'm not someone who's comfortable admitting people into my private domain, and I certainly don't relish uninvited guests. I was exactly the same as a child. At a very young age, I realized it was in my own best interests to keep my father's drinking secret, especially from my classmates at school. I soon became an expert. My primary defense strategy was to avoid making friends so that nobody would be tempted to call at my house and encounter my father. I achieved this by refusing to join in with playground games, turning down invitations to other children's houses and parties, and generally keeping to myself. My second defense strategy was to avoid going anywhere in public with my father. Unfortunately, that wasn't always possible.

An incident occurred, when I was fourteen years old, that had exactly the consequences I'd set out to avoid. We were driving back home from a rare, and particularly strained, whole-family visit to Aunt Sylvia's bungalow. My father asked my mother to park outside the local off-license, and she knew that nothing would be gained by objecting. He staggered from the car to the shop, then staggered out shortly afterward with a bulging carrier bag in each hand. By this stage in his life, the dimensions of his beer belly meant he was forever having to hoik up the waistband of his trousers, which would soon slide back down again over the bulge toward his hips.

As my father approached the car, I watched as his waistband slipped lower and lower. I knew what was going to happen. I opened the door and ran toward him, but I was too late; his trousers were already around his ankles, and his pale, skinny legs were on show for all to see. Rather than put down his precious cargo, he stood there, a look of panic on his face. I grabbed the bags from his hands, and he bent to pull up his trousers, almost toppling forward in the process. This scene may appear comical, but it wasn't. Not to me, not at the time. I looked around, hoping no one had noticed, and spotted a group of girls nearby, doubled up with laughter: Carol and three of her cronies from my class, all of whom — not unlike my delightful cousins — took great pleasure in discovering the vulnerabilities of others. I scuttled back to the car.

I know this sounds cowardly, but on Monday morning I told my mother I was too poorly to go to school. I used the same excuse on Tuesday. By Wednesday morning, she was threatening to call the doctor, and I resigned myself to the fact that I'd have to face the music. Entering the form room for morning registration, it seemed to me that every single one of my classmates was sniggering behind their hand.

"Hey, Sue, saw you and your dad down the shops on Saturday," Carol shouted. "Actually, saw a bit too much of your dad."

"Good job the police didn't catch him flashing himself at young girls," added one of her gang.

"Looked like he was off his head."

"My mum says your dad's a wino."

I stared at my desk and tried to block out the voices. It was impossible. Carol was the ringleader, going on and on and on; she just wouldn't stop. I did something completely out of character, something I've never done before or since. I stood up, went over to Carol's desk and slapped her, as hard as I could. She stumbled and hit her elbow on a radiator pipe just as our form teacher, Mr. Briggs, came in holding the register. I liked him; he was in his early twenties, slight, blond, kind. He taught English, but not to my class.

"What on earth's going on here?" he demanded, throwing the register onto his desk.

"Sir, it's Susan, sir," Carol sniveled. "She slapped me for no reason, made me hit my elbow. I think she's fractured it."

Mr. Briggs looked astounded.

"Susan, did you hit Carol?"

"Yes, sir." I looked down at my sensible school shoes.

He asked what had come over me; I mumbled that I didn't know. He turned to Carol, whose cheek was glowing red.

"Let's have a look at your elbow. Can you move it?"

After a brief examination, he told her there didn't appear to be any serious damage. She should go to the toilets, get a wet paper towel and hold it in place for a few minutes. Returning to the classroom, she stared at me with a twisted smile on her face, as though she was visualizing the torment she was planning to inflict on me.

When registration was finished and it was time for the class to file out, Mr. Briggs told Carol and me to stay behind. He asked why I'd slapped Carol, and I repeated that I didn't know.

"Carol, can *you* tell me?"

"It was just 'cos I mentioned her dad. We saw him staggering around drunk at the weekend, and I wanted to check she was alright."

"Is this correct, Susan?"

"She wasn't asking if I was alright. She was saying terrible things, calling him names."

Mr. Briggs told me I shouldn't ever resort to physical violence, whatever the provocation. But he knew it was completely out of character, so, on this one occasion, he'd let me off with a warning. If I did anything like that again, though, it would be straight to the head teacher for me. He told Carol he didn't want to hear that she'd been bad-mouthing my father again. When he asked if we both understood, we confirmed that we did.

"Right you two, get to your lessons."

The taunting continued, of course. What child gives up such entertainment just because a teacher says so? Carol and her friends took full advantage of having something to use against me. I did contemplate feigning a chronic ongoing illness, but I knew I couldn't stay off school forever. And anyway, I told myself, I was tough, already proficient at detaching myself from what was going on around me and stifling any emotional reaction to it.

The following week, Mr. Briggs asked me to remain behind again after morning registration. He said he knew a neighbor of mine who'd told him a bit about my father.

"How are things at home?" he asked.

"Great."

"Are they really?"

I didn't answer.

"Susan, I just wanted to let you know, my own dad had a drinking problem. I understand what you're going through."

I still didn't respond. He asked if my classmates had stopped teasing me, and I instinctively shook my head.

"Who's doing it? Is it still Carol? I'll have a word with her."

"Don't. It'll only provoke her."

"Alright, it's up to you. But if you need to get away from Carol's lot, you can come to my classroom at break time. And if you want any help, just say."

I went to Mr. Briggs's classroom at first break the next day — not because I couldn't withstand the bullying, of course, but because I prefer peace and quiet. While he was marking homework, I sat at a desk in the far corner and took out a novel. After a while, he looked up and asked what I was reading. I recall it was *Three Men in a Boat* by Jerome K. Jerome; he said it was one of his favorites. The next day, he brought in a P.G. Wodehouse novel he thought I'd enjoy. He said I could keep it; he had so many books he was pleased to make space on his shelves.

So this was my new routine. Each break

time, after the bell went, I would go to Mr. Briggs's classroom, take out a novel and read while he was marking homework and planning lessons. Sometimes he would bring in books for me and we'd discuss them. On a few occasions, he tried to get me to talk about what was going on at home, but I always sidestepped his questions. He told me it was best to keep my visits a secret, or the other pupils would be jealous, and I happily agreed. Mr. Briggs's classroom was my own personal oasis of order and calm, and I wasn't about to share it with anyone.

And then, of course, Edward had to get involved. He'd spotted a few books in my bedroom that had Mr. Briggs's name on the cover. Then he noticed that I wasn't in the playground at break times, and somehow managed to track me down.

"What do you do on your own all that time with Briggsy?" he asked, running ahead of me on the way home from school and blocking my path. I came to wish I'd been more evasive.

"He does marking, I read, he gives me books, we talk about them."

"Sounds dodgy to me. Teachers aren't allowed to spend time alone with their pupils like that, or give them stuff. I've heard about men like him."

"Don't be pathetic. He's just being kind."

Edward was distracted by the sight of his best friend, Steve (who was Carol's brother), riding his new skateboard along the opposite pavement, and I took my chance to push past him. I thought no more about it. Then, in the cloakroom a couple of days later, Yasmin — a quiet girl with whom, in different circumstances, I might have been friends — tapped me on the shoulder as I was putting on my raincoat.

"I think you should know, there's a rumor going around school about you and Mr. Briggs," she said.

"What rumor?"

"That you and him are having an affair."

"That's nonsense. Who's saying that?"

"Everyone. They're saying he's been giving you presents, like books and things, so he can have his wicked way."

She apologized for being the bearer of bad news, smiled sympathetically and left. I stood there, one arm in my coat sleeve and one arm hanging limply by my side. I was appalled that something so entirely innocent could be sullied by vile suspicions. The books, I thought, who knew about the books? Only one person, other than Mr. Briggs and me. People will believe anything if it's whispered to them, and Edward always was a spiteful little tittle-tattle. I intended to confront my brother as soon as I got home but, conveniently, he was having a sleepover at Steve's house.

The rumors, it seemed, had filtered upward very quickly, because before I'd even taken my homework out of my schoolbag, my mother received a telephone call asking her to accompany me to a meeting with the head teacher the following morning. She asked me what was going on, but I told her I didn't know. I didn't want to think about the stories that were doing the rounds. I hoped the whole thing would go away.

Once my mother and I were seated, the head teacher got straight to the point. She said it had come to her attention that there had been an inappropriate relationship between myself and a newly qualified teacher, Mr. Briggs. There were witnesses, more than one. She asked me to explain, in my own words, what had happened. I told her I'd been going to Mr. Briggs's classroom at break time to escape bullying by girls in my class. She asked whether he'd given me gifts. Yes, I said, but only secondhand books. Had he told me to keep it a secret? Yes, but only so other pupils wouldn't demand to stay in at break time, too. She leaned forward, expressed her sorrow at having to raise this, but had Mr. Briggs ever touched me, or asked me to touch him? I could be completely honest, no one would blame me, I wouldn't be the person getting into trouble.

"Definitely not," I said. "Nothing remotely like that. Not at all, never."

She looked at me skeptically, as if she'd known I'd deny it, whatever the truth. After reassuring my mother that she'd get to the bottom of this, the head teacher instructed me to return to class. My mother was tight-lipped as I kissed her goodbye.

The next day, there was a supply teacher at Mr. Briggs's desk. We were told he was off sick, and probably wouldn't be back before the summer holidays, which started in a couple of weeks' time. He didn't return the following term, and I never saw him again. I've no idea whether he was sacked by the head teacher, or walked out when questioned by her, or had always intended to leave at the end of the academic year. For me, it was back to the playground at break time, back to the taunts, which now were not only about my father. Eventually, after a few months, the rumors about Mr. Briggs and me became old news, and the main focus of Carol's attentions moved to a girl who she'd discovered was adopted and a boy who she'd decided was gay. She still tormented me about my father's drinking, but not with quite such gusto. I never forgave Edward, though, for destroying my place of sanctuary and wrecking what I still genuinely believe was an entirely innocent pupil-teacher relationship. I'd confronted my brother about it in the hallway as soon as I'd walked through the front door on the day of the meeting.

"Well, it was obvious he was a perv," he countered. "That's why I told Carol, when I was round at her and Steve's house, because I knew she was a friend of yours. And that's why I told the head."

Strangely, my mother was furious with me, even though she seemed to believe what I told her. There was something very unhealthy, she said, about a grown man seeking out the company of a teenage girl and plying her with gifts. I should never have accepted them. It might have seemed harmless to me, but I was naive; you always had to be on guard with men. Mr. Briggs was probably biding his time, gaining my trust, and who knew where on earth it might have ended? She put her arm around Edward's bony shoulders.

"Thank goodness Eddie was looking out for you."

■ ■ ■ ■

So here I was, landed with an uninvited guest. I would just have to make the best of it. I found I had no objection to Kate's vinous fantasy so, using the sturdy oak casket as a step, I retrieved a box of unused champagne flutes from the top shelf of the kitchen cabinet. She filled the glasses with the elderflower pressé, and we sat curled on opposite ends of the sofa, cushions forming barricades on our laps. There was an awkward silence as we both wondered what on earth to say to each other. Whenever I visit someone, I prepare beforehand a mental list of conversational topics in order to avoid such a situation arising. Kate was obviously not a person who thought ahead.

"Have you been up to anything fun today?" she ventured.

"Not quite what I'd categorize as fun," I said. I proceeded to tell her about my trip to the spa, including a description of my shallow aunt and cousins. She listened with commendable attention.

"They sound awful," she said when I'd finished. "I bet they were furious when you escaped without feeding their hunger for gossip."

Kate told me that, after spending several years working in the banking world, she was sick to death of superficial people. Apparently, she'd studied psychology at university, and had fallen into the world of "personnel" through sheer desperation for the steady income needed to repay her debts. She wasn't suited to it, personality-wise, being a bit of an introvert, and hated every second of her job. She was about to start a master's degree, and was aiming for a career in academia.

"It's what goes on inside that *I* care about," she concluded. "Not the labels on your clothes, or what car you drive, or whether you're popular or fashionable or good-looking."

It goes without saying that I'm not someone who likes to divulge personal information. There's too much of that sort of thing going on these days. People increasingly feel the need to validate their thoughts, emotions and experiences by sharing them with friends or even with complete strangers. On this occasion, though, buoyed by Kate's levelheaded views, I decided to explain the reason for the meeting with my aunt. I dispensed with the cushion, refilled our glasses with the ersatz champagne and began. I told her about my mother's recent death, the outrageous terms of her will, my strong suspicions of duress on the part of my brother, my intention to pursue court proceedings to have the will overturned and the investigations I was in the process of carrying out.

"What a can of worms," she said, also abandoning her cushion. "And you really think your brother tricked your mum into giving him the right to stay in the house?"

"Almost certainly. Tricked, bullied, bamboozled — I've yet to establish which. But I will."

"Shocking. Let me know if you need any help. It's a lot for you to cope with in your condition, and I need something to take my mind off things at the moment. I've got a bit insular, with it just being the kids and me at home. And I go past Birmingham regularly. My family live in Lichfield. If you're ever planning a trip up there let me know."

A surprisingly successful evening, all in all. I might even consider doing it again if I can think of nothing better to do.

Not being someone who bothers to check her mobile phone regularly, I found, when I got back from the office on Monday, that I had three missed calls. I seemed to be becoming quite popular. I dialed voice mail and listened to the first message while I was turning the cacti that fill my kitchen windowsill.

"Hello? Hello? Hello, Susan, love. Are you there? It's Auntie," squeaked the message. "Ooh, silly me, you're probably busy at work. I forget sometimes. Me and Uncle Frank are jetting off to the villa in Estepona this afternoon and I was hoping for a little word before I go. It's just, you know, what you were saying on Saturday, about the will and the 'live interests' or whatever that your mum's given Ed. You were saying you didn't know why she'd done it. Well, I've bin thinking about it — haven't bin able to sleep, which isn't like me. I've always slept like a baby. 'You sleep the sleep of the innocent,' Uncle Frank likes to tell me. Anyway, I think the reason your mum might have done it is because she was always worrying about Ed. I mean, because of the ops he had to have when he was little, and because of your dad's drinking. She read somewhere that it's all to do with genes. Used to go on about it a lot. She thought Ed would've inherited the drinking gene, and that his biology or whatever would've set him on the same path as your dad. 'The apple never falls far from the tree,' she used to tell me.

She thought it was her job to keep him on the straight and narrow. Well, I just wanted to tell you that. I mean, I'm not saying it was definitely the reason. It's just, I don't want you wasting your time with ferreting around and court cases and such like, when your mum was probably just trying to make sure Ed would be okay after she was gone. Right, that's me done. Off to sunnier climes for a few weeks. Viva España!"

What absolute rot. My mother wasn't a stupid woman; she wouldn't have given Edward the right to remain in the family home because of some perceived hereditary weakness. I concede that she often treated Edward like a tortured artistic genius who needed to be shielded from the harsh realities of existence, but in her heart she knew he was just a chancer who was after an easy life. We all have the ability to control our own destinies. It was apparent to anyone that Edward was a waste of space not because he was genetically preprogrammed to be, but because he'd decided to wallow in a mire of self-pity and self-indulgence rather than to clamber out, brush himself down and strive to become a hardworking, responsible citizen. And anyway, as my mother would have been fully aware, if Edward was biologically preprogrammed to have a weakness of character then so was I. After all, we have the same parents. My brother is nothing like my father, in any case. My father, on the occasions when he was sober, was intelligent, cultured and witty. Edward is none of these things. Further, and most crucially, my mother loved Edward and me equally.

Aunt Sylvia's theory was demonstrably wrong, and I intended to tell her so. Without listening to the other messages, I called her straight back in the hope of catching her prior to her departure for Spain. There was no reply.

The second voice mail message was equally maddening.

"Hi, Susan, Rob here. Ed asked me to call you. He thinks it's best if you two communicate through a neutral third party. That's me. Sorry to have to break this to you, 'cos I know you might not be too pleased, but Ed wants to change some of the rooms around in the house. He wants to convert your mum's bedroom into a studio for his art, and your bedroom into a music room. And he wants to put a pool table in the dining room. So he says it's time your mum's stuff was cleared out — you know, her clothes, toiletries, knickknacks, personal bits and bobs. He wants you to deal with it. Says it's too much for him, he hasn't got the faintest idea where to start, that that kind of job's right up your street. He wants to know when you're coming up to do it so he can make sure he's away. I'll be around, though, if you need a hand. He's told me what stuff he wants to keep. And I know you don't drive, and I've got my van, so if you want any stuff moving I'm your man." He gave his mobile phone number and asked me to give him a call.

Even though I'd predicted that Edward would set about desecrating our family home, and had been steeling myself against it, it pained me to hear his plans laid out so starkly. Pained and incensed. However, revenge, as the saying goes, is a dish best served cold. After a few deep breaths, I listened to the message again. It was, of course, a stroke of luck that I would be spending some time with Rob. He was next on my list of people to interrogate in the preparation of my court case; I needed to establish how deeply involved he was in Edward's scheme, and winkle out as much information as I could concerning my brother's actions and motivations. Rob would need to be handled with care, seeing as he was a coconspirator, so sorting out my mother's house would be the perfect

cover story and distraction. I could introduce my questions casually, without arous-
ing his suspicions and causing him to put
up his guard. With a little guile, I was sure
he'd be putty in my hands. I called Rob's
mobile number and left a message, saying
I'd be up in Birmingham the weekend after
next. I'd stay in my old bedroom for one
last night, before it was vandalized by my
brother.

The third message was from Wendy, who
I was surprised to discover had my phone
number.

"Hiya, Susan," went the singsong voice.
"Just phoning for a little catch-up. Don't
forget, me and Chrissie're waiting to hear
all about the baby. Give me a bell the moment you get this message. Bye."

I didn't return her call.

I found myself in a cell-like examination
room, marooned on my back, on what appeared to be a giant length of blue toilet
paper covering a raised trolley bed. My
belly, which had recently begun to resemble
the dome of St. Paul's Cathedral, had been
slathered in the familiar glaucous jelly. It
was the day of my amniocentesis test, and
the medical profession had chosen to treat
me with contempt. I'd been alone for what

felt like hours; I was taut with boredom and frustration.

The now-absent doctor, Dr. Da Silva, whose serious brown eyes and soft, rounded features gave him the look of a Labrador puppy, had begun by explaining the procedure to me. First, he'd examine my belly with the ultrasound machine to establish the precise position of the baby, then clean a small area of skin, insert a thin tube through my abdomen into the womb and extract a small amount of amniotic fluid. This would be tested and in a few days' time I'd be told whether the baby had Down syndrome or other chromosomal defects. He repeated what I'd already been told — that there was a risk of miscarriage. It was small, but nevertheless I needed to be aware of it. I could rest assured, the procedure wouldn't hurt. I informed him that I wasn't worried about the pain. I just wanted the damn thing over and done with. As he finished lubricating my belly there was a knock on the door and an anxious-looking nurse entered the room. She asked Dr. Da Silva, in an urgent stage whisper, whether he'd mind popping next door to give a second opinion on a little problem she had spotted.

"I'm so sorry about this, Miss Green. I

won't be long. Just relax and make yourself comfortable," he said, wiping the jelly off his hands and following the woman.

In the distance, I could hear voices: some urgent, some chatty, some angry, some placatory. There was a low background hum, whether from the water pipes running along the skirting board or from the mass of electronic equipment next to me, I wasn't quite sure. Above this was a steady tick. I craned my neck to locate the clock, which was on the wall behind me. Printed on its face was the word *Niceday*. Not for me. Underneath it were various exhortatory posters, Catch It, Bin it, Kill it; Coughs and Sneezes Spread Diseases: Stop Germs Spreading; We Value Your Opinion: Tell Us What You Think. I was more than happy to tell them what I thought. I thought it was completely unacceptable to direct a patient to lie down on a bed, raise it in the air with a foot pump, ask them to lift up their top and pull down their skirt, slather them with a mucoid substance, then leave them high and dry for hours on end.

I'd almost failed to make it to the amniocentesis appointment. I'd woken that morning with a splitting headache. After contemplating taking the exceptional step of spending the day in bed, I mustered my reserves of willpower, dragged myself to the bathroom, splashed my face with cold water and took a headache tablet. When I got to the Tube station, I discovered there were severe delays on the Northern Line due to an incident that morning. It would be very difficult to get to the appointment on time, and I pride myself on never being late for anything. There was no point even attempting the journey. I started walking back toward my flat, then changed my mind and headed for the bus stop. On the bus, I began to wonder whether I'd locked my French windows. I'd opened them at breakfast-time, and had no recollection of turning the key when I'd closed them. I pressed the bell and made my way to the front of the bus. As it drew to a standstill and the doors concertinaed open, I apologized to the driver, walked back down the aisle and regained my seat. It was unlikely that someone would break into my flat in the hour or two I'd be out.

On my march from the bus stop to the hospital, I suddenly remembered an important piece of drafting that was sitting on my desk at work. I really should have discussed it with Trudy the previous afternoon prior to submitting it to my head of department. He might be waiting for it, and I didn't want to appear unprofessional. I took my mobile phone out of my bag and dialed the number of the hospital to cancel the appointment. By this stage, however, it was five minutes to the allotted time and I was almost at my destination. I knew it was irrational to go to all the inconvenience of rearranging the appointment now that I'd come this far. I ended the call, put my phone back in my bag and walked through the doors of the hospital.

"Please excuse that interruption, Miss Green," said Dr. Da Silva, bounding back into the room. "Bit of an emergency. Where are we up to?"

"We're up to the part where I say I've got better things to do than lie around on a hospital trolley all day," I said, sitting up. I tore off a piece of the blue toilet roll that was covering the bed and wiped the gunk from my belly. It was as slimy and difficult to remove as some other unsavory substances I've encountered, and it took several pieces of paper before I was finally clean.

"But we were just about to get started," Dr. Da Silva said. "It wouldn't have taken long at all. It's really not a lengthy procedure. I'm sorry for the delay, but I was only gone from the room for a few moments.

These things do happen in a hospital." His puppy eyes were moist with regret. "Or is it that you've changed your mind about having the amnio?"

"No, not at all. I'm not a person who changes her mind." It was true, I wasn't. I never have been. Once I've decided on something, that's it. I hesitated, thinking back to the events of the morning. I realized it might appear to someone who didn't know me that I'd been frantically scrabbling around for excuses not to attend the appointment or, having attended it, not to go through with the test. They'd be wrong, of course. I'd tried to do the logical thing, but circumstances had conspired against me from the moment I woke up. That said, I don't like to be a victim of circumstance. It was important, I told myself, that I was not weak-willed or fickle; I had to be true to the person I was and always had been.

"Alright," I said, leaning back on the trolley bed. "Let's do it."

"Are you sure, Miss Green? You can take a few moments . . ."

"I don't want to discuss it, just get on with it."

He did so. I turned my face to the wall and gritted my teeth. It wasn't that painful, physically, just a sharp stinging sensation.

Something strange began happening to time as soon as I'd made my decision, though; the ten minutes the procedure took felt like an hour; the seventy-two hours during which miscarriage was most likely to happen felt like seven hundred and twenty; and the subsequent two weeks, when the miscarriage risk was still raised, felt like two months. When that time had passed, I felt strangely elated. The results, when I received them, were little more than the icing on the cake.

■ ■ ■ ■

NOVEMBER

■ ■ ■ ■

11

This month I finally commenced the process of sorting through my mother's belongings. It was a task toward which I had mixed feelings. I was keen to safeguard items of personal or monetary value in case Edward should take it into his head to dispose of them, but I didn't relish the prospect of the innumerable small decisions I'd have to make concerning each and every one of my mother's possessions. Neither, in my current state, was I looking forward to the physical effort involved. For those reasons, I hadn't been pressing Edward on the matter, and would probably have continued to let it lie, had it not been for the fact that my brother's unforgivable plans required the clearing of certain rooms.

I arrived at the former family home with my nerves jangling. Kate, who was delighted to have adult company on her journey north to see her parents, had picked me up after work in her wheezing Fiat. The offspring were in the back, already in their nightwear. She assured me they had been fed and watered, and would simply nod off en route. It's true, they did fall asleep, but not until they had spent the two hours during which we were stuck on the M25 variously whimpering, sobbing and howling. The lullaby CD, which was on a loop — Kate having rejected the rousing 1812 Overture that I thought would be beneficial on a tiring journey — was by that point on the fourth or fifth time of playing. After an all-too-brief interlude of calm, the baby woke again just before Oxford services, necessitating a stop to change his nappy and breastfeed him. Another full hour was thereby wasted. The experience was as horrendous as traveling by public transport.

I'd confidently expected to encounter Rob on my arrival, but there was a note on the kitchen table saying he was out, and would be back around midnight. "Catch you later," his message concluded. Did he really imagine I'd have any desire to stay up for him? The next day, opening my bedroom curtains (volcanic swirls, seemingly designed with the sole purpose of intensifying infantile fevers), I contemplated the view that had presented itself to me every morning of my childhood. Nothing had changed over the decades: rows of boxy hedges dividing the modest gardens that disappeared into the distance to left and right; sharp-edged lawns that had had their final cut before winter; neat sheds tucked away in corners, liberally coated in creosote against the increasing sogginess of the weather; the occasional ornamental fish pond or Alpine rockery adorned with concrete fauna. The leaves, which were billowing from the trees as the wind blew, would no doubt be raked into neat piles by the end of the day. If I was a less disciplined person I might have allowed myself to feel melancholy at the thought that I'd never again wake to this view. Such an emotion would be nonsensical, though. I was rarely happy here.

There was no sign of Rob when I entered the kitchen, but the empty beer bottle and toast-crumb-covered plate showed that he had, indeed, come home. I opened the cupboard where I knew my mother kept her cereal. The usual bran-based selection was still there, every packet, on inspection, way past its "best before" date. *What do these men eat for breakfast?* I was pondering, as Rob wandered into the kitchen in pajama bottoms and a bathrobe.

"Morning, Susan," he muttered, a dazed

expression on his face. "I heard you moving around. What time is it? Fuck, six thirty?" he added, glancing over at the clock on the oven.

"I've got a very busy day ahead of me."

"But it's the weekend." He ran his hands down the sides of his face and yawned. "Well, I suppose I'm up now. Here's the deal — you make us a brew and I'll crack on with breakfast. I can always go back to bed afterward."

Over oleaginous heaps of vegetarian sausages, eggs, beans and mushrooms, which I tackled nobly but ineffectually, he proceeded to prattle on about his business, as if I might care what he did to earn a crust. I was mindful, though, of my plan to be as amenable — friendly, even — as possible this weekend, so that Rob wouldn't be on his guard when I interrogated him. He told me that, after he graduated from art school, he'd drifted from job to job for a few years, mostly doing unskilled horticulture-related work. By his early thirties, he'd decided to get his act together, had completed a garden design course and had started his own landscape gardening company.

"So where does the traveling fit in?" I asked, with interest that was, of course, entirely feigned.

It was prompted by his divorce, he said. Incredibly, one of his clients had taken such delight in having the grounds of her house landscaped by Rob that she'd left her partner to live in penury with him. They married quickly, immediately after which it dawned on them that they didn't actually like each other very much. This ill-advised relationship somehow managed to limp along for a couple of years. His wife eventually jettisoned him for the owner of a pawnbroker's shop that she'd attended with the aim of pledging Rob's late mother's engagement ring. The marital home was sold and the equity divided equally between the once-again-very-comfortably-off former wife and the far-from-comfortably-off Rob. What a chump. He decided to spend some time traveling around India in order to "get his head back together." While he was away, it had dawned on him that the person with whom he should have been spending his life was a girlfriend from his university days, called Alison. He was going to set about tracking her down and wooing her back when work was a bit quieter.

"Business has been booming recently," he said. "I'm having to juggle two or three projects at the same time, so I've taken on another assistant. Plus, I completed on a house last week — bit of a wreck, needs totally gutting, but it's got potential."

"I'm delighted to hear things are working out for you," I said, dabbing my lips with my napkin and rising from the table.

I instructed Rob to wash up the breakfast things and tidy the kitchen while I made a start on my tasks for the day.

"Yeah, no problem, I'll do all that a bit later. Just going back to bed for an hour or so," he said, disappearing up the stairs.

I equipped myself with the necessary receptacles, took a deep breath and entered my mother's bedroom. It was unchanged from the weekend of my visit for the funeral, other than that the net curtains had been taken down from the window and were lying in a colorless heap on the floor. Everything was shrouded in gloom; the day was overcast, and the smutty bay windows admitted little of what sunlight there was. After switching on the ceiling light and the two fringed bedside lamps, I sat on the low stool in front of my mother's dressing table. I looked at my multiple reflections: one direct, face-on likeness in the large central mirror; and two more enigmatic, oblique versions in the narrow side mirrors. I was quite comfortable with the face-on image; it was the one I saw when I put on my makeup in the morning, or caught a glimpse of myself in a shop window. The side views, though, were unfamiliar, could almost be someone else. My hair didn't look as well-groomed as I'd expected it to; my profile wasn't quite as strong as I'd imagined; there was a sagging under the jawline that I didn't remember. It was unsettling to think that others could see aspects of me that I couldn't easily see myself. I imagined my mother sitting in front of this same mirror. I wondered whether she was at ease with her multiple likenesses, whether she felt confident that the different facets added up to a coherent, harmonious whole. And what about my father — had he ever sat here, contemplating his appearance, as I was doing now? Probably not. He wouldn't have wanted to see the person reflected back at him.

This was getting me nowhere. I had a job to do, and a limited amount of time in which to do it. Pulling out the main drawer of my mother's dressing table I was hit by the sickly smell of stale makeup. I opened an old powder compact and brought the small pink puff to my nose. The scent reminded me of the times my mother would lean over to kiss me good-night as I lay in bed. I always wanted her to stay longer, to hold my hand or stroke my hair, but she invariably had to go to Edward, who wouldn't settle until he'd had innumerable stories and lullabies, a mug of cocoa and checks for monsters in the wardrobe or under the bed. (He probably still won't. Is that Rob's role?) And, of course, once my mother had acceded to all of Edward's demands, she then had my father's to deal with.

I threw the face powder — together with compacts of blusher, palettes of eye shadow and tubes of frosted lipstick — into the bin liner on the floor next to me. To them, I added pots of face cream, hand cream and lip salve, along with hairpins, hairnets and rollers. That left only the framed family photograph, a pair of china candlesticks and a silver-backed brush, comb and mirror set, which I carefully placed in a cardboard box. After a moment's hesitation, I retrieved the powder compact from the bin liner and added it to the collection.

Next I opened my mother's naphthalene-infused wardrobe, which was crammed with dress-and-jacket and skirt-and-jacket suits in pale lemon, baby blue and lavender. I remembered her explaining to me, when I was a child, that she liked to stick to shades that she knew complemented her pale coloring and that would coordinate with each other. I told her that that was boring, but she was quite set in her ways. I filled three bin liners, destined for the charity shop, before the wardrobe was finally empty. I then turned to the chest of drawers, the contents of which were similarly destined, other than the tights and undergarments that I picked up between thumb and forefinger and put in the rubbish bag. It all felt like such a terrible invasion of my mother's privacy. In the bottom drawer, I found a misshapen buff-colored cardigan that used to belong to my father; one of his old favorites. I decided to retain it. Perhaps it would be useful to protect the contents of the box, I reasoned.

Inside my mother's bedside table, I found a fake crocodile skin box. This was where she kept her cheap bits of costume jewelry, which she chose to wear in preference to her more expensive items. I remembered having fun, when I was a small child, adorning myself with these baubles and standing in front of the wardrobe mirror, pretending to be the queen or Princess Grace of Monaco. For some inexplicable reason, I now felt impelled to recreate the scene. I draped half a dozen strings of beads around my neck, clipped diamanté earrings to my ears, pinned several enamel brooches to my black top and balanced a faux-pearl necklace on my head, like a tiara. I stood in front of the same wardrobe mirror and took in the regal effect. It was like being seven years old again — an age at which it was no less likely that I'd rule the country or marry a prince than that I'd be a teacher or a police officer or an airline pilot.

Rob, sure enough, had to choose that moment to knock on the door and enter, carrying two mugs of coffee. I'd thought he was still lounging in bed; more time must have passed than I realized.

"Christmas has come early this year." He smiled. "I mean, you look very decorative, very Bollywood."

I could feel the color rising to my cheeks, despite my efforts to subdue it. I struggled to think of a rational explanation for my ludicrous behavior but was unable to do so. I removed the items of jewelry and replaced them in the box, taking care not to give away my mortification by rushing. Having closed the lid, I sat on the Lloyd Loom chair in the corner of the room and accepted a mug, as though nothing unusual had occurred. Rob perched on the matching ottoman at the end of the bed. The coffee was instant.

"Looks like you're making headway," he said, oblivious to the awkwardness of the situation. "I guess it's hard, having to sort through years of stuff and decide what to keep and what to chuck. It's like drawing a line under a huge part of your past. That's probably why Ed couldn't face it."

"Couldn't face the hard work, you mean."

"I think he's just trying to stay strong. To move on."

I simply laughed. I was determined not to get into an argument, despite my urge to counter such poppycock. Surveying the room, Rob asked what I was intending to do with the furniture. I had to admit I hadn't yet formulated a plan; I have no room for it in my flat, but it'll come in useful when I receive my inheritance and buy a house. It'll have to go into storage until then.

When our coffee was finished, I suggested to Rob that he go outside to do what he does best — tidy the garden — while I continued undistracted.

"Are you always this bossy?" he asked, as he was leaving.

"Not bossy," I called after him. "Just organized."

Within another hour or so the task of clearing my mother's bedroom was complete. All that remained was the bare, dusty furniture and a pile of stuffed boxes and bin liners. The baby was squirming, enlivened either by the caffeine or by the vigorous activity of the morning. Lying down on the double bed, I stroked my bump in an effort to calm it. I heard the opening chords of "Perfect Day" drifting up from somewhere downstairs. As Lou Reed joined in, so did Rob. His voice was more tuneful, more controlled, than you might expect from someone so nonchalant. Perhaps he'd been a choirboy as a child. I recalled that my brother had also had a surprisingly tolerable voice when he was younger. He'd once had ambitions of singing in a band (of course) but found rehearsing for a couple of hours a week too much commitment. I closed my eyes and allowed my mind to drift along with the music. I thought about my own perfect day as a child.

It's our family's first morning in our rented holiday cottage in Cornwall, the summer before I start secondary school. My sleep hasn't been disturbed, and I haven't woken feeling sick with dread. When my mother hears me stirring, she comes in with a mug of tea. She doesn't just put it on the bedside table and leave. Instead, she pulls open the curtains and sits on the edge of my bed. The intensity of the light lends a cartoonish quality to everything around me. My mother's wearing a sleeveless cotton dress with pink-and-red roses on it, which I've never seen before, and her hair is twisted into a loose bun.

"What would you like to do today, sweetheart?" my mother smiles. "It's your choice."

While I'm thinking, I watch fairy dust drifting in the shafts of sunlight. I ask if we can go rock-pooling at the local beach. Without checking whether Edward's happy to do that, she agrees. My father also comes in to say, "Good morning." He's in holiday mode, in shorts and short-sleeved shirt, his sunglasses already tucked into his top pocket. I've never seen him look so healthy. As he hugs me and calls me his little princess, I smell no trace of alcohol on his breath.

We eat breakfast together at the wooden table in the back garden, which has a view all the way down the steep hill to the sea. Both sea and sky are such a soft, hazy blue that it's impossible to see where one ends and the other begins. No one quarrels, no one cries, no one storms off. Edward hasn't been reprimanded by my father this morning, so he isn't scowling or kicking the furniture, and my mother has no need to fight in his corner.

When we've finished eating, Edward asks my mother if we can go to the amusement arcade.

"Not today, Eddie. I'm going rock-pooling with my lovely daughter," she replies. He doesn't sulk.

My mother takes her time brushing and plaiting my hair, while my father butters bread for our picnic sandwiches. We don't want to miss a single minute of this rare and precious British sunshine, so my mother and I decide to walk to the beach. She asks my father if he'll drive down and meet us at the seafront. Because he isn't drunk, he doesn't refuse.

As my mother and I are sauntering along, looking at the almost tropically bright butterflies and wildflowers in the hedgerows, she isn't silent and detached; she asks me about the book I'm reading, how I'm getting on with my friends, how I'm feeling about starting my new school. We're still chatting when we arrive at the beach. Even though the rest of our family aren't there yet, my mother doesn't panic that my father might have started drinking and crashed the car. We sit on a sunny bench and wait. My mother takes my hand in hers and squeezes it.

We spot our car pulling into the car park, stroll over and help take the buckets, spades and folding chairs from the boot. We share the paraphernalia between us and carry it down to the beach. My brother asks my father to play Frisbee with him once we've set up our little camp. My father isn't drunk, so he says, "Great idea." My mother and I pick up our fishing nets and head off over the rocks. She isn't in a rush, she isn't anxious to get back and check on my father and brother, and time spools away as we're on our hands and knees, pushing aside curtains of seaweed and poking under rocks. We catch fifteen crabs and twelve tiny, darting fish. I've never seen so much life in one pool.

When my mother and I get back, my father still hasn't started drinking. We unpack our sandwiches, sit on our folding beach chairs and eat our lunch. My father doesn't slur his words or drop things; my mother isn't too preoccupied to listen to what I say and respond to it; Edward isn't hostile or belligerent. Later, we decide to play crazy golf at a little run-down place along the seafront. My father doesn't take his woven plastic shopping bag containing an emergency supply of cheap British sherry. Neither does he disappear for half an hour, then reappear flushed and staggering. We lose track of the scores, but no one cares who's won and who's lost. My brother doesn't have a tantrum when my mother tells him we'll have just one round of golf today, and my father has no cause to shout at him.

As the sun starts to dip in the sky, my mother drives back up the hill to our holiday cottage. My father, Edward and I walk, so we can detour to the shop on the nearby caravan site to buy ice creams. We pass the local pub without my father saying he'll just pop in for a swift half. Edward and I don't have to sit on the pavement outside, waiting and waiting for him to come out, and we don't have to endure looks of pity. My father doesn't stumble on the way home.

That evening, my father still doesn't go to the pub, and neither does he open a bottle. Nobody tells me how stupid and ugly I am. Nobody tells Edward he's a spoiled brat who's going to end up in Borstal. My father doesn't harangue my mother and they don't fight. We play Monopoly, which goes on for so long we finally agree to call it a four-way draw. When I go to bed, my father kisses me good-night; he still doesn't smell of alcohol. My mother comes to tuck me in, and sits on the edge of my bed again.

"Have you had fun today, sweetheart?" she asks.

"It's been the best day, ever."

Her face is luminous. She switches off my lamp and softly closes my bedroom door, and I realize I've felt no anxiety, no humiliation, no helplessness all day. As the light through the curtains fades, there's no shouting or screaming from downstairs. No doors are slammed. I don't need to hide in the shadows at the top of the stairs in case I have to intervene between my parents. There's no reason why I shouldn't fall asleep, and I do.

That's my perfect day. I may have embellished the truth a little.

After lunch, a doorstop sandwich that Rob messily prepared, I made a start on the dining room. In the corner by the window was my mother's bureau, at which she would write her letters and keep her diary. The drawers were crammed with dog-eared cardboard folders, some containing old, official-looking documents, which were unlikely to be of any importance now, and some containing personal correspondence from friends and relatives. I was tempted to dump the entire lot in the recycling bin to save precious time. In the end, I tied the personal folders together in bundles. I'd take them back to London and give them a quick once-over before disposing of them. The sideboard and dresser were full of items that weren't at all to my taste: heavy cut glass fruit bowls, vases and cruet sets; china figures of long-necked girls; brass knick-knacks. I was faced with a dilemma — I felt oddly reluctant to dispose of them, perhaps because they formed the tangible backdrop to my childhood. They weren't, however, things that I could imagine ever wanting to use or display.

Rob stuck his head round the door to check, yet again, how I was getting on. He'd obviously been instructed to keep an eye on me.

"I've been thinking," he said. "If it helps, I can store the furniture for you in my new house. I've got hardly anything of my own anymore, so it'd be a stopgap for me. We'd be doing each other a favor. And while you're about it you can put boxes of any stuff you're undecided about in my loft. You can have it back whenever you like."

A fresh dilemma — on the one hand, I didn't wish to be obligated to a virtual stranger, and someone who was in league with Edward at that. And it would mean I would have to have ongoing dealings with Rob, which I certainly didn't want. On the other hand, he was proposing a temptingly cheap and convenient solution, which in my current financial situation would be hard to turn down. The things I'd need to store were of no particular monetary value and of no interest to Edward, so it was unlikely that Rob would try to hold them to ransom. Plus, although the offer was almost certainly made to soften me up so I'd reveal information about my tactics, there was absolutely no possibility of that happening. I concluded, therefore, that it could do no harm.

"Might be best not to mention it to Ed, unless he asks," Rob said. "I mean, with you two not being on the best of terms. I don't know what he'd think about it."

Oh, good one, Rob, I thought. *Very clever, pretending you're not my brother's faithful sidekick and henchman. That's bound to win over my trust. Well, two can play — are playing — that game.*

Rob fetched a pile of old newspapers, plus several more cardboard boxes, and I allowed him to assist me in packing away the objects. It was the ideal opportunity — as we were both sitting on the floor in an informal manner and engaged in a mundane, repetitive task — to subtly probe Rob about the circumstances surrounding my mother's will. This is what I managed to get out of him (I've omitted my numerous prompts, together with the continual ums and ers, and the more major digressions):

"I'd only just got back from India. I was staying at a mate's house at the time. He's got a wife and family, and I didn't want to get under their feet, so I spent quite a bit of time with Ed at your mum's house. She was so kind, always made me feel welcome. In fact, she offered me the spare room straight-away, but I didn't want to impose on an old lady. On the day I witnessed the will Ed suggested I nip over in my lunch break to pick up a CD he'd been promising to lend me. When I got there, your aunt was sitting with your mum at the dining table. Your aunt greeted me like a long-lost friend, though I couldn't remember having met her before. As we were chatting, Ed went and got an envelope, then said he had to pop out. Your mum told me she'd written a will and she'd like us both to witness her signature. She got a pen out of the drawer in the sideboard, signed the will and then your aunt and I signed it. Afterward, your aunt tried to persuade me to do some gardening work for her. I explained it wasn't practical for me to take on the job because she lives too far away, but she was very persistent."

It all sounds so innocent, so spontaneous, doesn't it? I asked him what Edward knew about the contents of the will before it was signed by my mother.

"No idea. He never mentioned it to me. But like I say, I'd only just got back from abroad. The first I heard about the contents was just before you came up for the funeral. Ed got a letter from the solicitors after breakfast. Apparently, it said he was allowed to stay in the house for as long as he liked, and that it wouldn't be sold until he decided to move out. He was made up, but he knew you wouldn't be happy. Said something about putting the cat among the pigeons."

"What's he said about the will since then?"

"Sorry, Susan, but I'm in a bit of a difficult position here. I want to be open with you, but I don't want to be disloyal to Ed. All I can say is he knows you've done something at court to stop the solicitor dealing with the estate. He says you haven't got a leg to stand on, that you're wasting your energy. Says he'll just bide his time until you run out of steam. I don't think I've said anything out of turn there. I'm completely neutral in this. How're you planning to fight the will, anyway?"

Another award-winning speech: feigning total ignorance of the conspiracy, while giving away just enough information about Edward's thoughts to make it seem as though Rob, himself, is open and honest. I'm not that naive; I ignored his question.

By this time, the ornaments and trinkets were wrapped in newspaper and packed away in boxes. I was feeling frustrated by the lack of useful information I'd so far managed to winkle out. I turned my focus away from my brother and toward my mother. Closing the lid on the last box, and gathering together the unused newspapers, I asked Rob, casually, how she'd appeared in the last few weeks before she died. He rubbed the stubble on his chin and was silent for a moment, no doubt concocting a story.

"I suppose I'd say she wasn't 100 percent her old self," he said eventually. "She came across as a bit, sort of, distracted. As if her mind was elsewhere. She'd trail off mid-sentence, like she'd forgotten what she wanted to say. But all old people get like that. It wasn't anything out of the ordinary, nothing anyone would've worried about. Anyway, you spoke to her on the phone every week. What did you think?"

"I thought she was getting increasingly confused. I should've followed my instincts and brought forward my next visit. I could've protected her from Edward's scheming."

I realized as soon as the words came out that I shouldn't have said them in front of my brother's ally. Stupid.

"Ed wasn't scheming. He wouldn't take advantage of your mum. He was concerned about her. Always checking on her, making sure she was okay before he went out, seeing she had everything she needed, running errands. He was great with her. If you saw him in the pub with his mates, then saw him at home with your mum, you'd think he was two completely different people. He was really gentle and thoughtful when he was with her. She brought out the best side of him."

I must say that this is an aspect of Edward's personality that he's managed to keep concealed from me for more than four decades. Frankly, it's one that I don't believe exists. Rob's assertions were beyond credibility.

"But if she wasn't thinking straight, and Edward happened to put it into her head, even innocently, that he needed to stay in the family home . . ."

"I've got no reason to think that happened. Look, this is nothing to do with me. I don't know any more than you do. Sorry, but I'm a bit uncomfortable with this conversation. Let's talk about something else."

I have no idea what Rob thought he and I could possibly have to discuss with each other.

Later that evening, as I sat alone watching an episode of some gloomy Scandinavian detective series (Rob was at a friend's stag night celebration), I wondered whether my questioning had been too heavy-handed. If I tried a lighter touch Rob might still be fooled into disclosing information about my brother's actions and intentions, or about my mother's mental state. I didn't want to frighten him off. I resolved that, the following day, I'd deploy all my innate warmth and charm.

12

I was imprisoned between two filthy navvies on the front bench seat of a white Transit van; not a situation in which I'd ever expected to find myself. Rob was seated to my right, one hand on the steering wheel, the other tapping out the rhythm of the song he was humming. He was dressed in his work clothes, which, as usual, bore traces of every trench he'd excavated and bag of manure he'd spread. The equally malodorous goblin-like creature on my left was Billy, Rob's assistant and general dogsbody. Billy was a good head shorter than me, all bone and sinew, with deep wrinkles cross-hatching his cheeks. He had three stud-earrings in each ear and self-inked tattoos on his fingers. When he wasn't jabbering away, barely comprehensibly, he was twitching, scratching himself or rolling a cigarette. Sometimes all at the same time. I wouldn't have been surprised to discover he was out on day-release.

Climbing into Rob's van, I'd had to negotiate the yellowing newspapers and discarded paper coffee cups piled up in the foot well. The black vinyl seats were gashed in places, revealing the stuffing, and there was a thick film of grime over everything. I took the precaution of placing one of the newspapers on the seat before I sat down, in case my dry-clean-only black wool trousers were contaminated beyond salvation. The suspension of the van was obviously shot; every bump in the road was magnified a hundredfold and my bones were jarred in an alarming manner as I was repeatedly propelled into the air and jolted back down again. To be fair, Rob had been slightly abashed when he opened the van door for me.

"I don't usually carry passengers, other than Billy here. Hope you don't mind roughing it." Certainly I minded. It was necessary, however, for me to satisfy myself that my furniture and boxes would be stored safely.

We were bound for Rob's newly purchased house — a "hop and a skip" away, I was assured. As we hurtled over a particularly craterous pothole, Billy produced one of his previously constructed roll-up cigarettes. I didn't believe he'd actually light the thing until he began flicking at a plastic lighter. I take no pleasure in telling people what to do, but I had no alternative but to direct him, in the strongest possible terms, immediately to desist from his intended course of action. He didn't seem unduly put out, and I couldn't help thinking he was probably used to being given commands by police officers, prison guards and the like. Rob, though, was shaking his head.

"I don't think she means to put it so rudely, mate," he said, leaning around me. "It's just her manner."

"No probs. Sorry, love, I forgot you was in the family way," Billy said, squeezing my thigh just a little too high up for comfort. "You hardly look it. My missus was the size of a house by four months. Mind you, she's the size of a house, anyway." He chuckled away to himself, returning his cigarette to his tin. "Have you given up while you're carrying?"

"I don't smoke. I never have," I informed him.

"I thought you did," Rob piped up. "Years back, when we were all students. Everyone did in those days."

"You're mistaken. Perhaps you're thinking of someone else. I don't even remember meeting you." If I *had* ever done anything so contrary to logic and good sense, which I hadn't, I certainly wouldn't be admitting it to Rob.

"Nasty habit, anyway," said Billy. "Going to stop, myself, in the new year. So, what're you having?"

I explained to him that I had no idea. I was due to have another scan the following week, at which I could choose to find out. Whether it would be appropriate or desirable to do so wasn't something to which I'd yet addressed my mind.

"My missus was made up when we was told we was having a girl. Looking forward to dressing her up like a little doll and buying her My Little Ponies, she was. Then our Amy arrived, and all she wants to do is wear a football kit and kick a ball around. You never can tell. So what d'you want? A son or a daughter?"

Those two words pierced my consciousness like the snapping of fingers to someone in a trance. I repeated them to myself: *son, daughter.* I'd be a woman with a son. Or I'd be a woman with a daughter. Not only that, but fate had already made the decision for me. It wasn't something over which I had even a modicum of control. And then another word insinuated its way into my mind. If the baby was going to be a son or daughter, that would make me a *mother.* A child would look at me and think, not "estranged sister" or "work colleague" or "woman-I-sometimes-see-on-the-Tube," but "mother." That mattered. It mattered more than could be explained simply by logic alone. It mattered that I was not a disappointment, not a source of dissatisfaction, frustration or regret. I was confident my child would consider that I was fulfilling the parental role in an exemplary manner — *failure* isn't in my vocabulary — but what if . . . ? Billy was continuing to jabber on about how I'd get on fine without the baby's dad, that hardly any dads he knew stuck around for very long, but I was barely listening to him. "Mother."

"Susan, are you still with us?" Rob was saying. "You look like you're away with the fairies."

"I'm absolutely fine, thank you. Were you saying something?"

"I was just asking whether you wanted anything from the caf. I'm popping in for a couple of coffees for Billy and me."

"Oh, a pot of Earl Grey, thank you," I said, automatically.

That morning, I'd set my alarm for seven

o'clock and finished work on my old bedroom before Rob summoned me for yet another of his vegetarian truckers' breakfasts (if "vegetarian trucker" isn't an oxymoron). It had taken very little time to clear the room, my mother having depersonalized it as soon as I went away to university. The only things I decided to keep were a copy of *Little Women* that had belonged to my mother, and a copy of *Just So Stories* that had belonged to my father.

Rob was rather muted over breakfast, no doubt nursing a hangover from the previous evening. It had been after one o'clock in the morning by the time I heard his key in the door. I'd found myself unable to sleep until he returned, which accounted for my feeling uncharacteristically lackluster. The doorbell rang as Rob was in the garden emptying food waste onto the compost heap and I was flicking through the previous day's newspaper. Billy quickly made himself at home, tossing his jacket over the end of the banister, striding into the kitchen and throwing himself down onto one of the kitchen chairs. I gained the distinct impression that this was far from his first visit here.

"So you're moving some stuff out of your brother's house, are you, love?" he asked, blowing his nose on a grubby bit of tissue he'd produced from the pocket of his jeans. "I know Ed a bit, from The Bull's Head. Boss fella."

"This isn't my brother's house," I told him. "It belongs to us both equally, and it'll soon be sold."

"Oh, sorry, I got the impression your mum'd left the house to Ed. Sounded like he'd got plans for it."

"He's having difficulty coming to terms with the fact that he'll have to move out."

Rob returned from the garden, and Billy got to his feet.

"Right, governor, where do we start," he said, rubbing his hands together, probably at the thought of the overtime he'd be paid.

There was nothing for me to do but oversee operations as Rob and Billy grunted and strained under the weight of the boxes and furniture. While they were securing the contents in the van, I wandered from empty room to empty room. Each was filled with ghostly impressions of the objects they'd once held. Where the furniture had stood, the carpet was darker and plusher, protected from sun and wear, and the feet had left deep depressions. On the faded wallpaper were darker shapes of the pictures and mirrors that had once hung there. There was even a faint silhouette of the wooden crucifix that my mother had, in more recent years, hung above her bed. Despite these echoes of the rooms' previous lives, the memories they held were already dissipating, like smoke after a candle's been extinguished. In my old bedroom, I closed my weekend bag, which was marooned in the middle of the bare floor, and took a last look through my window. I picked up my things and closed the door behind me. *Enjoy your music room, Edward,* I thought, *because you won't have it for long.*

I perched on an upturned wooden packing case and sipped my flinchingly over-brewed tea while the two men unloaded the van and heaved the various tables, wardrobes and chests of drawers into position in the downstairs front room and two of the bedrooms of Rob's house. Next a set of stepladders appeared and my boxes were hoisted up to the loft. Rob was quite correct when he said his house was "a bit of a wreck." I concede that it was a potentially tolerable period terrace in an area not entirely without its attractions, but the kitchen, bathroom and decor had clearly been chosen by a color-blind lunatic in the 1970s. It had been touched by neither paintbrush nor pasting brush — nor, apparently, by vacuum cleaner or duster — since then. A very sorry situation in which to place my mother's treasured possessions. Beggars, however, can't be choosers.

When the job was finished, Rob handed Billy a couple of folded notes.

"Have a beer on us," he said, replacing his wallet in the back pocket of his trousers.

"Ta, governor. And good luck with the rest of your pregnancy, love. I can tell you're going to be a brilliant mum. You and the little one should come and live back here in Brum. It's much better than down that London. There's loads of parks and all sorts of stuff going on for kids. It's changed a lot since you was a girl."

"I'll bear your advice in mind," I assured him.

I accepted Rob's offer of a lift to New Street station, Kate having decided, most inconveniently, to stay an extra couple of days at her parents' house. As we were fastening our seat belts, he asked about the father of my baby. The directness of the question took me aback. I was going to tell him to mind his own bloody business, but I was still working hard on my friendly-and-amenable act.

"I'm not in a relationship with the father,"

I explained. "I've told him I don't need his assistance."

"Is he okay with that?"

"Not yet, but he will be. He still mistakenly believes he wants some sort of involvement."

"Why did you refuse, then? Did he treat you badly?"

"No, quite the opposite. If you must know, I've got three reasons for refusing — one, I don't want to be indebted to him morally or financially, two, I want to be free to make my own decisions about the child, and three, he doesn't really want the responsibility, anyway."

"Surely it's for him to know what he does and doesn't want. You can't just make his mind up for him. If he helps out financially or in other ways, that doesn't mean you owe him anything. You created the baby together, so you're both equally responsible. And the making-all-the decisions-yourself thing, well that's just not fair. I think you might have control issues."

I wasn't sure how much longer I could keep up the act. I could feel my mask slipping.

"What's your agenda, Rob? Are you a spokesperson for Fathers 4 Justice, or something? Because, otherwise, I'm not sure why any of this concerns you."

"I don't know anything about them. I'm not making a political point here. It's just . . . I've got personal experience which gives me a perspective on things that maybe you don't have."

"What kind of personal experience could you possibly have that's relevant to my situation?"

There was a long silence. I hoped my rhetorical question had closed the subject.

"When I was at college, I was a bit of a dick, if I'm honest," he began. I held myself back from saying that it came as no surprise. "I had quite a few girlfriends, and they didn't always last that long. There was one girl I was serious about, though — Alison — and she was serious about me, too. Only problem was, she kept nagging me to sort myself out. I was into all the usual student stuff, but just a bit too much into it, if you know what I mean."

"Not really."

"Nothing serious, just drinking too much, smoking too much, getting stoned most days — a bit heavier on the weekends. Then just before finals she found out she was pregnant. She was supposed to be on the pill. We talked endlessly, going round the houses. In the end, I said she should have an abortion, that we were too young to be parents. She agreed, but on the day she was booked into the clinic she had a stinking cold. They said she needed to go away, wait until she was better, then make another appointment. She never rearranged it. I kept nagging her, and she said she was going to do it, but time went on. After a few weeks, she said it was too late, she was going to keep the baby. I was shit scared. I didn't want the responsibility. I wanted to carry on going out with my mates, getting off my head on the weekends, spending my money on having a good time."

We'd been stationary at a busy crossroads for quite a while. The traffic lights had turned green and the driver behind was honking his horn. Rob crunched the van into gear.

"I don't really know why I'm going into all this. But there *is* a point at the end of it." He was quiet for a moment as he overtook a cyclist, then carried on with his story. "Eventually she told me to get my act together or piss off. I grabbed the lifeline. I said, at the end of the day, it wasn't my problem to deal with. It was Alison who messed up the contraception and her who'd decided to keep the baby, so she couldn't expect me just to do whatever she wanted. I told you I was a dick." More honking from the car behind as Rob's driving became progressively slower. He put his foot down on the accelerator and waved two fingers in the air; a wasted gesture, seeing as we were in a van.

"Alison left Birmingham and went back to live with her parents in Edinburgh. I didn't think much about the baby at first — I was too busy enjoying myself — but as time went on I started wondering. I didn't even know whether I'd got a son or daughter. Around the time of what would've been its fifth birthday, I decided to contact Alison. I was hoping it wasn't too late to get to know my child. I managed to find her parents' number, and gave them a call. They weren't particularly pleased. I expect they'd heard all sorts of terrible stories from Alison, most of which were probably true. They did say I'd got a son, that his name was James and that Alison was living happily with someone else."

Rob paused. I thought perhaps he'd finished, but after a sigh he continued.

"Alison's parents warned me not to try to contact her, she wouldn't want anything to do with me. I couldn't just leave it at that. I phoned and phoned, begging them to let me have her number. I explained that I just wanted to be a father to my son. They must've told her, because one night I got a call from her. She was very calm, very firm. She said I'd given up any right to see James when I walked away. He was a happy, confident little boy. He called her new partner 'Daddy.' She said I meant nothing to him, that my name wasn't even on the birth certificate. I could've fought to get access to James. Who knows, I might even have won. But I knew I'd done the wrong thing by walking away in the first place. I didn't want to do the wrong thing again by messing up their lives. I decided to leave them in peace. But every single day I think about my son, wondering what he's up to, what he looks like, what he sounds like. He's over twenty now. I've no idea whether he ever thinks about me. He mightn't even know I exist. I missed my chance to watch my son growing up. It's my own fault. I can't blame anyone else. I'm just saying, Susan, don't do this to your baby's father. Not unless you've got good reason to, not unless he's mistreated you or deserves it."

We were at the station car park by this point. Rob leaned his head on the steering wheel for a few seconds, then turned to me. I was going to say something firm to him, but he looked as if he might cry. Please don't, I thought. I'm not at all equipped to deal with men crying. Or anyone else, for that matter.

"Shit, I only wanted to give you the benefit of my experience," he said, sniffing and laughing. "Let's get your bags out of the back."

I accepted Rob's offer to carry my luggage onto the train, seeing as I was returning to London with far more than I'd set out with. On the way, Rob, calmer now, continued with his theme.

"Anyway, like I told you, I came to my senses when I was in India. Alison's the only one for me. She's the one I should've been spending my life with. I've wasted too much time already. I'm going to find her and my son, see if he can ever forgive me, and if Alison's not with anyone now, do my best to win her back. Make up for all the shit stuff I did when I was younger."

On the train home to London I thought about Rob's disclosure. I wondered if his intention had really been to make a heartfelt plea on behalf of excluded fathers, or if it had simply been to soften me up and make me better-disposed toward him. If so, it had almost worked; I'd almost felt sorry for him, momentarily. I reminded myself, however, that his problems were entirely of his own making. He'd behaved appallingly, and his girlfriend had undoubtedly suffered much more than he had, at least in the early days. I also reminded myself that, as Rob was Edward's partner in crime, it was unlikely that any of it was actually true.

With Billy's constant presence for most of the day, and Rob's "revelations" about his son, I'd had no opportunity to extract any further information concerning either Edward or my mother's will. It was fortunate that I'd be seeing Rob again in a couple of weeks' time. He was going to a gig in London with Edward, he said, so it would be easy enough for him to drop off the boxes I'd wanted to take back with me. Easy enough, too, for him to continue with his plan of getting me to lower my guard, he no doubt thought. Strangely, as I closed my eyes with the intention of having a short nap before Euston, I couldn't help recalling what an unusually deep shade of blue Rob's own eyes had been when he'd turned to face me in the van. It must have been a trick of the light.

In bed that evening, propped up with pillows, I sat looking through the cardboard folders that I'd retrieved from my mother's bureau. I'd hoped I might find some reference to her state of mind, or to her plans for her estate after she died, but the correspondence was, for the most part, too ancient to be of any relevance. There were thank-you notes from Uncle Harold, Aunt Julia and their sons for presents my mother had sent them over the years; letters from two old school friends who had moved to New Zealand and Canada, in which they reminisced about their shared childhood experiences; annual birthday cards from my father, which I noticed stopped the year I was ten; hand-made-at-school Christmas and Easter cards, mostly from Edward but a few from me; several barely legible letters from Aunt Sylvia, including one that had been torn into pieces then taped together, in which she expressed her deep gratitude for something unspecified; a typed letter of reference from my mother's boss at the university faculty office, saying that she was a reliable and hardworking employee; some letters and cards of condolence for the death of my father; and more in the same vein. I dithered about whether to keep anything, but finally decided I would dump the lot in the recycling bin. None of it told me anything I didn't already know, and anyway, I simply didn't have the space.

Next, I opened the hefty photograph

album, which I'd also brought back with me from Birmingham. The album began with my parents' wedding and ended just after I started school. The first photograph was a black-and-white formal, posed picture of the whole family outside the church after the ceremony. My mother looked shy, bashful — unaccustomed to being the center of attention. My father looked vacant, enduring what had to be endured in order to become a married man. I expect he'd had a stiff drink to help him through the ordeal. In contrast, Aunt Sylvia, standing next to my mother and wearing a long, lace-trimmed bridesmaid dress, was clearly having the time of her life. My mother was twenty-seven when she got married, which would put Aunt Sylvia at around twelve years old. At that young age, she'd already learned, from movie-star magazines, how to pose for the camera in a manner that displayed supreme (if misplaced) confidence in her own attractiveness. A skill that's never left her.

The rest of my mother's family had enthusiastically but ineptly cobbled together the poshest outfits they could, to mark one of their clan moving up in the world. Notwithstanding their best efforts, they looked stiffly awkward and graceless. My father's family, however, appeared quite at ease with the formal situation; wearing tailored three-piece suits and couture dresses and jackets, was nothing out of the ordinary for them. Despite their ease, the hints of suppressed frowns, pouts and smirks betrayed their various attitudes toward my father's union with my mother. Only the expression of Uncle Harold, my father's brother and best man, was as inscrutable as my father's — in my uncle's case the result of his army parade-ground training rather than self-administered anesthesia. It was odd to see my paternal grandparents in the photograph. I have no recollection of meeting them. I wonder if I ever did.

I flicked to a photograph in the middle of the album, which must have been taken a few years later. It was the day of my christening at the same church, a much smaller gathering. I was only a couple of months old. Unlike the wedding photograph, which was obviously taken by a professional photographer, this was a slightly skewed Kodachrome snap. The only member of my father's family who attended the occasion was Uncle Harold, who looked as staunchly dutiful as ever. My mother's family, also, was somewhat depleted; although my maternal grandmother was in attendance, my grandfather seems to have had better things to do that day. In the photograph my mother was holding me, looking ill at ease with the bundle in her arms. I suppose she'd only had a few weeks' practice. My father, serious, frowning, had his arm around her shoulders reassuringly. Aunt Sylvia, now seventeen or eighteen years old, was looking away from the camera, as though something on the ground to her right had distracted her. She was wearing a peach-colored minidress with white knee-high boots, a stark contrast to my mother's somber gray dress suit and matching pillbox hat. It's the only photograph I've ever seen of my aunt in which she isn't smiling.

"Well, you could all have looked a bit happier at my arrival," I said to the picture, before snapping shut the album, placing it on my bedside table and turning out the light.

A few days later I found myself trudging to the hospital maternity department in my lunch hour — another antenatal appointment, this one my twenty-week scan. I must say that I remain unable and unwilling to come to terms with the fact that, after forty-five years spent happily keeping myself to myself, both my body and my mind have now become public property. It's quite unbelievable how many people need to poke, prod, test and interrogate you when you're pregnant. Attending the various appointments seems to be a full-time job in itself, and my belly's been the subject of more intense scrutiny than that of the most industrious Turkish dancer. It's as if I've ceased to be a person in my own right, and have become merely a receptacle for another human being.

"So, Miss Green, are we going to find out the sex of your wee babby?" asked today's sonographer, a skinny middle-aged Scottish woman with cropped, tightly curled ginger hair. Since my encounter with Billy, I'd spent quite some time mulling over this question. Finding out seemed, to me, a little like opening your presents on Christmas Eve or flicking to the end of a novel when you have only read as far as the midpoint. It smacked of cheating, of a childish inability to exercise patience and self-restraint. I am, however, a very pragmatic person. I like to know exactly what's going to be happening and precisely when it will happen. That way you can guard yourself against unwelcome surprises and ensure that everything proceeds satisfactorily. If I knew the sex of the baby I could purchase the appropriate clothes and equipment. Not, you understand, that I'm the sort of person to buy frilly pink things for a girl and plain blue things for a boy, but I expect there will be some slight differences between the items I'd select. On balance, I decided to allow the sonographer to inform me of the sex of the baby. She duly did so.

Back at work Trudy beckoned me into her office, like a spy on a secret mission. She shut the door behind me with a suppressed giggle.

"So, what is it, Susan? Boy or girl?" She had a look of eager anticipation on her face.

"Oh, they couldn't tell. It was lying the wrong way round. I'll just have to wait until it makes an appearance."

Trudy couldn't have looked more dismayed if I'd told her it was all a mistake and I wasn't pregnant, after all. She walked back to her desk and slumped into her chair.

"Oh, what a terrible, terrible shame," she said. "That's so disappointing."

"Yes, isn't it?"

Well, it's one thing to have a quick flick to the last page of a book. It's quite another to read it aloud to all and sundry.

13

In the days since returning from my room-clearing trip to Birmingham I'd been revisiting my decision not to allow Richard to play a part in the life of my baby. I'd come to the conclusion, extremely reluctantly, that Rob might have a point. I had no reason to believe that Richard would cause any harm to the child, either emotionally or physically. Indeed, from his keenness to be involved in its upbringing, it might well turn out that he'd be a loving and attentive father, and a positive influence in its life. Bearing in mind my own early experiences, could I justify denying my child that? If I decided I *could* deny it, was it possible that the child would grow up to resent what I'd done, despite my explanation that I'd wished to preserve my independence? Further, was it right to overlook the effect that my refusal of contact would have on Richard? Judging from the years of regret Rob (truthfully or not) said he'd suffered as a result of his estrangement from his son, it occurred to me that to do the same to Richard could cast a shadow on his life. I'm not someone who backtracks from a decision that's already been made, but it takes a strong and secure person to admit they've been a little hasty.

St. James's Park had reached the climax of its autumnal display; the trees were still in almost-full leaf, but the foliage had turned copper, russet and ochre. The mid-November sun was bright and there was no evidence of the heavy mist of that morning. It wasn't a park with which I was familiar; Richard had been the one to suggest it, as a relatively quiet and pleasant place for an uninterrupted lunchtime rendezvous. Trudging along the path from The Mall (I was five minutes late, due to Trudy attempting futilely to initiate a conversation on the subject of how I was "feeling about things"), I spotted Richard sitting on the lakeside bench where he'd told me I'd find him. He was dressed in his usual immaculate way, as though he'd stopped to gather his thoughts before meeting the queen. His attire wasn't the first thing I noticed, though. My attention couldn't fail to be drawn to the fact that standing next to him on the wooden bench, and holding its head at an angle of haughty self-importance, was a large snowy pelican. Neither bird nor man was paying the other the slightest attention. Richard, himself, was engrossed in a paperback book, which I saw, as I neared, was *Madame Bovary*. Contrary to what you would expect from his rather reserved disposition, he's always been attracted to tragic heroines whose passions conquer their reason. I should have thought I was quite a surprise to him.

I was almost at the bench by the time he looked up from his book and gave me one of his most charming, fresh-faced smiles. I sensed that he still had hopes of winning me over.

"The lovely Susan," he said, carefully folding over the corner of a page, an uncharacteristic act that made me wince. After stowing the book in a pocket of his overcoat, he stood. I allowed him to peck me lightly on each cheek.

"You look blooming today."

I was already tiring of that adjective.

"Why is there a pelican next to you on the bench?" I asked.

"Oh, he's very friendly, this one. I come here to escape the hurly-burly, and I often find him next to me when I look up from my book. He seems to have taken a bit of a shine to me."

"But what's a pelican doing in a central London park at all?"

"Don't you know? There's a flock of them. Or is it a gaggle? No, actually I think it might be a pod. They've been here for over four hundred years — a gift from a Russian ambassador, originally. Peculiar creatures. I feel a strange affinity with them."

The pelican regarded me disdainfully, then raised its wings, jumped down onto the path and swaggered lake-ward. It was hard to believe that something could manage simultaneously to look so imperious and so absurd.

"Will you join me on the bench?" asked Richard. He took a neatly pressed handkerchief from the inside pocket of his overcoat, shook it out and swished at the seat with delicate sweeps of his arm. He then laid the handkerchief out flat next to him and patted it. We sat in silence for a few moments, watching the pelican nibbling, with his impractically long orange beak, at what must have been an itch on its puffed-up chest. Richard coughed.

"May I apologize for my inexcusable behavior the last time we met? I hadn't been sleeping well, and the situation regarding the child had been building up in my mind. I shouldn't have accosted you outside your office like that, and I certainly shouldn't have issued threats. I'd like us to forget everything that's passed between us in recent weeks and start again from a basis of mutual respect and harmony."

A group of four teenage girls, who looked like Japanese students (over-the-knee socks, quirky clothes, cartoony handbags), had stopped in front of our bench to admire the pelican, which was now shaking out his wings. One of the party began taking photographs of the others, who were making victory signs behind the bird's head.

"I have no objection to that," I said to Richard. "As I told you when I called, I've been giving more thought to your possible involvement in the life of the child. I may have been slightly premature in dismissing you before I'd examined the question thoroughly. It was important, though, to make it crystal clear from the start that I have no intention of adopting the role of pathetic, needy woman."

"Susan, I can't imagine anyone possibly thinking of you as pathetic and needy."

"Good. Now, what I want to say is that I've come to the conclusion, after weighing up all the various considerations, that it wouldn't be correct for me to exclude you entirely from the baby's life. So I've decided . . ."

I was interrupted midflow by one of the Japanese students — a smiley girl with her hair in beribboned bunches — approaching our bench, apologizing humbly for interrupting us and asking if we would take a photograph of their party with the pelican. Richard agreed to do so.

"You were saying?" he inquired, as he rejoined me on the bench.

"I was saying I've decided that some participation, on your part, in the baby's life wouldn't be unacceptable. Your involvement will have to be clearly defined and agreed between us before the birth, but I don't see why that couldn't be done amicably."

"Wonderful. You don't know what a huge relief that is to me. I know we can make this work for all parties concerned. I'll pop into Foyles this afternoon and pick up some books about fatherhood."

"I was going to suggest that," I said. "It's always best to read up on a subject well in advance."

A family, who had been talking in excited, Scottish-accented voices about the proximity of a rare Pokémon, stopped to look at the preening pelican. While the mother restrained her two young sons from prodding the real flesh-and-blood creature, the father approached Richard and me, again with a request that we take a group photograph. Richard agreed, begrudgingly this time. Rejoining me on the bench once more, he cleared his throat.

"So one matter's on the way to being settled — the extent of my postnatal involvement. There is, of course, another matter. Things have been said in the heat of the moment that neither you nor I really meant. We both needed time to come to terms with our changed situation before we could look again at our relationship. The fact that we're now singing from the same hymn sheet regarding the child indicates we've done that."

"Yes, I suppose we have."

"You know, of course, that I've never been keen on entering into a conventional committed relationship. But circumstances have now changed."

"Richard, I really don't think . . ."

"Let me finish, please."

Another group of tourists — this time Australian, by the sound of them — had gathered by the pelican. A middle-aged peroxide-blonde woman turned toward us.

"No, madam. No pictures," said Richard, a little too loudly. The bird, used only to murmurs of admiration, was startled by the unexpected noise and launched himself into the water. The Australians marched away, throwing resentful looks over their shoulders.

"Susan, we're both people who like things to be done by the book. I suppose it's traditional to go down on one knee at this point, but the pelicans have been busy and you're sitting on my handkerchief. Susan, our evenings together have meant the world to me. I think you might well be my soul mate. You're me in female form. Would you do me the honor of becoming my wife?"

"Your wife?" I asked, astounded. "Do you mean entering into a marital contract with you, or actually sharing a home?"

"One generally leads to the other."

I don't like to be caught off guard. The sole purpose of meeting Richard had been to bestow my munificence; to magnanimously confer on him what I'd decided it was morally right to confer. It had *not* been to negotiate any more personal sort of arrangement. My initial impulse was to tell him he could forget it. I stopped myself, however, and took a moment to think. Was it *really* so far beyond the realms of possibility? It couldn't be denied, the practicalities of looking after a baby would be even simpler to manage with two adults sharing the same household; and wouldn't it be even better, in terms of emotional security, for a child to live with both its parents, so long as those parents were able to get along amicably? Significantly, until the recent state of affairs, Richard and I had always seen eye to eye.

I mentally noted down everything in Richard's favor. He'd certainly been good company over the years; he'd never let me down, lied to me or hurt me. He was a smart, exceptionally well-mannered, pleasant-looking man with good taste and a steady income, and he and I shared many of the same interests. There had always been an attraction between us, and our more intimate encounters had been pleasurable. We'd never done anything "domestic" together, of course, but there was nothing to say that the good times we'd had within our strictly delineated boundaries couldn't translate into everyday life. In almost all respects he was the ideal life-partner for me. Balanced against that, though, was the fact that I'd never had the slightest desire to share my life. There was also the fact that I didn't have "romantic feelings" toward Richard, and neither, as far as I was aware, did *he* have them toward me. How important was that? I wondered. I looked at him hard, trying to decide whether I could ever feel more for him than I currently did. If such sentiments were going to develop between us, I would have expected them to do so by now. It was not entirely out of the question, but I was far from convinced.

"I do sympathize with your urge to do things by the book, Richard, but I don't think it would be a good idea. We'll get along much better as coparents than as husband and wife."

The pelican had emerged from the water again, and was eyeing me with what looked like contempt. Richard sighed, and slumped back on the bench.

"I suspected it might be too soon in our rekindled friendship to bring up the subject of marriage. I've taken you by surprise — you'll need some time to think about it. We can revisit the subject at a later date."

"I'm afraid there wouldn't be any point," I said, with more conviction than I necessarily felt. "I have to get back to the office. People will wonder where I am. I don't usually take a proper lunch break."

"Mummy will be so delighted when I tell

her I'm going to be part of our child's life. I'll be in touch to discuss the details. And as far as the other matter's concerned, we'll just leave it hanging in the air for the time being."

"It's not hanging in the air. It's gently floating to the ground, where it's going to stay."

"Hmm. We'll see about that. I sense that you're open to persuasion."

I allowed him to peck me lightly on each cheek once more, then retraced my steps along the path to The Mall. Glancing back, I could see that the pelican had jumped back onto the bench next to Richard, who was trying to remove his handkerchief from beneath its webbed feet.

14

A big-boned young lady were the words my mother used to describe her. "Beefy Brigid," Edward called her — actually to her face on one of the few occasions they'd crossed paths. I, personally, thought she looked like an Olympic weight-lifter. I wouldn't have dreamed of telling her that, of course. I did, though, suggest on several occasions that she might want to consider reining in her calorie intake for the sake of her health, appearance and self-esteem. Brigid would just slap me on the back heartily and say it was a good job she didn't easily take offense or I'd have no friends at all.

Brigid and I met in the first term at Nottingham University. We both liked to sit in the middle of the front row in lectures, so we often found ourselves next to each other. I was rather reserved in those days, and found her effusive bonhomie both infuriating (it felt like being battered by a tsunami of affability) and oddly soothing (I had no need to watch what I said, or even, for that matter, to say anything at all). At the end of our first year, spent in halls, it was Brigid who suggested that we flat-share, Brigid who found a suitable property and Brigid who made all the practical arrangements. I had no problem with allowing her to do so. She was the sort of assertive, forth-right person who would never be fobbed off with substandard accommodation or an unfavorable rental agreement. Our domestic relationship worked well, even when Brigid took up with Dermot, a rugby player even bigger than herself, and I — well, we will come to that.

And here I was, twenty-odd years later, sitting across the table from my old flatmate in a noisy Italian restaurant just off Chancery Lane. Since leaving university, Brigid had married Dermot, qualified as a solicitor, "dropped a sprog" as she called it and whiled away the early years of motherhood at a personal injury firm specializing in mundane slippers and trippers. She'd since retrained and was now a barrister with an exciting, radical chambers in Lincoln's Inn. Her caseload was of the type that often attracted media attention. Indeed, I'd recently seen dear Brigid interviewed on the ten o'clock news (a good job they invented widescreen television). Even though we both lived in London, I'd managed to limit our rendezvous to once every two or three years, aided and abetted by the busyness of her life.

"Who'd've thunk it," she said, smacking a great meaty paw on the table and making the cutlery jump in the air. "Old Susan 'I'm not the breeding type' Green up the duff. I remember you saying families were like prisons but without the hope of a release date. Well, you took your time coming round to the idea. Any longer and the train would've left the station." She took a large swig from her glass of red wine. "I'm almost out the other side now. Rachel's seventeen — one more year and she'll be off my hands. I've already started packing her bags." She took another large swig. "Honestly, though, motherhood's a doddle. I don't know what all the fuss is about. Just grab the nearest nanny and Bob's your uncle. Or your childminder."

Perhaps you can see why I befriended Brigid all those years ago, and why I've allowed our friendship to keep ticking over. Despite her exasperating sense of humor, she's a woman with a no-nonsense approach to life. It was for that reason, and more particularly for her legal expertise, that I'd suggested meeting for lunch. A few days earlier my — possibly naive — assumption that I had limitless time to investigate and prepare my legal case to overturn my mother's will was dealt a blow. I received in the post a document headed In the High Court of Justice, Family Division. It stated that I had eight days in which to "enter an appearance" setting out my case. If I failed to do so, probate would be issued to Mr. Brinkworth, allowing him to deal with the estate. The solicitor was clearly trying to call my bluff; I took that step, the matter could then only be settled by the court, with all the costs that would involve. He was no doubt banking on me losing my nerve.

"So have you finally given up the bachelor-girl life, or is this a solo enterprise? I mean, I'm assuming artificial insemination. Have you been finding alternative uses for the old turkey baster?"

"No, Brigid." I sighed. "It was insemination in the usual way, and no I haven't given up my independence. That's all I want to say on the matter."

"Fair enough, old girl. Your womb is your own business. As are your sleeping arrangements. So what brings you blinking out into the daylight? I haven't seen you for don-keys."

I paused for a moment as dishes were placed before us; a mozzarella salad for me and a mountain of linguine drenched in creamy sauce for Brigid, which she commenced shoveling into her mouth as though her plate might be whisked away from her.

"I want some legal advice," I said.

"Aha, an ulterior motive. What is it? Have the cops finally discovered you're running a drug-smuggling cartel from your flat in Clapham?"

Oh, the unparalleled wittiness of the woman. How I'd missed it.

"No, Brigid." I sighed yet again. "It's to do with my mother's will. She's given Edward a life interest in the house, so I'm not going to get my share until he decides to move out. Which he probably never will."

"What, your pothead bro's got the property?" she said, between heaped forkfuls. "You're going to have to do something about that, Susan, old girl. You don't want your dosh tied up ad infinitum. It could be yonks before you get your mitts on it, if you ever do. What was the mater thinking of? Did she forget about all the crap he's done over the years? Like what happened to your Phil, for God's sake. Though, now I come to think of it, she was the one person who didn't think any blame attached to Ed."

Perhaps Brigid's reference to Phil requires a little explanation. You may be surprised to learn that Richard wasn't my first partner, and neither was he the first person to suggest marriage. When I was younger, I had none of the silly, girlie interest in boys that others in my class had. I know people like to look for psychological reasons for every aspect of our personalities. If you want to go down that route you need only look at my closest models of masculinity, viz my father (alcoholic, unreliable) and my brother (lazy, vindictive). It could simply be, however, that I was aware from an early age that a close relationship with a boy or man — or indeed anyone — would undermine my freedom, dilute my individualism, take up precious time and cause the unnecessary expenditure of emotional energy. Looked at logically like that, it's astonishing that any rational person would want to engage in intimate relationships.

But then there was Phil, from up the road. He went to the same nursery school as I did, although I have no particular memory of him from those days. He went to the same primary school, and I do remember him from that time, vaguely, as a small boy with a pudding-basin haircut who was forever on the edge of things, on the sidelines; unobtrusive and easily overlooked. We ended up at the same local secondary school, and walked home the same way. It was probably when we were about thirteen or fourteen that he first spoke to me, after school. Initially it was about homework, tests and marks; later it was about what we'd read, listened to and watched on television. I wouldn't have described him as a friend at that time. I didn't need or want friends. He was just someone who happened to be going the same way as me, and who shared some of my interests. I tolerated him but was careful not to let him get too close, and I made it quite clear that he wouldn't be welcome to call at the family home.

In sixth form it transpired that Phil had chosen to take the same A levels as I had, so we had things to talk about on the academic front. People started thinking of us as girlfriend and boyfriend, but that wasn't the case at all. On the occasions he tried to get too familiar with me — when his conversation became too personal or intimate — I'd deliberately say or do something unkind to push him away. He made the mistake, in our first term of the lower sixth, of asking me to go to the cinema with him. I explained that that would never, ever happen. I didn't speak to him for at least two weeks after that.

Edward resented deeply the fact that I had a companion of sorts. On the way home from school he and his tight little coterie of misfits, rebels and dunces would trail behind Phil and me, making kissing noises, singing, "Suze has got a boyfriend," or, if that failed to rile me, trying to trip us up, barge us off the pavement or fire spitballs at us. It was to Phil's credit that he simply ignored Edward and his cronies, as faintly annoying but ultimately inconsequential insects.

I've been trying to track back to when and why Phil and I became closer. I think it must have been following my father's death. You might have assumed, from my references to my father's manifold faults and weaknesses, that I didn't care for him. If so, I've unintentionally misled you. I did. So, when my father died, I wasn't quite my usual resilient self. For the first time in my life I needed the support of another person. My mother was too focused on poor dear Edward. "A boy needs his father" was her repeated mantra. Phil appeared to understand how I was feeling: when I wanted to talk, when I wanted to be quiet. He invited me to the cinema again, to something subtitled (*One Deadly Summer*), I think, and I accepted. That led on to other evenings out and eventually — shortly before our A-level exams — I allowed him past the front door of our family home. We became, in the traditional sense, boyfriend and girlfriend. It's hard to believe it now, but it's true. I had a boyfriend.

Phil had decided to stay at home and go to Birmingham University, as he was required to provide practical and emotional support to his wheelchair-bound mother. He asked if I'd consider transferring from Nottingham to Birmingham University, but I declined. If our relationship was strong it would survive the geographical separation. If it was weak, it wouldn't. To further test it I insisted that we had no face-to-face contact at all during term time, a rule that I maintained until halfway through our second year. It turned out that our relationship *was* strong.

At the end of that academic year, as we descended the steps of the Birmingham Central Library, Phil dropped his book bag, turned to me and asked if I'd marry him once we'd finished our degrees. I told him I'd think carefully about his proposal and let him know my answer the following day. I spent that evening listing the pros and cons of marriage to Phil. On the positive side was the fact that he was serious, studious, quiet and amenable. In addition, I was used to Phil, and I certainly wouldn't want to go through the bother and effort of meeting and getting to know other possible partners in the future. On the negative side, could I be sure that he wouldn't try to fetter my independence, or prove to be unreliable and untrustworthy? Plus, I'd have all the hassle of divorce proceedings if he turned out to be a disappointment. I decided to reject the proposal. The next day I met Phil outside the Odeon cinema.

"So, what's the decision, then?" he asked, tracing the cracks in the paving stones with the toe of his shoe. His hands were thrust deep in the pockets of his corduroy trousers and he was carefully avoiding eye contact.

And then a strange thing happened. Instead of the words *I'm sorry, it's no,* I heard myself saying, "Yes." I was as stunned as he was. We both stood there staring at each other for quite a few seconds before the siren of a passing police car broke the spell. We hugged awkwardly, neither of us knowing quite how we should behave at such a significant moment. In the end, we marked it with two Coca-Colas and a large bucket of popcorn. So that's how I found myself engaged at the age of barely twenty. My mother seemed moderately pleased for me when I informed her of the fact. I remember she insisted I phone Aunt Sylvia immediately. My aunt, in her usual overdramatic and overemotional way, burst into tears of what I concluded was joy, rendering her even less coherent than usual. When I told Edward, his reaction was rather different.

"God help the poor bastard," he said, his face contorting with an expression that managed to encapsulate jealousy, malice and mockery. "Does he know he's letting himself in for a lifelong, nonstop barrage of criticism and disapproval? I think I'll have to have a word with him."

He did more than that. Much more.

"So, let's hear about your strategy. What's your angle of attack? What're your weapons and how big's your army?" asked Brigid, rubbing her mouth with the back of her hand.

"I'm planning a two-pronged assault," I told her, yielding to her well-worn metaphor. "Undue influence by Edward, and lack of mental capacity on my mother's part. I'm amassing troops on both fronts at this very moment." I explained my belief that Edward had pressurized my mother into doing something she would never, in her right mind, have considered doing.

"Hmm. Undue influence is a slippery fish. You'll have to get some pretty watertight evidence that your brother was up to no good. What've you got on him so far?"

When I thought about it, I had to admit: not a great deal. I told her what I'd managed to glean from my interviews with Aunt Sylvia and Rob. "But I know categorically and unequivocally that Edward engineered all this, even if no one else will come straight out and say so. It speaks volumes that the witnesses' stories show he knew where the draft will was kept and organized the signing."

"Not enough, old girl." She folded her arms across her ample bosom and fixed me with the matronly look she no doubt used on her less biddable clients. "I'm sure I don't need to tell you that bullheaded maintenance of criminality on the part of Edward isn't going to persuade a judge by itself. Unless you can get some real dirt — proof that he frog-marched her down to the solicitors' office with her arm twisted behind her back, or that he was threatening to unravel her knitting — undue influence is going to be a nonstarter. In fact, it might even turn the judge against you. They might decide you're just a green-eyed aggrieved sibling who can't come to terms with the fact that your mum put the needs of your brother before your own. Not that I'm saying you are, by the way. But it's much better to focus on what you can prove, and not muddy the waters with what you can't."

"But dropping the undue influence allegation takes the focus off Edward and trains it on my mother," I said. "It's like exonerating him from blame, and saying it was all down to her. I'm not letting him off that easily."

"Yes, but listen, old girl. I'll tell you what I tell all my clients, and what you must already know — it's not about occupying the moral high ground or achieving vindication of your beliefs, it's about winning the legal argument. Simple as. Shove all your feelings about Edward to one side and think, coldly and clinically, what you need to do to get your hands on half the proceeds of the sale of the house. Forget about trying to show the world that Edward's a bastard and you're a saint. If you confine your attack to your mum's lack of capacity, you can still say that her mental state left her open to self-serving suggestions by Edward. It's just that you're not claiming he set out with a malicious intent to force her into doing something against her wishes."

"I don't agree, Brigid. The facts need to be aired in court. I want to see a judgment, in black-and-white, stating that Edward is corrupt and immoral. This has been a very long time coming, and I'm not shying away from it now."

Brigid leaned back in her chair, which just about managed to withstand the force, and shook her head. "You're in danger of sounding like one of my obsessive clients. Step back from the case for a moment and think how you're going to convince the judge on the day. It's not going to be by raising all sorts of hyperbolic and evidentially unsupportable allegations against a family member, however well-founded you and I might believe them to be. It's going to be by producing incontrovertible, rock-solid evidence."

"Yes, I'm fully aware of that, but . . ."

"Okay, okay, old girl. Time's ticking and I can see I'm not convincing you. Let's move on to the lack of mental capacity question. What've you got on that?"

I told Brigid about the two strokes my mother had had prior to the drafting of the will. "To be perfectly honest, I didn't see a lot of her in her last months, but when I did see her I didn't think she seemed totally compos mentis. And even Edward's crony, Rob, admitted that she was vague. I've applied for her medical records, but the wheels of officialdom grind slowly. I've been told I should get them soon."

"Well, fingers crossed that that'll give you the proof you need. Ideally there'll be a helpful diagnosis in there, or expressions of concern about your mother's mental state. But you don't want to rely on that alone. You need some witness corroboration of how her medical condition affected her. Who was she close to? Who did she see on a daily basis?"

I'd already thought about that. "The vicar of her church — St. Stephen's — is the person she'd probably have confided in. I can visit him and take a statement. And her doddery old neighbors over the road. They told me, on the last day I saw her alive, that they were worried about her, but I didn't think they were worth taking seriously."

"Okay, old girl. Get all that evidence together and come and see me in chambers. I'll cast my eye over it and let you have my assessment. This is off the record. I'm not leaving myself open to a professional negligence claim if it all comes crashing down around your ears. And bear in mind that you could be in for some unpleasant legal costs if you don't win. It's probably not even worth asking, but are you sure you wouldn't rather choose the easy life? You could just walk away, concentrate on the impending sprogdom and wait for your inheritance to come to you in due course." She looked at me quizzically. "No, I thought not."

■ ■ ■ ■

DECEMBER

■ ■ ■ ■

15

I find it hard to believe it's now six months since sperm inadvertently met egg and the inexorable process of cell division commenced; it seems only days ago that that little plastic stick delivered its thundering verdict. In other ways, however, it feels like decades have passed. When I took the test, my mother was alive and well(ish) and there was a family home I could return to whenever I felt inclined. Now I'm parentless, rootless, adrift with no anchor. No, I retract that. I have no idea why such weak-minded thoughts have started to form in my head. As you're aware, I've always been the author of my own destiny. We can choose how to define ourselves, and I define myself as an autonomous and resourceful woman. What I lack in terms of family and other close personal relationships is more than compensated for by my rich inner life, which is infinitely more constant and dependable.

I can't help, though, but feel twinges of regret that my mother never knew about my pregnancy. What would she have made of it, I wonder? Would she have been shocked, worried, pleased? It's hard to imagine her having any of those reactions. She always treated my achievements with mild, disinterested approval and my disappointments with equally mild, disinterested regret. It was clear that she wished the best for me, but she also wished the best for the newspaper boy and the girl who helped out in the greengrocers. Edward's every minor success, on the other hand, was a source of intense joy and a cause for great celebration on her part, and his failures (which were regular and predictable) elicited sympathy or distress. My father would probably have been pleased about my pregnancy, so long as he wasn't expected to have anything to do with the child. His attitude toward Edward and me, on the occasions when he was sober, appeared to be satisfaction that he'd fathered offspring, mixed with annoyance at the practicalities of interacting with us. When he was drunk, satisfaction metamorphosed into euphoria and annoyance into seething resentment, admittedly aimed more at Edward than at me.

■ ■ ■ ■

As I was writing my short Christmas present and card list, Kate disturbed my peace yet again. She's taken to knocking on my door whenever she feels like it, particularly if she wants to share her frustration about her ongoing marital dispute. Apparently, sometimes Alex demands to see the children when it's inconvenient, sometimes he pleads unavoidable business commitments when he's needed; sometimes he treats Kate as though they're old friends, sometimes he treats her like his nemesis. I've told her on numerous occasions that she should just change her phone number, put new locks on the front door and forget she ever had a husband. Her response is always the same: "Oh, Susan, life isn't that simple." It makes me very grateful that Richard's position vis-à-vis the baby will be agreed well in advance of its birth. At least I won't have to engage in such irritating and time-consuming maneuvering.

With the lights of the baby monitor winking through the fabric of her cardigan pocket, Kate plonked herself down on my sofa, proffered the box of Quality Street she'd brought with her and told me about her latest dilemma: the arrangements for Christmas, less than three weeks hence. Kate wanted to visit her family in Lichfield over the festive period, but Alex said that that was unacceptable; he had no desire to spend Christmas Day driving to the Midlands and back just to spend a couple of hours with their children. I suggested to Kate that, if she felt compelled to reach a compromise rather than simply informing Alex what would be happening, they have one child each. Again, however, she was reluctant to follow my judicious advice.

Kate asked me about my own plans for Christmas, which up until this year I'd spent with my mother. Coincidentally I'd had a phone call from Aunt Sylvia only an hour or so earlier.

"Ooh, hello, our Susan," she cooed. "It's Auntie here. Just got back from the villa and wanted a catch-up. Bin thinking of you all the time we was away, wondering how you're getting on with your pregnancy. You must be quite big now, eh? Make sure you're putting your feet up. You don't want to get swollen ankles or varicose veins. I've always put my feet up for an hour or two in the afternoons, since I was in my twenties, and I've got the legs of someone half my age."

Sitting down on the sofa and resting my feet on the oak casket, I assured her that I couldn't have been feeling fitter. To be quite honest, that isn't entirely true. While I've had boundless energy from the time the morning sickness ceased, I've found, on several occasions in recent days, that a feeling of exhaustion has overwhelmed me without warning. I even had difficulty keeping my eyes open during what should have been a particularly productive in-house training day at work. Aunt Sylvia proceeded to prattle on about how a "nice deep tan" takes pounds off you, which are the best places to eat out in Estepona and how, if it wasn't for the girls and the grandkids, she'd be a permanent expat. "I'm a lady who can't abide being parted from her nearest and dearest, you see," she said. "That's just how I am. Family comes before anything else, even my own health and happiness. Talking of being with family, that's what I'm ringing up about. I bet you haven't got any plans for Christmas, have you, love? What with your mum having passed away so recently, God rest her soul."

"Well . . ."

"So, that's settled, then. You're staying with us. Wendy and Chrissie'll be here with the kids, so it'll be a houseful. Not that we're short of space. Your uncle Frank thought about guest accommodation when he had the house built. And the girls are dying to see you, so don't worry about feeling like a cuckoo in the nest. We've got a cozy little box room that's just the right size for someone on their own. We're going to have such a laff with the family all being together. I was forever telling your mum to come over for Christmas Day, but she always said she liked it to be just the three of you, and I suppose when your dad was alive she didn't want him causing a scene and ruining it for everyone. Come on Christmas Eve and stay 'til the day after Boxing Day. Ooh, I can't wait."

So that is, indeed, settled. Well, what were my other options? I haven't exactly been inundated with invitations for the festive period, and, although I do naturally prefer my own company, there's something about Christmas that causes a person to balk at the idea of being alone. Next Christmas, of course, I won't be.

"Why don't I give you a lift up to the Midlands again?" Kate said when I informed her of my plans. "Sod bloody Alex. If he wanted to spend Christmas with the kids he shouldn't have walked out on them, should he? He can fester in his gorgeous apartment with his gorgeous girlfriend and think about what he's missing. You know, I do appreciate you lending an ear. I feel much stronger since we became friends."

She passed the Quality Street across the sofa once more. I took a caramel swirl, then propped the box between us.

"I'm very pleased to hear it. Just keep telling yourself to think more like a feminist, and you'll come out of this on top."

"What do you mean? I *am* a feminist."

"I'm sure you're trying to be, but you have to learn to be more self-contained. You're too easily affected by the things Alex does. Your confidence was shattered when he left you, and you still let him get to you where the children are concerned."

"Anyone would be devastated if their partner ran off with someone else, leaving them with a newborn baby and a demanding toddler, whether they were male, female, feminist or otherwise."

"I wouldn't be. I've organized my life very carefully so that no one could ever cause that kind of devastation. Because I'm not reliant on anyone emotionally or financially, I can't be hurt. That's how a feminist is — iron-willed, Teflon-coated, in total control of every aspect of her life."

Kate unwrapped a toffee penny and put it in her mouth.

"That's not *my* definition," she said, sounding like someone with a mouthful of marbles. "As far as I'm concerned you don't have to be all, or even any, of those things to call yourself a feminist. What it boils down to is knowing that women are equal to men, and living that knowledge. It's about ensuring that that equality is recognized in the home, in the workplace, in public life. And it's about acknowledging that we all — women *and* men — are strong sometimes, weak sometimes, coolheaded sometimes, emotional sometimes, right sometimes, wrong sometimes. Locking away your feelings and vulnerabilities has got nothing at all to do with it. That's something else entirely."

She picked up the box and shook it at me invitingly. Resistance would have been both futile and unseasonal.

"I don't entirely disagree," I said, smoothing out the purple cellophane from my chocolate and adding it to the growing pile. "And I've got nothing against men in general, only against being treated as a second-class citizen. You must see, though, that a feminist would never voluntarily put herself in a position where a man could hurt her."

"That's like saying a feminist would never love, and that's obviously not true. Whenever you open yourself up to another person, same sex or opposite, you take the risk of being hurt. That's a simple reality of life."

"You're overlooking the centuries of oppression that women have suffered at the hands of men, sometimes even colluding in it. We're lucky we can choose to step out of the cycle. Why do the orange and strawberry creams always get left to the end?" I added, looking into the box.

"Not in my house — chuck me one. I'm not overlooking the lessons of history. But women have made huge strides in the last few decades. There's still a very, very long way to go, but maybe we feel more confident about acknowledging our vulnerabilities as well as our strengths."

"I don't have any vulnerabilities."

"Everyone does. You just hide yours, probably even from yourself. Try letting your guard down sometimes. You might find yourself pleasantly surprised by the consequences."

"You need to read *The Female Eunuch*," I told her.

"Okay, but you should read something

more current. The discourse has moved on, you know. It's like fairy stories. In the old days, the princess always had to get the prince, or it wasn't considered a happy ending. Then came the first wave of feminism, and that suddenly felt like a cop-out — no self-respecting princess would sell her soul by marrying a prince. (Chuck me another orange cream, will you?) It must've been a massive breath of fresh air after what went before. But, these days, fairy-tale endings come in all shapes and sizes. It's okay for the princess to end up with the prince, it's okay for her to end up with the footman, it's okay for her to end up on her own. It's also okay for her to end up with another princess, or with six cats, or to decide she wants to be a prince. None of those make her any more or less a feminist. It's about finding out who you are and what you want, and then being true to it."

"Maybe. You know, we mightn't always agree with each other, but I like the fact that you have opinions on things. At least you can be bothered."

Before she left, Kate gathered up the smoothed-out wrappers and put them back in the empty carton; something about making Christmas decorations with Ava.

■ ■ ■ ■

The following day Rob was due to drop off the items from my mother's house that I'd decided I could accommodate. He was driving down from Birmingham in the morning with Edward, off-loading him at a friend's house, then proceeding on to my flat. According to Rob, he hadn't told Edward either that he was storing items for me at his own house, or that he was delivering the boxes; my brother was under the misapprehension that he was visiting an elderly relative and Rob hadn't corrected him. A likely story. Why on earth would Rob be doing this if it wasn't part of a bigger plan concocted between the two of them? Did he have a subconscious resentment of Edward that made him want to act contrary to his wishes? It would be understandable, but I'd seen no evidence. Did he have a split personality? If so, he was keeping it well hidden. Was he perceptive enough to see that I was in the right and Edward was in the wrong? Doubtful. Could he have more personal reasons for wanting to help me? Obviously not; he hardly knows me, we have nothing in common and he's on a determined mission to win back Alison. The only logical explanation was that Edward, through his proxy, was keeping his enemies close.

"Ed's particularly angry with you at the moment," Rob had said on the phone when he called to confirm the arrangements. "If he knew where you lived he'd probably be battering the door down."

"And what's my dear brother's reason for feeling more antipathy toward me than usual?"

"He called in at the undertakers a couple of days ago to pick up your mum's ashes, and they told him they'd already given them to you. He's mad. He was going to phone you straightaway and tell you what he thought — he was saying you were a grave robber — but I persuaded him to calm down and take his time."

"So he cares about our mother's ashes so much that it's taken him over three months to think about collecting them? He's got no more legal or moral claim to them than I have. And you know what the law says about possession. He can do his worst, but I have no intention of relinquishing them."

"You shouldn't've taken them without telling Ed, though. It's a bit underhanded, if you ask me. But, hey, it's not my battle. I just thought I'd let you know he's on the warpath. He says he's been too laid-back in this will dispute thing because he's had other stuff on his mind, but he's going to start fighting back. He's going on again about valuables you took from the house after the funeral, and saying he's going to get them back."

All the above, I'm sure, was conveyed to me on Edward's instructions. I expect my brother thinks I'll be so intimidated by his wrath that I'll roll over like a little lapdog. He should have realized by now I'm a very different species.

As you know, I pride myself on my good manners and civility. Although Rob is my brother's coconspirator, I decided it would only be polite to invite him to join me for lunch in return for delivering the boxes. Politeness, though, wasn't the primary motivation for my cultivating our acquaintance further. I woke early — it was still dark outside — and pulled out some recipe books. I wondered what sort of food Rob would like. Being a gardener of sorts, I supposed it would be pork pies or pasties. Perhaps I could cook a beef Wellington or a stew with dumplings. Then I remembered he was a vegetarian. In the end, I decided to prepare a Spanish-style lunch instead. I wrote a list and headed down to the shops as soon as they were open. I spent the morning assembling a variety of tapas dishes, then cleaned, tidied, did my makeup and hair, and set about choosing an outfit that would combine weekend informality with classic style. Eventually, the meal, the flat and I were all as effortlessly organized and presentable as it's possible to achieve in half a day.

At the appointed time of one o'clock I sat down on the sofa to await my visitor. Whenever I heard a vehicle approaching, I got up to look through the bay window. Five past one: no Rob. Ten past one: no Rob. Quarter past, and I was beginning to think he must have had an accident; surely nobody would be so late without phoning with an explanation and apology.

I had my mobile in my hand to call him when I saw his familiar white van draw up behind Kate's car, which she'd parked in front of the house seconds earlier. I watched as the two of them greeted each other and exchanged a few words. A moment later he was carrying a stack of leaflets from her boot to our shared front door (she's recently started a campaign to oppose the withdrawal of funding from a local mothers-and-babies group). Noah was in Kate's arms, and Ava was walking next to her. I couldn't help noticing that Rob was acting in rather an over-friendly manner, causing mother and child to explode with laughter. He spotted me looking through the window and grinned, as did Kate. I went to the front door and opened it, while she was still fumbling in her handbag for her keys.

"You've met each other, I see."

"Yes, Rob's just introduced himself. He's kindly helping me cart this stuff from my car. You need at least four arms when you've got a baby."

"I'll carry them upstairs for you," said Rob. "Hi, Susan, by the way."

"I don't want to put you to any trouble. You're here to visit Susan."

"Oh, it's no trouble at all," Rob said, edging past my bump.

I was left alone in the hallway as everyone disappeared upstairs. By the time Rob eventually descended, looking pleased with himself, I was more than a little irritated.

"Right, shall I fetch the boxes then?" he asked. He lugged them in, one by one, and stacked them in a corner of the hallway. When he'd finished, he stood, rubbing his hands, waiting for me to say something.

"Before you go, I'd just like to point out," I said, "that I'm a very busy person, and if I make an arrangement with someone for one o'clock I don't expect them to turn up at quarter past."

"Lighten up, Susan, it's only a few minutes. There was an accident on the M6, so I was late dropping Ed off. I'm sorry, though, I should've given you a bell. Why don't I take you for a bite to eat to make up for it?"

"I have a prior engagement," I said.

"Oh, shame. Right. I suppose I'd better leave you to it, then. Another time, maybe."

Well, I couldn't let him assume I had nothing better to do all day than await his arrival. That would be a show of weakness, and who knows where *that* would lead? Once he'd sloped off I sat down at my kitchen table and looked at the tapas dishes. There was far too much food for one person; it would probably end up being thrown away. What a lamentable waste. I wasn't sure, at that moment, that I felt like eating any of it myself. When I returned to the sitting room, I spotted, through the bay window, that Rob's van was still parked outside; I could see him tapping out a text message on his phone. I hesitated. Would it really be weakness? Or just a sensible way of using up surplus food? Plus, I had my detective work to think about. I went outside and knocked on the window of Rob's van.

He wound it down and leaned out.

"There's been a last-minute change of plans," I told him. "You're welcome to share my lunch with me."

"That'd be great. I'll just finish sending this message to Ed." Updating his puppet-master, no doubt.

When I led him into the kitchen, Rob expressed surprise at the array of dishes.

"Wow. Do you eat like this every day?"

"A varied diet is important when you're pregnant," I explained.

Returning to the kitchen after a brief visit to the bathroom, I found that Rob had got up from the table and was standing by the work surface, studying, with more-than-innocent interest, the notes I'd made on duress and mental capacity in the drafting of wills. When he spotted me, he started wittering on about looking for a piece of kitchen roll to mop up some spilled olive oil. I turned my papers over so they couldn't be read, then threw a cloth to Rob. The spillage was almost nonexistent. I was about to confront him over his spying antics, but then decided against it. It would be better for my own counterespionage agenda not to reveal, at this stage, that I was on to him.

To my disappointment, I didn't manage

to extract from Rob any more information that was useful to my case, despite subtle and repeated probing. I concluded that he must either be cannier than he appeared, or must be used to giving evasive answers under close questioning. It goes without saying that he failed in his attempts to trick me into disclosing anything about my legal action. Having finished skirting around the edges of estate-related matters, we ended up talking about irrelevancies (among other things, on his part: his childhood in a small town on the Welsh borders, his hippie parents who were converting an old hayloft in Italy, his two younger sisters and their ever-expanding families; on my part: what I thought about life in London, why I hadn't gone on to be a solicitor or barrister after my law degree, the standoffishness of my father's side of the family).

Rob also updated me on his quest, telling me he'd joined Facebook but hadn't been able to find Alison on there. He wondered if she'd changed her name. He'd sent friend requests to two of her old flatmates, who he hoped would have some information on her current whereabouts. I wished him success. If anyone had happened to be in the room with Rob and me they would have thought we were two friends having a good-natured weekend lunch together, rather than members of opposing tribes assessing each other's strengths and weaknesses.

Before he left, I showed Rob my windowsill full of cacti, which I knew he, as a horticulturalist, would appreciate. I explained that this wasn't my complete collection; the other half was on my desk at work. Its extent and variety impressed him. Reaching out a finger to a large bunny ear, he talked about the way the cactus had evolved spikes, rather than leaves, in order to reduce the surface area through which it could lose water, while still providing some shade for the main body of the plant, often little more than a modified stem; many people, he said, wrongly assumed that spikes served only to ward off predators. He also remarked on the cactus's thick waxy skin, its well-developed root system and its broad, succulent trunk, all of which facilitated the storage of moisture or the minimization of its loss.

Putting a finger in the soil, Rob asked me how often I watered my cacti and whether any of them had ever bloomed. Apparently, to stimulate them to produce flowers, I should water sparingly during the dormant period (I *always* water sparingly), then give them a good drenching to mimic a brief rainy season. He picked up each of the containers in turn, remarking that several of the plants were pot-bound and would soon cease to thrive if they weren't repotted. And light, too, he said — they would benefit from being in a position with more direct sunlight, at least six hours a day. I must say, although I may have been impressed by his expertise in plant cultivation, I was more than a little disgruntled. I've managed to nurture some very impressive specimens without anyone else's interference. Admittedly, none of them has ever bloomed, but that's a detail.

Later that evening, as I was sorting through the boxes Rob had dropped off, I heard Kate's familiar tap on the front door. She was returning my copy of *The Prime of Miss Jean Brodie,* which I'd lent her a couple of weeks ago.

"I quite liked it," she said, "but I didn't get Miss Brodie. She didn't seem very likable. I can't enjoy a book if I don't warm to the main character."

"I disagree. I'd rather read about someone interesting than someone who's just nice."

"Talking about nice people," Kate said. "What a lovely man that Rob is. Very helpful. Very funny. We had a really good chat when we were upstairs."

"Did you? But I should warn you — if you're interested in him, do bear in mind he's a friend and ally of my brother, so deeply flawed and completely untrustworthy."

"I'm not interested in him." She laughed. "I've got enough on my plate at the moment. And anyway, he seems rather fond of you."

"Don't be ridiculous. For a start, he's on a mission to get back together with his ex."

"Well, all I know is that when he was up in my flat he was telling me he's never met anyone like you. He was talking about your dry sense of humor and your quirky way of looking at things."

"Kate, he's playing a game to get information about my legal case," I told her. "He's more devious than you'd think from his laid-back manner. I can only assume you've been reading romantic fiction again — something must be rotting your brain and clouding your judgment. I'll have to sort out some more literary classics for you. Have you read any Virginia Woolf?"

16

"Is it possible ever to know someone completely? To know all their thoughts and feelings, their hopes, their dreams, their sorrows and regrets, the parts of themselves they hide from public view? Only God can truly know us like that." The vicar smiled the beatific smile of someone blessed with certainty that he has wisdom and virtue on his side.

"Yes, I do appreciate that you're unable to give me a divine insight into the workings of my mother's mind or the state of her soul. However, I recall that she considered you to be a friend, and that you visited her regularly at home. I assume you're able to express an earthly opinion on whether she was rational and lucid in the last few months of her life."

The vicar — Jeremy he'd told me to call him, but I can only think of him as "the vicar" — put the leather-patched elbows of his tweed jacket on his desk and stroked his graying, man-of-the-people beard.

"I'd very much like to help you resolve your concerns. I can see you're hurt by the contents of Patricia's will. However, I've got to be careful of what I say. There are things that she told me — discussions we had — which were in total confidence. I wouldn't feel comfortable revealing all she unburdened to me. I'll do my best, though, to answer any questions that don't intrude on matters I believe she'd have preferred to take to the grave."

I had no idea what the vicar was talking about. My mother wasn't the sort of person who had secrets, certainly not from me. She was a simple, straightforward woman. Some people might even say boring — certainly an archetypal housewife and mother of her generation. I could only assume he was endeavoring to confer on himself the status of personal confidant. This didn't surprise me. I understand that vicars often have an inflated sense of their own importance, resulting from their congregations treating them as minor celebrities, founts of all knowledge or gatekeepers to the afterlife. His dog collar wasn't having the usual effect.

It was Christmas Eve. Kate and I had set off from London in the early-morning gloom, keen to avoid the worst of the mass exodus that would build inexorably as the day progressed. She was to drop me off at St. Stephen's Church so I could interview the vicar, and I'd then make my way to Aunt Sylvia's house by train and taxi. As usual, the offspring were squeezed in the back of the car, which was jammed full of luggage, child-related equipment and bulging black bin liners. "Father Christmas will be visiting us at my parents' this year," explained Kate with a wink. Both Ava and Noah were wearing snowman jumpers, and Kate had a Father Christmas hat pulled down over her ears. At least she wasn't wearing antlers.

It was more uncomfortable than ever in the tiny car. My seat had been pulled forward to accommodate a suitcase behind it, and I had to curl my legs to one side because a large, sharp-cornered parcel occupied most of the passenger foot well. My bump prevented me from utilizing the seat belt in the conventional way. Instead, I had to push the lap part below my bump and the diagonal part above it. The baby had recently started to press against my bladder, and no sooner had we managed to crawl out of London than I needed to use the services. I had a feeling it was going to be another long journey.

By the time I finally heaved myself from Kate's car outside St. Stephen's, the sky was as dark as nightfall and it was sleeting. Kate ran around to the boot and extricated my small suitcase and my large paper carrier bag full of presents. Disinclined though I was to waste my time and money buying gifts for people in whose pleasure I had absolutely no interest, it would, obviously, have been very poor manners to turn up at Aunt Sylvia's house empty-handed.

"Are you going to be alright?" Kate asked, as I maneuvered my bags into a barely manageable arrangement. The icy rain sliced at my cheeks and hands. "Shall I help you carry your stuff up to the doors of the church?"

"No, no, it's only a short way. There's no point in two people getting wet."

After exchanging hasty goodbyes and Merry Christmases, I shuffled along the slippery stone path, heaving my wheeled suitcase — on which I'd balanced the present bag — behind me. The umbrella did nothing to stop the sleet drenching my coat, my hair and my luggage. As I began to mount the worn steps leading to the doors of the church, the paper handles of the carrier bag gave way, and my carefully wrapped parcels tumbled out like favors from a piñata, landing in a shallow, muddy puddle by my feet. I must confess that I took the Lord's name in vain. I pulled open one of the heavy oak doors and wedged it ajar with my suitcase, then stooped awkwardly to retrieve my parcels one by one from the water; harder than it sounds when you have a belly like Father Christmas himself. I put the pulpy gifts in a pile in the small vestibule and pushed the door closed with an echoing thud.

I can see why people think of churches as places of sanctuary. Even from the vestibule I could smell the familiar, comforting aroma of old wood, furniture polish and candle wax. It was mixed with the scent of pinecones, which I established came from a decorated Christmas tree in the front corner of the church. Dotted around were arrangements of red-and-white flowers, tied in ribbon and trailing ivy. The only lights were near the front of the church, where an old woman in a housecoat was lovingly polishing a brass eagle lectern. She looked up, and I recognized her straightaway: Margaret, my mother's neighbor.

"Hello, Susan, dear. So nice to see you. Tut-tut, you're drenched. Come with me, I'll get some paper towels from the ladies to dry you off. Jeremy said you were coming to see him today. You're looking well. Pregnancy certainly suits you. When's the baby due?"

She shuffled toward a door hidden in the shadows just before the chancel, and I followed.

"In three months," I told her. "I'm glad I've seen you, Margaret. I wanted a word with you, too. I don't know whether you're aware of my mother's will."

"Yes, I am, dear. Edward told me he's allowed to stay in the house. He said there's some sort of argument about it. Not that I see him very often. He seems to sleep all day and entertain visitors all night. We used to see more of that Rob who was staying with him — he'd always stop for a chin-wag — but he's moved into his own place now. Wills are such a problem. People don't always end up with what they rightfully should."

We'd reached the toilets. Margaret grabbed a handful of paper towels and began dabbing at my hair and face. I'd normally have batted her away, but I felt too exhausted to bother. I stood there and allowed her to fuss over me. I was going to say "in a maternal way," but I don't recall my mother ever fussing like that. At least, not over me.

"All done. I'll just tell Jeremy you're here. I've finished my bit of cleaning and polishing for the day so I'm heading home now, but why don't you drop into ours when you've finished? You know where to find us."

The vicar proceeded to describe to me, with the usual pious embellishments, his initial dealings with my mother and the events surrounding her second stroke. I knew most of it already. My mother started going to church shortly after her first ministroke, about three years ago. The vicar immediately sensed that she was "a very spiritual woman"; she told him that walking into St. Stephen's "felt like returning home." She quickly threw herself into the life of the church: joining Bible reading classes, baking cakes for fund-raising events, helping with the flowers. The vicar had no sense that her thinking had been in any way impaired; she seemed to him to be an intelligent, sensible, capable woman who "found her faith to be a great source of comfort and reassurance."

My mother's second stroke, two years later, had occurred while she was serving tea from the trolley after the service (this one was a full stroke, although not catastrophic). The first the vicar knew that something was wrong was when the large aluminum teapot, from which she'd been pouring, crashed down onto the floor. My mother was standing there with an odd, twisted expression on her face. He and Margaret helped her to a chair, but she was unable to speak and didn't react to what they said to her. Someone phoned for an ambulance, while they reassured her that everything would be fine. The vicar found my mother's address book and phoned Edward, Aunt Sylvia and me. As it was a Sunday, I was able to travel straight to the hospital in Birmingham, where I found that my brother and aunt had already arrived.

You can imagine my distress at seeing my mother with tubes and monitors attached to her, and with no knowledge of where she was or why. That's by the by, though; my own feelings are irrelevant. The fact is, my mother's recovery was remarkable. She was out of hospital in less than a week, and within a couple of months — with medication, speech therapy and physiotherapy — was, on the face of it, back to her normal self. Initially, the vicar said, he called in on my mother almost every day, as our family home was only a few minutes' walk from the church. As she recovered, his visits became less regular, until she was able to resume attending church. Even then, he continued to call on her for afternoon tea once a week.

"Why did you do that? Do you visit all your parishioners at home?" I asked.

"I'd love to be able to, if I had infinite time," he said. "But, sadly, that's not possible. I'm afraid I have to limit my home visits to those who're housebound or who I feel would benefit from one-to-one ministry in the comfort of their own home. I continued to visit your mother because it was obvious to me, after the stroke, that she was anxious and depressed. She had a sense of her own mortality, a feeling that she didn't have much longer in this world, and there were things on her mind about which she didn't feel entirely at peace."

"What sort of things?"

"That, unfortunately, would be straying into matters which your mother revealed to me in confidence, and which I've already explained I don't feel able to disclose."

Again, the mysterious information. I decided to let it pass for the moment.

"Do you think the anxiety and depression affected her ability to think logically? Did it affect her judgment? Did she seem confused to you?"

"Those are difficult questions." There was a long silence while the vicar put his hands together, as if in prayer, raised them to his lips and closed his eyes. I wondered if he'd gone to sleep. With the radiator pumping out heat into his small office, and the atmosphere of serenity, I felt like I could have done so myself. Eventually, he opened his eyes.

"I'd say that, after the second stroke, Patricia could be a little confused about the small things. I mean, about where the flower arrangements were supposed to go, times of services and meetings, whether people wanted tea or coffee. Sometimes she forgot names of people in the congregation. Occasionally she'd come to church in the winter in a pair of sandals or in the summer in a thick overcoat. However, as far as the important things are concerned, I'd say she was completely rational and lucid. Her memory of the more distant past was perfect. She was fully aware of who she was, where she came from, who her friends were. And, I have to say, she was very clear about family relationships."

"But if she was confused about everyday matters in the present, was she capable of making an informed decision about the disposal of her estate? Could she have given proper instructions to a solicitor, or understood the contents of a will?"

"I'm sorry, Susan, I can only tell you the facts as I observed them at the time. I don't have the necessary medical expertise to give you the answers you're seeking. I certainly can't say whether your mother knew exactly what she was doing when she wrote the will. All I *can* say is that the confidences she shared with me may have influenced the decision she made in relation to the disposal of her estate."

I was, by this stage, hungry for my lunch, and worn-out by the journey and interview. I was also thoroughly fed up with the vicar tantalizing me with this allegedly confidential information that he claimed he'd been given by my mother; it was as if he wanted me to drag it out of him.

"Look, Reverend, let's put our cards on the table. If you know something that's relevant to my mother's will and you don't tell me, I'll just get a court order to compel you to give evidence. So I'd suggest that it's in your best interests either to reveal what you know or to stop implying that my mother entrusted secrets to you."

The vicar resumed his praying-hands, closed-eyes position, and the room once more fell into silence. After a deep sigh, he opened his eyes and looked at me.

"I very much sympathize with the situation in which you find yourself. But I'm caught between a rock and a hard place. *The Guidelines for the Professional Conduct of the Clergy* state that a person has the right to expect that a vicar will not pass on to a third party confidential information without their consent or other lawful authority. I think this is something about which I'm going to have to pray for guidance. As you know, Christmas is the busiest time of year for our church, and I won't be able to give it my attention for several days. Contact me in the new year and I'll have a decision for you. In the meantime, I wish you a happy and peaceful Christmas in the bosom of your family. Would you like me to pray with you before you leave?"

"No, thank you," I said.

Returning to the lobby area I found a hand-scribbled note in the place where I'd left the suitcase and sodden presents.

Stan popped down to pick me up in the car, so we've taken your things home with us. Come and join us for a sandwich and a cup of tea. Love, Margaret.

I could have kissed her. Almost.

By the time I left the church the sleet had passed and the sky had lightened a touch. I pulled my coat tightly around me against the bitter wind and headed up Blackthorn Road, sidestepping the icy puddles. It was strange to be walking along the path to Margaret and Stan's front door, rather than along the one to our own house across the road. I glanced over. Edward, it appeared, was away for Christmas; there was no car in the drive and the curtains were drawn. I wondered where he was. Not that I cared.

My discussion with Margaret and Stan went rather better than with the vicar. After a plate of egg mayonnaise sandwiches, followed by homemade mince pies with brandy cream and a small glass of sherry (what harm can it do at this stage?), we settled down in comfy armchairs in the sitting room. Stan put on a pair of reading glasses and began studying the *Radio Times.* I asked Margaret the same questions I'd put to the vicar earlier. She needed very little prompting.

"I'd say she was very muddled, wouldn't you, Stan?" said Margaret.

"Oh, yes, muddled. Definitely," he said,

not raising his head from the magazine.

"I kept saying she wasn't her normal self."

"Not her normal self at all," added Stan.

"I got the impression she wasn't really listening to me when we chatted. You know, as if she was just nodding along. You can tell sometimes."

"No, she didn't listen properly. Just agreed with what you said."

"And then she'd forget what we'd arranged to do. I'd call round all set for a trip out to a stately home and she'd be in her cardigan and slippers doing the dusting. I'd have to help her get ready."

"That's right. Get her ready." Stan chuckled at something he was reading in the magazine.

"If it wasn't for Edward living with her I don't think she would've been able to stay at home. Not that he's at all organized himself, but I think he got the shopping in and that sort of thing."

"He always did the shopping," said Stan, turning a page.

"And took her to doctors' appointments. But between you and me — and I'm only saying this to you because I know you don't get on with him — I never trusted him. I always thought he was taking advantage of your mum. You know, taking handouts from her when he should've had a job like any normal man."

"Not normal, that man."

"And the funny thing is — often when I knocked round for a chat with your mum he'd say she was busy, when I know for a fact she wasn't because I could see her pottering in the kitchen. He must've been up to something."

"Definitely something going on there." Stan took off his spectacles, gave them a polish and put them back on.

"If someone told me he'd taken advantage of your mum's confusion to get her to sign the house over to him, I wouldn't be a bit surprised. If anyone was going to get the house it should've been you."

"Mmm, should be yours, that house."

"So if you want us to sign something saying your mum wasn't in a fit state to make a will, dear, we're happy to do it, aren't we, Stan?"

"Oh, yes. Our pleasure. Have you seen the remote control, Peggy?"

Sitting on the train from Birmingham to Worcester, I felt very pleased with the way the afternoon had turned out. At last, in Margaret, there was someone who was prepared to step forward and acknowledge what had been going on. The vicar, on the other hand, had been a disappointment. That said, it sounded like he might well have some pertinent information that either God, or the court, would direct him to reveal. Bumping along in the taxi from Worcester station, however, my good mood began to dissipate. Had I really agreed to spend two days at Aunt Sylvia's house? Perhaps celebrating Christmas alone would have been the better option. "No," I told myself. "Positive thinking." For two days, I'd endeavor to suspend my critical faculties and succumb to whatever this family gathering entailed.

As my taxi disappeared down the long driveway and I walked toward the sprawling ranch-style bungalow, which was festooned with seasonal illuminations more flamboyant than Blackpool's, the front door of Wendine was thrown open. There, in the expansive chandelier-lit hallway, stood Aunt Sylvia, Uncle Frank, Wendy and Christine, all wearing reindeer antlers on their heads. Aunt Sylvia was holding out a set for me.

17

"Let's give you a tour of the bungalow, shall we? The girls can carry your bags to your room," said Aunt Sylvia, standing on her tiptoes to straighten my festive headgear. I gritted my teeth and tried not to think how I must look. I'd known the next couple of days would be an ordeal, but I hadn't expected the mortification to begin before I'd even taken off my coat. "It's got to be over twenty years since you were last here, and everything's changed. We must've extended and redecorated at least ten times since then. That's what comes from marrying a builder. If only I'd married a plastic surgeon, eh?"

My twin cousins, having played their part in the ceremonial greeting, had vanished along one of the corridors leading from the hallway. Aunt Sylvia and I came across their paunchy husbands — Dean and Gary — in the "games room." They had been joined by

Uncle Frank, now comfortably antlerless. There was a dartboard with properly laid-out oche, a table tennis table and full-size pool table. The main attraction of the room for the three men, however, was the well-stocked bar, complete with pumps and optics. They raised their whiskey tumblers to me, then went back to their conversation. Aunt Sylvia and I moved on to the snug, which was furnished with a cinema-sized television opposite a bloated leather sofa. Slumped on it were the four grandchildren, variously absorbed in phones, games consoles and laptops. They showed an interest in, and enthusiasm for, my arrival that was on a par with their fathers'.

Next on the grand tour were the lounge, the study and the morning room. There was a noticeable theme to the decor: the carpets and upholstery were cream; the fireplaces pale marble; the light fittings crystal; and the ormolu lamp stands, picture frames and mirrors gilt. Even the lights, tinsel and baubles on the Christmas tree were white and gold, as were the swags and garlands festooning the walls. Dotted here and there were bunches of white-berried foliage in glass vases and albino poinsettias in gilded pots.

"What do you think, love? I decided to go

for a classy look this time," said Aunt Sylvia. "If it was up to me I'd've had a lot more color and pattern, but my interior designer, Faye, said my taste was Texas whorehouse. Can you believe it?" She giggled. "I didn't take offense, though. I've known her for years. Uncle Frank used to get her to do the show homes. We agreed to compromise on Hollywood glamour. You know, Jackie Collins's style."

"Very . . . coordinated," I said, searching for a diplomatic word. I was going to play the part of gracious and cordial Christmas houseguest even if it killed me. Two days. Only two days. "A contrast to the outside of the house," I added.

"To be honest, love, that's a bit more me. Come along, I'll take you to the bedroom wing."

At the end of a wide corridor we arrived at what Aunt Sylvia described as the "box room." All I can say is that the boxes she had in mind must have been capacious and abundant.

"Hope you don't mind this room. I tried to get Wendy or Chrissie to swap, because you're the guest of honor, but they wouldn't budge. And I'm afraid you'll have to use the family bathroom," said Aunt Sylvia. "This room hasn't got an en suite. I hate going anywhere that doesn't have an en suite, don't you? You just get so used to having one. I'll get Uncle Frank to extend so you've got one for next time." After studying her reflection in the window and patting her heavily lacquered hair, she lowered the Roman blind and turned to face me. "I can't tell you how glad I am you came, love. This is going to be the best Christmas ever. Have a bit of a rest, and I'll give you a shout when tea's ready. You're not lifting a finger while you're here."

Within a few minutes of Aunt Sylvia leaving there was a murmur of voices and a cough outside my room. My cousins entered — without knocking — bearing my luggage. Wendy closed the door behind her with an ominous click and remained standing in front of it; Christine plumped herself down on the bed next to me. They had me cornered.

"We want to know all about the pregnancy," said Christine.

"You've bin ignoring our calls," said Wendy.

"We're worried about you. We want to know what's going on."

"Do you know who the father is?"

"Did he walk out on you?"

"How're you going to cope all by your-self?"

"Will you have to carry on working?"

"What'll you do for money?"

"Have you heard about the terrifying Down syndrome risk?"

"You could always have it adopted."

"I can't imagine how rubbish you must be feeling," said Christine, reaching for my hand. "With this being your first Christmas without your mum, and not only that but you're up the duff and on your own. You can't really get much lower than that, can you?"

How to react? In any other situation, I'd have told them it was none of their business and walked away. I'd done as much on numerous occasions when we were younger. Indeed, I could sense they were anticipating a combative response to their provocation and looking forward to some sport. But I was on their territory, trapped for two days, and I'd planned to give this family Christmas idea one good shot. I decided to try a different tactic.

"Oh, Wendy, Christine, I've got myself into a terrible mess and I don't know what on earth I'm going to do. The father doesn't want to know, my boss says I need to consider my position at work and I'm terrified about having a baby to care for. I'll need all the help I can get when it arrives. Thank goodness I've got you two on my side. I know you won't let me down."

I thought my performance was pretty convincing, but clearly not quite convincing enough. Christine let go of my hand and stood up.

"There's no need to be sarcastic. Do you think we're too stupid to realize? We're only trying to help you."

"That's right. Mum said to be extra friendly, and we was. Some people don't know when to be grateful."

"Oh, I *am* grateful," I said. "I really appreciate your concern for me. It's lovely to know how much you both care."

They stared at me — the antlers on their heads cocked at an identical angle — wavering about my sincerity or lack thereof.

"Well, we do care," huffed Christine. "We've bin told to."

Supper consisted of a Chinese banquet that arrived in several large crates from the local takeaway. My mother would have been horrified at the lack of home cooking.

"Who wants to slave over a stove on Christmas Eve?" asked Aunt Sylvia, using her long, berry-lacquered fingernails to prize cardboard lids from the multitude of aluminum trays spread out on the kitchen island. "There's enough of that on Christmas Day. Wouldn't it've been lovely to live in Victorian times and have a cook and servants. Bin born at the wrong time, I have. Right, Wendy, you get the crocks out. Chrissie, you get the cutlery and serving spoons. Susan, you just stay sitting on that stool. We're gonna have a buffet-style tea. Just fill your plates and grab a knife and fork. I'll serve you, Susan. A bit of everything?"

It was a free-for-all, with everyone — even the grandchildren, who had been hauled away from their electronica — piling as much food as they could fit onto their plates in double-quick time. Within minutes the kitchen was empty; the men had taken their plates to the games room, the children to the snug, and Aunt Sylvia, Wendy and Christine to the lounge.

"Come on, Susan, we're eating on our laps," Aunt Sylvia called. "We don't want to miss any festive TV programs. It's what a family Christmas is all about. Do you want one of the girls to carry your plate through for you?"

It was very different from the way I'd previously spent Christmas Eve. When my father was alive, the day would be dominated by his presence in, or absence from, the house. He'd be off and out before eleven in the morning so he could be the first person through the pub doors when they opened. He'd stagger back, quarrelsome, in the early afternoon. I'd do my best to avoid him by working in the kitchen with my mother, icing the Christmas cake and making mince pies, bread sauce and stuffing. We would listen to *A Festival of Nine Lessons and Carols* from Kings, and try to steel ourselves against the barrage of verbal abuse. The pubs would reopen at five o'clock, so we knew if we could withstand the onslaught until quarter-to we would be fine. I made sure I was in bed before closing time. I hardly remember Edward being around in the run-up to Christmas. I suppose he was off somewhere throwing stones at local cats or writing graffiti on neighbors' walls. Christmas Days themselves I can hardly bear to think about. The pubs were shut so the drinking was all done at home. Somehow, we managed to get through.

Following my father's death Christmas was a very different affair; we no longer had to listen out for the sound of his key in the lock, try to assess his mood or hide ourselves away. Edward remained equally elusive, though. Perhaps, by that age, he'd got used to doing his own thing. It suited me. If he was there we argued. The only drawback was that my mother would worry obsessively about where he was and what he was up to. After I moved away, I deliberately got the last available train to Birmingham on Christmas Eve, and the first train back to London after Boxing Day. Any longer at home — with the added torment of my brother's company — and I'd have gone mad.

"I love a Buck's Fizz on Christmas morning, don't you?" said Aunt Sylvia, popping the cork from a bottle as I entered the kitchen. She was dressed as if she was going to a party, in tight dress, high heels and full makeup. "Happy, happy Christmas, my love."

I'd expected the kitchen to be a hive of activity with preparations for Christmas lunch, but my aunt was the only one around. The children had woken at six o'clock to open their sacks of presents, and were now in the snug playing on their updated computer games and consoles. Everyone else was still asleep. I offered to help chop vegetables, but Aunt Sylvia said it was already sorted. "Marks and Sparks have chopped them for us," she said. "And stuffed the turkey crown and made the Christmas pudding and brandy sauce. Thank God for posh supermarkets. Remember the bad old days when you had to do everything yourself?"

Wendy and Christine sauntered into the kitchen together, half an hour later, dressed in identical fluffy pink dressing gowns and slippers. I wondered what their husbands made of the lack of differentiation in their appearance and personalities. Christine was slightly meaner, but that was the sole distinction I'd managed to ascertain between them. Following the obligatory exchange of Christmas well-wishing, Wendy grabbed two champagne glasses and filled them with Buck's Fizz, which the sisters knocked back remarkably quickly.

"The kids loved their presents from Santa," said Aunt Sylvia to Wendy and Christine.

"Oh, good," said Wendy. "I'll go and see them when I've woken up properly."

"I should hope so, too," said Christine. "We spent enough."

After breakfast, which was another help-yourself affair, there was absolutely nothing to do. Nothing at all. Aunt Sylvia placed the pre-prepared limbless bird in the oven, then snipped the tops off a few packets and emptied them into appropriate receptacles. The only job of any substance that needed to be done was the laying of the table, which my aunt instructed Wendy and Christine to do. It was as if she'd asked them to build the table themselves. Before they finally capitulated, there was a good ten minutes of "Why can't *you* do it?" and "It's not fair." I offered to lay the table myself, but Aunt Sylvia was adamant that I mustn't do a single thing. I was thoroughly bored. I suppose I could have chatted to the husbands, but I wasn't quite that desperate.

I decided to put on my coat and go for a walk. I headed down the lengthy driveway and along a country lane, having no idea where I was going but relishing the crispness of the air. It was a bright, cloudless day. I made it as far as the local village, where the congregation was emptying from a small, medieval-looking church. Several old ladies wished me "Happy Christmas" and we exchanged pleasantries about my pregnancy and imminent motherhood. I found a bench on the green and sat down in the sunshine. I closed my eyes for a few seconds. I felt quite calm and happy. Normally on Christmas morning I'd be deeply involved in the never-ending frenzy of basting, chopping and stirring. Perhaps this Christmas would turn out to be a good one, after all. Perhaps this was how and where I'd spend the festive period from now on; doing nothing, just relaxing. I opened my eyes and saw a grubby white Transit van approaching. It looked just like Rob's. But it couldn't be. Why would Rob be in Aunt Sylvia's local village? I watched as the van indicated left and turned along the lane that led to my aunt's house. I had an ominous feeling.

"Happy Christmas, Suze," said Edward, blowing a kiss. He was ensconced in an armchair in the lounge, where all the adults were now congregated, with his stockinged feet up on a padded footstool. He looked very much at home. I turned to Aunt Sylvia, who shrugged sheepishly.

"It was Wendy and Chrissie's idea," she said. "They thought it'd be nice to have the whole family together, and to forget about any past misunderstandings. I didn't tell you, love, 'cos they wanted it to be a surprise for you."

"And we couldn't invite one of you and not the other," said Christine, innocently. "That would be favoritism."

"He's apologized about what was said at the funeral, haven't you, love?" she said to Edward. "It was all down to stress, wasn't it?"

"Yes, Auntie," said Edward, with his best naughty-boy grin. "I was a bit tired and emotional. Ah, and here's my chauffeur."

"Happy Christmas, Susan," Rob said, entering the room through the door from the conservatory. "Your aunt invited me over with Ed. Thought it sounded fun. We've only come for lunch."

"It *will* be fun," said Aunt Sylvia, a little desperately. "Everyone always says, 'If you can't have fun at one of Sylvia's dos, you can't have fun anywhere.' Only problem is, it's thirteen for lunch now. Oh, well, we'll just have to count the baby. That makes fourteen."

I was livid. My cousins were well aware of the dispute between Edward and me, and the fact that we'd disliked each other for years. Their motive could only have been to provoke me further. Aunt Sylvia, who seemed very keen for me to stop the court case, probably thought I'd soften in my resolve if I saw my brother face-to-face. I wondered why Edward had gone along with it. I'm sure he had as much desire to spend time with me as I had to spend it with him.

Once again, the motive can only have been provocation. Unless, that is, he was simply lonely at Christmas. Poor little orphan Edward. And what was Rob doing here? Had he just come to cheer my brother on? I could sense that everyone was awaiting my reaction.

"Will you excuse me, please?" I said.

In desperation, I joined the children in the snug. I feigned interest in the computer games they'd received for Christmas, hoping they wouldn't notice my shaking hands and the tremor in my voice. They were quite pleased to demonstrate them to me. I was even encouraged by the ten-year-old (Leila) to play a game on her old console. It was inanely simple and repetitive, but I found it oddly calming to my jangled nerves. A few moments later Rob joined us on the sofa and watched over my shoulder as I played. I forgot he was there, so engrossed did I become in the childish game. I can quite see how one might become addicted if one didn't have an iron will such as my own. In that way, I passed a mind-numbing hour until Wendy stuck her head round the door to say that lunch was ready. I would infinitely have preferred to stay where I was.

"Ooh, isn't it wonderful having Susan here,"

Aunt Sylvia said, scanning the table. "And Edward, too, of course. All my family together at Christmas. I'm a lucky, lucky lady. Let's have a toast. To Susan. Thank you for joining our little get-together, and all the best for next year. It's going to be a fantastic one for you. I know it's scary. I know exactly what you're feeling. But everything's gonna work out for the best in the end." She raised her champagne flute, then took a large gulp.

"To Susan," murmured the adults at the table, mostly without enthusiasm.

"Oh, and to Edward, too." She raised her champagne glass again and took another large swig. I didn't partake in that particular toast. Aunt Sylvia had placed me at the head of the table ("I insist, you're our guest of honor."). She was to my left and Rob was to my right. Next to Aunt Sylvia sat Edward, and opposite him, next to Rob, were Wendy and Christine. The husbands and children were at the other end of the table. The good news was that we didn't have to wear our antlers. In any event, I'd slipped mine into the bin the previous night. The bad news was that Aunt Sylvia had produced thirteen Santa's elf hats from the sideboard. Edward turned his over, trying to make up his mind what to do with it. Christine grabbed it and plonked it over his greasy hair. He looked at me with a smirk, expecting me to make a fuss about my own hat. I didn't. I simply placed it on my head.

"That's one for the family album," he said, producing his phone from his pocket and taking a photograph of me. I smiled my brightest smile.

"So," said Christine, as we were finishing our main course. "What's the situation with Auntie Pat's estate now? Are you two still arguing about it?"

"Shush, Chrissie," said Aunt Sylvia. "We don't want to talk about all that today. We're just going to have a nice family lunch." Her voice, I noticed, was now rather slurred.

"But you said you were hoping they'd bury the hatchet. We've got to get it all into the open if they're going to sort it out."

"It's nothing to do with me," Edward said. "I'm just going along with what the brief told me. He says I can stay in the house, so I am. The dispute's between Suze and the executor. Though there are one or two matters I'd like to discuss with my dear sister before I leave."

"Let's drop it for now, shall we?" said Aunt Sylvia. "Anyone for second helpings, or shall I go and microwave the pudding?"

"Why *is it* that you're getting yourself all upset about the will, Susan?" asked Wendy sweetly. "Ed was Auntie Pat's favorite, so it stands to reason she'd leave more to him in her will."

"That's not true," I began.

"Wendy, leave it," said Aunt Sylvia.

"But, Mum, you're always saying Auntie Pat was only ever bothered about Edward. You said Susan must always've known that."

Aunt Sylvia leaned across and grabbed my arm.

"I'm sorry, Susan, love. I really, truly am." Tears were welling up in her eyes. She pulled off her elf hat and blinked them away.

"Sorry about what?" I asked, stunned by the turn of the conversation.

"Sorry she never loved you like she should. Sorry you were always second best. I wish I could've done something to make it alright for you, but it was out of my hands. Oh, Susan."

"Now, now, Sylv," said the usually silent Uncle Frank from the other end of the table. "Careful what you say. You know you can't take your drink. Let other people sort out their problems and you hold your peace."

"If I could just turn back the clock," Aunt Sylvia sniffed. "I'd . . ."

Uncle Frank got up from the table, came round to where Aunt Sylvia was sitting and almost lifted her from her seat.

"Come on, now. Time for a little lie down. The girls can finish serving lunch." With that he maneuvered her out of the room, my aunt tottering on her spindly heels.

"What was all that about?" said Christine to Wendy, who shrugged her shoulders.

"That was an interesting insight into the situation," said Edward, grinning. "Were you hoping Aunt Sylvia would be a witness for your case, Suze? I'd like to see how you're going to turn *that* to your advantage."

"I've had enough lunch," I said, standing and removing my elf hat. "I'm going to my room, too. Could someone please let me know when Edward's left?"

"Before you disappear," Edward said, also standing, "I want a word with you about Mum's ashes and her jewelry box. I want them back. You've got two weeks, then I'm going to the police. It's theft."

Out of the corner of my eye I could see Wendy's and Christine's beaming faces. This was exactly what they had been hoping for.

"Go to hell, Edward," I said.

An hour or so later I was lying on my bed,

trying and failing to read a page of *Contentious Probate Claims* (perhaps I should have brought some lighter reading material for the Christmas period), when I heard voices in the garden. I stood in the shadow, just to one side of the window, and peered out. If I craned my neck I could just about see Edward leaning against a protruding wall of the bungalow a little way along from my room. He was puffing on a roll-up, which he was holding between his thumb and index finger. Rob was standing next to him with a glass of beer in his hand. I cautiously opened my window a crack, my intention being to eavesdrop on their conversation. I'm not a natural snooper, but I felt it was justified in this particular instance; I might well find out something that was beneficial to my case. All's fair in love et cetera. I had to strain to make out what they were saying.

"You're getting soft in the head, mate." Edward's voice.

"I'm not soft. I just think you deliberately set out to provoke her. There's no call for it. Why don't you back off a bit?"

"Because she's a vicious little madam. You've seen what she's like. She does exactly the same to me, *and* some. I don't know why you're feeling so sorry for her all of a sudden."

"She's six months pregnant and on her own, among other things. And, you know, I don't think she *is* vicious. I think most of the time she's trying to do what she thinks is correct. She just gets it a bit wrong sometimes. It's the way she is."

"I can't believe I'm hearing this. Are we talking about the same woman? If I'm not mistaken, I think you've got the hots for my sis. I know you've always had a thing for domineering women. She'd eat you alive, though, Rob. You're much too laid-back to handle her. Steer well clear, if you value your sanity."

"Don't be stupid. You know I'm trying to get back together with Alison. All I'm saying is cut her some slack. You've got your mother's house. What do you need to rub her nose in it for?"

"Yeah, I've got the house, and she's trying to take it off me, if it's escaped your attention."

"Only because she suspects you were behind your mum writing the will."

"And do you think I was?"

"It's none of my business."

"Too right, mate."

My brother took a final deep suck on his cigarette, threw it onto the gravel pathway and ground it under the heel of his cowboy boot. He turned and disappeared through the back door, followed shortly afterward by Rob.

I closed my bedroom window. It was getting dark outside; I switched on the lamp, closed the blinds and sat on the bed. My initial response to the conversation was to question whether the whole thing had been staged by my brother and his friend. I concluded it hadn't. If they'd wanted me to overhear, they would have stood closer to my window and spoken in louder voices; I'd barely been able to hear what they were saying. Also, they would have said something to encourage me to believe that Edward was innocent in the matter. So, what to make of it all? It seemed, amazingly, that Rob was in the dark about whether Edward had tricked my mother into writing the will. Not only that, but he'd stood up to his friend. There was only one conclusion: he wasn't in league with my brother, after all. It looked like I'd seriously misjudged him. I wasn't, of course, impressed with his saying I got things wrong sometimes, but, even so, I felt disproportionately gratified by the turn of events. Delighted, even.

Then there was the fact that Edward had accused Rob of having a soft spot for me, which he'd firmly denied of course. Only a fool would think it could be true; Rob was single-mindedly focused on his ex, plus he was younger than me; he had friends; he had experience of proper relationships. The idea must have seemed odious to him. I hardly need to tell you, there was no interest at all on my part. He was clearly not my intellectual equal. And he was scruffy. And too tall. What else? I was having trouble remembering all his defects. His van could certainly do with a good wash.

There was a tap on my bedroom door. I opened it; it was Rob.

"We're making tracks, now," he said, leaning in the doorway. "It was a rubbish idea. I should've refused when Ed asked me to bring him. I thought it'd be good to see you, and that maybe you and he might, I don't know. He just can't see reason where you're concerned. With everyone else he really is a decent bloke. I hate seeing two people I care about fighting like this."

"Tell him to keep away from me in the future."

"I'm sorry he's spoiled things for you. Compliments of the season, anyway."

"And to you, too."

Unexpectedly, he moved toward me with

his arms open, and I allowed him to hold me in the sort of awkward festive embrace that is hard to avoid at this time of year. I can't pretend it was comfortable. My bump was, of course, an obstacle.

■ ■ ■ ■

JANUARY

■ ■ ■ ■

18

A new year and a renewed resolve on my part. The legal support acts were concluded, and it was now time for the main performance: proceedings in the Chancery Division of the High Court of Justice. I could have waited for Mr. Brinkworth to bring a case to prove my mother's will. That, however, would have placed him in the driving seat, which is where I fully intend to be (albeit, ironically, that I don't drive). I spent the first few days of January poring over textbooks in order to draft the statement of case. The court would be alert to the fact that a claimant is often willing to wound, but afraid to strike. I had no such fear. I set out my contentions regarding mental capacity and undue influence in robust terms, naming both Edward and Mr. Brinkworth as defendants. I was pleased with my work; worthy of a probate solicitor, I concluded, as I printed out and checked the final version.

In my lunch hour, a week into the new year, I walked the half a mile or so from my office to the Rolls Building on Fetter Lane — a brand-new, glass-fronted edifice that was an outpost of the Royal Courts of Justice. I located the Chancery Issue department on the ground floor, paid my fee and handed over the documents. The bored-looking clerk informed me that the court would serve them on my brother and the solicitor, who in turn would have twenty-eight days to file defenses. I'd have loved to see their faces as they opened their envelopes.

Recrossing the central atrium underneath the vaulted glass ceiling and exiting the building, I had a feeling of trepidation rather than triumph. I knew my case was legitimate and strong, but I'd have been happier if I'd managed to marshal more proof before I put the matter wholly in the hands of the judicial system. The medical records hadn't yet arrived, despite numerous phone calls by me and reassurances from petty officials; my witnesses were flaky, particularly Aunt Sylvia, whose irrational Christmas Day outburst was perturbing; and I was yet to find one conclusive piece of evidence of corruption on Edward's part. Time was now of the essence, though; I was due to give birth in a couple of months and I wanted the matter resolved before then. I was marching to a beat that wasn't entirely of my own choosing.

Hurrying down the Strand back to my office, I bumped — literally — into Brigid, who was thundering along in the opposite direction, trailing an overflowing wheeled document case.

"Twice in two months, that's a record. What're you doing in my neck of the woods, old girl?"

"I've just been to the Rolls Building. Proceedings are now underway against Edward and the executor."

"Good stuff. Who's acting for you?"

"I'm a litigant in person."

"Unwise, old girl, very unwise. You know what they say, 'A man who is his own lawyer has a fool for his client.' Don't forget I said I'd look over the papers for you. Give my clerk a ring. Must dash, got an ex parte application listed at two. Ta-ta."

With that she was off, barging her way through the lunchtime pedestrian traffic with her document case in tow.

It had been a unique start to the year. The

morning before New Year's Eve I'd received a phone call from Rob. I hadn't expected to have any further contact with him until I was in a position to retrieve my belongings from his house. He said he'd been invited to a party in Brixton, only a short walk from where I lived, and asked whether I'd like to go along with him. He assured me that Edward wouldn't be there; my brother was celebrating in Birmingham with a gang of friends of which Rob wasn't a part. I said no. Why on earth would I (a heavily pregnant woman) want to go out on New Year's Eve (the wildest night of the year) with a man I hardly knew, to a party at the house of people I'd never met? I told him I preferred to see in the New Year quietly at home. He tried to persuade me of the merits of a sociable celebration, but I told him he was wasting his breath.

Coming off the phone I had a heavy-hearted feeling that I couldn't quite define. Not disappointment, exactly; that would make no sense, seeing as it was my decision to decline the invitation. More like glum resignation, perhaps to the sheer inevitability of the decision I'd made. You might find this hard to believe, but I've never celebrated New Year's Eve. I'm not a person who has close friends, and my acquaintances have never thought to include me in their celebrations. Richard, during the years of our arrangement, always had commitments elsewhere on that particular night.

When I popped upstairs to tell Kate about Rob's ludicrous invitation, she reacted with unexpected enthusiasm.

"Susan, you've *got* to go," she said, pressing down the sticky tabs on the nappy of the uncooperative Noah, who was kicking his legs like the pistons of an engine. The flat was messier than ever. Kate was about to start her master's degree, and there were now books, pens and notepads jumbled up with the customary domestic debris. "He's a lovely guy. You'll have a great time. What else have you got to do?"

"I couldn't possibly go," I told her. "I'd be expected to make small talk with people I have no interest in. And I'm quite sure there'll be dancing. What's more, I don't want anyone to get the wrong idea. If a man and woman attend an event together it gives the impression they're a couple."

"And what would be so terrible about that?" said Kate, doing up the last popper on Noah's dungarees and sitting back on her heels.

"It would be humiliating," I explained. "He's obsessed with this Alison, and I'm due to give birth in a few weeks. He'd be mortified if people assumed we were in a relationship and that he was the soon-to-be father, and I'd be equally mortified at his mortification. Plus, more important, I don't want people thinking I'd choose someone like Rob as my partner."

"Why?"

"Because he's not like me."

"In what way?"

"He's not cultured."

"Are you sure? He seems pretty well-educated to me. Anyway, you don't have to share a partner's tastes in everything for a relationship to be a success. Look at Alex and me. We always loved the same things."

"But Rob's a manual laborer."

"He designs and landscapes gardens. And if he *was* a manual laborer, what difference would that make?"

"And he's friends with Edward."

"That just shows how independent-minded he is — that he's prepared to befriend someone who's an adversary of his best mate."

"Kate, listen carefully. I *do not* want a personal relationship, even if that's what's on offer, which it very definitely isn't."

"Fair enough. Then just go along to the party as pals and have some fun. Do something different. You're a wonderful woman, Susan, but you're very stuck in your ways. You've had the same job for years, you've lived in the same flat for years, you never go out and meet new people. You hardly go out at all these days. I know I mightn't seem like the best person to give advice, because I've had a few confidence issues recently, but I'm getting back out there again. Don't you sometimes feel a bit claustrophobic? Like you just want to kick down the walls and do something really crazy and different and out-of-character?"

"I'm having a baby, in case you hadn't noticed, Kate. How much crazier and more out-of-character can you get?"

"I know, and I can see how you're changing already. I just want the best for you — you're my friend. And it seems that Rob wants to be your friend, too. Stop saying 'no' to everything and start saying 'yes.' What's the worst that can happen? A bit of embarrassment, a bit of awkwardness. And what's the best that can happen? You might meet some interesting people, have some new experiences, enjoy yourself. Tell Rob you'll go. And you can blame me if you have a rubbish time and never speak to me again. Come on, Susan, pick up the phone."

She can be like a Rottweiler sometimes.

We were silent, watching Noah trying to pull himself forward on his tummy to get something just out of his reach. He'd be crawling soon.

"So?" said Kate.

"What are you doing on New Year's Eve?" I asked.

"I haven't decided. Alex is having the kids for a couple of days because he missed out at Christmas. Why?"

"I'll go to the party if you come, too," I said. "That way no one will get the impression that Rob and I are a couple."

"Okay, done." She looked very satisfied with herself.

I went back downstairs and phoned Rob. He expressed delight at the fact that I'd changed my plans, and he had no objection to Kate coming along, too. I was going to a party. A New Year's Eve party. With two other people. If you'd told me that a year ago, I wouldn't have believed you.

That night, as I was lying on my back feeling the twisting and flexing of the new life inside me, I thought about what Aunt Sylvia had said on Christmas Day. I'd tried to push it to the back of my mind — as, it appeared, had everyone else by the following morning; it was as if nothing untoward had happened. During the course of Boxing Day my aunt was as bright and breezy as usual: pestering us to join in charades; producing a new set of cringe-worthy party hats; making plans for a big family get-together in Estepona when the baby arrived. She remained so until my departure. As I was climbing into my taxi, she held on to the door and leaned in.

"You know I'm always there for you, don't you, love? I wish you'd drop this silly dispute with Edward, but if you're dead set on going on with it I'll support you. Just write down what you want me to say and I'll sign it."

"But it has to be the truth," I said. "I'm not asking you to lie. I want you to give your honest opinion."

"I know, love, but I'm just a silly old woman. You know the truth better than me. Maybe I didn't really notice what was going on with your mum. I get caught up in my own little world sometimes. You just write it down for me."

Despite her erratic behavior and acute self-centeredness, Aunt Sylvia seemed genuinely to have my best interests at heart. I was glad she would support my case, but I wished she was more reliable in her recollection of events. Her claim that my mother cared for Edward more than me was troubling, even though it was unfounded. What if the case came to court, and she said as much in evidence? No, I told myself, that wouldn't happen. Aunt Sylvia had been tipsy and confused on Christmas Day. If it came to a hearing, I'd make sure she was well coached.

I had no alternative but to wear a black trapeze dress to the party. It was the only item of clothing I had in my maternity wardrobe that looked even vaguely like something a person might wear for a night out. In the last week or so I'd started suffering from swollen feet and ankles, so along with the billowing tent I wore support tights and comfortable low-heeled shoes. Of course, you can always dress up an outfit with costume jewelry (which I have in abundance from my evenings out with Richard) and artful hair and makeup.

When I finally finished getting ready and looked at myself in the full-length mirror, I wasn't too displeased with the overall result. Until, that is, Kate knocked on my door. I'm not sure I'd ever seen her legs before; they were usually encased in jeans or jogging bottoms. She was certainly not reticent about revealing them this evening. She was wearing a short, sleeveless midnight blue velvet dress with silver high-heeled sandals. Her long hair, which was usually scraped back into a ponytail, was loose and swishy. *Youthful, lively* and *fun* were the words that came to mind. There rose inside me a pitiful wish that I hadn't persuaded her to come along to the party. The thought was perverse. I suppressed it.

Rob, who was staying at a cheap hotel nearby, arrived over ten minutes late. He'd obviously failed to learn his lesson from his last visit. I drew his attention to his poor timekeeping, but all he did was roll his eyes. Dealing with members of the opposite sex isn't that dissimilar from training a dog; you need to be firm and persistent.

"I'll be the envy of all the men at the party, turning up with two such lovely women," he said, as Kate and I were putting on our coats. Hmm. Rob had made a bit of an effort himself. Gone were the khaki combat trousers, baggy sweatshirt and donkey jacket, and in their place were dark-colored jeans, a charcoal-gray jumper and Crombie-style overcoat. He smelled of soap and aftershave instead of soil and manure. Obviously, he still looked gangly, and his unruly hair would have benefited from a good trim.

We walked the half mile to the party, Kate cursing her heels that she said she'd pulled out from the back of her wardrobe.

"I'll be walking home barefoot," she said.

"I'll give you a piggyback." Rob laughed. Good to see them getting on so famously.

The party was in a Victorian semi-detached house off Acre Lane — palatial by London standards, in that it hadn't been subdivided. One of the hosts, Lizzie, had been at college with Rob and Edward in the early 1990s and now worked in a community arts center. Her partner, Liz (unwise to choose a life-partner with the identical name, in my opinion), ran a small gallery. As we entered the hallway, Rob embraced them both, then turned to introduce me.

"This is Ed's sister, Susan, who I was telling you about yesterday. And this is her friend Kate."

There was a crush in the kitchen, especially near the drinks counter, but a short man in a novelty Christmas jumper, noticing my bump, shouted, "Make way for the pregnant lady." With those magic words my path cleared. Kate spotted a couple of women from her local mums-and-babies group on the other side of the room. They waved her over. After sloshing prosecco into a pint glass, she abandoned Rob and me and half danced across to where they were standing. So much for having a chaperone to ward off any presumptions of coupledom. As it turned out, though, there wasn't quite as much embarrassment as I'd feared. When introductions were required, Rob referred to me as "my friend"; in response to questions implying that he was my partner or the father of my baby, he said, smilingly, " 'Fraid I don't have that honor." And whenever the conversation was heading toward the subject of my domestic situation, he neatly steered it in another direction.

Surprisingly, Rob's friends weren't, for the most part, the uncivilized rabble I'd imagined. I began to relax somewhat and even to enjoy myself. Rob found a couple of free chairs at the dining table, and we engaged in conversation with a plump woman and a skinny man — a potter and a stained-glass craftsman — who Rob hadn't seen since his college days. At one point Kate, flushed and breathless, tried to persuade us to join her in the dancing room. I was pleased to have the excuse of my swollen ankles; Rob said he was too comfortable where he was. After what felt like only an hour, Lizzie — or it could have been Liz — announced that it was five minutes to midnight and that we should charge our glasses.

"You'll toast the New Year with champagne, won't you?" asked Rob.

"Yes, why not," I replied. He eased through the throng to the drinks counter.

I may not have been to a New Year's Eve party before, but I've seen enough films to know exactly what happens; on the stroke of midnight there occurs a torrent of kissing, hugging and general physical contact, the thought of which was excruciating. Taking advantage of the fact that everyone was occupied with popping corks and filling their glasses, I found the bathroom and locked myself inside. As the chimes of Big Ben filtered upstairs, followed by cheering and the singing of "Auld Lang Syne," I perched on the edge of the bath. I stayed there for quite a few minutes, enjoying the peace. I thought about the events of last year, and about the year to come, as is traditional at such a time. My life, as I'd so carefully organized it, was shifting, adjusting. Perhaps not entirely for the worse.

When I eventually rejoined the party, Rob was scanning the room anxiously. His face relaxed when he saw me.

"Susan, where were you? You missed the chimes. I thought you'd gone home."

"No. Nature called. Here's to the New

Year," I said, accepting the glass that Rob was proffering. I was resigned to the fact that the occasion would have to be marked by some sort of embrace. To head off anything more demonstrative, I gave him a quick peck on the cheek. It seemed to make him happy enough.

Rob absentmindedly held my hand as we walked away from Liz and Lizzie's house. There was no need; I'm neither a child nor an invalid. It was a frosty night, though, and I had no gloves, so I didn't protest. After a minute or two, he seemed to realize what he was doing and let go. Kate had decided to stay at the party with her two friends. They were having a night off from husbands and children and were keen to make it last as long as possible. As Rob and I walked along, he described the delights of his cheap hotel, which he regretted booking; the carpets were stained, there was fluff in the corners of the bathroom and his bedroom was so cold he could see his breath as he exhaled. On a whim, sensing where the conversation was heading, and feeling I owed Rob a favor for his assistance with my mother's effects now that I knew it wasn't part of Edward's plot, I informed him that he was welcome to spend the night on my sofa if he so wished. He did.

When we got home, I found I was livelier than I'd have expected at almost one in the morning; I had no desire to call it a night, and neither, it turned out, did Rob.

"Got anything to drink?" he asked, throwing his coat over the arm of a chair. "The night's still young and so are we. Well . . ."

I found a bottle of cooking brandy at the back of a cupboard and poured him a glass. I asked what he'd like to do.

"Dunno. Have you got Netflix? Or, I know, what about a board game? I play a mean game of Risk."

"I think I might have a Scrabble set from when I was a child."

"Let's dust it off, then."

At my request, Rob crawled underneath my bed — a feat that was now well beyond my capabilities — and managed to locate it in a box of other childhood games. He set it up on the kitchen table, and I made us some hummus on toast while he updated me on his quest: one of Alison's old flatmates had informed him that she'd been married and divorced, and he now knew the surname she used on Facebook. He'd sent her a friend request and was awaiting a reply. I told him I hoped he heard back soon.

We played two games; I won both, but, to

be fair, he put up a pretty good fight. I hadn't guessed, from his conversation, that his vocabulary was so extensive.

"I'll get you back another time," he said, folding the board and pouring the letters into the bag. "You had the advantage 'cos you're stone-cold sober. Wait 'til the baby's born and I can ply you with drink. Sorry, that sounded a bit creepy."

We followed up Scrabble with a few rounds of gin rummy, using a tatty pack of playing cards that had belonged to my father. Rob was the overall victor. I didn't mind too much; I'd forgotten how much fun it is playing games.

It was almost three o'clock by the time we agreed we should turn in. I wasn't sure I'd ever voluntarily stayed up that late before. I gave Rob a sheet, a pile of blankets and one of my pillows, then put the oak casket containing my mother's ashes next to the sofa for use as a bedside table. He seemed a little taken aback when he realized what it was, then shook his head and laughed.

"Only you," he said. I have no idea what he meant.

19

It was the most restful sleep I'd had for many a week; no waking in the small hours with troubled thoughts about the legal dispute or impending motherhood. Perhaps it was due to the late night or the small glass of champagne I'd drunk just before we left the party. I was woken shortly after eleven by a voice calling through my bedroom door.

"Just wondering if you're awake."

"I am now."

Rob strolled in and perched on the edge of my bed. A member of the opposite sex in my bedroom, and me in my nightdress — it was inappropriate, to put it mildly. I must say, though, with Rob it didn't feel unnatural or threatening; he's rather like a child who has yet to learn the niceties of social etiquette. At forty-three. Nevertheless, I pulled my quilt up to my neck.

"My stomach thinks my throat's been

cut," he said, "but you haven't got much in. What about going out for brunch? I know a place in Battersea that does a great veggie fry-up."

It was New Year's Day; I had nothing to do, nowhere to go and no one to meet. I could see no particular harm in Rob's proposition. Strange, I know, but I found I was becoming accustomed to his company. He might be rough-edged, but he was unexpectedly easy to be around. While he was retrieving his bag from the hotel and I was getting ready, Kate came down, bleary-eyed and disheveled, on a hunt for paracetamol. She asked what I was up to today, and I told her about brunch in Battersea.

"Oh, I like that place. Can I tag along?" she asked.

"Perhaps not, on this occasion. Arrangements have already been made."

She raised her eyebrows and said "Ooh" in quite a silly way.

The café was busy and we had to hover by the counter, waiting for a table. Rob ordered a Bloody Mary, and I had the virgin version. The place had a morning-after-the-night-before feeling to it: warm and fuggy; smelling of fried food and fresh coffee; muted Miles Davis playing in the background. By lunchtime, we were finally seated and our breakfasts had arrived (mine a full English to satisfy what had recently become an almost limitless appetite, Rob's a "textured vegetable protein" facsimile).

"You don't remember me from the old days, do you?" said Rob, leaning his elbows on the small table. I said I didn't. "I was in my first year at college with Ed when we met, so that means you were in your third year. You came along with Phil to a couple of parties that Ed and me were at. I was struck by how grown-up and sophisticated you were compared to the rest of us, a bit above it all. I wanted to talk to you but, to be honest, I was intimidated. You wouldn't have wanted anything to do with me anyway, seeing as I was two years younger and you were engaged. I suppose Phil must've dragged you along 'cos he and Ed had become friends while you were away."

Yes, it's hard to believe. My quiet, studious, socially awkward fiancé, Phil, who was reading Classics at Birmingham University, had become friends with my rebellious, anarchic, party-going brother, who was dabbling in painting at the city's School of Art. Edward, who had hounded and hassled Phil when we walked home together from school, had now decided he was friend material. It was beyond coincidence that the timing corresponded with our engagement.

Throughout my studies in Nottingham, Phil and I had written to each other once a week. In his first letter after I went back to university for my final year he mentioned that Edward had called round and had persuaded him to accompany him to the pub. I had an uneasy feeling about it. In my reply, I asked what reason Edward had given for inviting him. I warned him to be careful. Phil said Edward just wanted to be friends with his future brother-in-law, which he thought was admirable. He said not to worry. His subsequent letters that term described further invitations from Edward, to the pub and to student parties. Phil had even decided to join Edward and his friends on a trip to the Lake District. They were going to camp in a valley, next to an inn, walk in the mountains during the day and quench their thirst in the evening. Edward and his arty gang fancied themselves as nature-communers and poetic wanderers, following in the noble footsteps of Ruskin. The trip was, apparently, great fun.

During the Christmas holidays I went with Phil to a party thrown by one of Edward's friends. It was in a three-story Georgian house owned by a local benefactor and rented out cheaply to art students. From observing Phil, it was clear that he was in awe of Edward and his self-consciously unconventional friends. It was also clear that they, in turn, regarded him as an exotic pet (in their world it was the quiet, studious Phil who was the novelty). I didn't enjoy the party. The alcohol-and-cannabis-induced idiocy was incomprehensible to me. In addition, I found their ribbing of Phil to be demeaning. I couldn't understand why he tolerated it. On the way home, we argued. A few days later, Phil suggested we go to a New Year's Eve party thrown by another of Edward's friends. I refused. We spent the evening watching television with my mother.

The following term Phil's letters — although just as friendly and affectionate — became less regular. There was even a week when he didn't write at all. There were no longer any references to nights out with Edward, but I believe that that was because he knew I didn't approve, rather than that they had ceased. In the subsequent university holidays Phil said there was another party at the student house we'd been to at Christmas. He said it was Easter-themed fancy dress, that it would be a big event. I allowed myself to be persuaded, very much against my better judgment. Phil decided to go as an Easter chick, in a costume Edward had sourced for him. I refused to dress up. Wisely, as it turned out, because Phil was the only person in fancy dress. It had been a joke on the part of my brother and his friends. At the party, Phil played along, intermittently flapping his wings and chirping; I felt humiliated on his behalf.

In the summer term of that year, Phil's erratic letters became erratic notes — just an odd paragraph or two hoping I was getting on well with my revision and finding time to enjoy the sunshine. I put the terseness of his correspondence down to the fact that he was studying hard for his finals; after all, we were still engaged and were planning to move to London together as soon as we'd found jobs there. In July of that year, I invited Phil to accompany my mother to my graduation ceremony in Nottingham. I didn't invite my brother. Phil said he was very sorry, but he'd already arranged to go to the Lake District once again with Edward and his friends. They were staying in the same campsite next to the inn, and planning a ridge walk up Striding Edge to Helvellyn. He said it was a swan song to the academic year just gone and to the group of friends; once we moved to London he doubted he'd see them again. I was furious with him, but he was determined. I suspected that Edward was behind the scenes directing his responses. In the end, I had no choice but to go along with it. Anyway, he was right; once we'd moved away from Birmingham he'd be having no further contact with those people.

Phil's mother didn't have a contact number for me in Nottingham, so I didn't get the news until I returned home the day after my graduation ceremony. Nobody could explain quite how it happened; it was a dry, sunny, windless day and visibility was good. "Accidental death" was the coroner's verdict. I pieced together my own picture of the sequence of events from evidence given at the inquest and from snippets of information gleaned from Edward's friends. The group — six young men in total, including my brother and fiancé — had set off from their campsite at nine o'clock in the morning with thumping hangovers. They had taken numerous breaks on the ascent of the ridge: to take photographs, to sketch views and to recover their breath after steep sections. With the exception of Phil, they all found the going tough. They weren't exactly the most healthy-living bunch of students.

As the sun rose higher in the sky they shed their jackets and put on their sunglasses.

None of them had proper walking gear; it was jeans, trainers and canvas satchels rather than walking trousers, boots and backpacks. They were fortunate it was such a fine day. Phil went on ahead a few times, calling back from minor peaks that they were nearly at the summit. As they reached him they would see another higher peak looming before them. The heat of the day built, and his incessant joking started to irritate them. Around midday, Helvellyn not yet conquered, they decided to stop and eat the packed lunch they had had the good sense to order from the inn the night before (breakfast had consisted of Mars bars and stale cheese-and-onion crisps washed down with flat Coca-Cola).

At some point after lunch Phil wandered off, his camera and binoculars around his neck. The remaining five men made pillows from their jackets and bags, and lay back in the baking sun. By around one o'clock they were fully rested, and decided to set off again. Phil hadn't returned. It was assumed that he was absorbed in taking photographs or studying the view. They waited a few minutes. When he'd still not reappeared, they started calling his name. One of their party — Ian — scrambled down to a protruding granite platform to get a better view of what was below. Tentatively peering over the edge, he saw Phil, inert, on a scree slope, hundreds of feet beneath. It was before the days of mobile phones, so help couldn't be summoned immediately. With a rising sense of panic, the group split up. Edward and Ian would make their way down to Phil, the other three would return the way they had come and alert the mountain rescue service. My incompetent brother and his friend never managed to reach Phil, instead ending up utterly lost and disoriented. The helicopter crew, once they had recovered the body, had to return to the mountain to locate and rescue the wretched pair.

On hearing the news, my mother's response — after wiping her eyes with a handkerchief and saying what a tragedy it was for Phil and his mum — was to fret about how the traumatic experience would affect Edward. My natural reserves of self-discipline and willpower enabled me to deal with the situation, although I found I had no desire to leave my bedroom during the subsequent days. I expect I needed a good rest after the hard work I'd put into my finals.

The funeral was tiny, just Phil's wheelchair-bound mother; his estranged father, who he hadn't seen for over ten years; a couple of people from university; and the group that had been on the mountain. Edward turned up at the church just after the service started and left as soon as it finished. The wake was held in Phil's mother's cramped sitting room. In a slurred whisper, Ian admitted to me that, after lunch on Striding Edge, Edward had rolled a couple of joints that the group had passed around. Phil wouldn't have been used to it. Poor innocent, naive Phil. I'm not saying Edward deliberately killed him. But he lured him into his group to get at me; introduced him to a lifestyle to which he was unaccustomed and unsuited; and supplied the drugs that affected his judgment. See what sort of person I have for a brother?

Immediately after the funeral I packed my bags and left for London. When I returned for the inquest, I managed to track Edward down to one of his favorite pubs. Not surprisingly, we ended up rowing. He refused to admit responsibility for the circumstances that led to Phil's death. He called me paranoid and malevolent, and claimed I was trying to divert the spotlight away from myself. I told Edward he might just as well have stood behind Phil and given him a shove. Edward said he probably threw himself off the cliff to avoid having to marry me. Later, my mother appeared bothered.

"I heard what happened in the pub. I don't want you saying hurtful things to your brother, Susan. You know he's got a sensitive nature, just like his father. I don't want him going off the rails. He's not tough, like you."

It was some months before I returned home.

"No, as I've told you, I've no recollection of you at all," I repeated, piercing the yolk of my fried egg with my fork.

"Well, I haven't forgotten you. Over the years, Ed's talked about what you've been up to, but I wasn't sure we'd ever meet again. Funny how things work out."

"Indeed. It's fortuitous that we've become reacquainted, otherwise I'd have spent a fortune on storage charges."

"That's one way of looking at it, I suppose."

"So, are you managing to carry out the renovations to your house around my mother's furniture?"

"Yeah, everything's going well. I've put in a new kitchen and bathroom, and made progress with the decorating. I'm going to be sanding floors when I get back. I'm grateful to Ed for giving me a roof over my head, but you need a place of your own. I'm not seeing so much of him now I've moved out — I'm so busy working on the house."

"That must be a relief for you."

Rob put down his knife and fork and took a swig of his Bloody Mary.

"He still doesn't know we're friends. I mean, he knows I was around when you were clearing out those rooms at your mum's house, but that's all. There were one or two people at the party last night who might be in contact with Ed, though, so I probably need to come clean before he finds out from someone else. He'll go crazy, but he'll have to accept it. I'm neutral in this thing between the two of you."

"He'll probably think I'm deliberately befriending you to get back at him," I said, dipping a button mushroom into the runny yolk.

"And are you?"

"Of course."

He laughed, unsure whether I was telling the truth. As was I.

"You know, over the years Ed's talked quite a bit about his childhood," said Rob, through a mouthful of cold toast. "About your dad's problems with booze. If you ask me, the bad blood between you and Ed can be traced back to that."

This is what happens if you let down your guard; people think they can tread wherever they like. My territory was being invaded.

"I'm *not* asking you."

"Sounds to me like you dealt with it in totally different ways. Ed by going out all the time and you by locking yourself away. He told me he wanted to feel that you were both on the same side, but that you were always so cool and distant he couldn't tell what was going on in your head."

"I'm sorry, Rob, but this isn't a subject I wish to discuss with you. You know nothing about our family."

"Agreed. I only know what Ed's told me and what I've worked out by reading between the lines. It's just that it'd be great if you two resolved your differences. Maybe if you could both see where the other one's coming from it would help. Ed's really not a bad person."

"Hah."

"You're just very different personalities. He's not great at managing his life. It sounds like your mum was overprotective toward him, maybe because of your dad. I'm not saying he didn't take full advantage of that, but because he was used to her doing everything for him he expects people to help him out. I think the opposite's probably true of you. It sounds like you had to cope by yourself."

"Rob, that's enough. I don't go in for this kind of cod psychoanalysis. I have no interest in what Edward's told you, or what you've surmised. It's none of your business."

I hadn't quite finished my breakfast, but I was finding it heavy-going and indigestible. It had been an error of judgment. I beckoned the waiter over and asked for the bill.

"What shall we do now?" asked Rob, as I put on my coat, looped my scarf around my neck and picked up my handbag.

"I don't know what *you're* doing, but I'm going home to work on some draft documents for my court case against Edward. Here's twenty pounds. That should cover my meal and drinks. I hope you have a good journey back to Birmingham."

I placed the note on the table.

"God, Susan, are you on your high horse *again*?" he called after me as I maneuvered my way through the packed café. "Just hang on a mo 'til I've paid."

I didn't look back.

Five minutes later, as I was puffing along the street in the direction of Clapham and rummaging for my phone so I could order a cab, Rob's van bumped up onto the curb just ahead of me. By the time I drew level with it, he'd wound down the passenger-side window.

"Hey, lady, going my way?" he called.

I ignored him and continued walking. He drove on ahead, then pulled over again. As I drew level with him for a second time, he leaned across the seats.

"Come on, Susan, be reasonable. Okay, I might've been a bit tactless, but there's no need to go off in a huff."

I stopped to face him.

"I'm not 'in a huff.' I've never behaved in a way which would merit such a description. I'm just demonstrating to you that your line of conversation was unacceptable."

"I get it — no talking about yours and Ed's childhood. Fine. But that doesn't mean you have to stomp off."

"I'm not 'stomping off.' Again, I've never behaved . . ."

"Yeah, yeah. So why don't you get in the van, then, and let's not waste any more of the day. Allow me to show you a good time — I'll take you to Kew Gardens."

"Why would I want to do that?"

"Because, as I'm sure you're aware, they've got a very impressive collection of cacti. Go on, you know you want to."

He opened the passenger door and swung it open. After a brief hesitation, I climbed in. I couldn't deny it, Rob's proposition was more than tempting; there were some uncommon specimens on show, and I hadn't been to Kew since my earliest days in London.

Rob and I spent the majority of the afternoon in the Princess of Wales Conservatory, which houses the cacti and succulents. The atmosphere was thick with exotic scents, and the climate-controlled heat was welcome after the raw chill outside. I felt myself slowly defrosting as we ambled along the pathways, our coats and scarves in our arms. Rob explained that there were ten sectors within the glasshouse, the main ones being the dry tropics and the wet tropics. The eight remaining microclimates included a seasonally dry zone, which contained desert and savanna plants, and areas for carnivorous plants, ferns and orchids. It was as though he'd swallowed the guidebook whole and was regurgitating it. A not unimpressive feat. When I said as much to him, he told me that Kew was his place of pilgrimage, one to which he returned with regularity; the cultivation of flora was like a religion to him. I admired his passion.

As the sky outside the glasshouse darkened and the crowds thinned then trickled away, it seemed like the place belonged just to Rob and me. Standing in the dry zone, next to a particularly magnificent and spiny Golden Barrel cactus, inquisitiveness got the better of me; I couldn't help asking him what this was all about. Why was he choosing to spend time with me, when he could be back in Birmingham in a pub with Edward? Or be taking in the sights and smells of Kew Gardens with one of his other London friends? He shrugged.

"Well, I suppose it's because we're mates. I get bored of hanging around with men all the time. It's good to have platonic female friends. Plus, I don't know anyone who knows as much as you do about cacti. I've found it's a bit of a niche interest." He laughed. He laughs a lot.

20

It was a dismal day in the most miserable month of the year, and I wasn't going to work. Trudy had reminded me I'd hardly taken any of my annual leave entitlement for this financial year, and suggested I use it up by extending my weekends. She said I'd benefit from the rest now that I was so heavily pregnant. I wasn't convinced; without my routines I feel like a dinghy cut free of its moorings. As it turned out, though, her suggestion proved to be a timely one. My mother's medical records had finally arrived in a hefty parcel the previous morning, and I suspected it would take quite some time to study and interpret them.

Kate had nipped down first thing to say she was dropping the children off for an overnight stay with Alex, and to ask whether I'd like to see a film at the Brixton Ritzy that evening. I suspected her taste in film might not be the same as mine, but unusually I wasn't put off by that. Perhaps my pregnancy hormones were affecting my critical faculties; or perhaps it was just that I couldn't remember when I last went to the cinema with another person. I accepted the invitation. After Kate had returned upstairs, I checked my phone for messages and found an email from Mr. Brinkworth. I made myself a mug of tea and sat down at the kitchen table to read it.

I have received your claim form, and have today lodged at court the acknowledgment of service. As you are aware, I refute your contentions, and I am currently in the process of drafting my strong defense and counterclaim.

Your brother attended these offices yesterday. I advised him to instruct his own solicitors; conflict of interest prevents me from representing both myself as executor and your brother as one of two beneficiaries who are in dispute. During the course of our brief meeting, Mr. Green said he had reported your theft of your mother's ashes and her jewelry box. The police officer told him they would not wish to become involved in a family dispute at this stage, and advised him to raise the matter with me. In an effort to resolve the issue, I propose that we agree a neutral third party hold the items in safekeeping pending resolution of the court case.

I would also point out that, now that proceedings have been commenced, legal costs will escalate. To avoid the possible depletion of your mother's estate, I suggest that an effort be made to settle this matter through mediation. Kindly confirm your agreement. I will put the same proposal to your brother through his solicitors.

So, formal mediation is it, Mr. Brinkworth? The solicitor wouldn't be proposing such a move if he was entirely confident of his case. Where was the room for negotiation, though? Either the will was watertight and Edward was entitled to stay in the house, or it wasn't and the house should be sold. Perhaps Mr. Brinkworth thought my brother could be persuaded to vacate the house by a specified future date now that proceedings had been commenced. Even if that were the case (which I doubted), I wouldn't want to forgo the pleasure of seeing Edward in court. As far as the jewelry box and ashes were concerned, I couldn't see what I'd gain by handing them over to a third party. Besides, the casket was valuable to me. I decided not to bother replying.

My phone beeped. A text message from Rob. Just checking in to see how the lady of leisure is getting on. Since New Year's Day he's taken to texting or calling at odd times, mostly late at night. I've even initiated contact myself, on occasion. The reason is, I'm having great difficulty sleeping in these final weeks of my pregnancy, due to a combination of backache, heartburn, leg cramps and urgent trips to the loo, and Rob's a night owl. It's therefore only common sense that we help each other fend off boredom in the early hours. Our conversations tend to meander from one subject to another, until I can no longer remember where we started. I suppose I should come clean. I've actually started to enjoy talking to Rob, looking forward to it, even. On the nights he hasn't rung, it's felt as if something was missing. Peculiar, I know.

While I was typing a reply to Rob, I became aware of a dull ache in my lower back. There were jobs to be done, however, and nobody but I was going to do them, so I sent the message, grabbed a handful of carrier bags and set off down to the high street with my list. By the time I got back to the flat, I was feeling more off-color — nothing serious, just a headache and odd twinges in my abdomen. I decided it would be sensible to rest after unpacking my groceries; I'd return to bed and read a book. Undressing, I noticed a dark red stain on my underwear, not unlike the start of my period. I rushed to the toilet. More blood, fresh and red this time. I was going into labor. But it was weeks too early, and this wasn't how it was supposed to start. I grabbed my maternity folder and found the number of the hospital. The nurse was businesslike, asking how many weeks pregnant I was and about the symptoms I was experiencing. My voice was breathless as I answered.

"I think we'd better have a little check on baby," she said. "There's nothing to worry about. We just need to make sure everything's okay. Have you got someone who can bring you in?"

"No. Wait, yes, I think so."

What was happening? I was so stupid, stupid, stupid to think all would be fine. From the day I'd found out I was pregnant, I'd carried on with my life almost as normal, taking my condition as a given, as something that would run its forty-week course and end in the delivery of a baby. I couldn't believe, now, that I'd been so naive. I was forty-five years old — an "elderly primigravida" — ancient, in maternity terms. There were innumerable things that could go wrong: with the baby, with the pregnancy, with me.

It must be my fault, I thought. Had I overexerted myself that morning? The shopping trolley had been full, and one of the wheels had been sticking, so I'd had to shove it to get it to move. And then my bags were so heavy I'd had to stop to rest several times on the way home. I should have ordered my groceries online. Or maybe I'd eaten something unsafe — I'd read somewhere that pineapples could bring on labor, and I'd had a fruit salad the day before; or perhaps I'd eaten something that was past its sell-by date — food poisoning can be dangerous in pregnancy; or it could be the result of a virus or an infection — a couple of my colleagues had been ill recently. I tried to calm myself, to order my thoughts, but it was impossible. I stumbled upstairs and hammered on Kate's door. Thank God she was back from dropping the children off with Alex.

"What's going on? Is the house on fire?"

"I'm bleeding. I have to get to hospital. I think I'm having a miscarriage." There. I'd put it into words.

"Hang on a sec, I'll get my car keys."

On the way to the hospital, I voiced my concerns to Kate. What if something had happened to the baby? What if I walked out of the hospital alone and no longer pregnant? What if all this had been for nothing? On the other hand, what if I was about to give birth to a living, breathing infant? I wasn't ready. I'd hardly thought about it, really, in practical terms. I hadn't bought any clothes or equipment. I hadn't read the manuals on how to look after it. I was planning to do all that next month. Kate reassured me.

"If you're in labor I'm sure nothing bad will happen. You're over thirty weeks now. And the baby'd be kept in the hospital for a while. I've got everything you could possibly need for a newborn, up in the loft. But it's probably a false alarm, so stay calm."

"We're just going to listen to baby's heartbeat, darlin'," said the rotund Afro-Caribbean midwife as I lay on a bed in the small room. My own heart was pounding. She pressed the ice-cold monitor against my belly and moved it up, down, left, right. "Ah, that's it. Would you like to hear?" I nodded. She turned up the volume on her device, and I heard a deep, regular thud. What a lovely sound.

"I'm going to give you a quick internal now, if that's alright," she said. "Slip your undies off and put this sheet over your lap."

I never expected to find myself lying naked from the waist downward, legs akimbo, with a neighbor sitting next to me. I suppose I could have asked Kate to leave, but I discovered I didn't actually care. That's what pregnancy does to a woman.

"Well, I can't see any signs you're going into labor," the nurse said, snapping off her rubber gloves once the examination was concluded. "But we'll need to observe you and the baby for a while."

A fetal heart rate monitor was strapped in place and wired up to a machine next to the bed. Listening to the hypnotic sound, I put my hands on my belly and felt a small bulge appear and disappear. A fist, perhaps, or a foot. *Please,* I thought to myself. *Please help me keep my baby safe.* Kate headed off to find the café, and returned shortly afterward with two cardboard cups with plastic lids. I'm not the sort of person who enjoys eating or drinking from disposable containers. That is, I never used to be. Maintaining such standards, though, is tumbling down my list of priorities. I shuffled up the bed and accepted the cup.

"I keep meaning to ask, have you decided

on a birthing partner?" Kate asked me, removing the lid and blowing on her drink.

"I don't need one."

"Don't be crazy. Nobody should go through it alone. I've given birth twice, so I know the ropes. I'm applying for the role."

As if to display her credentials she described, in gruesome and intricate detail, the births of her own two children. It was like listening to a war veteran recounting his part in a particularly hard-won battle. I've always known I'm perfectly capable of enduring labor and childbirth without someone to hold my hand, metaphorically or otherwise, but, to my surprise, I found it reassuring to think of Kate being there.

"Okay," I said. "You've impressed me with your firsthand experience — the job's yours."

Eventually the midwife returned with a tired-looking junior doctor who, after checking the notes and charts, asked me a few brief questions.

"Right," she said. "Baby seems fine at the moment. But there's no obvious reason for the bleeding and I don't want to take any chances, particularly in view of your advanced age. We'll keep you in overnight for observation and see how things develop."

It's difficult for me to admit this, but, as

the doctor turned away, I cried. Proper tears, rolling down my cheeks and landing on the starched white pillows of the hospital bed. Kate leaned over and put her arms around me. I buried my face in her long hair. She smelled of warm milk and clean laundry. I can't remember the last time I cried. In fact, now that I come to think of it, I have no recollection of ever having done so, although I suppose I must have, as a small child. It's strange how something you never planned or desired can have such an effect on you. As you know, I never wanted to be a mother. More than that: I positively recoiled at the idea. If you'd told me a year ago that in twelve months' time I'd be in the late stages of pregnancy, I'd have been horrified; I'd have done everything in my power to prevent it from happening. And how do I feel now? Now I feel that my world has changed.

If it had just been my own health at issue I'd have said the medical profession was making a lot of unnecessary fuss, and discharged myself. But my desire to escape had to be balanced against other consider-ations, and those considerations weighed more heavily. A stay in the hospital was what it had to be. I gave Kate my front door key and a list of items I'd need: nightwear, toiletries, reading materials, etc. I wondered how I would have coped with these practicalities without her.

The ward to which I was transferred was small; just six beds. Jen, the woman in the bed to my left, was a teacher in her late thirties, quick-witted and loquacious. She helped to take my mind off my situation by relating her own story. Like me, she'd made a conscious decision never to have children. A few months ago, she'd had a contraceptive coil fitted, but, unknown to her, she was already pregnant. She continued to have periods, and it was only when she went to the doctor to complain of feeling bloated that a pregnancy test was carried out. She was over six months pregnant. The coil couldn't be removed, and she was at serious risk of miscarriage, so she would have to stay in the hospital until she gave birth. Considering it was less than a week ago that she discovered she was pregnant, she was coping with remarkable equanimity.

Jen introduced me to the other women on the ward. The girl in the bed to my right was fifteen — obese, pale and puffy — and had just been diagnosed with preeclampsia. The doctor had told her they needed to deliver her twin babies by cesarean section as soon as possible. Her tiny, wrinkled grandmother was a constant presence at her bedside, other than when she went for a cigarette break. Neither of them looked very happy. Two of the three women on the other side of the ward were experiencing complications in the late stages of their pregnancies and were being closely monitored. They had been there for several days, and already appeared to be the best of friends. The third woman — the saddest case — had been told that her baby's heartbeat had stopped. She was due to be induced and give birth, knowing that her baby would be stillborn. She kept the curtains closed around her bed most of the time, not wanting to converse with the mothers-to-be.

Inevitably, Jen asked about my own situation. There was something about the sisterly atmosphere in that ward — diverse types of women going through different kinds of adversity, but leveled by what our bodies were doing to us — which made me feel I had nothing to hide. I told her the whole story. She said I was "one tough mama." A strange way of putting it.

"But — and tell me to mind my own business if you like, I'm a nosy so-and-so — why were you so reluctant to let this Richard have some involvement in the first place? It's going to give you a break now and then. And why would you have any doubts about taking the money, if he's offering? Most single mums have to chase dads to pay."

"Because I've never wanted to be reliant on anyone else," I explained. "If you have sole charge of your own destiny no one can let you down."

"Yeah, but we're about to become mothers, touch wood. We're stepping onto an emotional roller coaster. We'll never have complete control of our own lives again. But sometimes you have to lose something to gain something."

Kate returned at visiting time with the items on my list. At last, I could get out of the horrendous hospital gown I'd had to put on when I was transferred to the ward. Jen introduced Kate and me to her slightly dazed-looking husband, who seemed to be dealing with the news of his imminent, unplanned fatherhood with good humor equal to that of his wife. I actually passed a not unpleasant couple of hours in the presence of these three people.

When the visitors had gone, my fellow patients settled down to read, listen to headphones or sleep. The thoughts of earlier that day came back to me: what if my body wasn't up to it? What if I was just too old to carry a baby to full term? Even though there were a few weeks left to go, perhaps it would be better if the baby was delivered now. An incubator would do a better job of protecting it than me. I asked the nurse, who was making the final checks before lights-out, if that was possible.

"Don't be thinking like that. Signs are, everything's going to be okay. Your body knows what to do."

The next morning, I woke up feeling much better. The baby had been wriggling all night, which had reassured, rather than annoyed, me. When I went to the loo, I found that the pad I'd been told to wear was spotless; the bleeding had stopped. Maybe things would be alright, after all. Jen, on the other hand, had woken with pains in her abdomen. She'd been given painkillers, and the curtains were pulled around her bed so she could rest. In the absence of my companion the day dragged. The woman whose baby had died inside her left the ward early to be induced. A nurse packed her belongings into a bag and the bed linen was soon changed. Just before lunch, the girl with preeclampsia was wheeled out for her cesarean section. Following the operation, she would be going to the postnatal ward, along with her twin babies. It was odd to think that within the hour she would be a mother, at fifteen. I wished her the best of luck for the future.

Just as I was thinking I'd have to spend another night in the hospital not knowing what was going on with my body, the consultant appeared at the end of my bed. He was tall, thin, authoritative. After examining my notes and charts, and muttering to the nurse, he finally turned his attention to me.

"Right, Ms. Green, would you like to go home?"

"Is it safe? For the baby?"

"Oh, yes. It seems a small blood vessel burst inside you, which caused your bleed, but I have no concerns. The baby is obviously happy, and you're a picture of health, so I can see no reason why I shouldn't discharge you. Go home, take it easy and enjoy the rest of your pregnancy."

I must admit that, as he moved away to the next bed, I felt tears welling up in my eyes once more. I wiped them away with the edge of the sheet.

Kate turned up as I was finishing getting dressed. She helped me pack my things. Jen, who was feeling a little better and had pulled back her curtains, expressed jealousy at the fact that I was going home; she would probably be in the hospital for weeks. She asked me where exactly home was. It turned out she lived only a few streets away.

"We can go on pram walks around the Common when the babies arrive," she said, scribbling down her phone number on a scrap of paper. I liked her. It wasn't as horrendous an idea as I might have thought a few months ago. "By the way," she added, as I was about to leave, "I never asked. What're you having?"

I hesitated. Why not? "A daughter," I said. "I'm going to have a daughter."

21

It was gone midnight when Rob called me on my mobile phone, in a state of high excitement. He told me that, to his delight and amazement, Alison had accepted his Facebook friend request, and they'd exchanged a series of messages. She'd confirmed she was recently divorced, and told him she had three grown-up children, all of whom had left home for university and work. Her own career in hotel management was flourishing. Rob said that, when he subsequently spoke to her on the phone, it was as if the intervening years and the falling-out had never happened. James had been asking questions about him, apparently, and Alison thought it was time to consider a reconciliation between father and son. She invited Rob up to Edinburgh so they could meet first, without telling James, and then decide how to proceed. Rob was ecstatic. He was traveling up to Scotland that weekend.

Since that call a few days ago, I've received no communication from Rob. It's completely understandable. Alison was his first and only love; he was desperate to get back together with her. His priorities, now, are elsewhere. I'm thrilled for him, naturally, and I hope he'll be very happy with his reconstituted family. Although I'd become accustomed to our daily and nightly phone and text contact, the fact is that Rob has only ever been the custodian of my furniture while it's in storage, nothing more and nothing less. There's no reason why his newly rekindled relationship should change that. Unless, I suppose, he decides to move up to Edinburgh, in which case I'll have to make other arrangements. A minor inconvenience. There's nothing to justify any feelings of regret or disappointment on my part.

In any event, I've had other matters to distract me: I was to meet Richard at a busy pub on High Holborn. The location had been a compromise; I wanted a businesslike meeting, so I rejected Richard's suggestion that we go to a restaurant or to one of our previous haunts. At least, with this plan, I could stop by briefly after work, have a quick drink, sort out what needed to be sorted out and be home by dinnertime. I arrived first. The crowds parted as I entered, and people at the bar stood aside. I was getting used to this; no longer did I have to stand in packed Tube trains, queue in the post office or wait my turn in the sandwich shop. After ordering a lime and soda for myself and a gin and tonic for Richard, I squeezed into a seat at a corner table near the constantly opening and closing door. I watched the throngs of people spilling onto the pavement outside the pub, gulping down drinks, smoking and generally behaving in the raucous way that young professionals behave on a Friday evening straight after work.

The arrangement to meet had been made a few days earlier, when Richard and I had bumped into each other in the Oxford Street branch of Marks & Spencer, of all mundane places. The shop was buzzing with January sale shoppers, but the lingerie department was relatively quiet. I'd grown to unforeseen proportions, and supplementary purchases were urgently required. As I was metaphorically weighing up the items on offer, trying to decide which were the least aesthetically displeasing, I happened to glance across to the nightwear section, where I spotted a man who, from his side profile, looked the spitting image of Richard: impossibly even features, precisely cut and coiffed hair, parade-ground posture, impeccable dress. He was with a tiny, slightly humpbacked elderly woman wearing a bobble hat. She was holding a pink floral nightdress in front of her. The man-who-looked-like-Richard nodded his approval. How strange that he should have a doppelgänger in London, although they do say we all have one wandering the earth somewhere. I'm not sure I'd like to meet my own; I prefer to think of myself as a one-off.

The man-who-looked-like-Richard followed the elderly woman as she moved away from the nightdress rack. As he did so, I caught his eye. It *was* Richard. We both looked away — I, because I didn't wish to engage in conversation while holding a double-pack of maternity bras; he, perhaps, because he was uncomfortable being seen in such a banal situation. With my intended purchases under my arm, I headed for the tills via a circuitous route. It seems that Richard's thinking was identical; we arrived simultaneously at the same point, but from different directions.

"Susan, what a wonderful coincidence," he said, his expression giving the lie to his words. "I've been meaning to call so we can get everything agreed, you know, well in advance."

"Aren't you going to introduce me to your friend?" asked the small woman, in a strong Northeastern accent. Newcastle? Sunderland? I regret to say I've never been able to tell the difference.

"Mam, this is Susan. Susan, this is my mam — er, mother — Norma."

"Oh, I've been dying to meet you, pet. I've been badgering Richie but he said not until everything's sorted out between you. Seemed to think I'd put a spanner in the works, but I'll not interfere. What's gone on between you is no business of mine."

"Pleased to meet you," I said, holding out my hand, which she squeezed with both of hers.

"Look at you, Susan! You're a picture. I notice you're carrying very high. That means it's a girl."

"Good guess."

Richard smiled. "Well, I never."

"Ah, just wait 'til I tell the family," she said. "They'll be over the moon." She grabbed the undergarments, which I'd been endeavoring to conceal, and thrust them into the hands of Richard, who was already holding the pink floral nightdress. "You go and pay for these, while me and Susan here

have a little wander. I'll see you by the car-
dies." She threaded her arm through mine
and we headed off. I was in no rush, and
had no objection to spending a few minutes
in the company of this old woman — soon
to be my baby's grandmother — who reminded me a little of my own mother. Also,
I admit, I was intrigued, and keen to learn
more.

"So, do you live near Richard?" I asked.

"Me, oh, no, I live in Gateshead, with one
of Richie's sisters. I love visiting him, but I
couldn't live down here, pet."

"But I thought Richard was born and
brought up in Sussex."

Norma chuckled. "No, he'd never left
Gateshead until he was eighteen. Did really
well in his A-level exams and got a place at
Cambridge University. We were all so proud
of him. And then he moved down to London
when he graduated. I understand why.
There wouldn't have been any work for him
where we live. You can't tell he's from
Gateshead anymore, of course. He started
talking posh when he was at university, to
fit in I imagine, but he's been doing it so
long now it's just how he speaks. I sometimes think he's a bit embarrassed about
the way I talk, but he still invites us down
to visit him, so I can't complain."

This was certainly shedding a new light on Richard. I'd never have guessed that he was a self-invented person, but, then again, perhaps we all are, to a greater or lesser extent. We'd reached the knitwear section, and Norma was riffling through a rack of oatmeal-colored cardigans. She asked me to find her size, and I duly did so. She turned to me.

"You know, I'm not an old fuddy-duddy, Susan. Things have changed since I was a lass, and I don't blame you for not jumping on Richie's proposal just because you're having a bairn. That can be a recipe for disaster. I know he can be a bit — now what's the word? — *detached* from the real world. He's always been like that, since he was a wee lad. But his heart's in the right place, and I can tell he wants to do what he can. So do I. This'll be my eighth grandchild. I've resigned myself to the fact that I won't see this one like I see my others — most of them live a few streets away — but I hope I'll get to know her."

"Richard and I are going to sort things out."

"I know you are, pet. Speak of the devil."

Richard appeared at my side and handed me a carrier bag. I tried to reimburse him for his outlay, but he said it was the very

413

least he could do, all things considered. After arranging to meet a few days hence, Richard and his mother shuffled off, arm in arm, to continue their shopping trip. Heading down the main aisle, she turned and called to me, "Can't wait to see you again and meet my new granddaughter. Come and visit us in Gateshead."

Once he'd tired of holding open the door for the constant stream of people entering and leaving the pub, Richard finally joined me at the gloomy corner table. I realized, now, why it was the last unoccupied one in the pub; it was directly underneath the speaker pumping out dance music. The usual greetings and civilities out of the way (conducted, through necessity, with voices raised), I took my portfolio and pen from my briefcase.

"Right, I only have half an hour, so let's get down to business. I'll make notes of our discussion, type them up and send them over to you for your agreement."

"Great idea. That way there'll be no misunderstandings."

"Sorry, no what?"

"Misunderstandings."

"Exactly. Number one — place of residence. Obviously with me. Once I've received my inheritance, which will be very soon, I'll buy a flat that's better suited to a family of two, so you can rest assured there'll be no compromises on the domestic front."

"Sorry, Susan, I missed all of that," he said, leaning into my personal space, then quickly withdrawing.

I repeated myself at top volume, articulating my words as distinctly as I could.

"Oh, yes, certainly. I've always accepted that the child will live with you, Susan, and I have no doubt that you'll organize everything in a suitable way."

"Good." There was a loud and prolonged cheer from a group of men at the bar. I waited for it to subside before continuing. "Number two — regularity of contact between you and the child. I was thinking once a week."

"Did you say once a week?" Richard shouted. "If so, that's perfect. I'm usually up in London on Wednesdays and Thursdays, as you know, so either of those days would be fine. And she could stay with me in my hotel on Wednesday nights. I'm assuming she could accompany me to meetings and to the shows I'm reviewing."

"I should think so. I understand they're not much trouble when they're little. They just sleep all the time."

"Excellent. I'll purchase one of those baby slings. So much more convenient than a pram in theaters and galleries."

"And when she's born you can come to the hospital to have a look at her, even if it's not a Wednesday or Thursday."

"Very accommodating of you, Susan."

"What was that?"

"Accommodating!"

I nodded, took a sip of my drink and scribbled down what we'd agreed so far. My throat was feeling sore from raising my voice.

"Number three," I shouted, "weekends. I'm assuming you'd like to take her to Sussex from time to time. I was thinking one weekend in four."

"I'm not sure I can agree to one weekend a year."

"Oh, for heaven's sake, can you ask one of the bar staff to turn that music down."

Richard was gone for some time, but his mission must have been successful, as the volume was soon lowered to a tolerable level. As he regained his seat, I repeated item number three on my agenda.

"That's precisely what I'd have suggested," said Richard. "I can meet you at Waterloo station for the handover. Once she's old enough to make herself understood, do you think it would be acceptable to put her on the train in London and I'll meet her at the other end?"

"I don't see why not. After all, it's important to encourage independence from an early age. Moving on. Number four — holidays."

"I don't generally take holidays, as such."

"Neither do I, Richard, but I understand that children enjoy them."

"Well, shall we say twice a year, for a week in the spring and a week in the autumn? I'm so looking forward to showing her the European capitals."

"That's agreed, then. Obviously on dates to fit in with school holiday times. Which leads me on to five — decisions about the child's education and other such practicalities. I'm happy to listen to your views on such matters, but, as the main carer, the final decisions must always be mine."

"If it was someone other than you, Susan, I might object, but I know your thoughts on such matters are likely to accord with mine, so I'm prepared to accede to that."

"And finally, number six — the financial side, which we haven't seen eye to eye on so far. I'm very much against taking money from you, but I know you feel strongly that you want to contribute. I've decided on a compromise. Each month I'll itemize the precise amounts of money I've spent on the child, for food, clothing, books, etc. I'll allow you to pay 50 percent of the total, and not a penny more. I wish to make it clear that under no circumstances will I accept any money for myself. I won't be morally indebted to you."

"Understood and agreed."

"As far as I'm concerned," I said, gulping down the last of my lime and soda, "we've covered everything that needs to be covered."

"I must say, I think we can congratulate ourselves on a job well and amicably done. Some people would've made a meal of all this, but we're both too sensible and pragmatic to get bogged down in detail. I'm very much looking forward to putting our agreement into practice. What is it, eight weeks now?"

"Seven weeks and two days."

"Even better. There *is* just one other item for the agenda, though, before we go our separate ways," said Richard. "The one we left hanging in the air last time — the question of marriage."

"Richard, I appreciate your offer, but, let's face it, it's not what either of us signed up for. Our relationship was like an affair — the evenings out, the nights in hotels, the distinction from the everyday. And just like, in an affair, the parties generally have no intention of leaving their spouses, I'm pretty sure neither of us ever envisaged spending the rest of our lives together."

"Perhaps your lack of enthusiasm might be justified," he said. "I've been giving it some more thought over the last few weeks. My aim, all along, has been to do the right thing, and if you'd changed your mind and thought marrying was an attractive option, then I'd happily step up to the mark. But I must say, I'm not certain I'd make a great success of the living-with-someone bit of marriage in the long-term. I have my own particular ways of doing things, as I know you do, and I can't imagine how I'd fit around another person's habits and routines. My proposal still stands, of course, but if you're determined to reject it I'd understand completely."

"I can set your mind at rest, Richard. If we were to marry it would be a complete disaster. I have no intention of accepting your proposal."

"Well, let's shut the door on all that business, then. This has been a very productive evening. I knew, in my heart of hearts, you'd feel that way. Neither of us will ever settle down with a partner. We're much too set in our ways."

I suppose it would be hard for me to disagree.

■ ■ ■ ■

FEBRUARY

■ ■ ■ ■

22

"What're we looking for?" Kate asked, picking up the packet of Post-it notes I'd skimmed across the kitchen table.

"Any reference to mental health concerns, however fleeting or minor," I said. "Confusion, memory loss, anxiety, depression. Also highlight any drugs prescribed. Use the pink Post-it notes for symptoms, yellow for diagnoses and green for medication."

"Hang on a minute, let me write that down."

I hoped I was doing the right thing allowing Kate to assist me. She was studying a pseudoscientific subject at postgraduate level, so she couldn't be entirely devoid of logic. The fact was that, since my discharge from hospital, my mother's medical records had simply been sitting in a pile on top of the casket, waiting for me to do something with them. Even *mental* exertion was beyond me. At the beginning of this month, however, I was prompted to take action. I'd received in the post defenses to my claim: one from Mr. Brinkworth and one from a firm that said they had been instructed by Edward. The court documents contained nothing that I didn't know already — they were little more than bare denials of my allegations — but I knew it was high time I mustered my evidence. When I told Kate about my task for the weekend, she offered to help; I suspect her motive was more to escape the essay she was supposed to be writing than to share my burden.

"Our campaign against the closure of the mums-and-babies group's going well," Kate said, scanning the first sheet in her pile. "We've had so much support from local people, especially parents and grandparents."

"Fascinating," I said, "but I think we'll concentrate better if we don't engage in idle chitchat."

"Okay, boss."

Kate was examining the notes relating to my mother's first admission to hospital, two years before her full stroke. After turning over a few more pages she looked up.

"They keep referring to her having a TIA. What does that mean?"

I reached for my laptop and looked it up.

"It stands for 'transient ischemic attack,' " I said. "It's the medical term for a ministroke. She had temporary paralysis on one side of her body, and her voice was slurred. It only lasted a few hours. I didn't even bother coming up from London, because by the time I heard about it she was completely back to normal. Or so she said."

"Didn't you want to see her to check?"

"There didn't seem any point. I believed what I was told."

I'd been sure, at the time, that I was doing the correct thing. If my mother had wanted to see me after her ministroke, she would have said so, wouldn't she? Telling Kate, however, I felt — not guilty, exactly — maybe a little shamefaced. I was starting to wonder if, perhaps, the rational decision isn't always the best decision. We went back to our reading.

"It says the MRI scan showed she had a small blood clot causing a temporary disruption of the oxygen supply to her brain," Kate said. "She was prescribed a drug called clopidogrel."

I turned to my laptop again. "It's what they call an antiplatelet medicine that prevents blood clots from forming. It's precautionary — if a person has had a ministroke their risk of having a more serious one is increased." I checked the side effects, but found nothing that would have affected my mother's thinking.

"It looks like she only took it for a few weeks, anyway," said Kate. "She told the outpatients' clinic she was getting headaches and wanted to stop. They prescribed low-dose aspirin instead."

"Any other medication?" I asked.

"Doesn't look like it. The notes say the doctors were satisfied with her recovery. They discharged her to the care of her GP."

The bundle of records I was studying related to my mother's second, more major, stroke. They began with her emergency admission to hospital following the incident at church. There were pages and pages of data: clinical observations; blood pressure, heart rate and temperature charts; hematology and cytology results; and medication administration records. There were also reports of CT and MRI scans. The notes said my mother had had a left hemisphere ischemic stroke, caused again by a blood clot in her brain — this time larger. She'd been treated with something called a tissue plasminogen activator drug to break up the clot, and had been put back on the anti-platelet medication, together with warfarin to thin her blood and beta blockers for high blood pressure. There was an abundance of medical terminology, some of which I understood but most of which I'd check later. I wanted to get on to meatier stuff.

The doctors noted that my mother was responding well to the treatment; within days she started to regain the use of her paralyzed right hand and had sufficient control of her voice to make herself understood. This accorded with what I remembered from the time; my mother appeared to be recovering so well from the stroke, in fact, that I returned to London before she was discharged from hospital. She had Aunt Sylvia and Edward visiting her every day, after all, and I knew that a backlog of work would be building up on my desk. And I recall that Richard had tickets for a concert at the Barbican that I particularly wanted to attend. Despite the numerous reasons why it made sense for me to return to London, I must admit that I now question whether I should have waited until my mother was discharged; perhaps I shouldn't simply have assumed she'd make the same rapid and complete recovery as she had from her ministroke.

I turned to the outpatient notes, which related to my mother's regular appointments at the hospital following her discharge. The first pages concerned physical matters: the usual checks on her blood pressure and heart rate, and discussions of how she was getting on with her medication. Then came a page of much more detailed notes. Now this was getting interesting. My mother reported to the doctor that she felt upset about small incidents that had never used to bother her, like next door's cat coming into her garden to do his business or the milkman delivering the milk after breakfast was finished. Although she knew she was getting matters out of proportion, these things were almost unbearable to her at the time. My mother also told the doctor that she kept misplacing things — keys, her purse, her address book — and forgetting what day it was and what she was supposed to be doing. It made her feel stupid and angry with herself. She was determined not to let anyone know what was going on, and she was sure she was hiding it well by writing detailed lists and reminders for herself. However, it was exhausting putting on a show. She said she felt down in the dumps. The hospital notes recorded that my mother was referred to a neurologist and a psychiatrist for further tests and assessments. At the conclusion of these she was given a diagnosis: vascular dementia.

"Oh, no," I said. "Oh, God."

"What've you found?" asked Kate, looking up in surprise from the last sheet of her pile.

"Dementia. My mother had something called vascular dementia."

"That's a bit more serious than confusion. Didn't she tell you? Didn't you realize?"

"I knew something wasn't right, but she hid it well. I only visited her a couple of times after her stroke, so I didn't see all the signs. I don't think my aunt knew either, though, and she saw her regularly. Poor, poor Mum."

We sat in silence for a few moments. "On the positive side — and I don't mean to be callous," said Kate, "this is fantastic for your court case, isn't it? I mean, it's not fantastic that she had dementia. That goes without saying. But you can't change history — she had it and that's that. You must feel satisfied knowing you were right all along."

"I suppose so." Kate was correct. This was exactly what I'd been hoping to find. Strangely, though, satisfaction wasn't my primary feeling.

"If she'd told me at the time, I could've visited her more often. I could've helped. I could've shielded her from Edward."

Kate wasn't really listening to me; she was

caught up in the thrill of the detective work. "I'm just looking up vascular dementia," she said. "It says here symptoms can include slowness of thought and difficulty in planning. It also says there's no specific treatment. What was the hospital doing for her?"

I went back to the notes. "It says she was prescribed antidepressants in addition to all the other drugs she was taking. She was also given advice on lifestyle changes and referred for occupational therapy. It looks like that was to help her manage everyday activities. It probably helped her disguise her problems." I turned over another sheet. This one was about her care plan. The notes recorded that a meeting had taken place at which my mother and Edward were both in attendance. My brother had agreed to be her primary carer and, consequently, no additional home support was organized. My mother was advised that she was entitled to claim state benefits to pay Edward for the care he'd need to give her. She told them she'd already submitted an application.

I went through the rest of the papers. More of the same: reviews of medication; notes of discussions about problems with memory and planning; further tests and assessments. The doctors told my mother that her condition appeared to be stable, for the time being, but that she should continue to take her medication regularly as any further clots could cause deterioration. It was noted, often, that Edward was in attendance at the appointments. So that was it. I now had proof, not only that my mother was suffering from a medical condition that would have affected her ability to write a will, but also that Edward was fully aware of that fact. Indeed, he was benefiting financially from her need for assistance. I could understand my mother's reasons for not telling me about her diagnosis. She was a proud woman; she wouldn't have wanted people feeling sorry for her. But why would Edward keep it from me, if not for nefarious reasons? The more I thought about it, the more my sorrow at my mother's diagnosis was replaced with rage at Edward's duplicity.

I was now certain that a judge would declare the will invalid, and that the estate would be dealt with under the rules of intestacy; that is, the house would be sold straightaway, and the proceeds would be divided equally between Edward and me. It felt like we were entering the endgame. I should have been feeling happier.

The following week, during my lunch break, I called in to see Brigid in her Lincoln's Inn chambers. Her attic room was about the size of a broom cupboard, and was accessed via a steep, winding staircase, the ascending of which was far from easy in my heavily pregnant condition, and can't have been much better for the hefty Brigid. Her desk was laden, not only with the expected briefs and files, but with dead potted plants, used coffee cups, sandwich wrappers and miscellaneous receipts. It reminded me of her bedroom in our shared flat.

"So, what've you got for me?" Brigid asked, clearing a space in the middle of the desk with a sweep of her brawny arm.

I passed her my claim form and statement of case, together with the two defenses, which she spent a few moments perusing. I explained to her what I'd discovered in the medical records, and showed her the most significant pages. Finally, I informed her that Margaret, my aunt and the vicar could — to a greater or lesser extent — attest to the fact that my mother was suffering from forgetfulness and confusion.

"You've missed your calling, old girl. I always said you should've gone for the bar."

"Dealing with the paperwork would've been fine," I said. "It's the people that would've been the problem."

"Tell me about it."

She looked at the sections I'd highlighted in the medical records. "This is exactly the evidence you need in a matter like this," she said. "Have you heard of a case called Banks v Goodfellow?"

I told her I'd read about it in the course of my legal research. The case established that, when someone makes a will, they must understand the act they're carrying out and its effects; the extent of their property; and the claims to which they should give effect.

"That's right. And he or she mustn't be affected by a disorder of the mind that — and I'm quoting here from memory — 'poisons his affections, perverts his sense of right or prevents the exercise of his natural faculties.' Generally speaking, if a will appears rational and doesn't contain any irregularities, mental capacity is presumed. But the case of Vaughan v Vaughan established that if there's evidence of confusion or memory loss, it'll be for the people seeking to rely on the will — i.e. Mr. Brinkworth and your brother — to establish mental capacity. And another case says that an irrational disposition in a will can rebut the presumption of capacity. So the medical evidence, combined with the fact that there's no logical reason why your mother would give preference to your brother over you, is all in your favor."

"That's exactly what I thought."

"A slight note of caution, though," said Brigid. "The issue isn't whether the person *actually* understands what they're doing, it's whether they've got the *mental capacity* to understand. The more complex the estate, the easier it is to prove lack of capacity. The fact that it's a very simple will with only two beneficiaries doesn't exactly help you."

"But with vascular dementia she probably wasn't capable of understanding all the implications of a life interest."

"That's what I'd be trying to argue."

"And then there's the undue influence."

"Oh, yes, the strong-arm tactics. You know I've never been keen on going down that road. Undue influence requires coercion. The deceased had to have been pressured into making a will they didn't want to make. In your favor, what amounts to coercion varies with the strength of willpower, and if the willpower's weak due to mental frailty, less force is required to overcome it. The problem is, it's possible to be influenced to do something without that act being against your will. So, if Edward simply badgered or nagged your mum into giving him a life interest in the family home that's not enough. The court will need to be satisfied, on the balance of probabilities, that Edward did more than that — that he actually *forced* her to make the will *against her better judgment*. You haven't shown me anything to prove that."

A young barrister knocked and stuck his head round the door. Brigid told him she would be with him in a sec.

"So, Susan," she said, standing, "my advice is, forget the undue influence and focus on mental capacity. The medical records, supported by the witness evidence, give you a reasonable case on that issue. Get those witness statements drawn up and signed as soon as possible, and serve your evidence to the other sides. Hopefully they'll capitulate without the need of a hearing. Best of luck, old girl. Don't forget my cut of any winnings."

A couple of days later I received a call at work from the vicar of St. Stephen's.

"Miss Green, I'm so pleased I've got hold of you. I've been thinking carefully about the issue we talked about on Christmas Eve, and I've been praying long and hard for guidance. I've come to the conclusion that I have a moral and ethical duty to disclose the matter that your mother told me in confidence, now that she's no longer with us."

"About time," I said. I'd actually forgotten all about the vicar's allegedly top secret information.

"Yes, I'm sorry it's taken me so long, but it's been a very difficult decision for me to make. In the end, I've been swayed by the fact that it's something that will have an impact on you personally, and possibly on the way you act in the future. Also, before she died, your mother was wrestling with the question of whether to tell you herself. I believe that she may well, ultimately, have decided to do so. I feel that those considerations outweigh my duty of confidentiality to your late mother."

"Fine. I'm sure God will understand your reasoning. So what is it?"

"Ah, well, it's not the sort of thing I could possibly divulge over the telephone. Come and see me in the vestry and I'll explain it to you."

"You do realize I live a hundred miles away, and I'm eight months pregnant?"

"I do, indeed, Miss Green, and I'm sorry to put you to the trouble, particularly in your delicate condition. But I'm sure that, if your mother knew I was going to tell you this, she would want me to do it in person."

As it turned out, I'd been considering making yet another trip to the Midlands. I'd now typed up witness statements for the vicar, Margaret and Aunt Sylvia, and I wanted to oversee their signatures personally.

"Alright. What about next Friday afternoon?" I said.

"Super." There was a pause. "You might want to bring along a friend or relative for support."

23

Kate clambered up into the loft above her flat, while I simultaneously held the ladder steady and thwarted Ava's and Noah's efforts to follow her. A few moments later, she reemerged with a bulging holdall full of newborn-baby clothes, which she lowered down to me.

"Throw them in the washing machine and they'll be as good as new," Kate called as she disappeared back through the hatch. Next, she brought down a Moses basket, followed by a black bin liner full of bedding and a first-stage car seat. "There's not much more you need at the start, other than a bag of nappies."

"But where am I going to put all this stuff?"

"You'll find somewhere. Think of your flat as a TARDIS — you'll be amazed how much you can cram into it."

I offered to pay her, but she refused.

"We'll stick them back up there when you've finished with them. Who knows? Maybe one of us'll need them again in the future."

"Hilarious."

That evening I opened the holdall and spread out the contents on the sitting room floor: bodysuits, vests, cardigans, jackets, caps and mittens. Everything was unbelievably small; it called to mind the clothes I'd had for my Tiny Tears when I was little. I'd taken that doll almost everywhere with me, from the day I unwrapped it on my third birthday, to the day — five years later — that it mysteriously vanished from my bedroom when I was out Christmas shopping with my mother. She said I must have taken it with me and forgotten where I left it. I knew better. Edward looked very pleased with himself when we returned home, exhausted from battling the city center crowds. It was only later that evening that I realized why. I had no proof, though, and my mother was furious with me for making such an accusation.

"I wouldn't put it past the little brat," my father had slurred. "He gets away with murder in this house."

As I was tidying away the baby clothes, the

phone rang. I glanced at the display; Rob's number. I'd heard not a whisper from him in almost a month. Inexplicably, I felt a sense of trepidation as my hand hovered over the receiver. I snatched it up a second before the answer machine clicked in.

"Hello."

"Susan, it's great to hear your voice. It feels like an eternity."

"I suppose it's been quite a while."

"The time's just vanished, I've been mad busy."

"I see."

"It all went brilliantly, Susan, I've had an amazing time. It was a bit awkward with Alison at first. She was sussing me out; making sure I'd really changed and wasn't still the arse I was twenty-odd years ago. I must've convinced her. She decided to take some time off work, show me the sights of Edinburgh and introduce me to her parents and her other two kids. One's at college in the city and the other one's doing an apprenticeship at a local joinery firm."

"How lovely."

"It was. Everyone was so friendly — the complete opposite of when I contacted the family all those years ago. The past's been forgiven and forgotten. It probably helps that they've got a new villain now — Alison's ex-husband. Sounds like, compared to him, I wasn't so bad."

"I assume you met your son."

"Eventually, yeah. He's started a PhD at the University of Liverpool. Alison suggested we visit him together so she could introduce the two of us, so after about a week in Edinburgh we drove down. I can't explain what it was like — saying it was the best day ever doesn't do it justice. I wasn't mentally prepared for meeting him, though. I knew, rationally, that he was a twenty-three-year-old man, but subconsciously I was still thinking of him as a boy. In fact, he was as tall as me — maybe a bit taller — and stockier. And he had this great bushy beard. He's an amazing guy — Alison's certainly done a wonderful job."

"I'm glad you got on with him."

"We more than got on. I wouldn't call it a father-son relationship. I don't think that'll happen after all these years. But we definitely bonded. Alison stuck around with us in Liverpool for a few days, then went back to Edinburgh, but James insisted I stay on. There was a spare room in the house he rents, which I used. It was great just hanging out with him. We visited John Lennon's childhood home, went on a Beatles tour, took a ferry across the Mersey. Then I suggested I show him Birmingham, so he came and stayed with me. I took him to where his mum and I met, and to a few of our old haunts. He left this morning. We're going to make an effort to see each other regularly."

"I expect you'll be seeing Alison regularly, too, now you two are together again."

He laughed. "Actually, we're not together."

Not together, I thought. *Not together.*

"I'm sorry to hear that. You must be very disappointed."

"Not in the slightest. When we finally met each other, I realized straightaway how ridiculous the whole idea had been. I'd built up a rose-tinted picture in my head of what Alison was like and how it was when we were together, but it wasn't true then and it certainly isn't now. I think she's great, I got on well with her, she was friendly and funny, and maybe if I'd wanted to pursue it she might've been interested, she might not. But there was no spark there at all, as far as I was concerned. It's pretty crazy that I've spent all this time obsessed with a person who never really existed, other than in my imagination. I've been an idiot. Alison and I'll stay friends, though. We've got James in common, and we're a big part of each other's past. But she's not part of my future.

I've been doing a hell of a lot of thinking these last few weeks. And I'm so sorry I haven't called for ages. I've been in a little bubble — real life has been suspended. I'm going to make it up to you."

"There's really no need."

"There is, as far as I'm concerned." A pause. "Anyway," he continued, "tell me what you've been up to?"

"I've been busy with paperwork for the court case," I told him, finding that I was relaxing into the conversation. I explained what I'd discovered in my mother's medical notes. He was surprised; Edward had never mentioned the diagnosis of vascular dementia. On the subject of Edward, he said that the two of them had had a falling-out. My brother knew we'd been to the New Year's Eve party together; he'd called Rob a double agent and a treacherous, backstabbing bastard. I couldn't help smiling. I told Rob about my pregnancy complications and my stay in the hospital. He said he wished Kate had called him so he could have visited me. He was very sorry he hadn't been around for support.

Our conversation must have lasted over an hour, although I wasn't watching the clock. Toward the end, I just happened to mention that I'd be traveling up to the

Midlands by train on Friday to meet the vicar and to organize the signing of the various witness statements.

"That's perfect. I'll meet you at the station and drive you wherever you want to go."

I declined his offer, perhaps not as firmly as I might have done, but he stood his ground.

"You need someone with you," he said, "because of your health scare. You don't want to be on your own if something happens again."

I admit I felt very happy indeed that he'd insisted; it would certainly save on both time and taxi fares.

I was uncharacteristically fidgety and unsettled on the journey to Birmingham. I couldn't identify the reason; perhaps it was anxiety about meeting the vicar or about seeing Rob, but neither made sense. I tried to focus on the baby-training book I'd bought the previous week. I realized, however, that I was reading the same paragraph over and over again. Kate had told me to ditch the book. She said that babies couldn't be trained like performing chimps; that you just had to "do what comes naturally." That's fine for her to say, but what if it doesn't? A groundless thought; of course I'll know what to do.

Squeezing through the ticket barrier at New Street station, I saw him before he saw me. He was looking at the arrivals board and checking his watch. I experienced a jolt of recognition; it was nothing to do with his appearance — it was something else. The sensation was a little like opening your front door after a long period away; a feeling both that you're reencountering something familiar and that you're seeing it anew. Rob spotted me and came striding over. When he reached me, he stopped, hesitated, then seemed to make up his mind. I found myself reciprocating his greeting. I confess I even buried my face in his donkey jacket as he buried his in my hair. A line had been crossed. Utterly ridiculous, I know. I feel pitiful even recounting this. I have no idea what on earth we must have looked like: a small, heavily pregnant, immaculately turned-out woman, and a tall, floppy-haired workwear-clad man. My brain had clearly left my head.

I was surprised to discover that Rob had cleaned his van, inside and out. He'd even put a rug over the filthy seat, and hung up an air freshener. Not exactly limousine service, but an improvement on the last few times. En route he told me that work had been slow recently; it always was in winter. While he'd been away in Edinburgh and Liverpool, Billy had been overseeing the renovation work on his house. It was now almost finished, and he thought he could sell it for a good profit. Coincidentally, a friend of his with a successful landscape gardening firm in London had called him to say he was receiving far more inquiries than he could possibly handle. He'd asked Rob if he'd like to join forces. It was a shrewd proposition, Rob thought; there was a bigger potential client base down south, and he had nothing tying him to Birmingham. He appeared to want my approval. I don't know why. I told him his commercial and domestic arrangements were none of my business.

"Maybe. But it'd help if I knew what you thought."

Rob continued to sketch out his embryonic plans, and was still doing so when we pulled up next to the lych-gate of St. Stephen's Church. He jumped out of the van and came round to the passenger side to help me maneuver myself down.

"Shall I come in with you?" he asked. "Bit of moral support?"

"No, I'm really not expecting this to take

long. Just wait for me here."

Rob was in the graveyard examining the headstones when I shoved open the church door and thundered back down the path a few minutes later. He picked his way across the wet grass and met me at the lych-gate.

"One call down, two to go," he said, after I'd heaved myself back into the van.

I didn't answer. I just stared straight ahead.

"Susan, are you okay? Shall I drive you to Margaret's?"

A pause.

"I think I'll leave that for another time."

"It's your call. Are we heading straight to your aunt's house then?"

"No, no, I don't want to go to Worcester. Definitely not."

"I thought you were going to spend the night there. Won't she be expecting you?"

"Did you not hear me, Rob?" I snapped. "Are you deaf or stupid? I don't want to go to Aunt Sylvia's house. I don't want to go to Margaret's house. I don't want to go anywhere."

"Come here," said Rob, endeavoring to put his arms around me. "I don't know what that bloody vicar's said, but I can see it's upset you. Do you want me to go in there and break his legs?" I pulled away and leaned my forehead on the passenger window. "Sorry. Let's get you back to mine," he added, starting the engine.

On the journey to Rob's house I thought about what had happened at my meeting with the vicar. It had been ice-cold in the vestry this time; the heating system was playing up, and the antiquated two-bar electric fire was doing nothing to counteract the February bitterness. We sat in our coats and scarves, the vicar with the addition of a tweed cap and fingerless gloves. I began by showing him the brief witness statement I'd drawn up in his name, which summarized the facts he'd told me last time we'd met. He read through the statement, then placed it on the desk in front of him. He put his hands palms-down on top of it.

"I'm sorry, I'm afraid I can't sign this in its present form."

"Why not?"

"It's not that I disagree with anything you've written, but there's one further matter that needs to be included if I'm to give evidence in this case."

"And that is?"

"It's best if I just come out with it. Susan, your mother was feeling very down in the dumps in the last few months of her life. She'd been keeping a secret. She suspected she might soon be meeting her maker, and was agonizing over whether or not to open up to you. Can I ask — have you ever seen your birth certificate?"

"No," I said. "My mother lost it years ago." I'd never bothered obtaining a copy. I suppose I might have done if I'd wanted to apply for a passport or a driving license, but I'd never been tempted to do either. "What's that got to do with the matter in hand, anyway?"

"Your mother didn't lose your birth certificate. She hid it."

"Why on earth would she do that?"

"She didn't want you to stumble across it, because if you found it you'd see that she wasn't your birth mother. My dear, I'm very sorry to have to tell you this — you were adopted by your parents when you were a few weeks old."

"Ha. She really was losing her marbles," I said. "She actually thought she didn't give birth to me?"

"This wasn't a delusion. We had many, many discussions on the subject — on the moral dilemma of keeping it a secret from you and the pain it would cause should you find out about it. The story she told was too convincing and plausible to be a product of her imagination. I know it must be a terrible shock to you."

"This isn't true. This is a lie. I would've known if I'd been adopted. I would've sensed something. Everyone's always said how much I look like my parents. Where's the proof? I've only got your word for it. For goodness' sake, *you* could be making it up for all I know."

"If you're finding this hard to accept — and I understand why you would — may I suggest that you look at your birth certificate? Your mother told me where she kept it. I think she might have been anticipating a situation such as this."

"So where did she say it was, then?"

"In her jewelry box. The lining in the base is loose. She hid it underneath. I really am very, very sorry."

"So you should be, passing on preposterous stories like this without checking your facts. It's unworthy of you and your position. I'm going to make a formal complaint to the bishop or synod or whoever."

I grabbed the unsigned statement that was still sitting on the desk in front of the vicar and left.

Stepping into the hallway of Rob's house, I

was hit first by the warmth — welcome after the heaterless vestry and drafty cab of the van — and second by a smell of paint, wood varnish and wallpaper paste. The place had been transformed from a bare shell into something almost resembling a home.

"I have to make a phone call," I told Rob, handing him my coat.

"You can do it in the living room. I'll put the kettle on."

Kate's mobile rang at least half a dozen times. Finally, she answered.

"I need you to do me a favor," I said. "Can you use the spare key to let yourself into my flat and get my mother's jewelry box down from the top shelf of the book-case?"

"No problem. Hang on a minute."

I heard the jangle of keys, footsteps on the stairs, the sound of locks being opened and the burglar alarm being deactivated.

"Right, I've got the box. What do you want me to do with it?"

"Take the upper shelf out, empty the base and see if the lining's loose."

Noises of fumbling.

"Yes, it is. There's a piece of folded paper inside. It looks like a birth certificate."

My heart was thudding, my hands were damp. I thought I might drop the phone.

"Can you unfold it and read out the names of the baby, the mother and the father."

"The baby is Susan Mary Green. Oh, it's your birth certificate. The mother's name is Sylvia Grainger. Under father's name it's blank. What's going on, Susan? Are you okay?"

"Thank you for doing that," I said. "Can you put everything back where you found it and lock the door behind you?"

I hung up. I felt sick; the room began to dissolve, like watercolor paints leaching into one another. I lowered myself into an armchair and leaned forward, elbows on knees, head in hands.

Things were beginning to come back into focus as Rob entered carrying a tray laden with a stainless steel teapot, mismatched mugs and a packet of chocolate digestives.

"This'll sort you out," he said, setting the tray down on a low table. He looked at me. He saw that it wouldn't.

"Do you want to talk?"

"I'm not feeling well. Could I possibly lie down somewhere? Just for a while."

"The baby's not coming, is it?"

"No, nothing like that. I just need to rest."

He led me upstairs, saying he only had

the one bed at the moment, but that I was welcome to use it. The room was austere; freshly decorated and yet to be personalized. The only indication of the room's occupant was a pile of horticultural books on the bedside table. After pulling back the covers, Rob helped me take off my shoes.

"I'll ring your aunt and tell her you're not coming. I've got her number somewhere from when she wanted me to do her garden. Sleep for as long as you like. I'll be downstairs if you need me."

I closed my eyes, but there was no possibility of rest with the pounding in my head. My aunt was my mother and my mother was my aunt; my father wasn't related to me at all. It was almost impossible to take in. I tried to work it out. Aunt Sylvia was fifteen years younger than my mother, so she would have been seventeen when I was conceived. That was a few years before she married Uncle Frank. My mother would have been in her early thirties, married to my father for six years. I couldn't understand how Aunt Sylvia could have given away her baby. A baby she'd carried, just as I was carrying mine. Neither could I understand why my parents would want to adopt someone else's child. And why did they all hold on to their secret? I'd never gained the impression from any of them that our relationships were other than they appeared to be. Aunt Sylvia had visited our house with an annoying regularity, but she did have a very close relationship with her sister. And she'd always been keenly interested in what I was up to, but I'd assumed that that was just her nosy nature. Aunt Sylvia: silly, vain, self-obsessed. The thought that I was her daughter appalled me. My childhood — everything that had been said or done to me, everything I'd experienced or felt — was based on a lie.

An hour or so later, I drifted back downstairs. It had turned dark outside; the curtains had been closed, lamps lit and a sputtering gas fire switched on. I heard the sound of a radio coming from the kitchen, where I found Rob sitting at a table reading the local newspaper. He stood up as I entered and asked how I was feeling. I apologized for my peculiar behavior. I explained that the vicar had told me something about my mother that had shocked and upset me. He asked again if I wanted to talk about it; I told him I didn't.

"Are there any hotels nearby?" I asked. "There are things I need to discuss with Aunt Sylvia. I've decided to go to her house in the morning, so there's no point getting a train back to London tonight."

"Forget it," Rob said. "You're staying here."

To be honest I needed the company. I was in no state to be on my own. We passed a somber, rather domestic evening together. I helped Rob prepare the vegetables for the recipe he was following, then watched as he busied himself at the hob. We shared a bottle of wine; I needed it. Once we'd eaten, Rob washed up the dinner things and I dried. We talked about our recent work projects, about how Birmingham had changed over the years, about films we'd both seen or wanted to see, carefully skirting the subject of what I'd been told at St. Stephen's. Toward the end of the evening, I could see that something was playing on Rob's mind. As I was about to go up to bed, he broached the subject.

"Shall I sleep on the sofa, or shall we share? It's a king-size, so there's plenty of room for the two — I mean three — of us."

I was unprepared for the suggestion. Obviously, if I'd had time to think about it, or had been a little more my usual self, I would have had no hesitation in instructing him, unequivocally, to sleep on the sofa.

"I don't know," I said. "It's your house —

it's up to you."

"Okay then, we'll share."

I suppose I could have told Rob I'd decided I'd prefer to sleep alone, after all. But I didn't. I have always been a person who deplores inconsistency.

And waking the next morning, finding his warm body molded to the back of my own, and his arm draped across my bump, it was — well, it wasn't entirely unwelcome.

24

"It's a shame you couldn't've come yesterday, 'cos you've missed Wendy and Chrissie. They were devastated not to see you, but they had to head off at the crack. They've gone skiing. I can't remember where. It sounded Eastern European, but that can't be right. Uncle Frank's seeing them off at the airport. He'll be back before lunch. Rob phoned yesterday to say you were under the weather. It can happen when you're this late on, if you don't take it easy. I was just the same when I was carrying the twins. 'Sylvia, stop racing around like there's no tomorrow,' Uncle Frank would tell me. But you know what I'm like. I can't sit still for a minute. That's how come I stay so trim."

She broke off, momentarily, at the sound of tires on gravel.

"Oh, Rob's driving off. Is he not coming in? I was looking forward to a natter with him. I've seen a Michelangelo's *David* that'd look brilliant by the gazebo, but I want his artistic opinion. Ta-ta, Rob, love — I'll see you later. Susan, I can't tell you how thrilled I am you two've got together. He's such a catch. I've always liked a man with his own business. You'd be fighting me for him if I was twenty years younger."

All of this before I'd crossed the threshold of Wendine, or even said 'hello.' Earlier that morning I'd explained to Rob that his role for the day was simply one of taxi driver; his presence at my meeting with my aunt would be a hindrance. He said that was fine by him. There was a house and garden designed by Capability Brown nearby, where he could happily while away a couple of hours. Perversely, however, as I watched his van disappearing down the long drive-way, I almost regretted that I hadn't allowed him to accompany me. The burden of the matter I was about to raise with my aunt was heavy on my shoulders.

Standing in the kitchen while we waited for the coffee to brew, I made a monumental effort to engage in chitchat with Aunt Sylvia on the important topic of whether she would suit a fringe. Eventually, once we had considered the subject from every possible angle, she pushed down the plunger on the cafetière and bent to peer at its contents.

"Might've bin brewing a bit too long. Wake up the little 'un good and proper, this will," she said, straightening, and patting my belly affectionately.

She took two flower-patterned china mugs from the cupboard, poured the coffee and added three spoonfuls of sugar to one of them. She paused with the spoon midair.

"Sugar for you, love? I know I shouldn't, but I've always had a sweet tooth, ever since I was a little girl. 'Sylvia, you're sweet enough already,' my dad used to say, but a little of what you fancy does you good."

I declined. She went over to the fridge and returned with a canister and a bottle.

"Squirty cream or milk?" she asked, adding a thick swirl to her own mug.

"Black, please."

"Ooh, aren't you the sophisticated one?"

We were seated on cream leather sofas in the lounge, facing each other across a glass-topped Louis XIV–style coffee table, on which lay the statement I'd drafted. Aunt Sylvia leaned forward, turned to the last page and signed it, without even glancing at the contents. I suggested she might want to read it through first, but she said there was no need.

"You're better with words than me, love. I know it'll all be right."

I'd wrestled with the question of whether, in the changed circumstances, I should still ask Aunt Sylvia to sign the document. In the end, I decided I would; whatever the outcome of today's discussion, I still needed witness statements to back up the medical evidence in my case against Edward.

"Now that that's out of the way, tell me what you've bin up to," Aunt Sylvia said, picking up her mug and spooning the cream from the top.

"I went to see the vicar of St. Stephen's yesterday."

"That's nice. He was a very good friend to your mum. Always looks well-turned-out, even though he's got a beard."

"He said Mum had a secret."

Aunt Sylvia put down her mug and spoon, and began brushing fluff from her skirt.

"Did he, love? I wonder why he'd say such a thing. I suppose everyone has a few skeletons in the closet, though. I'm sure it wasn't anything important. I should've brought some biscuits in with us. I've got some lovely Scottish shortbread. Would you like one?" She stood up.

"Apparently Mum told him I was adopted."

460

I was calm, much calmer than I thought I'd be. My aunt sat back down again. The color rose from her neck to her cheeks.

"She *was* muddled, though — you've said it yourself. We've all said it, haven't we?"

"Not about this. I know who's named as 'mother' on my birth certificate. I've come here today because I want to hear it from you."

"I don't know what you're talking about. I mean . . . Oh, Susan, love," Aunt Sylvia cried. "Oh, I don't know what to say."

"What about telling me the truth? It's about time someone did."

"It shouldn't've come out like this. I didn't think Patricia still had that birth certificate. She told me she'd destroyed it after the adoption was finalized. When did you find it?"

"Yesterday. It was hidden at the bottom of Mum's jewelry box."

"I can't imagine what you must be thinking."

She stood up once again and stumbled round the coffee table to join me. She tried to grab my hands, but I pulled them away, then heaved myself along to the far end of the sofa.

"Don't," I said. "Please don't touch me. I just want the facts."

"Susan, I wanted to tell you, ever since you were a little girl. But I couldn't, could I? Patricia was your mum. She was bringing you up as her own daughter. It wasn't for me to rock the boat. It would've upset the whole family — your mum, your dad, your grandma and grandpa, Uncle Frank. And it would've confused you. I did what I thought was for the best. I went along with what everyone wanted."

"Then why didn't you tell me as soon as Mum died?"

"I thought about it, honest I did. But you were grieving. And then I found out you were in the family way. I didn't think you should have to cope with this, as well. And I would've had to tell Wendy and Chrissie. Uncle Frank knows. I told him before we got married. He had the collywobbles about going through with the wedding, but he stood by me in the end. I'm going to tell the girls as soon as they're back from wherever it is they've gone. Once they get used to the idea, they'll be over the moon you're their sister."

"I'm not interested in whether you tell them or not — that's a matter for you. All I want," I added, slowly and firmly, "is the truth about my birth."

From the hallway came the sound of a

telephone ringing. My aunt made as if to get up, then changed her mind. We both listened, wordlessly, waiting for the caller to hang up or for the answerphone to click in. Eventually it stopped. Aunt Sylvia cleared her throat.

"Susan, love, I was so young." So began the story of my birth. "I was only seventeen when I found out — still living at home. It was less than a year since I'd left school, and I'd only recently got my first job — in the tie department in Rackhams. I had all the boys after me, but I always went so far and no further. Other than that one time. When I realized I was pregnant, I was horrified. It felt like my life was ruined." She shook her head, as if to dislodge the memory.

"You could've had an abortion, if I was such a terrible mistake," I snapped. "You didn't *need* to bring an unwanted child into the world."

"Don't say 'unwanted.' It wasn't like that. I never once thought about a termination. It wasn't that I disapproved — I knew a couple of girls who'd done it and hadn't had any regrets, but for some reason I decided straightaway that I wasn't going down that road."

My baby was pressing uncomfortably on

463

my bladder. I shifted position on the slippery leather sofa.

"So how come you just gave me away?"

Aunt Sylvia flinched.

"When I started to show, I knew I couldn't keep it to myself any longer. The only person I could think of to tell was your mum. She was married to your dad by then, and living across the city, so we didn't see so much of each other. I met her at the Kardomah Café one Saturday during my lunch break. I was shaking like a leaf when I told her. I thought she'd go mad. She was fifteen years older than me, remember, so she was more than just a big sister. She was so understanding, though. She asked who the father was, and whether he'd do the right thing. I told her it was just someone I'd met at a dance — that I'd never seen him before or since. 'Everything'll be alright,' she said. 'I'll explain it all to Mum and Dad. Whatever they say, I'll stick by you.' "

Aunt Sylvia rose to fetch a gold tissue-box holder from the sideboard, while I tried to assimilate the fact that I was simply the by-product of a one-night stand. She settled back down on the sofa and dabbed the corners of her eyes, careful not to smudge her heavy makeup.

"I felt so guilty telling your mum, and putting all the worry on her, but she was true to her word. She came round to ours the next day, sat your grandma and grandpa at the kitchen table and just told them. Like it was nothing at all to worry about. Your grandma was blubbing and your grandpa looked like he was going to wallop me. Then they started saying things like, 'What're the neighbors going to think?', 'How're you going to support it?', 'How're you ever going to get a husband now?' I didn't have any answers. Your mum did, though. She must've bin thinking it all through. 'Am I right that you're not going to have any support from the father?'

" 'Yes,' I said. 'And am I right that you don't want this baby to ruin your life?'

" 'Well, yes,' I said. 'Then there's only one solution, Sylvia.' It was obvious where this was going. 'I can't just give it away to a stranger,' I told her. 'Not to a stranger. To me and Clive.' "

"Why would she do that? It was your mess, not hers. It's a big sacrifice to make, even for a sister."

"It wasn't a sacrifice for her. You see, your mum and dad had bin trying for a baby since they got married. There'd bin three pregnancies and three miscarriages one after the other. She felt like time was ticking. Your mum was in her thirties and she thought she wasn't going to be able to carry a baby herself. I think she decided it'd happened for a reason. I remember she'd got it all planned out. 'Sylvia can tell her boss she's going to stay with relatives for a while. She'll have to resign, but hopefully they'll take her back. She can go to Auntie Gladys's in Rhyl until the baby's born, then she can come back home as if nothing's happened. Nobody'll be any the wiser. And Clive and me can adopt the baby. That way we keep it in the family, and everyone's happy.' Your grandma and grandpa calmed down a bit after that. Two problems solved in one fell swoop, you see — your mum's childlessness and my unplanned pregnancy."

"Very neat and tidy. Everything swept under the carpet."

"Nobody even bothered asking me, love. They all just assumed I'd go along with it. So I did. I couldn't see any alternative. But the week after I gave birth to you, when your mum and dad came up to Rhyl, I didn't think I could hand you over. You were so beautiful. Your eyes were the bluest blue I'd ever seen, and the tufty hair on top of your head was the softest I'd ever felt. While they were nattering to Auntie Gladys, I wrapped you up in a shawl and tucked your little bunny next to you — I'd knitted it in the last month before you were born — and just held you and held you and held you."

My Bunnikins. It had always been my bedtime favorite; it was now wrapped in tissue paper in a shoebox at the bottom of my wardrobe. I'd always thought my mother had knitted it for me.

"When your mum and dad left, they took you with them. I've never cried so much in my life. I kept saying to myself, it wasn't as if you were gone forever. I could still see you whenever I wanted. I'd still be able to cuddle you and talk to you and watch you grow up."

Aunt Sylvia sniffed, took a deep breath and smiled at me. I turned away, toward the white marble mantelpiece. It was crammed with framed photographs of Aunt Sylvia, Uncle Frank, Wendy, Christine and the grandchildren. I noticed that, at the end nearest me, there was a small, heart-shaped silver frame containing a black-and-white photograph of a newborn baby. If it was Wendy or Christine, there would be an identical picture in a matching frame. There wasn't.

"Anyway, I stayed behind in Rhyl for a couple of weeks, until I'd got over the birth and looked almost back to normal. It all worked out just as your mum had planned. The neighbors knew nothing about it and Rackhams took me back. Your mum used to bring you to visit every week. At first it was hard, seeing you in her arms, and then having to say goodbye to you all over again. But then, I suppose, I just got used to it. You became Patricia's daughter, my niece."

"How convenient for you," I said, turning back to face my aunt. She flinched again, but continued with her story.

"Everyone was surprised when your mum became pregnant a year later, but we assumed it would end in miscarriage like the others. This time, though, she managed to carry the baby all the way. I've never seen her as happy as she was the day Edward arrived."

"I can imagine."

"To be honest, I was green with envy when I saw her with her little family. Eventually, I met Uncle Frank and had the twins, and the rest is history. I'm so sorry, Susan. I'm sorry your mum and dad never told you the truth. But you can see, can't you, that none of this was my fault? I just did what I was told. I wish things'd bin different, but you play with the hand you're dealt. Now that you know the truth, I won't have to pretend anymore. You're *my* girl now. You always will be."

The eyeliner and mascara were forming inky pools in the corners of Aunt Sylvia's eyes. She dabbed them again with a tissue.

"And what about my biological father? I need to know everything you remember about him."

Her expression changed from pitiful to fearful.

"I'll just have to gather my thoughts, love. I'm going to pop to the little girl's room. I'll be back in a jiffy."

I was beginning to feel claustrophobic; the ceilings of the lounge seemed too low, the carpet too thick, the air too heavy with perfume from the scent diffuser on a nearby card table. I struggled up, walked through the door to the conservatory and gazed through the window. The sky was steel gray, and there was a fine drizzle; the sort that seems little more than mist but drenches you in seconds. The branches of the trees were bare, and there were no signs of life in the sodden flowerbeds. I watched a solitary magpie land on the bird table, realize there was nothing for him and fly away. After a while, Aunt Sylvia appeared in the doorway, looking resigned.

"I'm getting myself a glass of sherry before

I carry on. Dutch courage. Can I get you one?"

"No, thank you," I said.

When she returned, carrying a crystal glass, she suggested we make ourselves comfy in the lounge again.

"I'd rather stay here."

"But it's so chilly. Never can get the orangery warm in the winter."

"I really don't care."

I eased myself into a wicker armchair, and Aunt Sylvia, reluctantly, did the same.

"So? What about my father?"

"Susan, I wasn't sure whether to tell you this. Nobody else knows but me — not even Uncle Frank. I could carry it with me to the grave if I wanted — it'd probably be easier for everyone if I did — but I'm going to tell you. You deserve to know the whole story. No more secrets, eh?"

Aunt Sylvia looked down at her hands and started twisting a large diamond-encrusted eternity ring round and round on her finger.

"Like I said, I was only seventeen at the time, although people used to say I seemed much older, 'cos of the way I dressed — you know, like a film star. I always looked up to your mum. She had it all — a husband, a house, a job, enough money to buy nice things. It's hard to remember, but your dad was an attractive man in those days. He was thirty-two, well-respected in his field — whatever that was — and very charming. The fact is, I had a bit of a soft spot for him. Of course, he was already drinking too much. Everyone knew that."

"He was an alcoholic."

"I know, love, but in those days he seemed like someone who just took it a bit too far, like Oliver Reed or Richard Harris. His drinking came across as rebellious, not weak and destructive like it was later. Nobody guessed how it would take him over."

"How is any of this relevant?"

There was a long pause. I could hear the faint tick of the ormolu carriage clock through the lounge door, and the buzz of a tractor in the distance.

"The evening in question we'd bin at a family wedding. It was cousin Shirley's — remember her? Lives in Australia now."

I nodded.

"It was on a Friday," she continued, "and I had to get up early for work the next day, so I decided not to stay to the end. Shirley said, why didn't your dad give me a lift home, then come back to the reception? He wasn't keen, because he was enjoying himself, but he'd just got a new car, which I think he quite fancied showing off, so in the end he agreed. He'd already had a few drinks, but people didn't bother so much in those days. On the way, he was joking with me, saying I looked like the Brigitte Bardot of Birmingham. When we got back to your grandparents' house, he decided he'd come in and have one for the road. He knew where my dad kept his whiskey."

"I don't know why you're telling me all this. I want to know about my biological father, not my adopted father."

"I'm getting there, love. I'm leading up to it." She picked up her sherry glass, took a sip, then carried on. "I was already feeling a bit tipsy. I didn't usually drink, but I'd had a couple of Babychams that night. I put a Tom Jones record on the gramophone and started dancing. Your dad got up and joined in. We were in fits of laughter at first, doing silly moves."

She took another sip from her glass, and I noticed that her hands were trembling. I had a sudden sense of where this was leading; I hoped against hope that I was wrong.

"Well, let's leave it at that." She sighed. "It was just the once. I regretted it straightaway, and I could tell he did, too. He left soon after and I didn't see him again for weeks. I never told him I was pregnant."

"No!"

"The only time he talked to me about it was after your mum had come up with the idea of adopting the baby. He turned up at my counter in Rackhams late one afternoon, shortly before I handed in my notice. All he said was, 'Is it mine?' I said, 'Yes,' and he said, 'I'm sorry.' That was it."

"Please God, no." I squeezed my eyes shut.

"The next day your mum phoned to say your dad had agreed to adopt the baby. She never knew he was your real dad. At least, *I* never said anything. I did sometimes wonder, over the years, whether your dad might've told her when he was drunk, but if he did she never let on. She'd banned anyone in the family — even me — from talking about the adoption. We all just acted like you were hers. You're the first person I've ever told." She knocked back the rest of her sherry and put the glass on the table. "You must see, Susan, none of it was my fault, or your dad's. He'd never shown any of that kind of interest in me before. It was just a few minutes of madness for both of us. I don't regret it now, though, because look at you. You're a wonderful girl, so clever and beautiful. I couldn't be more proud of you. And you're going to give me another grandchild. The only thing that makes me sad is thinking about what you had to go through with your dad's drinking. I know it was tough for you. It was tough for me, too, standing by and watching. If I could've taken you back I would've. But I couldn't."

Aunt Sylvia was finally silent. She appeared to be awaiting a reaction from me, but I was as incapable of responding to her as would be a statue carved from a block of ice. Her story of my conception resounded in my head like the edge of a glacier shearing off into the ocean. My blood was a frozen river; icicles of pain were piercing my head, jabbing behind my eyes, in the roots of my teeth. There was a sharp ringing in my ears, and it seemed that the air in the room was searing my lungs.

"You do understand, don't you, Susan? Say you do, love. Say you don't hold anything against me. I'm glad you found out, honest I am. This can be a brand-new start for all of us, now everything's out in the open."

She was pawing my arm and looking at me pleadingly.

"You've made the facts very clear to me." I shivered. "But please don't expect me to say you weren't to blame."

"Susan, you don't understand what it was

like in those days. It was still a shameful thing to be an unmarried mum. Maybe not so much in London, or among trendy, arty types, but where we were from, well, my parents wouldn't've bin able to live it down."

"I do know what it was like. I'm not stupid. But I also know what *you're* like. You've always been a flirt. You can't even say hello to a man without turning on the feminine charms. Everyone knows that. You were jealous of your sister, and you wanted what she'd got. You seduced my father when his self-control was undermined by drink, then were too spineless to face the consequences of your actions. Yes, I do understand. I understand completely."

"It wasn't like that at all, Susan."

I felt desperate to escape, to get away from this woman who didn't seem to have any awareness — not the slightest inkling — of what she'd done. I ignored her cry of self-pity and checked my watch; I'd been at the bungalow for almost two hours. With fortuitous timing the Big Ben chimes of the doorbell echoed from the hallway. I pushed myself out of the wicker chair and made my way through the lounge to the cloakroom. Aunt Sylvia tottered after me.

"Stay a bit longer, love. Let's talk some more."

"We've said everything there is to say to each other," I told her, as I wriggled into my too-small coat.

"But we haven't. We've barely started. Don't walk out on me like this. Ask Rob to come back a bit later. I'll make us a bite to eat."

I shook my head and pushed past her to the door.

"You did what you did. Every action has an equal and opposite reaction. You turned your back on me, and now I'm turning mine on you."

On the journey from Aunt Sylvia's to the station, Rob endeavored to establish from me why I'd ushered him straight back to the van as soon as I'd opened the front door, and why my aunt's face looked like melted candle wax. I told him we'd been going over family history. He clearly sensed there was more to it than that.

"I'm here when you feel ready to open up," he said.

He might have a long wait.

To avoid any further unwelcome references to what had happened at Aunt Sylvia's, I asked Rob about the garden he'd visited that morning. He was still describing it in mind-numbing detail when we reached the outskirts of Birmingham.

Rob switched off the van's engine in the multistory car park and turned to me in the gloom.

"Susan, before you go I've got a proposition to make. This mightn't be the greatest timing, but 'he who hesitates is lost,' as they say. And after what happened last night I feel I'm on firmer ground."

"Nothing happened last night, other than that we slept in proximity to each other. To be more accurate, you slept and I tossed and turned."

"Alright, but listen. You know I've been doing a lot of thinking since I met up with Alison. It's as if I've had blinkers on for months, and now I've finally taken them off. I can see the whole picture."

"I don't have much time, Rob. Can you get to the point please?"

"Okay, right." He took a deep breath. "Well, you know I told you I'm toying with the idea of relocating to London and merging my business with my mate's?"

"Yes."

"Well, what do you think about us moving in together?"

"What on earth are you talking about?"

"We can rent at first, if you're worried about the commitment. You must've worked out what I feel about you, and I've been getting the message that you feel the same. Disregard the fact that we've only known each other properly for a few months — when something's right it's right. We're very different, but we complement each other. You know the saying, 'The whole's greater than the sum of its parts'? That's us. You'd be good for me and, well, I'd be *fantastic* for you. And at our age why waste any more time?"

This was the last thing I needed; I already felt under siege, bombarded, almost overwhelmed by wave after wave of assault on my psyche. I wasn't sure how much more I could take. Far from making plans to share my life with someone, all I wanted was to get home, lock the door, switch off my phone and shut out the world. Recent events had proved what I'd known all along; other people couldn't be trusted.

"That's a ludicrous idea," I said, fumbling in my haste to unfasten my seat belt.

"I know, but what the hell?"

"Why do you think I'd want to live with you, when I've never, ever had any desire to share my life with anyone? I enjoy my own company, I value my independence, I like doing things my way. I don't want some great lumbering man messing up my house and getting under my feet. And you're wrong to assume, just because we seem to get on with each other, that I have other sorts of feelings for you. I have a train to catch in fifteen minutes. I really don't need this, Rob."

With difficulty, I bent, grabbed my handbag from the foot well and thrust open the van door.

"I notice you haven't actually said 'no,' though."

"No. Under no circumstances. Absolutely not. Is that clear enough for you?"

■ ■ ■ ■

MARCH

■ ■ ■ ■

25

I should be celebrating the fact that I'm on maternity leave — no more wedging my colossal belly into packed commuter trains, no more suffering my colleagues' infuriating tics and inane chatter, ample time to pursue my own interests — but I find myself in a state of limbo; I'm unable to think how to fill each endless, empty day. This month, if all goes well, I'll become the mother of a baby daughter. I believe the appropriate feeling is one of nervous anticipation, but I'm barely thinking about it. How can I contemplate what lies ahead when I'm ensnared by the past?

It's only in recent days that I've reached the depths of this all-engulfing despondence. The morning after my return from Birmingham I had, in fact, woken with rekindled spirit. I was angry, fired up. It was time to take back control. I'd deliver the deathblow in my court case, get the house and contents sold, and move on with my life, free of any remaining ties to my family and the past. Clean, clinical and quick.

I sent the witness statement to Margaret, who signed and returned it within a couple of days, then I fired off emails to Mr. Brinkworth and to my brother's solicitors, Lawson, Lowe & Co. I attached copies of the most damning pages of the medical notes (the ones referring to my mother's diagnosis and its debilitating symptoms) and of the statements by Aunt Sylvia and Margaret. I told Mr. Brinkworth that my evidence proved it had been negligence of the worst possible kind for him to take my mother's instructions without seeking confirmation from a doctor that she knew what she was doing. I said that validity was no longer an issue; a will written by an elderly lady with vascular dementia could never stand up to the court's scrutiny.

In my other email, I pointed out to Lawson, Lowe & Co. that the medical records showed their client had been fully aware of my mother's diagnosis, and so would have known she was vulnerable to pressure from him. He'd kept that information secret. In light of my evidence the court would be highly suspicious of a will that conferred a benefit on Edward greater than that which was conferred on his sister. I demanded that both Mr. Brinkworth and Lawson, Lowe & Co. stop playing games and concede defeat. I was supremely confident they would do so. My evidence had demolished their case. I congratulated myself; it was a job well-done on my part. If anyone thought I'd sit back and let events unfold — that I'd allow myself to be a victim of other people's negligence or treachery — they had made a very grave miscalculation.

I was almost tempted to phone Trudy to ask if I could return to work and carry on as normal until I went into labor. I don't see the point of finishing three weeks before the due date; it gives your mind too much freedom to wander onto hazardous terrain. It would be humiliating going back to the office, though, after the disproportionate fuss that was made on my departure. Trudy had wanted to organize a maternity leave send-off at the Thai restaurant across the road, but I told her I'd derive no pleasure from such an event. My intention was to walk out through the swing doors on my last day of work as though it was a normal Friday evening.

I became suspicious when, at five o'clock on the day in question, tables were pushed to one side and bottles of wine appeared from my colleagues' bags. Contrary to my request, Trudy had planned a surprise drinks party. I smiled politely while she burbled on about how the office would descend into anarchy without me, how they would miss my wry sense of humor, how the baby would have the most efficiently organized life of any baby, ever. There were toasts and numerous gifts, which I was cajoled into opening in front of everyone. Trudy's gift was a breast pump and a packet of breast pads ("I used to leak milk everywhere in the first few weeks," she said, much to the obvious disgust of Tom). Tom's own gift was a Babygro with *Straight Outta Compton* on the front ("Thought it was your era," he said with a smirk). Lydia's confidence-boosting gift was a DVD instructing me how to get my body back in six weeks ("You used to have such a lovely figure"). Inevitably, I was bullied into making a speech myself. I managed to dredge up some seemingly heartfelt words; I'd been to enough of Trudy's own maternity-leave-dos to know the score.

Once the public mortification had ended, I made my escape. I'm sure no one noticed, just as, despite their declarations to the contrary, no one will notice my absence for the next six months. Annoyingly, I had to bear the far-from-inconsiderable expense of a cab all the way home to Clapham; not only was I grappling with gift bags decorated with various species of baby animal, I also had a large cardboard box under my arm into which were packed my cacti. I didn't trust any of my colleagues to look after them; no doubt they would drench them, completely disregarding the fact that such plants have evolved to thrive in arid conditions.

I'd expected the defendants' surrender to be immediate. As the days passed, however, I began to feel a little less bullish. On the first morning of my maternity leave, I received the two emails I'd been waiting for. I sat in the armchair with my laptop, put my swollen feet up on the casket and opened the first one, from Lawson, Lowe & Co.:

We have taken your brother's instructions on your recent email and attached documents. Our client freely admits that he has always been fully aware of your mother's diagnosis, which she asked him not to disclose to any other parties, including family members. We have recently interviewed Mr. Shafiq, your mother's consultant. He will confirm that, whilst her condition affected some of her day-to-day activities in minor ways, it didn't affect her ability to understand the extent of her estate, the act of making a will or the claims to which she should give effect. This testimony puts the medical records in context and defeats your claim of lack of mental capacity on the part of your mother.

We are also in the process of drawing up a witness statement by the Reverend Jeremy Withers, who contacted our client to inform him that you are not the biological daughter of Mrs. Green. I note that you have omitted to disclose this fact, despite it being highly relevant to your mother's reason for making the will. As well as giving evidence about your relationship to Mrs. Green, Reverend Withers will testify to the fact that she was concerned about how our client would cope after her death, particularly in view of their close bond: a further reason for making the will.

In all the circumstances, we have advised our client that he is in a strong position. He will therefore continue to resist your claim robustly.

The second email was from Mr. Brinkworth:

The fact that the medical records show your mother had vascular dementia does nothing to alter my position: it was not incumbent on me to seek medical advice before drafting your mother's will, because there was nothing in her behavior to suggest that she was not fully aware of what she was doing. Your brother's solicitors have now informed me of the new evidence that has come to light, from which it is clear that your claim cannot succeed. I am caught in the middle of what amounts to a dispute between your brother and yourself concerning your mother's true wishes. I would urge you one last time to reach a compromise with him to put an end to these misconceived proceedings.

I reread the two emails. It was as if I'd played a seven-letter word in Scrabble, only to find that my opponent can not only do the same, but can use a triple-word-score square. I hadn't reckoned on my mother's own consultant downplaying the impact of her symptoms and attesting to her competence. Neither had I reckoned on my adoption — which I'd thought was known only to the vicar, Aunt Sylvia, Uncle Frank and me — being dragged into the proceedings. I could imagine how Edward must have felt when he was told I was adopted; how he must have chuckled with glee and rubbed his palms together. I'm sure he felt vindicated, not only with regard to my mother's will, but with regard to everything he's ever said or done to me.

That bloody vicar. Did he really believe he was behaving ethically by telling Edward, or was he just trying to cause mischief? Either way, it had devastated my case. I thought about what Brigid had told me — "an irrational disposition can rebut the presumption of capacity." The fact that my mother had appeared to have no reason to favor Edward would have put doubt in the minds of the court concerning her competence to make a will. Now there *was* a possible reason. For the first time, it occurred to me that perhaps my mother's giving Edward the right to remain in the family home hadn't, in fact, been an act of dementia-induced irrationality. She'd fully intended to benefit him over me.

I didn't bother getting dressed that day. I lay on the sofa watching mindless television programs, flicking from channel to channel in an effort to find something to numb my senses. My breath was shallow and my heart was racing. I realized that the focusing of my energies on winning the court case had served to distract me from other, less welcome, thoughts. They started crowding in.

"And ye shall know the truth and the truth shall set you free." That was what the vicar had called to me as I hurried from the vestry. Some verse from the Gospel of John. I beg to differ with the venerable saint. I know the truth now. I know that I was an embarrassing mistake, the outcome of a transitory, meaningless encounter between two people who had no feelings for each other. I know that my biological mother cared so little about me that she was pre-pared to give me away; that, for the woman who I believed was my mother, I was a consolation prize, a stopgap, just in case a real son or daughter didn't come along; that I was tricked, fooled, lied-to by my family for my entire childhood, my entire life. And does the truth make me feel free? It does not. I feel imprisoned by it, defined by it. I was never who I believed I was; far from being the protagonist in my own story I've simply been a minor character in someone else's.

I haven't left the flat for a week; the spring sunshine seems too bright and the noise from the streets too clamorous. I had my grocery shopping delivered today, so I wouldn't have to venture out. Not that I'm eating much. Kate keeps knocking on my door to ask if I'm okay. I tell her I'm worn-out, that the late stages of pregnancy are taking their toll and I need to rest. She's offered to come and sit with me, but I haven't let her beyond the front door. I'd rather she didn't see the flat; I haven't bothered tidying, or cleaning — or even showering — for days. She doesn't know I was the product of an affair between my father and aunt, or that I've been outplayed in the court case. I don't want to talk about either, but I can think about nothing else.

Rob's been bothering me, too, telephoning every day. I've told him not to waste his time. I have no news, nothing to say to him. Just the once, he referred to his feelings for me and to the stupid idea of our moving in together. I told him if he mentioned it again I'd stop taking his calls. He says he'll drop the subject for now. He won't seem to go away, though. Aunt Sylvia's been telephoning as well, alternating between landline and mobile. I don't pick up. In fact, I'm so sick of deleting her answerphone messages that I've unplugged the machine. I don't need it.

I have no idea why Aunt Sylvia's keen to make contact. The whole pregnancy-and-baby thing must have been such an inconvenience to her. No doubt her main concern, when she was carrying me, was that her figure might be permanently ruined. If she'd kept me, I'd have been nothing more than an embarrassment; I'd have cramped her style and ruined her chances of getting a good husband. I don't suppose she had a moment's regret after she handed me over to my mother and father. What a relief it must have been to get back to her single, unencumbered life, free to flirt and flaunt herself. I bet she's hardly thought about our true relationship since. In fact, knowing how vacuous and self-absorbed she is, I wouldn't be surprised if she'd completely forgotten she gave birth to me until I reminded her.

I've been spending a lot of time looking again at the photograph albums I brought back from my mother's house. The image of my christening — where my mother looks awkward, Aunt Sylvia looks distant, most of the guests look grim — it makes sense now. They were all acting out their parts, going through the motions. The albums contain hardly any other photographs of me as a baby, just a couple of my mother holding me, stiffly, on what looks like a park bench, and one of my father cradling me in his arms. My mother isn't smiling in either of the pictures. Why not? After all, it was her idea to adopt me. Maybe she found the demands of new-motherhood harder than she'd anticipated, or perhaps she had difficulty bonding with a baby that wasn't her own. My father, on the other hand, looks almost happy. I expect it was because he'd got away with it. He'd managed to pass on his genes to the next generation, and no blame had attached to him. In fact, he'd have been hailed as a saint for taking on someone else's child.

Not surprisingly, there are numerous photographs of my brother as a baby: Edward naked on a blanket; Edward in the arms of his grandma; Edward in his pram, his cot, his pushchair — later in his high chair, on his tricycle, holding his favorite teddy. Sometimes I'm there in the background. Occasionally I'm the subject of the photograph, too, but squeezed into the edge of the frame as an afterthought. My mother was the main photographer of the family — the sole one as my father's drinking escalated. The ratio of pictures of Edward to pictures of me says everything that needs to be said. I wonder how I could have failed to notice it before.

■ ■ ■ ■

I started the court proceedings to fight for justice, fairness — to secure for myself what I believed my mother would have wanted me to have. I realize, now, that that wasn't what the case was about. What I wanted was to prove that Edward and I were equal in my mother's eyes. I wanted a judge to pronounce in open court that she wouldn't, if she'd been in her right mind, have favored my brother. Of course, I always knew she cared for Edward more than for me; the evidence was plain for anyone to see. Sometimes, though, self-preservation causes us to look away.

My mother worried that Edward had inherited a genetic weakness of character from my father; that he'd descend into alcoholism or drug addiction without her perpetual vigilance. She said it was our duty to protect him. I wonder whether, if my mother had known that I also share my father's genes, she would have worried about me, too. I doubt it. She considered me to be entirely free of any kind of emotional frailty or vulnerability. She never bothered to look closely enough. I suspect, now, that the reason she never revealed that

I was adopted was that she thought I'd abandon Edward to his fate if I knew he wasn't my brother. The ongoing deception was a desperate attempt to ensure that there was someone to look out for her son after her death.

I used to think that what distinguished Edward's experience of childhood from my own was the way in which we responded to my father's drinking. I'm sure an amateur psychologist would claim that it caused me to be serious beyond my years, to want to be in complete control of my life, to judge myself — and others — harshly. Equally, they would claim that it caused Edward to be impulsive, irresponsible, needy. I suspect that such an analysis might be more accurate than I'm prepared to admit. But I'm not sure, now, that that was the only distinguishing feature. I think that what set my childhood apart from Edward's was that I was never loved, and my brother was.

Enough. I've come to a decision. I get out my laptop and write two emails: one to Mr. Brinkworth and one to Edward's solicitors. I suggest a meeting, on neutral territory. It should take place as soon as possible, in view of my impending due date. I shower, wash my hair, dress and waddle down to the high street to buy milk and bread. When I get back, I load the dishwasher and fill the washing machine, then spend time straightening my flat. Finally, when order is restored, I empty a cardboard box from the cupboard under the stairs and put the casket containing my mother's ashes inside it. I screw up balls of newspaper, which I pack tightly into the gaps. I seal it, round and round, with almost a whole roll of parcel tape, then write Edward's name and the address of our family home on the top in black marker pen. I go online and book a courier company to collect it. It wouldn't be appropriate for me to hold on to my mother's ashes. She would have wanted them to be with her son. It's regrettable, but it's no great loss. The casket will never be more than a footstool to me.

26

I pour a glass of water from the carafe that has been placed in the middle of the conference table, take a sip, then unzip my portfolio. I'm beginning to wish I hadn't arrived at the mediator's office so early. I thought I'd gain a tactical advantage by doing so — I could choose the best place to sit, and would have time to organize myself before Edward arrived — but as I wait I can feel my nervousness intensifying. Nonsensical. There's no reason to be anxious; I know exactly what I'm going to say.

I've been suffering from chronic heartburn since I woke this morning. I decided to skip breakfast, but I'm regretting my decision. The sound of my rumbling stomach is thunderous. As well as this simultaneous hunger and sickness, I'm experiencing uncomfortable tightening sensations across my belly. They started the day before yesterday. I've read all about them: Braxton Hicks contractions — practice contractions — the body's way of preparing for what it'll have to do in the next few days. I want this meeting to be over and to be safely back home.

I look around the characterless meeting room: long blond wood conference table with a dozen matching chairs at regularly spaced intervals; thick, green carpet, which deadens sound and makes the room feel cocooned. On the table, as well as the carafe, there are glasses, notepads and pens laid out in front of each chair. Rather excessive. There'll only be four of us: the mediator, Edward, his solicitor and me. It was Mr. Brinkworth who suggested this particular firm of solicitors to act as mediators. He's seen them at work before and was impressed. He said, however, that there was nothing to be gained by his own presence at the meeting. If an agreement is reached between Edward and me he is, without admitting negligence, prepared to draw up the consent order and bear his own costs. His offer to take a financial hit indicates to me that he feels, at least partially, responsible for this mess.

At just after eleven o'clock the door opens and in puffs a well-groomed Asian man with a glossy, Conker Brown attaché case. He's followed by Edward, who's carrying a dog-eared, tea-stained cardboard folder. My brother looks awkward, out of place in the professional environment. Yet again he's wearing the ensemble that's become his outfit of choice for formal occasions: black jeans, shirt and suit jacket; metal-tipped bootlace tie; and black cowboy boots. I can smell the unmistakable fragrance of eau de pub that precedes him wherever he goes.

"Hey, sis," he says, affecting a saunter as he follows his companion to the opposite side of the table. "Oh, hang on a minute, I can't call you that anymore. How're you doing, Suze? Not long to go, I see."

He practiced his opening lines on the journey here; I can tell.

"Very well," I say. "Thank you for your concern."

"I'm Mr. Green's solicitor, Sajid Iqbal," says the dapper man. He leans across the table with his hand extended. "I know you haven't got legal representation, Miss Green, but don't feel at a disadvantage. I'm just here to listen and take notes, and to offer my client advice if he wants it."

"I can assure you, I don't feel at a disadvantage."

"Well, this is all very nice, isn't it?" says Edward, pushing his chair back from the table, stretching out his legs and knitting

500

his fingers together behind his head. This manifest nonchalance used to annoy me, but I can now see it for what it is — an act. He feels as awkward as I do. I notice how much older he looks under the room's harsh lighting; how gray his hair is becoming at the temples, how lines radiate from the corners of his eyes. Being a full-time party animal takes its toll.

The door opens again and the mediator comes in — a woman in her late fifties wearing a dove-gray trouser suit and crisp white shirt. Her immaculately styled blond hair is in a French pleat. She sits down at the head of the table, puts on the pair of bifocal glasses that are hanging on a gold chain round her neck and opens her file.

"Good morning, everyone. I'm Marion Coombes. I'll be acting as your mediator today. I prefer an informal atmosphere, so I suggest we use first names. Is everyone in agreement? Good. I should begin by explaining it's not my role to pass judgment on the rights and wrongs of the case, but simply to open up channels of communication between the parties with the aim of finding common ground. I've looked at the papers, and I'm hopeful that a compromise can be reached before the close of business. I'd like to begin by briefly summarizing the facts of the case, then each party can have their say."

She looks down at the notes in front of her.

"I see that Susan and Edward are the daughter and son of the late Patricia Green. Under the will, Edward has a life interest in the family home. Susan claims that the will is invalid — Edward and the executor refute that. Evidence and witness statements have been served by all sides and stalemate has been reached. The next stage is a full court hearing. Is that correct?"

I nod. Edward and Mr. Iqbal exchange whispers.

"Just in the interests of accuracy," says Edward, running a nicotine-stained fingernail along the wood grain of the conference table, "Susan isn't my mum's daughter — she's adopted. She isn't biologically related to us."

"Ah, yes," says Ms. Coombes. "Reverend Withers raises that issue in his statement. Do you wish to respond, Susan?"

I can feel another practice-contraction coming on. It's as if a wide belt's been placed around my abdomen and is being yanked tighter and tighter. I try to breathe steadily and rhythmically, to ride the wave. It subsides.

"Yes, I'm adopted," I say, "but I wasn't aware of the fact until very recently. I'd like to add, though, also in the interests of accuracy, that I *am* biologically related to my mother — Mrs. Green — and to my brother."

"How d'you work that one out?" Edward asks.

"Aunt Sylvia was my birth mother. So Mum was my biological aunt as well as my adopted mother."

"Aunt Sylvia's your mum? You're having me on."

"Do I look like I am?"

"Well, I can't see the family resemblance, personality-wise, but I'll take your word for it. One day you're my sister, the next day you're no relation at all and now you're my cousin. This is a bit of a roller-coaster ride for me."

He laughs nervously and surveys the room. No one else is laughing.

"There's another twist in the track. Or maybe a switchback. I am your sister."

"Meaning?"

"Meaning we've got the same father."

"What, Dad and Aunt Sylvia? Now you really *are* taking the piss. He always used to say what an airhead she was. Silly Sylvie. There's no way he would've done the business with her."

"I can assure you, I wouldn't make up something like this. If you don't believe me, you can phone Aunt Sylvia."

Ms. Coombes and Mr. Iqbal have been scribbling away.

"Well," says Ms. Coombes, looking up from her notes. "We've had some very interesting disclosures here, though we've yet to see where they take us. It seems, Edward, that Susan is your cousin and natural half sister, as well as being your adopted sister. Do you accept what she's told you?"

"I suppose so." Edward seems wrong-footed. I notice he has a twitch in his left eye. He rubs it with his fist. "Yeah, okay. I'm not sure what to make of it, but okay. It doesn't really affect anything, though. I mean, she still wasn't my mum's real daughter. Sorry, Suze, but that's just how it is."

"You're right, Edward. I wasn't her real daughter." I turn to Ms. Coombes. "There's something I want to say before we waste any more time. Is that alright?"

"Yes, certainly. There are no rules of procedure here. Go ahead."

I address my brother again.

"Edward, I'm going to be completely open. This is hard for me, and it'll be the one and only time I say this to you — or probably to anyone — so listen carefully. When I found out I was adopted, I was shattered. I'm prepared to admit that. It was like a hammer had smashed my recollection of our childhood into fragments. I was overwhelmed with uncertainty. But after a while I came to realize that that was what needed to happen, that it was long overdue. I spent days going over past thoughts, feelings and events. In trying to piece everything back together again I had to examine every memory to see how it fitted into the new picture. I looked with a fresh perspective at my relationship with Dad and Mum — even with you. There are things about Dad's behavior toward us that I'd tried for years to avoid thinking about. I don't need to tell you what — you know yourself. As far as Mum's concerned, I saw it clearly — that she'd never loved me in the same way she loved you."

Edward purses his lips and shakes his head. I ignore him and continue.

"It forced me to think again about what she would've wanted to happen after she died. I still believe I'm right — that Mr. Brinkworth should've obtained a doctor's opinion before he drafted the will of someone with dementia, and that you pressurized, or at least influenced, Mum to make a will. If I wanted to, I could carry on with the court case to try to prove that. But I've come to the conclusion that, despite my belief about the lack of validity of the will, its contents are probably not inconsistent with what she would've wanted. She was fully aware that you're incapable of looking after your own affairs . . ."

"Thanks, Suze."

". . . and she would've wanted you to have a secure place to live after she died, even if it meant I never received my inheritance. I haven't come here to negotiate. I've come to tell you my decision. I've decided that I'm not going to pursue the court case any further. You can stay in the house for as long as you like — for the rest of your life if you want. My only condition is that you pay your own legal costs. I'm not going to be out-of-pocket because of other people's dubious conduct. You can tell Mr. Brinkworth to draw up a consent order and I'll sign it."

My brother is silent. I can't read his expression. I'd expected a whoop of delight.

"This means you've won, Edward, in case you didn't understand what I said. You've got what you wanted."

"Well, that's a very constructive move on

Susan's part," says Ms. Coombes. "I wasn't expecting such a significant concession so early on. Edward, would you like to discuss this settlement offer with your solicitor before you respond?"

Edward leans forward and puts his elbows on the table.

"No need. I haven't come here to parley either. First things first — I want to say again, Suze — I didn't put any pressure on Mum to write a will. I know you'll never believe me, because you've always had me down as some kind of crook, but just use your common sense. If I was going to go to all the effort of forcing her to make a will, don't you think I would've made sure I got the lot, instead of just the right to live in the house plus a half share when I move out? Did that never occur to you? But, the main thing you should know, Suze, is that I never even *wanted* to stay in the house after Mum died. I only moved back in in the first place because she needed somebody to help her. I hate the fucking place."

Mr. Iqbal coughs politely.

"Sorry for the language," Edward said to Ms. Coombes. "But that house has got too many bad memories. When I'm there, I feel dragged down. Not only that, it's way too big for me. I can't stand the poxy neighbors, always telling me to turn my music down at night. And there's a massive garden to maintain. I hate gardening. And also, by the way, even if I did want to live there — which I don't — I can't afford to. The council tax is sky-high and the heating bills are astronomical. I've seen a brilliant studio flat in the center of town, where you pay a maintenance charge and you don't need to do anything to it. I'm planning on selling up, using my half of the proceeds to buy the flat, then renting it out while I go traveling for a couple of years. I need to get away. I need some sun. I'm thinking southeast Asia. The rent'll pay all my expenses. I went to see the estate agents a couple of days ago, and they've already been to take photos. They say it's a highly sought-after area for families 'cos of the good local schools. I should be abroad before the start of summer."

He leans back in his chair again.

"So actually, Suze, *you've* won."

This isn't what I was expecting. It takes me a few moments to grasp what Edward's said. My wait is almost over — I'll have my inheritance. It makes no sense to me, though.

"If you hate the house so much why did you tell me you wanted to carry on living there? Why didn't you agree to put it up for sale straightaway? Why have you been opposing the court proceedings?"

"I dunno. Habit, I suppose. We've always fought. It's what we do. When I saw how angry you were with me about the will, it got me riled. You wound me up with all your crazy allegations. The harder you attacked me the more you made me dig in my heels. I wanted to rub your nose in it. It's your own fault. If you'd been nice about it all in the first place we wouldn't be here today. You would've got what you wanted months ago."

"That's beyond ridiculous. I wouldn't have thought even *you* would behave in such a juvenile manner. We've wasted all this time and effort and money just because you wanted to score points?"

Edward laughs.

"We've had some fun, though, haven't we, Suze?"

"Well, this is very unusual," says Ms. Coombes. "I don't think I've been involved in a case like this before, where both sides have so readily conceded defeat. So, let me summarize the position. Edward, you're going to vacate the family home and put it on the market. Under the terms of your mother's will that means the proceeds of sale will then be divided between the two of you. The court proceedings will be terminated by an application to the Chancery Division for a consent order. All parties to bear their own costs. Are you both in agreement?"

The mediator looks from one side of the table to the other.

"I can't believe Edward's pushed it this far, but yes, that's fine by me," I say. An understatement. It's more than fine.

"Fine by me, too," Edward says.

"Thank you all for your levelheaded and practical approach to today's meeting, which has resulted in a very satisfactory outcome all round. Good morning, everyone."

Ms. Coombes picks up her file, rises and leaves the room with a gracious parting nod of her head.

"Easiest morning's work she's ever had," Edward says, standing and stretching. His nervousness has dissipated. He looks relaxed, content. "Thanks, mate," he adds, turning to Mr. Iqbal and shaking his hand. "Sorry you didn't have much to do, but I needed you here in case she tried to pull a fast one. You never know with my sister." He winks at me.

Mr. Iqbal says he can just about make the one o'clock train back to Birmingham. After snapping shut his attaché case, and swiftly polishing finger marks from it with the sleeve of his coat, he hurries out. Edward loiters, watching me putting my papers away in my portfolio.

"So . . ." he says.

"So?"

"So when's the baby due?"

"Yesterday."

"Bloody hell. No wonder you're the size of an elephant."

"Thanks."

"No offense."

I feel another tightening of my belly, stronger than before. I breathe in, pause, then breathe out. Breathe in, pause, breathe out. It takes a while to pass.

"Are you stuck? Can you get out of that chair alright?"

"Of course I can."

I struggle up, using the edge of the table for support. We walk out of the solicitors' offices and take the lift together down to the ground floor. There's an awkward silence. As we step into the marble-floored lobby Edward touches the sleeve of my coat.

"You know, Suze, you're wrong. She did love you, too. Why would she leave you half of everything if she didn't? You and Mum just had a different sort of relationship. To

511

be frank, I was jealous of the way she treated you — like an equal. It's not as much fun as you might think, always being cast in the role of the irresponsible child. She knew you didn't need her help — your life was always going to turn out fine."

"That's not the way I see things. But we'll never know. I don't always find it easy to work out people's motivations."

"Join the club."

We've descended the steps to the pavement outside the office building. We hesitate.

"Well, good luck with the birth and everything."

It feels unnatural, contrived, but I say it, anyway. "Thanks. Good luck with the traveling."

This is it. This is the moment I say goodbye to my brother and we go our separate ways, never to trouble each other again. But it seems that that isn't to be.

"Oh, no," I gasp.

It starts as a warm trickle, quickly becomes a stream, then a gush. It lands on the pavement between my legs, splashing my shoes.

"You're kidding me. Is that what I think it is?"

"Oh, hell." All I can do is stand there looking at the puddle I've created.

"What do we do?"

"I don't know."

"Are you having the baby?"

"I don't know."

"You must know. Are you having contractions?"

"I've been having them for a couple of days, mild ones. They're getting stronger, though."

"Okay, let's not panic. People do this all the time. I've got the VW parked a couple of minutes away. I'll give you a lift to the hospital."

He takes my arm and we step over the puddle, which is beginning to trickle toward the curb.

"Just one thing . . ."

"Yes?"

"If you give birth in my car I'll be deducting the cost of a full valet from your share of the estate."

27

While I'm trying to reach Kate on the phone, Edward relishes his part in the unfolding drama, delighted to have an excuse to overtake other vehicles on the inside lane, jump traffic lights and make liberal use of his horn. At one point, he leans out of the window and yells abuse at an elderly woman on a pedestrian crossing, telling her to get a bloody move on as his sister's about to give birth in his car. Formerly, I'd have been both furious and humiliated at finding myself at the mercy of Edward, but — really — what's the point?

My contractions have switched up a gear since we set off. The sensation is unpleasant, rather than agonizing; more like bad backache, combined with stomach cramps and period pain. As each one floods over me, my bump becomes hard as rock. I can cope easily, with steady breathing. I'm in control.

On my third attempt to call her, Kate finally picks up the phone. She says she'll whizz the kids over to a friend's house and meet me at the hospital with my maternity folder and overnight bag, which I've had packed and ready for at least a month. When the call is ended, I use my phone to time the contractions. They're roughly every five and a half minutes, and last about thirty seconds.

"Slow down," I tell Edward. "I'm not quite at the rush-to-hospital stage. There's a while yet before the baby arrives."

"Are you sure?" His foot eases off the accelerator a little.

"Believe me, Edward, I wouldn't lie. You delivering my baby is not part of my birth plan."

"Phew. Well, we can take a little detour, then. There's a record shop near here that I've been meaning to have a nose around."

I tell him to forget it. I have no intention of sitting in the car, bored and uncomfortable, while he spends hours drooling over rare vinyl. In response, he swerves round a right-hand corner much too fast. I lean toward him, then grab the edges of my seat to steady myself. He pouts for the rest of the journey.

■ ■ ■ ■

By the time we manage to find a space in the patients' car park, I'm finding the discomfort more of a challenge. A contraction of unexpected intensity hits me as we cross the busy foyer area of the hospital; I stop and grab Edward's arm.

"Er, that actually hurts," he says.

"Same here."

When the moment has passed, we join the queue for the lift, and just about make it down the long corridor to the birth unit before the next contraction strikes. I clutch Edward's arm again as he explains the situation to the woman behind the desk. A dark-haired midwife, who introduces herself, with a Spanish accent, as Claudia, leads us to a small room and asks me to make myself comfy on the bed. Edward slumps onto a chair in the corner, relieved to be handing me into someone else's care. Once Claudia has timed my contractions and taken my pulse, temperature and blood pressure, I explain my birth plan to her. Completely natural: no medical interference, no artificial pain relief and no other drugs, under *any* circumstances. I know how doctors and midwives like to take charge, and I'm determined to avoid a cascade of intervention. She smiles to herself as she makes notes. Next, she asks me to change into a hospital gown, after which she'll feel my bump and give me an internal examination. I tell Edward to wait outside.

"It's fine for your birth partner to stay, if you'd like him to," she says.

"He's not my birth partner, he's my brother."

"Perhaps not, then. It's lovely to see a brother supporting his sister, though."

She kneads my abdomen, then uses her fingers — without even looking — to check how far my cervix has dilated. Three centimeters, she tells me. I've got a long way to go. She'll pop back to see how I'm getting on. Edward returns as I'm having another contraction. I hold on to his arm once more and breathe steadily. In the distance, I can hear a woman screaming, and another making mooing noises. I have no intention of behaving in such a manner. I've always been very good with pain. Whenever I grazed my knee as a child, I would find the first-aid box, clean my own wound and apply a plaster. Edward, in the same situation, would be squealing for his mummy.

"Funny, me helping you when you're in

childbirth, after all we've been through," my brother says when I let go of his arm.

"I'm finding it hysterical."

"I've missed you, you know, in a strange sort of way."

"That's hard to believe."

"I have, as a matter of fact. Mum was the glue that held us together. I've been thinking in the last couple of months that, now that she's gone, we might never see each other again. And when I think that, I feel a bit, you know, kind of sad. Who am I going to argue with, if not my own sister?"

"I'm sure you'll have no problem finding someone. And by the way, not all siblings fight. It doesn't have to be like that."

"I know, but we never stood much chance from the start. We were preprogrammed to fight, with Mum fussing over me nonstop and you being such a daddy's girl."

"I was *never* a daddy's girl. He treated us equally badly."

"It was obvious you were the apple of his eye, though. You were academic, like him, and quiet and thoughtful and well behaved. I was a troublemaker, as far as he was concerned. I could never compete with Miss Goody Two-shoes."

"He wasn't bothered about either of us, Edward. All he cared about was where his next drink was coming from."

"Seems we remember things differently yet again. But truth is subjective — everyone has their own versions. Maybe both of ours are equally valid."

Uncharacteristically deep for my brother.

"Perhaps," I say. "But my truth is just a little bit more valid than yours."

After the next contraction, I tell Edward he's played his part by conveying me to the hospital; there's no point him hanging around. He says he doesn't think he should leave, that I need someone with me.

"Alright," I say. "But only until Kate arrives, absolutely no longer."

"Great. I'll just shoot outside for a quick ciggie, and be back before the next contraction."

He isn't. I bend over, clench my teeth and grip handfuls of sheet. I'm not going to make a noise. I'm *really* not. Women's bodies are designed for childbirth, so the pain can't be more than we can bear. Mind over matter. As the contraction ebbs away again, I notice, through the small window on the other side of the room, that it's dark already. I feel alone. Edward's right, I need someone to help me through this. I don't want to do it all by myself.

It goes without saying that I want my friend Kate here with me; she'll be a calm, capable, reassuring presence. Not only that, she's been through it before, she knows the score. I can't stop thinking about Rob, though. I know he won't be much use in practical terms, but he makes me smile, in spite of myself. I think of all he's done for me over the last few months: helping with my mother's belongings, storing furniture, driving me around, looking after me when I was devastated by the news of my adoption, phoning and texting me when I couldn't sleep, being steadfast, despite my coolness toward him and despite Edward's disapproval. I wonder whether I've ever thanked him for any of it. It's obvious to me now: I want him by my side through this, and afterward, too. It's not exactly a revelation. I suppose I've known for a long time, but I didn't want to admit that I, just like everyone else, might be subject to such irrational feelings, feelings that shave away your outer layer of protection and render you exposed and vulnerable. Can I really allow that to happen?

What seems like hours later, but is probably only minutes, Kate comes running in, throwing my bag onto the chair. She looks keyed up.

"Here we are again. How's it going?" she asks, plonking herself on the edge of the bed. "You look hot. Wait a minute." She gets a flannel out of my bag, wets it in the sink and places it on my forehead. Another contraction; she lets me grip her hands, hard. I hear myself making strange little grunts as I hold back the screams. When it's passed, I relax.

"I thought your brother would be here. Has he just dumped you and run?"

"No chance. He's not one to miss out on a bit of free entertainment. He thinks he's going to be hanging around for the whole performance.

"Speak of the devil," I add, as Edward slouches in. My brother and my friend haven't met before. He looks her up and down appraisingly; she looks him up and down disapprovingly. An expression of resignation crosses his face, as he realizes she knows too much about him.

"You can go, now Kate's here," I tell him.

"I just asked the midwife," he replies. "She says you can have two people with you."

"Bugger off, Edward. The thought of you supporting me through childbirth is so grotesque it's almost comic."

"Well, shall I just wait outside, in case you

change your mind?"

I decline; he looks thwarted. As he's sloping out of the delivery room, I call after him, asking if he'd mind letting Rob know the baby's on its way. His face screws up into an instinctive sneer of disapproval, but he must do as I request, because within minutes my phone's ringing. I'm in the throes of a wrenching contraction, so Kate delves into my handbag and answers the call. She relays to me that Rob's chucking some stuff into a rucksack and jumping into the van. I say to tell him he shouldn't put himself out, but he won't be deterred. Admittedly, it's an odd time to be making a life-changing decision, but perhaps there's something to be said for choices based on instinct rather than on meticulous design. I have a sense that I won't regret it.

"Tell him yes," I pant to Kate, as she's about to end the call from Rob.

"Yes, what?"

"Just yes."

There's a change of midwife, as one shift finishes and another one starts. Claudia wishes me the best of luck for the future. The thin-lipped new midwife looks old, tired and bored; she can't be far off retirement. She introduces herself as Ann as she flicks through my notes, barely glancing at me. The contractions are continuing to intensify; they're every three minutes now, and lasting almost a minute. After a brief examination, Ann says I still haven't dilated much. All that effort for nothing.

Kate offers to massage my shoulders and back. It doesn't help at all; it just annoys me to be pawed and pummeled, and I tell her to stop. I have an electronic nerve-stimulation device in my bag, which will distract me from the pain. Kate gets it out, attaches the four sticky pads to my lower back, and passes me the controller. I switch the machine on and feel a mild tingling sensation. The next contraction is building up. I press the boost button on the machine. The contraction floors me, and I find myself making strangulated animal noises.

"It didn't work," I pant, as the contraction subsides. "It did sod all."

"Maybe you need to turn it up to maximum strength. Here, give it to me." She twists a knob, and the tingling sensation intensifies. It's as infuriating as Kate's massage, but I stick with it. While we're waiting for the next contraction Kate roots around in my bag to see what I've packed.

"Oh, Bananagrams. That's a good idea."

"No, it's not," I cry as the pain starts to

build again. "Throw it out the window. I don't want to play any silly bloody games." I hold down the boost button as the contraction reaches its climax. Compared to the power of what my body is doing to me, it has about as much effect as someone tickling me with a feather. My breath comes fast and shallow.

"Remember your breathing techniques," Kate says. "Look at me. In through your nose, out through your mouth. In through your nose, out through your mouth."

I ignore her. I know it's panic breathing, that I should listen to my birth partner, but I can't. I feel light-headed. The contraction passes, and I pull at the wires attached to the sticky pads.

"Get these stupid things off me. This machine's worse than useless. Whoever makes them should be sued. I'll have to get by with nothing at all."

"You don't need to. You can ask for pain relief."

"No way. Birth is a natural process. Women managed it in the olden days without anesthesia, and there's no reason why we shouldn't do the same nowadays."

"Yes, but some things have improved since then. People used to die in childbirth."

"Thanks for reminding me."

As the next contraction starts building, I grip on to Kate again. I'm starting to feel overwhelmed by wave after wave of pain, each one getting bigger and longer and stronger.

An eternity passes, then Ann comes in again, this time accompanied by a male student midwife.

"Hmm. Still only four centimeters dilated," she says to the student after examining me. "Minimal progress. Of course, there's a much greater risk of a long and difficult labor with older ladies. The muscles of the womb don't work so well."

"Is everyone deliberately trying to undermine me?" I shout. "Has anybody got any positive words of encouragement here?"

"You're doing a great job," Ann says, unsmilingly.

After what feels like another eternity there's a knock on the door and Rob enters. I'm pleased to see him — much more than pleased — but, for some reason, that feeling expresses itself in the form of copious tears and snot. It occurs to me, as I wipe them away on the sleeve of my hospital gown, that I'm not at my most attractive. Rob doesn't seem to notice; he comes striding over to the bed, bends down and puts his arms around me. The skin of his stubbly cheek feels cool in comparison to the stuffiness of the room. He smooths the hair back off my face, and I realize it's drenched with sweat.

"I'm afraid I'm rubbish company today," I manage. "And I'm about to get worse," I add, as another contraction starts building. I clutch at the sleeves of his jacket.

"Don't forget about the breathing."

"Shut up. You're as annoying as Kate," I gasp.

"I've been Googling childbirth," Rob says, as the pain subsides and I let go of him. "I could apply for a job as a consultant obstetrician, I'm such an expert." He turns to Kate. "Do you want to take a break?"

"I wouldn't mind. I need to make a few phone calls and I'll grab myself a sandwich."

"So, how're you doing?" he asks, when she's gone. He straightens my hospital gown, which is starting to fall off one shoulder.

"Not great. It's been hours. I should be nearly ten centimeters dilated, but I'm nowhere near. I'm going to have to ask for pain relief."

"Why wouldn't you?"

"I wanted to do it naturally."

"That's all well and good, but if you need it, you need it. Shall I grab the midwife?"

I hesitate, then nod. *Failure,* I can't help thinking to myself. And then I think, *but who gives a shit?* Within minutes the "gas and air" has been set up and I'm given a mouthpiece to hold. I suck at it greedily. It makes me feel light-headed, as though I've had a few too many glasses of wine. It doesn't take away the agony, but I feel distanced from it; from everything.

"So, did you get my message?" I ask Rob between contractions, my head reeling.

"You mean the minimalist 'yes'? A bit cryptic."

"Not cryptic at all, unless you'd prefer to forget the question you asked me in the van."

"What do you think?" He takes my hands and kisses them. "But should you be making life-changing decisions at a time like this? When you make up your mind, I want you to be compos mentis. I don't want you waking up tomorrow morning thinking, 'What the hell have I done?' "

"This isn't spur-of-the-moment, you idiot. It's just that it's taken an extreme situation and pharmaceutical assistance for me to pluck up the courage."

"Well, that's decided, then. We're going to be a family — you, me and this little one, when she decides to show her face."

It sounds extraordinary: a family.

Kate returns at some point. Time is starting to slip and slide. The "gas and air," which gave me some relief, has stopped numbing the pain and is simply disorientating me. The contractions are excruciating; I've given up trying not to scream. Rob sits on one side of the bed and Kate sits on the other, both holding my hands. They keep telling me how well I'm doing, to keep it up, that it won't be much longer now. Ann comes in and examines me once more; still hardly any progress, despite all the time that's passed. She tells me we need to do something to speed things up. She'll put me on a Syntocinon drip, which will make the contractions bigger, and hopefully cause my cervix to dilate. Maybe now's the time to move from "gas and air" to pethidine, she says. I'm beyond caring. I just want this agony to be over and my baby to be safely out of my body.

I'm given an injection in my thigh, a catheter is inserted into my arm and I'm hooked up to a drip. Monitors are strapped to my belly to measure my contractions and the baby's heart rate. When the pethidine starts to kick in, the pain's still there, but seems separate from my body. I feel elated, as high as a kite. My impulse control has been switched off, and I find myself telling Rob, in between thumping contractions, that he's the kindest, funniest, sweetest man I've ever met. I love his unruly hair, and the straightness of his nose, and the mole on his cheek and his blue, blue eyes. I've even got used to his excessive height. He laughs. He says he loves me, too, that he rather likes Susan-on-drugs. He might ask Ann if we can take some pethidine home with us.

I turn to Kate.

"I remember thinking how cool he was the first time I saw him at a student party. He used to look like the lead singer of a grunge band, so laid-back and sure of himself. On a completely different planet from me."

"Hang on a minute," says Rob. "You kept telling me you couldn't recall ever meeting me."

"Well, I wasn't going to admit you'd made an impression, was I?" I pant, as the next contraction comes crashing over me. "You should know — even *I* tell white lies occasionally."

The initial elation from the opiate drug ebbs away and I feel spaced-out. When I'm not contorted with pain, I listen to the steady drumbeat from the baby's heart rate monitor and stare at the screen next to the bed, where numbers are changing at random and a wiggly line is going up and down. Rob and Kate take it in turns to talk to Ann, then try to explain things to me. I'm having difficulty understanding what they're saying.

There's another change of shift, and Claudia's back. She's surprised to see I'm still here. The pain is ramping up fast; the pethidine must be wearing off. Claudia says there's been a bit of progress with dilation, but I think she's just trying to keep me positive. At the next contraction, I scream that I've had enough, I can't do it. Claudia says she knows I was clear in my birth plan that I didn't want an epidural, but she can see I'm not coping well. She asks if I've changed my mind.

"Yes," I say. "Yes, please. Please give me an epidural."

The wait is endless and I lose any last remaining shreds of self-restraint. Eventually, an anesthetist comes in. I'm asked to sit up, bend over, and I'm given an injection into my spine. It works like magic; the agony starts to subside, then disappears completely, although my body feels like I've run ten marathons back-to-back. I'm hugely relieved that the pain has gone, but I'm scared. Things have spiraled out of my control; none of this was part of my plan. My baby should be here by now, safely in my arms. Instead she's in limbo, waiting for me to push her out. And I can't. I just can't seem to do it. Claudia feels my belly, and says, with a concerned frown, that my contractions are getting weaker rather than stronger. The rhythm of the baby's heartbeat is less regular, and there are intermittent silences. Each time the sound stops, I hold my breath until I hear it start again. The midwife leaves the room and comes back almost immediately with a doctor. They look at the printouts from the monitors, and whisper urgently about fetal distress. Rob goes to talk to them, while Kate pats my arm reassuringly. I notice she looks done in. She must have been here almost a full night and day.

People crowd around my bed. The doctor tells me the baby isn't happy, that it's all gone on too long. They need to carry out an emergency cesarean because I've failed to progress in the first stage of labor. Do I understand? I do; my body's well and truly let me down this time. More important, it's let my baby down. I'm handed a clipboard, with a form attached. I sign my name without reading it. The doctor says we should make our way to the theater, and Rob asks me whether I want him or Kate with me during the operation. I can't answer; all I can think is that I want the baby out safely, as quickly as possible. They must have decided between them, because Rob is at my side as they wheel my bed down the corridor. He whispers words of encouragement, but my mind's elsewhere. My baby's stuck inside me. In distress.

A screen is erected across my chest to hide what's going on. Rob, who's changed into blue scrubs like the medical staff, sits in a chair pulled up close to my head. There are a lot of people in the room; doctors, nurses, midwives, all wearing masks. Someone explains what will happen, but I can't take it in. I'm terrified. Is she hanging in there, or has my body failed her completely? There are murmurs, metallic sounds, a suction noise, and I feel a tugging and pulling. Then my baby is held up above the screen for me to see. She looks limp, purple-white. I thought she would be given to me immediately, but she's taken away. Nobody speaks, and I can't see what's happening. Rob grips my hand tightly. There are tears streaming down his cheeks. I can see he's trying to choke them back, trying to be strong for me. It's no good. He lowers his head to mine, cheek to cheek, and our tears mix together. I close my eyes. Then I hear a high-pitched squeak, and another. The midwife appears from behind the screen with a bundle wrapped in a white cotton blanket. It's placed on my chest. I see a small pink face, and a tiny mouth opening and closing, looking for something to suck. My baby. My beautiful, beautiful baby.

28

When the doctors have completed their morning rounds, and there's a hiatus in the bustle of the ward, I open the rain-streaked envelope Rob found on my front doormat yesterday. Inside, I find a greeting card showing a woman at the wheel of a red convertible, her blond hair streaming out behind her. Underneath are the words *Congratulations on passing your driving test.* I open the card; it's from Edward. I can just about decipher his scrawl:

"Hey, Suze. Rob told me it all went well (in the end) and that you've produced a niece for me. Would've dropped into the hospital to give her the once-over and see whether she looks like her old uncle, but a mate's just asked if I can fill in as roadie on his tour, and we head off tomorrow. Am leaving the sale in the capable hands of Mr. B. Will be back in Brum in a couple of months for a quick stopover before I go traveling. Maybe we should do something with those ashes while I'm home — scatter/bury/whatever. Can't think where Mum'd want them deposited. Can you? Aunt Sylvia might know — but she'll probably want to build a replica Egyptian tomb in her back garden. Anyway, have a beer on me to celebrate. I'll give you a fiver when I see you. If I remember. Ed x."

I turn it over. On the back is a postscript:

"Sorry about the card. Was in a rush, and only read the word 'Congratulations' in the newsagent's. You might as well hold on to it — it'll save me buying another one if you do pass your driving test one day. I mean, who knows what you'll do next?!"

I put the card with the small pile of rubbish that's accumulated on my bedside cabinet, then change my mind and stand it next to the more conventional cards I've received from Rob, Kate and my colleagues at work. Every atom of my body tells me I shouldn't let Edward near my daughter — his behavior toward me over the years has disqualified him from any entitlement to be a part of our lives. Not only that, he'd be a terrible role model for her as she grows up.

There is, however, a tiny, flickering notion in my head: that by excising him completely I might be depriving her of something. That there might be a void in her life, perhaps even in my own. I need to extinguish that thought; it can only be a manifestation of the high levels of oxytocin surging through my veins. I'm relieved he's going away.

Richard has been to visit. Rob phoned him to tell him the good news while I was in the post-op recovery room waiting to be transferred to the ward. He called in to the hospital the next day, dumping a very large parcel at the foot of my bed. I wasn't in any fit state to unwrap it, so Richard told me what it was: a chemistry set. He'd always wanted one himself when he was a child, but the family could never afford one; his daughter wouldn't miss out as he had. Standing next to the cot, Richard stared and stared at the baby, responding to my observations with disjointed replies. I said he was welcome to hold her if she woke; he left very soon afterward. He's in a state of shock. I understand; he'll get there, in time.

Rob's been busy browsing estate agents' websites. At visiting hour, he kicks off his boots, stretches out his long legs on the hospital bed next to me and switches on his iPad to show me details of rental properties. He's keen to have a decent-sized garden. In fact, that seems to rank above all other requirements, as far as he's concerned. He doesn't mind how far out of London we live, but I tell him I need to be within easy commuting distance of my office. As he scrolls through the listings, I think again about the wisdom of our plan. He needs to be stopped before he wastes any more time on this search. I tell him I've come to the conclusion that it's not such a good idea, after all; I've changed my mind. Rob puts down the iPad and turns to me, propped up on one elbow. He says he knows it's all very quick, he doesn't want to rush me, he'll wait until I'm ready. There's been a misunderstanding. I explain I've changed my mind about renting. It's vital that I stay on the London property ladder — if I step off I may never be able to get back on — so I think we should buy. His expression changes quickly from dark to light.

To manage Rob's expectations, I tell him we'll purchase the property as "tenants in common" rather than "joint tenants." That way our shares will be defined by law, which will make it much easier if we decide we've made an appalling mistake. Plus, as tenants in common, if one of us dies our share would pass to our next of kin rather than to each other. Rob laughs when I explain this to him. Whatever I want to do is fine by him, he says.

Our discussion's interrupted; my daughter's woken. Her tiny fists are punching the air and she's making squeaking, creaking noises. Rob picks her up and cradles her in his arms, bouncing her and patting her back. He's a natural, and she senses it; his sisters have five children between them, so he's had practice. She's calm, but not for long. Rob just won't do when she's hungry. He passes her over to me. I unbutton the top of my nightdress and she latches on. I bend down and put my cheek against her downy head. I need to think of a name for her; I can't keep calling her "my daughter" or "the baby." Obviously, family names are out of the question. I don't want to give her a common name like my own, but neither do I want to give her one that's silly or ostentatious. And I don't want a name that can be shortened — *that* can lead to all sorts of aggravation. I thought, perhaps, an abstract noun, like Hope or Joy, but I'm not one to advertise my feelings. Rob's first suggestion was "Roberta." I presume that was his idea of a joke. Next, he suggested giving her a name that's already been shortened, like Kate, Meg or Nell. Nell. Little Nell. Rob looks up the meaning: bright shining one. It fits.

Nell's fallen asleep on my breast while she was feeding. I remember the baby training manual said you should wake them up again when they do this so they don't think they need to feed to get to sleep. As if I'd do that to her. I gently slide my finger into her mouth to disengage her, and pass her to Rob so he can put her back in the clear plastic crib next to my bed. She stirs, chirps a little, but the mission is accomplished with success. A moment later, Kate pushes through the ward's heavy swing doors, carrying Noah on her hip and holding her daughter with her free hand. Ava gazes at Nell, with her nose pressed flat against the walls of the crib. Noah sits on his mother's lap and plays with a cloth book while we chat. Kate says that, when she was in my flat picking up some clean nightclothes, Aunt Sylvia called. My aunt was overjoyed to hear that I'd had the baby. She asked Kate to pass on her love to us both. She also asked her to say she's told my cousins she's my mother, and that they're speechless with delight. More important, Aunt Sylvia wanted Kate to tell me she's changed the name of her bungalow from Wendine to Swendine. She's had new signs made for the gatepost and porch, and she's got new headed notepaper and calling cards. She was most concerned that I know that.

"Changing the subject," Kate says, "I've got a suggestion." A divorced mother she knows from the mums-and-babies group has told her she's looking for another single-parent family to buy out her ex's share of their house. The two cohabiting mums will then be able to help each other with child-care and domestic chores. Kate says she's a great woman, and it's a nice house, not far from where we live now. She's very tempted. If she goes for it, Rob and I can buy her flat from her and un-subdivide the house. It's not a bad idea. In fact, it might even be a fantastic idea. I like where I live, and so does Rob.

Kate also updates me on the latest news about her campaign against the withdrawal of funding for the local mums-and-babies group. She's received an email from the council this morning; the funding will definitely stop. It's wrong. Kate's told me all about the group; families in the area rely on it. I may even need it myself. I wonder aloud if it's possible to sue the local author-ity. I tell Kate and Rob that, when I'm back on my feet, I'll do some legal research and send a few emails. And I'll phone my very useful friend Brigid to ask if she'd like to drop in to meet Nell. People always want to see new babies.

"Oh, hell," says Rob, "not another bloody legal dispute."

"I'll have so much time on my hands while I'm on maternity leave, I might as well put it to good use. Plus, it'd be a shame not to use all the skills I've picked up over the last few months."

"I'm not sure you're going to have quite as much time as you think, Susan," says Kate. "But thanks for the offer of help." She turns to Rob. "Don't look so worried. It's different this time. It's for the good of the community, not some misguided personal fixation."

Rob sighs, theatrically.

Visiting time passes quickly this evening. Kate, Ava and Noah head off, along with the other patients' relatives and friends. Rob leaves his things next to my bed while he nips to the bathroom. He says he'll be back in a minute to say good-night. The ward goes quiet again, or as quiet as a ward can when it accommodates six newborn babies and their mothers.

I'm itching to start my new life with Nell, but I've been told it'll be one more night before I'll be discharged. I'm in pain from the cesarean section, but it'll be manageable at home with a little pharmaceutical assistance. I look across at the crib. Nell's still in a deep sleep, lying on her back, her rosy face turned toward me. Her arms are raised from the elbows, and her hands are palms-up next to her plump cheeks; her legs are bent at the knees and splayed like a frog's. She has a tag around her slender wrist with my name on it. I made her; she belongs to me. If I stretch out my hand from where I'm lying in my hospital bed I can stroke her cheek; her skin feels soft and pillowy, hardly more than a puff of warm air. I gently reposition Bunnikins, my old knitted rabbit, who's sitting in the corner of her crib, watching over her as she sleeps.

From time to time Nell twitches or snuffles. I expect she imagines she's back in her cocoon. I don't think she wanted to leave; I can already tell that she and I are alike. It's odd — since she was born, matters of certainty and uncertainty have swapped places. I was convinced I'd know exactly how to handle the practical side of caring for a baby: how to change her nappy, how to hold her when she's feeding, how to bathe her, but I admit I feel inexperienced and clumsy. Conversely, I was very far from convinced that I could love my daughter straightaway. I'm amazed, now, that I ever doubted it. I'm beginning to understand how my mother must have felt when she held her own baby for the first time; how Aunt Sylvia must have felt when she gave me away.

My aunt (I can't call her anything else yet) said she spent a week with me in Rhyl before my mother and father came to claim me. She couldn't fail to have bonded with me over the course of those few days. I know she would have been taken aback when she first felt the solid corporeality of the living creature she'd produced, and then been amazed that her own body could bring into being something so remarkable, so perfect. She would have looked at the world afresh and wondered what magic there was in it that could cause such a thing to exist. I can see it all perfectly in my mind, Aunt Sylvia with her new baby: she lets my fingers close around one of her own and is shocked at the strength of my grip, so tight it seems as if I never want to let her go; she looks into my eyes and can't bear to be the first to look away; she holds me close to her skin while she feeds me; she rocks me in her arms when I'm fretful, listening to my breathing deepen and slow; she whispers secret thoughts to me, thoughts she'd be embarrassed to share with anyone else; she watches my chest rising and falling as I sleep, my almost-translucent eyelids flickering, and wonders whether I'm dreaming. She has dreams of her own, about who I'll grow into, how I'll look, walk, talk. Will I be like her? Or like my father?

Knowing all that Aunt Sylvia must have felt, it's hard to comprehend how she managed to hand me over. She was only seventeen years old; twenty-eight years younger than I am now. Even with my own strength and resilience, my years of experience and my knowledge of how time heals most things in the end, I couldn't bear to give up my baby. How much harder would it have been for someone so young? I can see her kissing the top of my head, passing me over to my mother, then feeling the negative weight, the absence. She wouldn't just be going back to life before the baby; there would now be a child-shaped hole. Why didn't she say "no" when the idea was put forward? Why didn't she refuse to hand me over when they came for me? I thought, when I first discovered the truth, that it was because she cared more about herself and her own future than she did about mine, but now I think I was wrong. I think it was because she wanted the very best for her daughter; more than she believed she, herself, could provide.

It's no wonder, now that I come to think of it, that Aunt Sylvia used to call at our house so often. I know she enjoyed spending time in my mother's company, but her desire to see *me* — to watch me growing and changing — must have been just as important, if not more so. The simple fact is, I'm nothing like her. I hope she hasn't been disappointed; I hope she understands and forgives my lack of ease with life. It's not just genes that create a person, after all. I expect there were numerous times when she wanted to tell me she was my mother. But it would have been difficult for her to do that when she'd made a promise to her sister. And how do you go about telling your niece that she's your daughter? Where would you start? I ask myself, can I forgive Aunt Sylvia for giving me up, for keeping the secret? Perhaps. I'm not ruling anything in or anything out; I'm going to wait and see. The world seems bigger, louder and more colorful than it did a few weeks ago, a few days ago. At the moment, I'm not entirely sure who I am in relation to it. But that's fine.

Rob's back from the bathroom, stowing his iPad in his canvas shoulder bag, putting on his jacket and gathering up his things. He takes his mobile out of the back pocket of his jeans and checks the time.

"Wish I could stay longer," he says, "but I suppose I'd better make tracks before the ward sister catches me. It's ten-past already."

He leans over and kisses me on the lips.

"Who cares what time it is?" I say. "Stay a bit longer. Pull the curtains round and join me on the bed. No one will even know you're here. Forget the stupid rules."

"What, Susan Green saying 'forget the rules'? That's not something I ever expected to hear."

"Just shut up and do it."

" 'Just shut up and do it'?"

"Just shut up and do it, please."

"How can I refuse when you ask so nicely?"

He puts down his bag, takes off his jacket and throws it across the back of the chair. I watch from my bed, propped up with pillows, as the curtains slowly close around us.

ACKNOWLEDGMENTS

The seed that grew into *The Cactus* was planted during my creative writing master's at Manchester Metropolitan University. Many thanks to my fellow "whiskey drinkers": Angie Williams, Bryn Fazakerley, Paul Forrester-O'Neill, Saiqa Khushnood, Steven Mepham and Liz Middleton. Their friendship, encouragement and first-class reading skills enabled the seed to germinate and push through to the light.

Plants thrive best when tended. I'm hugely grateful to Jane Finigan for being such a champion of *The Cactus;* her support and expert guidance have been invaluable. Thanks also to Juliet Mahoney and everyone at Lutyens & Rubinstein for nurturing this book, particularly while Jane was on her own journey into new-motherhood. David Forrer at Inkwell Management has been another steadfast champion, for which I'm very grateful.

Many thanks to Erika Imranyi at Park Row Books in the United States and Lisa Highton at Two Roads in the UK for adding *The Cactus* to their collections, and for their faith, enthusiasm and fantastic editorial input. All plants benefit from being in the ideal location, and from a little pruning and training. Thanks also to Natalie Hallak and the rest of the team at Park Row for their hard work and diligence, which have allowed this book to settle so well into its new home.

None of this would have been possible without the support of my family and friends, who are soil, water and light. Special thanks to my dear friend, Beth Roberts — my daily inspiration — who gave me the courage to take my first step onto new ground and the determination to keep going through those rocky patches. Finally, love and gratitude to Simon — my first reader — and to Gabriel and Felix, for their endless patience and understanding while I was busy cultivating *The Cactus.*

ABOUT THE AUTHOR

Sarah Haywood studied law and has worked as a solicitor, an advice worker and as an investigator of complaints about lawyers. She now lives in the UK with her husband and two sons. *The Cactus* is her first novel.